THE
VALUE
OF
NOTHING

JOHN TAGHOLM

THE VALUE OF NOTHING

A MODERN OPERA

QUARTET BOOKS

First published in 2019 by Quartet Books Limited
A member of the Namara Group
27 Goodge Street, London, WIT 2LD

A catalogue record for this book is available from the British Library

ISBN 9780704374713

Typeset by Tetragon, London
Printed and bound in Great Britain by
TJ International Ltd, Padstow, Cornwall

for Lucas

'...a man who knew the price of
everything and the value of nothing.'

OSCAR WILDE,
Lady Windermere's Fan

Radix malorum est cupiditas

OVERTURE

T he boy stood in front of the familiar wall, a backdrop of jagged shapes and lurid colour, and felt the first tremors through his legs. He stepped back into the shadow of the building to merge with the graffiti, just another shape amongst the patterns.

The sun was setting on the other side of the old building, casting its dark outline in front of him, beyond which the mass of lines swept outwards in a great curve, silver parallel threads tinged with pink. Invisible to the world, he waited for the sounds to follow, faint at first like a distant avalanche, but growing stronger, the roll of drums played low, not an ominous tone but a signal of promise.

He looked at his watch, which glowed in the half darkness. 20:01. The train had left on time and was now two minutes out of the Gare de Lyon at the start of its long journey. He remembered when he had first seen it, about three months earlier, snaking alongside the rue Coriolis, almost within touching distance of the apartment blocks. The words above the carriages announced *Paris-Milano-Torino* and he had watched by the roadside until the last carriage had disappeared.

It was the start of an obsession, but it wasn't until his third sighting of the great train, from the tracks where he now stood, that he had seen the girl.

It was coming closer, the low rumble of the wheels transmitted into the stained wall against which he was leaning. In the gloom he was smiling and his eyes were wide open. He was certain she would be on the train. She carried his dreams of escape into a world he could barely imagine.

And then the great bulk of the train was on him and he watched the lit windows move past, still slow enough for him to register the passengers inside. He was counting the coaches as the earth shook beneath him. She was always in *Voiture 14* and the light from the windows came and went across his face, his smile revealed then lost. She was in the same seat and as usual there was no one opposite and she was alone. His eyes followed her and even in that brief time the image was burnt into his memory to be recycled later and shuffled at will. She had hair cut short around her neck and pushed up from her forehead and her eyes were dark. He was not really conscious of these observations, which were not sexual, but more a confirmation of something almost religious, the physical manifestation of hope to carry him through the long days. He watched her eyes and even though for one brief second they looked in his direction, he knew they were not focused on him.

Then she was gone, along with the deep roar of the engines finally released from the restrictions of the terminus. As the last carriage flashed by, he stepped on to the track and into the warm slipstream, so strong that it sucked him forward two paces. The red light on the last carriage began to recede and within seconds the train had roared around the massive brick embankment holding the 12th arrondissement at bay and disappeared from sight. Long after it had gone he stood waiting until the turbulent air had settled and the sounds of Paris had reasserted themselves.

His watch told him that it had all been over in four minutes.

He was small for his age, just twelve years old and the watch, a chronometer, was too big on his wrist. He wore it only when he was alone. He ran his hands over its face, although his eyes were on the empty track ahead.

'Fucking Arab.'

A shout from behind brought him back to his senses and he turned to see two policemen running towards him. He took off across the tracks to his right, towards the old signal box. A local train was heading for the station and he judged that he had time to get in front of it so that the *flics* wouldn't see him double back towards the footbridge. The train's horn gave a low bark of warning but he had plenty of room to spare and for ten seconds or so he ran alongside the carriages. Although the train was going considerably faster, he was hidden until he got to the old steps where he crouched down by the crumbling brick balustrades. The policemen were making their way towards the signal box, as he knew they would, so he climbed up to the *passerelle*, and squeezed through the bent and rusting bars of the wrought-iron gate topped with barbed wire. The footbridge was not much more than two metres wide, but it ran for almost a kilometre, a narrow rule across the thirty or so lines that divided the Bois de Vincennes from the old warehouses and the dual carriageway alongside the Seine. These tracks were one of his playgrounds and he sat over them and laughed as he watched the policemen stumbling over the sleepers trying to find him. Dusk had almost become night and it was dangerous for them as the trains moved relentlessly in and out of the terminus. The dials of his watch shone even more clearly and he absentmindedly slipped his most treasured possession up and down his wrist and rested his head on the dusty guard rail. He pictured her speeding into the darkness, the train moving towards its top speed, the world flashing by, rushing the woman towards her exotic and undefined destination. His own world measured no more than eight kilometres square, an area loosely defined by the great stations of the capital and the wilderness of tracks they spewed from their ever open mouths. He was an immigrant, an alien, a foreigner, a stranger and so was this land in front of him, territory that didn't belong to Paris any more than he did, ignored like he was. He felt companionship here, an empathy with the place that was always prepared to welcome him and where he could be himself.

He lived in a shanty town behind the Gare du Nord and the Gare de l'Est, his home, a shack of wood and tarpaulin, built on a deserted goods' track a stone's throw from the Périphérique. He was a child of the Paris that no one knew. Although barely half an hour's walk behind Sacré-Coeur, it might just as well have been another galaxy. He was not of that world and he had been taught to despise it, to regard the honey-coloured centre of the city as a dangerous illusion, a deliberate deceit to lure the eye away from the truth. He lived on the raw edge of the city, kept at bay by poverty and hatred and, in some ways, he was happy to have it this way. That is, until he saw the woman on the train, who had somehow become a conduit to somewhere else, a fabled world to which he couldn't ascribe any shape, or indeed have any real hope of ever being able to do so.

A line of grey soot marked his forehead, a stigmata of his condition. The track along which she had departed was now in complete darkness, the future shut off and unavailable. Youssef Tigha trudged off the bridge to make his own journey across Paris, but before he did he had one more task. He slipped the watch from his wrist and slid it into his pocket. Arab boys didn't wear chronometers. He would hide it later in the den above the tunnel.

No child should have witnessed what Youssef had seen in his short life and his face was older than his years. Although there was in his walk a certain youthful innocence, this was deceptive for his childhood was never lived, never fulfilled. There was nothing for him to grow out of, or build on for the future and the child in him lay trapped and unknown. He was misshapen, he knew, not on the outside, unless you counted the deep lines on his face, but inside, out of sight, where the imbalance had given him enormous self-reliance at the cost of any hope of love.

He stole an apple and an orange from a stall outside a shop near the Gare de Lyon and finished the first by the time he reached the new walkway created on the arches of the old railway near Place Bastille. This is how he lived, hand to mouth, moment to moment, the future simply a disappearing train, the present a series of unplanned events that took him through each day, longer in winter than in summer, an eternal loop from which he saw no escape.

On the wide pavement in front of the new opera house he saw a poster of a singer, her image contorted in misery or love and he stopped and brought his hands to cover his face. His mother was coming towards him again, floating, flying, real and not real and his face, should anyone have looked at him, was of horror and disbelief. He could not move, held rigid by the scenes released in his mind but somehow more present than reality. This normally happened at night and he would sit bolt upright, panting trying to rid himself of the images. They would go, he knew, but only to hide in wait for him again, to catch him when he least expected it, like now.

Somebody pushed him out of the way, swearing abuse and he came back to the here and now. His beating heart began to slow and he trudged onwards towards the Place de la République, where he gave the orange to a family who spent most nights there, unrolling their bedding when the crowds began to thin around midnight and neatly packing it up again in the early morning, to wash in the fountains, a family with two young daughters, neat, clean and homeless. He knew they were about to be moved on, driven out after the terrorist attacks. In a way, he took pity on them, not that his face showed it. He handed the orange to the younger of the two daughters, her face framed in a red headscarf and turned away before she smiled at him from the gloom.

ACT ONE

I

Round Mary was waiting, crisp and efficient as ever, a folder tucked against her ample bosom, her lipstick applied with glistening efficiency despite the hour. Nothing about her indicated that she had risen well before dawn to travel across London on a series of night buses and early Tubes.

'Good morning, Mary.' Michael Finistere took the folder from his PA. 'Is it there?'

'Waiting for you,' she said.

He was already reading his itinerary as she rustled ahead of him to call the lift. It was shortly before seven and his driver had brought him in from Beaconsfield before the rush hour had begun, a regular journey that got him to his desk before most of London was properly awake.

'Who's meeting me?'

Although it was all written down, Mary's response betrayed no sign of irritation.

'Erik Mollet, along with his assistant, Claude Papon. I think you've seen them before.' She knew he had, but it was better that she softened her response.

'At least I won't have to speak French,' Finistere said, stepping into the lift, his back to his assistant. 'I'd frankly rather learn Japanese.' He was thinking of the last time he had seen Mollet, in some swanky restaurant up by Montparnasse. Mollet spoke excellent English, even if it was with an irritating American drawl, but he had joked with the waiter in French and there was a palpable wall of exclusion between the Frenchmen and himself. Michael Finistere liked to be in charge and, in French, he couldn't be.

In the lift, he was aware of Round Mary's bulk at his side. 'Any problems getting in?'

Mary knew this was only a way of filling in time and that her boss had about as much interest in her as he had in the French language. 'No, it was an easy run, thank you.'

'It's my mother's birthday today. Would you send her some flowers? And can you do one of my notes.'

Mary Houlihan did indeed know how to fake Michael Finistere's signature and compose the sort of loving note that was probably not only beyond his imagination but also clever enough to be safe from detection by his elderly mother. She also knew that he called her Round Mary behind her back but at least she had the satisfaction of knowing that, but for her, certain elements of his life would crash around his feet.

The lift arrived at the top floor and she led the way through the double glass doors to the roof. The sun was now above the horizon, just to the east of the Shard, an orange balloon about to be pierced. Although the blades of the helicopter were still, Finistere nevertheless stooped as he walked under them towards the metal steps. By now he had forgotten her, wrapped in a schedule of events that she had organised on his behalf. She would get a Eurostar and join him later, as the idea of travelling with him in the back of a helicopter would appeal to neither of them.

'Morning boys,' Finistere said to the crew, all of whom he recognised. In recent months this had been a trip they had made together on several occasions and there was an easy male familiarity amongst them. He strapped himself into his seat and spread the folder on the table in front of him, hearing the pilot seek clearance for take-off. He looked out of the window as the helicopter rose slowly above Farringdon Road and wheeled over Smithfield Market, heading southwards to cross London. If he had been able to look behind, he would have seen Round Mary still standing on the roof, her substantial form diminishing as they gathered speed and height. Michael Finistere's affection for his PA was strictly limited and fringed with irritability, since he was aware that she regarded herself as the pillar supporting his private life and probably his business world as well. In truth, he had chosen her primarily for her looks, for his other assistants, picked with different criteria, had merely led to complications.

They flew due south, the sun on his left and he lowered the blind on the sprawl of south London. He was not keen to look down on the Battersea estate where he had been brought up, nor at New Covent Garden market where his father had worn himself to death. Unlike his father's, Michael Finistere's hands were perfectly manicured and they shuffled the papers in front of him, smoothing down the order of play for the day ahead. A cup of green tea was placed on the table but he barely acknowledged its arrival. The expensive watch on his wrist told him that he had two hours to review the papers that he had already memorised.

If Michael Finistere gave the impression that he had a cavalier disregard of facts and worked only by instinct, it was an act he cultivated, for he was always meticulously prepared. He would carry no documents in Paris, nothing that spoke of the homework and minute preparation he always did. His father had shown his graft on his face, which was worn and sallow even before his fiftieth birthday. It wasn't going to happen to Michael Finistere and although he didn't believe in psychological mumbo-jumbo, he could see that the only way in which he was his father's son was in his determination to be his precise opposite.

He heard the pilot check in with French air traffic control and they clattered towards the coast. The helicopter wasn't the quickest way of getting to Paris but he could travel virtually door to door and, thank heavens, he didn't have to sit with other people.

Going over Calais, the pilot pointed out the gash of land that was the remains of the migrant camp but Michael Finistere wasn't interested. His thoughts were on Erik Mollet, the man who would greet him in the capital, small, dark, typically French and an ex-rugby player. He had a sneaking regard for the man whom he saw as a worthy rival and one not to be trusted an inch. Mollet had been a scrum half and although Finistere had never played the sport, he had seen footage of the diminutive player in his pomp and admired his elan, a thought he nevertheless kept to himself.

A text confirmed that Mary had organised flowers for his mother and that she was about to leave the office for St Pancras. He read a copy of the note she had composed on his behalf:

Dearest Ma, your favourite peonies on this special day as you continue to bely your age. With love from your loving son, Michael. x

For reasons he didn't want to explore, he would have found it difficult to write even a small message like this. His mother was an admirable woman but he didn't understand her world, her circle of friends or the things she found important. She was simply a presence who loved him unconditionally and he took that for granted and barely gave her a second thought.

The pilot informed him that they were just approaching the northern suburbs of the city and had about fifteen minutes to go. He pulled up the blind and in the distance he could glimpse the Seine snaking its way through Paris. The helicopter was beginning its slow descent towards the Montparnasse tower, but Michael Finistere's eyes weren't looking towards the black monstrosity which marred the city's skyline. Down below he was trying to locate the reason for his visit. He could see the main railway line that would later carry Round Mary into Paris and his eyes followed it until it arrived at the Périphérique. They were still too high to make out any detail but he could see the shape of the great warehouses and the old railway lines that fed into them. His eyes were fixed on the spot until they were over and beyond it and the pilot was making preparations for the exacting task of landing on the small pad at the top of the skyscraper. Michael Finistere didn't want to watch so he returned to the papers on the table and waited until he felt the touch of the wheels and the sound of the engine being throttled down.

'There we are, Mr Finistere. Paris in all its glory.'

'Thank you, boys. Perfect as ever.' He was referring to the flight and not the city. He kept his head down and his eyes straight ahead as he made for the door that led to the lift. He was met by one of the tower's bevy of pretty PR assistants, who took him downstairs to his waiting car. The traffic was hopeless, as usual, on the way back to the centre of town and his hotel. His bags had been sent the day before and Round Mary had booked his usual suite at the Hotel Lancaster where the manager was waiting to greet him. Michael Finistere took all this as a matter of course, nothing more or less than what a great deal of money can bring.

The rooms managed to be neither masculine nor feminine, a mix of cool greys, pale blues and white with the odd pink silk cushion to offer the mildest of contrasts. All was silent inside despite the Avenue des Champs-Élysées thundering by not far away. He had just over an hour before he was due to meet Mollet and his team. He stripped off his clothes and lay naked on the thick carpeted floor. He had a big body but he was trim and lean with no sign of fat. He straightened his legs, pointing his toes forward like a ballet dancer, before raising them a few inches from the floor. He began to make small paddling motions, his arms by his side, his head perfectly still. He continued to do this for twenty minutes, with only one pause, before standing and running through a series of further exercises aimed at stretching his muscles. He always did this before an important meeting, a way of clearing his mind and becoming more relaxed. He went through to the shower, turning on a stream of cold water and standing motionless beneath it.

Drying himself, he walked over to the wardrobe, where his clothes had been hung and laid out. He put on a clean white shirt and attached the gold cuff links his father had given him. The dark blue suit was one of many he had made in London. His tie was grey silk, as was his handkerchief. It was an eve of battle routine, a process of focusing. Ridiculous, he knew, when he would shortly be standing in a slum in northern Paris, but necessary for him. He transferred his wallet and keys, took an appraising look at himself and even as he was checking his watch his phone rang and it was Mary to tell him his car was downstairs. It was quicker to take Eurostar to Paris than fly by helicopter. He took her efficiency for granted. Well, if he was truthful, he took her completely for granted.

He had several views of himself in the soft lighting of the mirrored lift. For a moment he had the impression that he wasn't there, that only his reflections existed. He frowned at the various images of himself and he experienced a faint wave of unease, that somehow he didn't exist, that he was merely an illusion. The lift doors opened and he stepped away from himself.

Round Mary was waiting in the foyer and he handed back the folder she had given him earlier in the day and she placed it in a leather bag. They had made the trip to the warehouses before and although less than a mile away, they were at the mercy of the Paris traffic, so, at Mary's suggestion, they had left plenty of time.

'What do you think of this place?' he asked her.

She assumed he meant Paris rather than the hotel. She knew he had little time for either but he didn't allow her time to reply.

'I don't know how people live here. A dirty city, if you ask me.'

'It has its charms.'

'Really? You could have fooled me.'

Mary, who was used to his abrupt dismissals, merely assumed that he was getting in a combative mood for his upcoming encounter with Mollet.

'They drive like idiots. And rude. Jesus.'

She kept quiet as the car rolled on towards the Porte de Clignancourt, where it thrummed over the big cobbled intersection before dropping under the bridge that brought the railway lines into the Gare du Nord.

'Look at that. People living under here.' He was pointing at the shacks built under the concrete flyover. 'It's meant to be a civilised country. I ask you.'

The car turned right and then right again into a large car park, where a line of articulated lorries were parked in echelon along a wire fence. He could see the man he assumed was Claude Papon leaning against his car, smoking.

'And that's another thing. They still smoke.'

Mary knew her boss had once smoked heavily and now had the zeal of a convert.

'C'mon, let's go and make a few million.'

He walked towards the man and even before he'd stopped to shake hands he asked where Mollet was.

'He's up there,' Claude Papon told him, nodding his head back to the old brick warehouse behind him. 'Shall we join him? You're not quite dressed for this sort of thing,' he said, looking from Mary to Finistere.

'There's more where this one came from, don't worry.'

They followed Papon through a gate and along a rubbish-strewn path to a wooden door set into an even larger door that they had to stoop to get through. As the door closed behind them, Michael Finistere experienced the same apprehension that he'd had in the lift, a sensation new to him and one for which he could give no rational explanation.

2

Youssef Tigha watched the group enter the building, his curiosity
alerted. He was perched on a brick parapet over a disused railway
tunnel now overgrown with buddleia. He had seen them before
on several occasions walking between Clignancourt and Maillot but this
was the first time he'd observed them going into the old warehouse that
he often used as a place to hide and play.

He scrambled along the brick ledge and down to the recently erected
metal fence where, over a period of time, he had worked loose two of the
upright zinc spears. He pushed them apart, squeezing through the narrow
gap before moving the metal bars back together again. He scuttled under
the massive concrete supports of the railway until he came to the first of the
old brick warehouses. He waited here to be certain that the group hadn't
posted someone on the door of the bigger warehouse beyond. As certain
as he could be that the road was clear, he sprinted over to the larger, more
imposing old brick building.

The windows rising geometrically above him had all been broken but
the metal frames on the upper stories defiantly remained. Although it was
unlike any building back home, Youssef liked its look and feel, its propor-
tions comfortable and easy on the eye, especially in contrast to the concrete
blocks all around, which although more modern, were already stained and
without dignity. It was a good place to lose himself.

He reached the door and found that it was still open. Pushing gently
against it, he peered into the darkness. He knew this space well and even in
the dead of a moonless night he was able to find his way around. He had
explored the floors, five in all, each as large as one of his father's old fields
back home and he climbed the staircase, looking in at every level.

Even before he got to the top, he could hear the murmur of their conversations and he slowed down, taking care where he trod for fear that the

scrunch of glass underfoot would alert them. A small wooden partition wall separated the stairs from the large open space of the warehouse floor and Youssef waited until the distant chatter had built up before daring to peek around it.

What he saw made his eyes widen in surprise. The figures stood in the middle of the floor, lit by a series of lights that made the rest of space dark in comparison. They were gathered around what Youssef took to be the largest toy he had even seen. He could see buildings and roads, railway lines with small trains, a park with water and trees and small people along the paths so real that he expected them to move at any minute.

A man with a long stick was pointing at parts of the model and on an enormous television screen in the gloom of the warehouse other pictures emerged. This was the most exciting discovery he'd made in the city and he stood quite openly in the frame of the tongue-and-groove wall that had once supported a door. He knew that the spill of light would make him almost invisible. He spoke a little French but his English was good and he picked up various familiar words floating across the open floor.

He sank down on his haunches and listened to the distant conversations.

Erik Mollet was the ringmaster, his long stick a magic wand with which to entrance his audience. 'And so, this is the complete concept. I think you must agree that my modellers have done a first-class job. Narrow your eyes and come in close and it might just as well be the real thing.'

Michael Finistere, who had sat through countless presentations from groups and individuals keen to lure him into spending his money with them, was reasonably impressed. It can't have been cheap to make such a perfect scale model, nor to have it presented in such a theatrical way, but he wasn't going to swoon in front of Mollet and his sideman.

'Very neat Erik. So where are we standing exactly?'

Mollet looked suitably pleased and stepped forward to direct his pointer. 'We are precisely here. And if you look at the screen, I will show you in even more detail.'

In the distance the two old brick warehouses appeared, floating in the darkness. 'You'll recognise that we are in the larger of the two, on the left. Now watch.' Like a conjuror bringing a rabbit out of a hat, the building slowly dissolved to reveal an empty site. And then, in an animated sequence, two new buildings magically appeared and, in front of them, a stretch of water with a fountain firing a thin spurt of water almost to the height of the new buildings.

'*Voilà*,' he said with a flourish.

Finistere looked at the screen, refusing to be impressed. 'Good job it's never windy in Paris,' he said, looking down at the model, 'for those buildings would get very wet.'

He didn't like the idea he was being tickled under the chin, seduced by bright lights and beautiful images. Next week his own board was meeting to approve the final financial package for the project and he would have to deliver his verdict. It was bad enough dealing with British planning regulations and red tape but here, even if they did still operate under the broad umbrella of the EU, local house-rules and restrictions existed to catch the unwary. There were none of these outlined in the presentation, he noted.

'Where are the problems?' he demanded.

'Problems?' It was Papon.

'Oh come on, don't make out you don't understand the word, Erik. Where. Are. The. Problems?' he repeated, enunciating each word clearly. He took the stick from Mollet and swept it above the board. 'Where are my millions going to come unstuck? It's a reasonably shitty site that hasn't been used for years and it's bang next to a main railway line. What might we expect to go wrong? Perfectly reasonable question. C'mon, Erik, you were an international scrum half, so you're used to ducking and diving.'

'Ducking and diving? I don't think I understand.'

Round Mary was ostensibly making notes. So far, the meeting was taking a familiar form. It was the sort of rough and tumble that Finistere enjoyed, the deliberate shaking of the trees and ritual banging of the chest.

'Make a note, Mary. Translator for the next meeting. I would hate anything to get lost in translation.'

Mary duly made a note on her pad and couldn't help recalling the minutes of the board's last meeting in which her boss had outlined the potential profits at the various stages of this development. What he was doing now had something of the playground bully about it, a bigger boy pushing around a smaller classmate, only in this case it was money that was the muscle.

'I'm forever being asked to part with my money, gentlemen and I'd like to know where the pitfalls are.'

'Pitfalls?'

'Translator. Definitely.' Finistere stooped down to brush accumulated dust from his shoes with his clean white handkerchief.

Mollet had moved back into the shadows as Papon had taken the floor. Now he stepped back into the light and gave an easy laugh. 'You're right of course, Michael. We will define a list of the risks as we see them and reconvene. But in the meantime, are you not just a little bit excited at all this?'

'Sure. But it's still only a toy, isn't it?'

Mary, whose legs were now beginning to ache, would have laughed along with Mollet if she had the chance. The truth is she found him rather attractive, even though she knew he played in a league above hers. Nevertheless, his easy Gallic charm and courteous manner appealed to her and she couldn't help but smile.

'I thank you for all this,' Finistere said without conviction, moving away from the model, 'and I'd be grateful if you'd send the video stuff to Mary when you can. When shall we reconvene? Tell you what, I'll give you a day and we'll meet again here on Wednesday lunchtime. Should be time enough.' And might spoil your lunch, he thought.

The boy saw the loud one leave the group into the gloom of the large open space, so he had to move quickly to arrive at the bottom of the stairs in good time. He needed to get across the exposed ground in front of the brick warehouses before they emerged behind him. Once hidden behind the far wall he was able to watch them all depart, the loud man and the big woman first and the other two about ten minutes later. He watched them secure the small middle door and, with a cursory glance over the building, return to their car, parked beyond the lorries.

Youssef waited until he was sure they had gone before turning towards the back of the warehouses. Entry points to the two buildings had been secured some months ago and all the ground-floor windows were boarded or barred. Graffiti covered most of lower sections and notices warned against trespassing. In amongst the buddleia and hawthorn at the back of the building, Youssef pulled away several rusting corrugated-iron sheets to reveal a patterned manhole cover, perhaps once upon a time used for the delivery of fuel, the boy didn't know. What he did know, though, was this was his point of entry, one he'd been using regularly since he'd discovered it.

It was dark underneath, more so when he'd pulled the cover back in place and he felt his way along to the internal door which, although always closed, was never locked. Once opened it was lighter and he took the stairs two at a time to the top floor. The lamps that had lit up the middle of the room had been turned off, but there was enough daylight filtering through the industrial windows to wash over the model.

Youssef had never seen anything like it before and he stood for a long time just taking it in, wondering who could be clever enough to make something so real. He moved slowly around the outside and marvelled that wherever he stood the amount of detail was the same, that if he screwed up his eyes he could be one of the little figures on the paths.

It was only when he had completed a circle that it began to dawn on him that he was looking down on his own territory. There was the railway bridge under which he slept and the road that led to Clignancourt and on the other side, the one that went to the station. But where was the old railway line alongside which his camp had been built and all the other huts? In an instant, he saw that he had been excluded again, that his paltry shack and the rest of the encampment built in and around the concrete pillars were absent along with many of the other landmarks that made up his home.

Youssef saw that it was all going to change, to be torn down and rebuilt and that he would be discarded along with the old buildings. At first, he had been transfixed by this new world but now he realised that it would replace his own, however temporary, existence.

When he made a second tour of the model, he could see it more clearly and understood his predicament exactly. He had gained his perspective and it told him that he didn't really exist, that the world went on without him, for he was powerless. He leaned forward and touched one of the small figures, carefully outlining its shape. And then, out of the corner of his eye, he saw there were more figures, a child with its parents, but they were almost out of reach. The pointer was resting against an iron column and with this he loosened the little family and swept it nearer. He picked them up and held them in the palm of his hand, before taking them around to the far side of the model. Here it was easy to put the figures under the bridge and he experimented with the best position. He separated the child from its parents and put him – he had decided it was a him – on the top of an embankment wall at roughly the point he had made his camp among the buddleia. The parents he left in the shadow of the railway bridge. They were lying down.

3

Mary Houlihan's legs still ached, not that she would show this in front of her boss who believed that everyone should keep up with him, unable to acknowledge that sort of weakness in others and especially, she knew, in himself. He was already on the phone in the back of the car laughing with a chum and discussing a place to meet for dinner that evening. He had a network of male friends that all seemed to share his indefatigable energy and who were united by another common currency, money.

She heard him settle on the Savoy Grill and she made a note in her diary of the rendezvous and time. It was likely that he would forget or that it would be superseded by another, better offer. She sat in the front with the driver listening and understood that she didn't really figure in his life but was merely a useful adjunct and she wondered if everyone was like that for him, available but never properly connected. Her phone buzzed and she saw that a link to the video had been sent by Mollet.

'Is that Mollet?' Finistere said from the back of the car and she saw that her boss had been copied in on the email, not that he would have been able to retrieve the file from Dropbox, or anywhere else for that matter.

'When you reply, get him to email the details of Wednesday's meeting as soon as possible. That should keep him busy.'

She did as she was told, in a politer form, of course. Finistere had a natural suspicion of the French, seeing them all as unreliable schemers not to be trusted. But then, he thought that of most people and it was this instinctive caution, she presumed, that had made him very rich.

She was going back to the Lancaster with him, where he wanted to review the footage before he flew back to London. He had asked her to keep the suite on even though he wouldn't be staying that night and to book it again for the Wednesday. She was being asked to stay over in Paris to fix the interpreter and do whatever was necessary for Wednesday. Mary hadn't expected to be offered the suite for the night, nor would she have wanted it. She was happy in the small Left Bank hotel she had organised for herself and where she had stayed in the past. The car was to sit outside the hotel and wait until he was ready to return to Montparnasse. It was a strange way to lead your life, she decided, but in some small way she was part of it, a thought that sometimes made her uncomfortable.

The suite was about the same size as her London flat and better furnished, although she wouldn't have chosen the understated neutrality of the place, its clear fear of offence.

'Not sure about that Mollet. What do you think?'

She almost told him she didn't agree but kept her counsel knowing that the question was rhetorical in the first place.

'It was all a bit too neat, didn't you think? Like a very deliberate way of covering over the cracks.'

'Quite impressive, though,' she offered.

'Too impressive if you ask me. Have you sent the email yet?'

He didn't look at her as he asked the question.

'Of course.'

On her laptop she downloaded the file from Dropbox and she sat behind him as he watched the various sequences used to augment the scale model. She was only too aware that this was the endgame in a process that had begun over six months earlier and that his last-minute apprehension was a familiar self-imposed caution before the final commitment. She thought he was right to move carefully in these final moments, but there was something unappealing about his singular disregard of other people's efforts. Then again, she wasn't faced with the sort of decisions he had to cope with.

The images of the new development played before them, Finistere giving the impression that he was only half watching.

'Bloody fountain. Waste of time, if you ask me.'

'Impressive, though,' she said for the second time.

'You're easily taken in. Expensive and pointless.'

She was thinking of the giant fountain in Switzerland that she had seen on holiday and of the other fountains people travelled to see, the Trevi Fountain in Rome, or the ones in Trafalgar Square, expensive and serving no other purpose than to please. She wanted to say wasn't this enough but again remained silent.

'What do you think of it?'

She was surprised to be asked, as if her opinion mattered.

'I thought you were going to make a lot of money from it. Isn't that the point?'

He got up and paced to the far end of the room, moving to the window to look down on the plane trees. This was all quite familiar to Mary, the careful treading down of the ground before the point of no return had been reached. It was as much an act as a display of justifiable caution.

'What was wrong with the original buildings? I thought they were rather fine.'

'That's not my responsibility,' he said, still looking out over Paris. 'Anyway, they're about to fall down.'

There was an edge to his reply, a tone that she hadn't heard before and if she hadn't known him better she would have described it as doubt.

'It's a perfectly good modern development. And I do like the fountain.'

'Hustle that document out of them would you. I want to think about it for as long as possible. And make sure you get a good interpreter, one we can trust. I don't want someone who's going to bat for both sides. Order some tea, would you? If there's anything else, I'll call you.'

She did as she was told and then packed up the laptop, announcing that she would see him the day after tomorrow but would keep in touch in the meantime. He didn't say a word and was still looking out of the window as she left. She was annoyed that he hadn't asked her to stay for the tea, but glad to be out and away from the intense and one-sided nature of their exchanges.

Down in the foyer, she slipped off her leather shoes and put on a pair of trainers intending to walk to her hotel, down to Place de la Concorde, where she would cross the river to walk along the Left Bank to rue Jacob. It had been a long day and she was looking forward to clearing her head of a surfeit of Michael Finistere. Not that she disliked him, just that the process of being with him was unequal and therefore unsatisfactory, not so say exhausting. The walk would do her good.

Michael Finistere watched her leave the hotel, surprised to see her wearing trainers. She must be trying to lose weight, he thought. He wouldn't have minded a stroll in Paris himself but he was leaving for the helicopter within the hour and anyway he was preoccupied with a vague uncertainty, similar to the feeling he'd experienced earlier in the lift. Images of the development played in his mind and he saw the new buildings with absolute clarity, as he did the stages of development, the detailed lines of costs, the risks and the returns. Yet he felt there was something missing, a vital or hidden part and this disturbed him, like the broken spring in a bed at night. The development was going to be called Les Merchandises, not his idea but once upon a time the old warehouses had stored goods for use in Paris. It wasn't this that bothered him but a much vaguer malaise that seemed to hover around him, a cold mist that he was unable to dispel.

Crossing the Seine, Mary thought of the Liffey back home in Dublin and the days she would walk over to St Stephen's Green to meet friends. How different her life was now, although not necessarily happier. Not as simple, certainly, but then she had deliberately wanted to complicate it and as her mother would have told her, it's your bed, you lie in it. She wouldn't want the world of Michael Finistere, but she had somehow found herself part of it, albeit a tiny cog in a much larger machine. She was an optimist though and broadly happy with herself, even her size, though she was often told she should lose weight, even by her doctor. What did he know, she thought? She was only twenty-eight and had her life in front of her and if occasionally she wanted to throw a sharp object at her boss, she was learning a lot and right now she was walking through the heart of the Left Bank to her hotel and supper in the small bistro opposite. What was wrong with that?

Youssef lay on the wooden pallets that he'd made his bed. In the hut that he'd helped construct, they ran along the far wall and were slightly raised from the floor that often got wet when it rained hard. Over the months he'd been there he'd improvised bedding so that by now he was reasonably comfortable. He had begun to pin odd pieces of material to the walls to make a varied patchwork to soften the wooden planking. He looked up to the ceiling and imagined the railway lines beyond. He knew they went to Calais where he was told his brother might be living. They had fled together after the planes had bombed their home but he found it hard to remember all the details of that journey, for he had been concussed, Suliman later told him. They had become separated when the dingy that took them across the sea began to sink and the waves had pushed them apart. When the strong arms pulled him out of the sea, he found that he was alone. How he knew his brother was still alive, he didn't know, but he had convinced himself that as long as he kept thinking he was alive then he would be. He shut his eyes and tried to sleep but a hundred memories fought for his attention in the darkness and out of nowhere his mother was flying towards him again, a momentary vision that seemed to last forever. Why did she never see him, why wouldn't her eyes look his way? The image was never more than that. It never became anything else. All he ever got was this one image that always, like now, caught him unawares and had him sitting upright on his makeshift bed. He hadn't meant to think of her but then she arrived, horribly there but not there, clear but not real or normal. He waited for his breathing to change and as he did so he replaced the image with one of his own choosing, the giant model in the warehouse. It spread itself in front of him and he lay back to see it and looked carefully for the figures he had carefully placed.

He could feel sleep slowly overtaking him, his body melting into itself. When he awoke sometime later it was quiet and he was left with the residue of a bad feeling, that all was not as it should be. Then he knew what had awoken him. In his dream he had seen the little figures swept away by something much larger that he couldn't describe, his home smashed. He saw the model buildings broken, the fountain destroyed, everything tipped at wild angles, the streets cracked. And in the middle of all the chaos there was a long white stick and a man's hand. He couldn't see the rest of the body, just the hand that raised the stick and brought it down so violently on to the model that the buildings jumped in the air and the people spilled on to the floor.

Youssef sat on the edge of the pallets and put his head into his hands. Was he ever to find peace or would he always be haunted like this, never able to sleep but always at the mercy of forces he seemed unable to control?

He stood outside the hut and listened to the rumble of Paris and the distant sirens that always seemed to fill the air.

4

The police came just before dawn, as they usually did, drumming their batons against their shields like ancient tribesmen. Usually there was no real purpose to their visits beyond harassment and he lay in bed as they moved noisily through the camp, banging on the doors, shouting abuse and occasionally dragging an individual from his bed with shouted insults. He waited his turn, the commotion getting louder until his own door was yanked open and an anonymous dark figure hidden behind a helmet and visor, his body protected by armour, yelled at him to stand before yanking him out and pushing him against the rough wooden planking of the hut. His arms were forced up as the man screamed at him a torrent of words he didn't understand. This might be one of my dreams, Youssef thought as a way of comforting himself, perhaps it is not really happening in reality but only in one corner of my mind. The policeman went into the hut and proceeded to rip the materials off the wall, pull the pallets apart and destroy the bed. As he left, he spat at the boy's feet. The pattern was always the same, an aimless act of pure vandalism with the purpose of making their lives so miserable that they would decide to move on. It had happened to him across Europe, but it was worse here, the ugliness of the police behaviour and the squalor of their surroundings merely highlighted by the beauty of a city that he knew people travelled from all over the world to see. There was no one to complain to, no authority that would take up their cause and so silently, as dawn began to give shape to their surroundings, they began to reassemble their world, Youssef re-pinning the fabrics to the walls and deciding, in a minor act of defiance, to change the pattern and make a different patchwork, before restoring the bed. By the time the sun had appeared above the Périphérique, what he called his world had been restored, just as the jams had re-formed on the busy road. The events of the morning were still waiting to be given meaning.

It was Tuesday and he set off for the market in rue de Bretagne for breakfast. He had got to know several of the stallholders who in return for doing odd jobs would feed him and occasionally give him money. It helped, he knew, that they thought he was quite handsome, but that was not always to his advantage and there was one greengrocer who always came to stand too close and looked at him in a strange way.

This morning he was early enough to help unload the lorries that had just returned from the wholesale market. He had a knack of making himself useful and although he was clearly resented by some, on the whole he was accepted. It was the closest thing he had to family. He was given apples, cherries and bananas, some of which he ate, the rest he kept in his rucksack for later. He was amazed at the quantity of food he wheeled through to the stalls and the casual way some of it was discarded.

He was halfway through the morning, bringing in several boxes of carrots, when he stopped in mid-action. A combination of events that had troubled him now appeared to make sense and he pushed the waving carrot tops with even greater purpose. In a life that had become so dislocated, Youssef was conscious that this was beginning to happen more often, that instead of simply being at the mercy of events he had it in his power to seek solutions and work out answers. His transition from child to man had been abrupt but he was now aware that it had taken place and that he had changed. He took comfort in this, that the part in him that was dependent and helpless was in the process of being replaced.

Between them, the stallholders gave him assorted loose change and he left rue de Bretagne with almost twenty euros and enough food to last him a few days. The purpose of being in Paris was staying alive and right now he could see ahead two, maybe three days, which in the scheme of things was a lifetime. He crossed in front of the Gare de l'Est and then the Gare du Nord, working his way northwards. It was midday before he arrived at the camp but before going to the hut his dream of the night before prompted him elsewhere.

He entered the warehouse through the manhole, going first to the second floor where, on one of his earliest visits, he had discovered a series of metal lockers. He had chosen the least accessible one to store some of his very few private possessions, although he had another secret place for his prized watch. He now added most of the food and all but a few euros to the locker. He knew, though, that this safe haven was soon to be taken from him and he climbed to the top floor with a sense that once again his world was in peril and in danger of being lost.

The figures that he'd moved, the parents sleeping and the boy keeping watch nearby, were still there, silent and waiting for him. He understood the plan even more clearly now and was able to fit the buildings and roads in front of him on the model into the picture of what he knew to be real and, he was sure, soon to be destroyed. The increasing police raids signalled that they would shortly receive another more serious visit in which their huts would be razed to the ground and they would be moved on. Last night's dream was a premonition but it had taken him most of the morning to relate the dawn raid to the planners' model. He didn't want to destroy this beautiful toy but he was angry that he had been eradicated from it, just as his home town had been obliterated around him regardless of the fact that his family had lived there for hundreds of years. Who cares when you drop bombs from high in the sky or sit removed in a posh office and design a lovely model like this? Then you don't need to think of people, certainly not people like him. He felt invisible, dust on a bigger man's jacket waiting to be flicked away.

He went around to the far side of the model where he confirmed that the old railway line that led to the tunnel, above which he had his camp, now didn't exist. Too frightened, he'd never ventured far into the tunnel and he didn't have any form of light to help him. No matter how long he looked at the plan, Youssef couldn't understand how the planners had managed to eradicate something so large. But then this is what happens, he decided, the consequences ignored. He looked at that corner of the model for a long time and thought of the group that had stood around it the day before, the noisy man in the suit with the big woman and, just like earlier in the day, an idea came to him that somehow – and he didn't know how – seemed absolutely right.

He returned to his locker, took out a few more euros, and left the build-ing, covering the manhole cover with the sheeting. He set off back down towards the Gare du Nord, happy to have the next task in front of him, one that would take him through the afternoon. His father had been like that, never still, always doing this job or that and although it made him sad to think of him, this was a happy recollection and his thoughts absorbed him so that he reached his destination before he knew it. He stood in front of the shop as he had several times before, only now he had a purpose.

The window, which had been lined with a sort of orange paper to protect the displays from the sun, showed a range of toys, from cars and model cranes to dolls and small prams. At first he couldn't see what he wanted. He was nervous about entering for fear that he would be spoken to in rapid French or thrown out for being an Arab, but he plucked up courage and went in. It was a wonderland of toys, more than he'd ever dreamed of or thought could exist. Youssef lost his self-consciousness and he wandered around the magical interior until he saw what he was looking for, perfect in every way but for the price. He shook his head, a gesture that must have been seen by one of the assistants, a young woman who asked, first in French and then in English, if she could help. Hardly able to look at her, Youssef brought out the ten euros in accumulated change and showed it to her. She smiled and now it was her turn to shake her head. She pointed deeper into the shop and showed him something similar to the one he'd been looking at, offering it to him to hold. Youssef nodded his head and gave her the money, which she took, handing back two euros and then his purchase wrapped in a brown paper bag.

Youssef had a real sense of purpose as he strode back up the rue des Poissonniers towards the warehouse where once again he went through the procedures of getting into the old brick building. He climbed the stairs with a mounting sense of excitement out of all proportion to what he was about to do, although by now he had attached a symbolic importance to it. He went straight to the far side of the model and from the brown bag removed his purchase, which he held in his hand, turning it first one way then the other. He then placed it on the model and moved it around, deciding whether it could be seen from all angles, before returning and adjusting its position. He repeated the exercise twice more before he was happy. His final act was to take the figure of the boy and stand it next to the new addition to the plan and then, with half-closed eyes, assess them in relation to their surroundings. He declared himself happy and returned to the second floor to put the remaining money in the locker. He was still carrying the brown paper bag and he looked inside it before throwing it away. Inside was the white paper receipt. He took it out and saw that he should have paid ten euros for his purchase. The assistant had in fact let him have it for eight, allowing him to keep two euros. He sat down on one of the lockers and thought through what had happened. He understood then that she had done it deliberately, an unexpected act of kindness, an event so rare in his life that tears formed in his eyes. He dropped his head and watched his tears absorbed in the dust of the floor, glad that no one could see him cry but grateful also for the relief it seemed to give him and the weight that seemed to lift from his chest.

Finally he got up, knowing exactly what he was going to do, even though the idea didn't exist before his tears.

5

Mary Houlihan had about her a certain persistence, a quality from which Michael Finistere benefitted but never chose to praise. She approached finding a suitable translator with admirable logic, one that was helped by Google but finessed by her. By ten o'clock that Wednesday morning, sitting in a café in the rue du Bac, she had a list of ten possible candidates, four men and six women and with the crumbs of her breakfast croissant on the empty plate in front of her and a fresh *café crème* by her side, she began the process of whittling down the group.

After an hour and another coffee, she was left with three possibilities who, at various points in the unfolding day, would come to see her in the rue du Bac. Not long afterwards, the list was reduced further. Reporting her progress to her boss, he had told her he didn't want a man. 'It's bad enough having to negotiate with men as it is and I don't want another,' was his curt response and so she phoned and stood the candidate down.

Mary had been taught French rather well by a particularly enlightened nun who had spent some time working in northern France. She had been unconventional too and made them discuss real issues – politics, art, boys – in a way that didn't make the learning too arduous. Mary wouldn't be able to hold her own in French in a quick-fire conversation, but her comprehension was good, even if her vocabulary let her down, and the subjunctives, of course.

Mary knew the first woman wouldn't do in the time it took for her to walk from the café entrance to her table. There was a mouse-like plainness about her that she knew would set Michael's teeth on edge and even though her strong and clear voice belied the way she looked, her boss would have lost interest in her well before she spoke.

She ate lunch and waited for the other candidate hoping that her instincts on the phone were going to be justified. She was watching the rue du Bac go about its business when a copy of the email from Erik Mollet to Finistere arrived on her laptop. She saw that there was confirmation of the following day's meeting and an attached list of what Erik had called, Mary thought quite amusingly, 'Pitfalls and Problems'. She was just about to open this when there was a cough and she looked up to see a smiling woman who immediately introduced herself.

'Hello, I am Sophie Arditti. We spoke.'

Mary shut her computer and rose to shake her hand and only then registered how tall the other woman was. Her English was only slightly accented and she had an engagingly open face. By the time she sat down again she had probably made her decision, but over the next twenty minutes it was nice to be proved correct.

'I won't beat about the bush,' Mary said, 'but Michael Finistere, the man you'll be working for is, shall we say, not easy. He's direct and quite rude and as we say, he doesn't take prisoners. He's very demanding and one of the most important things he demands is total loyalty. He doesn't speak French, he doesn't like the language and he's not keen on the French either. So...'

'Thank you for being so straightforward. I admire it,' said Sophie Arditti, clearly not put off. 'My father felt the same about the English. But then he was Italian.'

'And I'm Irish, so perhaps we all feel the same way. And, to add to the list, he's also a bit of misogynist.'

'I assume you want me to take the job?' Sophie said and because she was still smiling, Mary knew that this was the woman.

'Well, I hope you'll take it. There is an important negotiation tomorrow with the French developers to whom my boss is about to release a great deal of money. Before he completes the deal he wants to know what the pitfalls are. It was an English word they didn't understand.'

'*Les pièges*,' Sophie said. 'We all want to know about those. Especially with a *misogyne*, almost the same word.'

The two women laughed. Later, after they'd agreed a fee and arranged to meet at the Lancaster at eleven the following morning, Mary sat alone and felt pleased with her day's work. Compared with a typical day with Michael, it was simple and stress free and she blessed her good fortune. It has to be said that there was an element of deviousness in Mary's satisfaction, for

Sophie was a handsome woman and in her experience Michael Finistere might soften his usual combative behaviour in her company.

She opened her computer and returned to the list of *pièges*, saying the word out loud. There were ten and as she read through them she tried to put herself in Michael Finistere's place. She imagined him approaching the document with his usual prejudice and suspicion. She wondered what he would make of the contaminated industrial soil, or the need to put in special rubberised foundations to absorb the vibrations caused by passing trains. And what about the extremely expensive safety measures to ensure that nothing from the site would fall on the tracks during construction? When she'd been through them all, she imagined that she had reached the same conclusion as her boss. There was nothing here that they didn't know already. These were the major pitfalls and problems associated with the demolition of the existing buildings and the building of the new development. Michael Finistere would want to know what had been left off.

She stared out of the window for a while and then paid the bill, leaving to walk up to the nearby taxi rank, where she asked to be taken to Porte de la Chapelle. Perhaps, she surmised as they rumbled across Paris, something of Michael Finistere had rubbed off on her after all.

She would have liked to see the scale model again but she had no key to access the building where it was kept. She walked up and down in front of the handsome buildings with the list of *pièges* in her hands, before turning towards the dual carriageway that flanked the northern boundary of the development. For a while it was on the same level as the site, before it dropped under the massive concrete bridge. She hadn't realised before but old railway tracks existed between the road and the site. This became clearer the lower she went and it was only then that she remembered Finistere's comment in the car the day before. She had been sitting on the opposite side, so she hadn't registered the shanty town of huts that had been built on the tracks and under the protection of the bridge. Groups of men were sitting around a fire made of broken pallets and a young boy was scrambling up from the boundary fence of the development.

Only now did Mary begin to feel uncomfortable, not simply because she was a lone woman in a rather isolated spot, but because she didn't want it assumed that she was prying. She walked on quickly and as she did she saw that the old railway lines entered a tunnel, something that was impossible to see from the road.

The smell of burning rubber followed her as she came out of the underpass and began the slow climb towards Clignancourt. She had been frightened, she admitted to herself, and she resisted the impulse to turn around and look more carefully at what she had seen.

She had a map of Paris in her bag and when she reached the massive junction at Clignancourt, taking a table outside a café, she began to study it. She thought about ordering a glass of wine but settled on tea instead. Even the map she had, reasonably detailed, hadn't marked the old railway. It made her want to return, to check the evidence of her own eyes and confirm the existence of the shanty town that she estimated could not be more than two or three kilometres from Montmartre.

She saw that there were a series of minor roads that would take her some of the way back but there was no other way to get beyond the main railway tracks than under the bridge. She knew one thing, that Michael Finistere would not have wandered around these parts by himself and this very thought made Mary decide to return the way she had come. So after the tea, made in lukewarm water and rather undrinkable, she marched off down into the underpass again with a resolution she didn't entirely feel. The view from this direction was different and she was able to note the number of huts, about fifty, she estimated. The deserted railway tunnel she saw was covered in graffiti, the tracks running into the darkness of the open mouth.

This was a strange no man's land, a patch that appeared to have been forgotten, certainly no part of Paris that she had been taught existed. It was hard to believe that the glorious buildings lining the Seine were only a short walk away. This was indeed a different Paris.

Mary saw how the tracks split behind the site of the new development and she tried hard to remember if they had ever been mentioned at the many meetings she'd attended to take notes. As the road rose on the other side, she looked through metal railings at the rusting tracks and the encampment, wanting to take a photograph on her phone, but at first deciding this wasn't wise. In the end, she put logic aside and quickly snapped a picture, a spectator on the other side of prison bars looking into a cell.

Later, back at her hotel, she looked at this picture, blowing it up so that she read the multi-coloured graffiti around the mouth of the tunnel, mocking reminders from those who'd left if not their names, then their marks. There was litter all around and the rusting lines spoke of little or no use. This space was just a wilderness but one in which people lived and had to survive.

Later Mary confirmed with her boss that she had found a translator, sending her details and informing him that she was coming to the hotel at eleven, which would give them time to meet and get used to one another. She imagined what line of attack Finistere was planning for tomorrow, for she knew he wouldn't make things easy, far from it. She debated whether to send him the photo of the track and tunnel but couldn't imagine that they had got this far without taking it into account.

She felt pleased with herself not simply for having gone up to the site, but for being brave enough to walk alone through the underpass. Mind you, in thinking about it she gave an involuntary shudder and tried not to imagine what might have been. She decided she would have the drink that she'd denied herself earlier, walking round to her bistro to take an early supper. She thought about Michael Finistere and his own dinner at the Savoy Grill. She knew what he would have been drinking because he always ordered the same wines, a Chassagne-Montrachet and a Volnay. He was a creature of habit and she couldn't decide whether this was because he knew a great deal about wine and had concluded these two were the ones he liked best, or if he had picked on these two wines simply because, at their exorbitant price, it was safe for him to order them.

He called later to confirm that he'd received the agenda for tomorrow's meeting.

'What did you make of the list?' he asked.

As if he really cared, she thought. 'I imagine you knew most of that anyway.'

'Sure, but it helps us focus on what they might have left out.'

Mary could almost hear the mirth in his voice. This was a game he loved, meat and drink to him.

'What about this translator woman? I take it she's good?'

'I think you'll like her.'

'A looker?'

'I'll leave you to decide. She has a nice smile, certainly.'

'Dinner last night was a waste of time,' he said, shooting off at a tangent. 'All Ridley can do is talk about his golf handicap and you know what a bore that can be.'

Well she didn't, as a matter of fact. 'I can imagine,' she said. 'But dinner must have been nice.'

'Oh sure, but at those prices it needs to be. I'll take you there one day.'

He'd said this before on more than one occasion. 'That would be nice,' she said.

'Well, I'll be there by eleven. Behave yourself.'

She was left holding the phone wondering how it was possible to have a conversation with someone and feel no connection at all.

6

He put down the phone and picked up the list that had been sent by Erik Mollet. He wasn't in Beaconsfield but in his small flat off Shepherd Market in Mayfair. It had once belonged to a whore, or high-class escort as she liked to be called, a fact he told everyone who came there. Finistere enjoyed seeing their reaction and accordingly he had various stories, some true and others figments of his imagination, to embroider the basic facts. The truth was, he knew the prostitute and indeed several of her chums, and he would often be entertained by her in this very room. She told him that she had been left the flat by a grateful client, a fact he was hard pushed to believe until he saw the deeds that were, as she said, in her name. She had needed to sell and for once Michael Finistere didn't drive a hard bargain and both parties were pleased with the outcome. To seal the deal, they had sex for the final time in front of the old fireplace against which he was leaning. It was a bachelor pad, not dissimilar from what it had been then, except it wasn't only bachelors she entertained, but anyone who could afford her fees. And, of course, he had entirely renovated the place, even if he could remember the old decor as if he was standing surrounded by it now.

He sat by the small desk in the window with the view down on to what was the old market. He imagined how shocked Round Mary would be if he told her the story of the flat and what had gone on in here but he thought her strict Irish Catholic sensibilities might not have coped. He transferred his thoughts to the list of Pitfalls and Problems and read through them again, although by now he could virtually recite them blindfold. They were more or less what he knew already, a rehash of some of the early site assessment exercises they'd conducted almost half a year ago. In a way, he was slightly disappointed in Mollet. He would have been wiser to add one or two more to keep everyone on their toes. Even then, though, he doubted if the Frenchman and his team would have been giving him the full picture. Michael Finistere didn't suffer from cold feet but something was bothering him and if the flat had been big enough to pace around that's what he would have done. Instead, he phoned Stuart Phelps, who sat on his board and was the nearest thing an owner like Finistere could have as a right-hand man.

'Stu, it's me. You've got the list?'

'Sure have. Nothing we didn't know is there.'

'Why should I be worried then?'

'Because you always are.'

Stuart had been at the same school and probably knew, or thought he knew, Michael Finistere better than anyone. He'd done any number of deals with his friend and had seen this last-minute concern on more than one occasion.

'Nothing else specific has cropped up, has it? We've made heavy contingency plans in relation to every item on the list. Assuming all the properties are sold, we'll make a killing, enough for the odd case of good Burgundy anyway.'

Michael liked his old friend, one of a group of males he could trust.

'I'm going over there again tomorrow.'

'Do you know something we don't?'

'No, but just like my Dad's hands used to ache before the weather turned cold, I've got this odd feeling.'

'Do you want me to come over with you?'

Finistere appreciated the offer but it wasn't what he was after. He didn't need to have his hand held, but someone to give shape to his apprehension, to supply facts to support his feelings or at least to indulge in speculating what might be wrong.

The year before, Michael Finistere made a hundred million pounds. He didn't have to work, but the idea of not never really crossed his mind. Others might have said to him that money was simply a drug, that without it, or at least without the process of making it, he couldn't exist. He'd heard all the stories and indeed he'd helped foster one or two. As much as he felt no guilt about the money, he also appreciated that very few people understood what having a great deal of money really did to your life. Once the process of making it was underway, what followed was the infrastructure to keep it. The web became more complicated as time went by and looking after money, as Michael often told his clients, was a full-time job. His father would never have stopped, of that he was sure. If the money had flowed in like it had for his son, he would have felt compelled to go on for fear the tap might close. It was a compulsion.

Youssef Tigha pushed the coins together to make a pattern. Then he stacked them in their various denominations, but each time he counted the amount was still the same, just over twelve euros. It was a comfort to have so much and yet it wasn't enough to buy what he really needed, even if he wasn't sure he'd have the courage to use it. He decided to take half the money, closing the door on the locker and taking a little pleasure in the knowledge that at least some of it was left. He checked the model and its new additions before he left the building and made his way northwards towards the stadium, next to which there was a garage. He had once asked for work here, but had been chased away. He remembered, though, that in the shop he'd seen what he now sought.

'What do you want, kid?' the voice shouted almost as soon as he walked in. The manager was large and unshaven, wearing dirty blue overalls on which he rubbed his filthy hands.

Youssef pointed to the displays to one side of the payment kiosk and the man looked behind him. Yellow stars proclaimed that everything was just five euros. When the man turned back, Youssef was holding out the change he had in his hand. The man came over to look suspiciously at it before moving aside to allow Youssef to pass. When he got to the counter, he picked the one he wanted and the man tore it from the cardboard mount and gave it to him.

'Now piss off you little Arab.' Youssef didn't have to understand all the words to know what he was saying. He made to walk past the garage manager but in front of him he paused, pressed the torch and saw the beam light up the man's face.

'Get out of here you bastard,' he yelled and he made to hit Youssef, who ducked and ran to the door. 'And don't come back you little fucker.'

Not all shopkeepers in Paris were kind.

That was the easy bit, Youssef thought as he prepared himself for what was to come next. At least it was daylight and would be for a few hours yet. He returned to the camp, tucking the yellow torch into his pocket before heading for the tunnel entrance. He'd been this way so often before the men around the brazier barely gave him a second look. He usually clambered up the steep sides to his camp above but instead he stood in front of the dark mouth of the tunnel plucking up the courage to enter. He moved cautiously forward. He'd been this far before and he waited for his eyes to adjust to the darkness. He could feel his heart beat and he tapped his trouser pocket to reassure himself that the small torch was there. He didn't know what good it would do but he was surprised that the longer he stood there, the more he could see. He inched forward, as much concerned about the darkness ahead of him as what he might step in or what might run across his path. He knew he should wait before turning on the torch for he wanted to be far enough into the tunnel for the other men not to see him. He got the sense that the track was dropping very slightly as it turned slowly to the left and when he eventually pressed the back of the torch, he saw that he had been right for the beam at first picked up the curving wall to his right. He caught the light reflected in a pair of eyes and he heard a creature run further into the tunnel. There had been enough rats back home for him to be used to them and he continued to follow the curve of the tracks. He didn't want to turn around for he imagined the curve of the tunnel would have blocked out the daylight at the entrance.

Youssef kept his fear at bay. The torch, although not powerful, was strong enough to show him the brick walls on either side although its beam didn't penetrate far into the darkness directly ahead. Another rat darted across his path and he was glad he was not wearing shorts. The air was stale and unused and unnaturally still.

At first the shapes looming ahead disconcerted him and his instinct was to stop and turn off the torch. The sudden complete darkness took him by surprise and he quickly turned the light back on. It took him a moment to regain his balance before he walked towards the objects in the tunnel. The torch caught the red of a lamp and he saw that it was mounted as a warning on the back of a wagon. It was filling most of space but Youssef squeezed along one side, concerned about the size of the carriage towering above him. The beam of the torch picked out the shape of another just beyond and his curiosity was only just more powerful than his fear. He was rewarded for his efforts, for just after this second truck it seemed to be slightly lighter and even without the torch he could make out a platform to his left. He hoisted himself up, feeling the layers of dust under his fingers and as he did so he became aware of another sensation, fresher air, a mild current that from time to time fought free of the stale mustiness of the tunnel. Youssef shone the torch against the wall along the platform and he could see some double doors. He was cautious now, afraid of what he might discover.

The handle of the first door was layered with dust and it clearly had not been used recently. He turned it and pulled but nothing happened and he assumed it was locked until he pushed and almost fell forward. He was in what felt like a huge storage space although the weak torch couldn't reveal its true dimensions. He risked uttering a sound that seemed to be absorbed into the emptiness around him. He had lost his sense of direction but he knew he couldn't have come that far and the turn in the tunnel would surely have led back towards the warehouses. His torch revealed a bench to his left and he sat down.

He couldn't believe all this existed underground, a lost world. The small torch couldn't give him the scale of the place, but he sensed that it was large. He could tell that he was alone and sitting there in the dark underground cavern he felt calm and not even the rustle of hidden rats could disturb this. He would need to explore more but this was beyond his small torch.

He returned the way he came, excited at this lost world, knowing that if the camp was destroyed he would have somewhere to flee, a sanctuary where it was dry and warm.

7

Mary was laughing to herself. It was early on Wednesday morning and she was imagining Michael Finistere going through the routines of departure from London unable to issue a series of demands and questions in her direction. A colleague had been deputed to be early that morning, an efficient, pleasant woman but one who didn't quite have the robustness to cope with his demanding and unrelenting behaviour. Mind you, Finistere had already been on the phone asking her to confirm exactly where they were meeting Mollet's team, something she had already done in an email late the night before.

'And have we got the suite for tonight?'

'Yes, it's booked for tonight and tomorrow, just in case.'

'Just in case what?'

'Contingencies, I think you said.'

'Right. What's the forecast?'

'Not good, I'm afraid. I hope you get clearance for Montparnasse.'

'It would be typical of the French to stop us. There's always something.'

At this rate, she thought, a self-fulfilling prophesy. 'I'm sure it will be fine.'

'Have they invited us to lunch?'

'Not as yet. If they do, do you want me to accept?'

'You might as well.'

The question-and-answer session went on for about ten minutes. Although it was only six-thirty in the morning, Finistere was already into his stride.

'And the translator woman, what's her name, Dotti was it?'

Mary sometimes wondered if her boss did this deliberately. He had a forensic memory when it came to facts and figures and she had thought, on more than one occasion, that he was only playing at forgetfulness.

'Sophie Arditti.'

'That's the one. You've taken her through the drill, haven't you? I want her absolutely on my side.'

'I've made that very clear, yes.' And I've added one or two extra observations about you, Mr Finistere. 'Did you call your mother?'

'Oh bugger. I'll do it later.'

Ten minutes later Mary Houlihan stepped out of her shower and dried herself in front of the full-length mirror on the wall of the small bathroom. She always thought she looked smaller naked. The breasts were large, to be sure, but they didn't sag and they were firm on her upper body. Yes, her hips were large, but she regarded them as a given that no amount of dieting would ever change. Her legs she was proud of and they somewhat belied the hips above, tapering as they did to good ankles. Perhaps her face could do with a little more definition and seeing her hair flattened on her scalp, she asked herself if it shouldn't be shorter. She knew that it was often difficult to see oneself but assessing the image in front of her, Mary Houlihan declared herself not altogether displeased.

The previous evening, returning from her reconnoitres in the underpass, she had bought some new underwear and once she had dried her hair she took each garment and held it in front of her. She stepped into the knickers and pulled them into place before clipping on the matching bra. Mary was a dark redhead and her skin was white, so the emerald green silk underwear defined her well and when she pulled the high-leg panties a little further up her hips they complemented her shape. Although she would not have admitted that Erik Mollet had anything to do with the purchases, she nevertheless would not have minded him seeing her now.

She finished dressing, completed her make-up, combed her hair and finally curtsied to herself in the mirror laughing again as she did so. Mary Houlihan looked good when she laughed, something of an impish six-year-old girl breaking out.

By the time she came down to breakfast she had decided to have her hair done and speculated if she had time before Sophie's arrival at eleven. She doubted it but asked the receptionist, a formidable woman, probably in her mid-fifties, if she could recommend a salon nearby. There was a place around the corner that was always open early, she was told, but whether they could do her she had no idea. It was a risk, Mary knew, but she decided to take a chance and shortly after nine she arrived at the salon to see that each of the chairs was in use. As she stepped inside, one of the hairdressers beckoned her over, appraising her hair even as she did. Mary explained what she wanted and Miriam, her name was clipped to her shirt, looked at her watch and said she had to get 'her lady' ready for work and would be ten minutes.

Mary Houlihan's hair had remained just about the same for as long as she could remember and so to trust its change to a hairdresser she'd never met in a strange salon in a foreign city was taking a chance and only afterwards did she wonder why she had taken the risk. Once Miriam had taken hold of her hair, quite firmly and confidently, she relaxed as she was asked in slow French whether she would prefer it like this, or like that. For the second time that morning her hair was sprayed flat on her skull and by clever manipulation of the long strands, Miriam gave her an idea of what she thought would work. Mary agreed and for the next hour watched as her cut hair fell on her shoulders and on to her lap and she underwent a sort of transformation that was both external and internal. Miriam had given her a parting, almost masculine in style, short around the ears and sides, the rest pushed back and slightly raised. It made her face seem lighter and thinner and with it the rest of her body. She couldn't believe the change, nor, indeed, where the courage had come from to do it. She was delighted and so was Miriam, especially with the tip Mary left. She felt the air around her face and head as she returned to the hotel and laughed out loud for the third time that morning.

'They're re-directing us to Le Bourget,' the pilot called back to him.

'What the fuck. Why?'

'Thunderstorms and high winds. Too dangerous to land in the city centre. I've radioed ahead and told the car to pick us up there. We'll get to the airport before we would have arrived at Montparnasse, but it's a bit of schlep, about seven miles, into town. I'm sorry.'

Finistere decided to go straight to the development and he called Round Mary.

'Typical,' he said, 'the French won't let us land at Montparnasse and have rerouted us to a place called Le Bourget, wherever that is. Tell Mollet and his mob we'll see them on site. I'll have to take a chance on the translator. Apologise to her, would you? I hope this is not an omen.'

The day had begun badly. Earlier his car had been delayed picking him up from the flat and the only way he could be sure of getting to Farringdon Road in time was to take the Tube to Chancery Lane and walk. He hadn't been on the Central Line for years and it was rush hour. It was an experience he never wanted to repeat.

They had about sixty miles to go and the journey in the helicopter had been bumpy, particularly as they left the Channel and hit the French mainland. The pilot had warned him as they flew into cloud but the sudden drop in height took him by surprise. He was wearing a seatbelt, which kept him in place even as his body tried to rise. No, things were not going well this morning but were, he had to admit, in line with his mood. 'Some days are just like that,' his father had often said, as though it was a matter of fate and there was nothing you could do about it.

Mary spoke to a woman in Mollet's office to say she and the translator would be arriving separately from Finistere, who had been delayed but would be coming straight from Le Bourget and, traffic permitting, should be on time.

The car that would have been taking them all to the meeting had been rerouted to pick up Finistere so Mary and Sophie ordered a cab. The translator, who was wearing a grey linen jacket and skirt and a white silk shirt, took it all in her stride. She looked very elegant and Mary thought that her boss might be slightly mollified when he saw her.

They arrived at Les Merchandises slightly early and sat in the car waiting for the others. Mollet and Papon pulled into the trailer park shortly afterwards and Mary introduced them to Sophie Arditti. They chatted rapidly in French and she assumed, from the gist of the conversation, that the men were flirting with her. Mary was surprised then when, as they walked to the wooden doors, Mollet leaned his head towards her and complimented her on her hair. '*Bien chic,*' was how he summed it up.

Youssef watched them from within the buddleia, noting that the loud man was missing. He saw the group go in but hesitated before he made a move. A few minutes later another car arrived and the loud man got out, smoothing down his suit. Even from this distance, Youssef could see that he wasn't happy and he appeared to be grimacing as he hurried towards the doors. He was carrying the briefcase the fat woman had been holding the day before last.

The boy was more confident about approaching the doors, already aware of the floor they were going to, but he needed to hurry because he wanted to see their reaction when they saw the model.

He crept up the stairs and once more peered around the wooden partition. He was just in time to see the lights turned on and the model come to life. There was another member of the group, dressed in grey, who was speaking both French and English, but he couldn't see her clearly.

The big woman was already holding the briefcase and the loud one had moved next to the new woman to shake her hand. He was quite a long way from the group and the sound of their discussions came and went. The new woman had her back to him as she chatted to the loud man, who seemed happier. Then the introductions were over and the two groups separated and he thought the meeting was about to begin. The woman in grey had moved to the side of the loud one, who was about to begin speaking. Now that Youssef could see her more clearly, there was something about her that made him want to go closer. Then Youssef took a sudden intake of breath. He shook his head and blinked. Was this possible? Could this be the woman from the train? This was about the distance he always watched her from the tracks and the more he stared, the more he was sure. She was here, she existed. This was the dream made real and he brought forward one of the images of her in the train, framed in the carriage window, part of a fantasy that was in the process of becoming reality in front of him, the same face, the same eyes, yes those eyes. And with this recognition came fear.

Michael Finistere was going to be on the front foot from the start.

'As you know,' he said, 'this charming woman, Sophie Arditti, is going to help us make sure there are no difficulties understanding some key issues today, so that we know exactly what…' here he referred to some notes he had made, '…*les pièges* might be for us all. I hope I make myself clear. If not, I'm sure Ms Arditti will.'

Mollet was quick off the mark. 'We are delighted to welcome *Mademoiselle* Arditti.' And then, in French, 'I'm sure we will understand each other perfectly.'

At this point, Sophie turned to Finistere and translated.

This is how it continued.

'Let me thank Mr Mollet and his team for coming up with the list of pitfalls and problems so quickly and for all the work they put into this magnificent scale model of our development.'

Sophie did the translation and only then did everyone automatically turn to the model. Michael Finistere was about to continue when he stopped, walked closer and then pointed to the far side, over the miniature buildings, the pretend roads and cotton-wool trees, the little figures and cars, across to the northern edge of the development.

'What the fuck is that? Has someone been using this as a toy?'

Sophie duly translated but by then everyone had followed Finistere's pointed finger.

8

The figure was giant, about three stories high in relation to the first of the proposed new buildings, but still only a toy figure. It was dressed in dayglow orange and at the end of its outstretched arm it was holding a red flag. Just behind and protected by it were the smaller figures of the mother, father and child. It was a wonder they hadn't seen it from the start, for it was so out of scale with its surroundings. In fact, had it been the right size it would have been entirely in keeping and might have been regarded as an amusing addition by the model's makers. They all peered forward to look more closely.

'How did that get there?' Mollet said in French, looking at his two assistants. 'Did you change it?'

Sophie translated, although Mary had understood. Finistere walked around the model to get a closer look, leaning in towards the orange figure before prodding it with his finger. The arm holding the flag waved slowly up and down and a shadow came and went over the smaller figures just behind. He was about to ask whether this was some sort of joke but this immediate reaction was checked and he closed his mouth. Someone had put the figures there deliberately.

'Some sort of prank, Mollet? French humour? I thought that was the domain of the English.'

'I don't know,' the Frenchman said, honestly. 'I'm certain it wasn't there the other day, but then I can't say I looked that carefully.' And then, in rapid French to Claude Papon: 'This place is sealed, isn't it? No one can get it?'

'Absolutely,' Papon said. 'But I will check.' He left quickly towards the stairs.

Sophie explained the exchange.

'So, not a joke then Erik?' asked Finistere, smiling. He liked to see the French discomforted. In fact, he now chuckled and said, 'I wish I had thought of it myself,' for the figure represented some of the apprehensions he'd been having about the project. He shook his head. '*Pièges*, eh Erik? Perhaps that little fella is trying to tell me something.'

Mary looked down at the figure whose arm was still slowly rising and falling. Like her boss, she too thought it was a warning but perhaps not in the same way that Finistere did, for she saw the protective nature of the larger figure standing in front of the family. She'd seen similar, larger-than-life-size mannequins on the French motorways, flagging a warning to approaching drivers to slow down. Then she thought of her walk through the underpass, past the shanty town and the men gathered around the burning pallets on the tracks, before she looked again at the model. It was difficult to correlate the geography of the layout in front of her with the reality outside, for the dual carriageway and the underpass were missing from the model and the major railway lines were merely represented by a grey-painted embankment on which cotton-wool trees had been stuck. She saw, though, that the little figures of the family that were protected by the giant in orange were placed at the far end of the model, at a point where the dual carriageway and the underpass would be and, more specifically, the deserted railway line around which the shanty town was built.

Claude Papon had returned to report that he'd been around the outside of the building and that there were no signs of forced entry. Sophie once again translated.

'So they did it themselves,' said Finistere, pointing at the figures and continuing to enjoy the moment. 'Clearly some form of advanced computer animation, wouldn't you say?'

Youssef watched as events unfolded in front of him, transfixed at the impact the orange figure had on the group but then alarmed as one of the men broke away from the group to come rapidly towards him. Youssef turned and fled to the floor below, where the layout was the same, and he hid behind the wooden partition. He was unable to hold his breath and he was certain the man would register his panting and the beating of his heart, but he heard him race down the stairs towards the outside door. Youssef didn't dare move and a few minutes later the man returned, taking the stairs two at a time back to the top floor. When he thought it was safe, Youssef followed.

*

Finistere was again conducting ceremonies.

'So, pitfalls and problems, Erik. Let's pretend the figures are exactly that, simply toys, meaningless. Tell me more. The deal on the table is for two hundred and fifty million, give or take, yes? A quarter of a billion pounds for which my company takes the proceeds of the sale of the five hundred and fifty apartments at around half a million each. Assuming they sell, that is.' He had picked up the white stick and was now pointing at the new buildings. 'Then a percentage of the commercial rents and a little slice of the service charges.'

'And,' said Mollet, 'the fee for using your money in the first place.'

'Of course,' replied Finistere.

'A good deal, wouldn't you say?' the Frenchman said.

'Then why is that figure telling me to stop.'

'It's only a toy, as you said.' Mollet's face was serious.

Still holding the white pointer, Michael Finistere wandered away from the group towards the tall metal windows that lined the open space on both sides. Many of the panes of glass had been broken and he peered through the jagged remains on to the desolate site beyond. He knew it took vision and no little bravery for these projects to see the light of day and that it was impossible for all contingencies to be covered. The margins were large, though, and the rewards considerable, more for his group than Mollet's, as he was risking more money. He was conscious, however, that any delays in the redevelopment would be his liability. He caught a glimpse of himself in one of remaining panes and stopped. His hair, short, formal, parted had resisted all attempts to conform to current fashions, so it had never been long, nor wound in a pony-tail, nor shaved to a stubble. Since he was in the gym at five most mornings, his face had maintained its shape over the years. He was less ready to admit that his views had remained similarly unchanged and that he had arrived at middle age much as he had left his teens, his instincts and prejudices intact. On the whole, he was pleased with this stasis, which he regarded as maturity.

However, on this stormy morning in Paris, he was still unable to account for his feelings of unease.

He returned to the group. 'Persuade me,' he said, handing the stick to Mollet, who gave a theatrical bow.

Erik Mollet had come to the conclusion some time ago that Michael Finistere was a formidable and unpredictable opponent with an uncanny knack of sensing the weak points in any deal.

'There are many difficulties with this site, as you know. I have tried to explain them all during our various meetings and I attempted to encapsulate them in the paper I sent.' He pointed the white stick at the orange figure and pushed it over.

'Here's one,' he said. 'Since we bought this plot several years ago, the migrants have started to live here.' He jabbed the stick on the northern extremities of the plan. 'I will admit, on this model they are not represented, but we have the cooperation of the police and the mayor and they will pose no problem. I'm told they're about to be moved on any day now. So that will be the end of one of the problems.'

Significantly, all this was said in French and Sophie Arditti explained in English, even taking the pointer from Mollet to give emphasis to her words.

When she'd finished, Finistere nodded his thanks. 'And it's as easy as that, is it?' he said, clicking his fingers. 'The police move in and they go. Like Calais.'

'Like Calais,' echoed Mollet.

'Except they haven't all gone from Calais, have they? Some have moved on, but others are still arriving.'

'Paris is different. This is the capital city.'

'I can take your word on that, can I?' Finistere said in a voice that belied that he could. 'Won't the buggers keep returning? You know what they're like. Our government called them a swarm. Even the shortest delays will cost us both money, me more than you.'

'Yes,' agreed Mollet, 'it is a joint risk, but manageable. You've seen how the police work here. They have their ways.'

Youssef heard all this in French and English, so his comprehension was doubly confirmed, his conclusions underlined and highlighted. As he had suspected, they were going to be moved on, driven out yet again on their unhappy, broken journey across Europe.

The Frenchman was still talking, although by now Youssef had stopped listening, his eyes drawn to something else. The big woman had put the bag down and the group were being asked to look at the top end of the model, at the area where Youssef had placed the figures. One of the other Frenchmen turned on the television and the main lights were dimmed. Youssef could see old black-and-white pictures of railway tracks, presumably the ones on which the camp was built. He wasn't interested in what was being said for his attention was still fixed on the bag resting against one of a line of metal columns that supported the great roof. The decision was made in an instant, the process of risk assessed in a blink of his eyes and he moved into the dark interior of the space to stand behind one of the iron pillars. There were three more between him and the bag.

'Once upon a time, these railway lines helped bring goods into Paris, which were stored in this and other great warehouses. Those lines will have to be taken up and the channels through which they ran filled in. This is another problem, a not insignificant task.'

Youssef wasn't listening to this or the commentary on the old newsreel and he was only partly aware of the sound of the steam train spilling out from the large plasma screen. By now he had reached the penultimate column, his eyes, like that of a big cat hunting, fixed on the briefcase. His stillness belied the speed that followed and he quickly and silently covered the ground to the bag and snatched it up. He ran back along the line of columns, heading towards the door. He was half way there when he heard the cry.

Michael Finistere, unimpressed by the steam train huffing its way across his project, had turned to look at Sophie Arditti and the shape of her lips as she translated Mollet's running commentary. His eyes dropped down over her body and he liked the way she wore her clothes, the shape of her breasts under her jacket and the way she stood. But then his eye was taken by a very different shape moving in the periphery of his vision further on in the gloom of the warehouse. Shielding his eyes from the spill of the down-lights above, he could make out the shape of a boy running across the empty floor.

'What the fuck.'

At this, the rest of the group turned to look at Finistere but seeing him stare into the body of the warehouse, they adjusted their eyes to follow his. Mary knew what had happened even before she confirmed the empty space at the foot of the metal column.

'The bag's gone,' she said.

'You mean the fucking briefcase?' Finistere shouted. 'What's in it?'

'Everything.'

It was an incongruous sight to see Michael Finistere, neatly clad in a tailored suit and wearing immaculately polished black leather shoes, sprinting towards the exit and for a moment they all watched. He was fit and reached the doorway before the others had reacted. Finistere heard the soft but urgent pad of feet below him and raced after the sound. His smooth leather soles on the concrete steps were not ideal and they slowed him down, almost causing him to slip over. Even so he reached the ground floor with remarkable speed and burst through the outside doors certain that he'd see the boy on the open carpark space, but the only movement in the desolate scene was the rain bouncing from the roof of a parked lorry. The boy was nowhere.

Finistere turned back in, the shoulders of his suit soaking wet. The boy had to be inside and he walked slowly towards the interior of the ground floor.

Youssef heard his approach. He was standing just behind the door that led to the basement and then on to the hatch that would take him to the exterior. In his hand was the piece of wood that he had used to wedge shut the door from the inside, for there was no lock. He knew that whoever was following him would try the door and he reckoned he only had seconds before this would happen. He had just forced the pole under one of the door's panels and jammed the other end to the floor when he heard the feet stop on the other side. He saw the handle turn and he knew that whoever it was would next try to force the door open. He ran to the hatch and pushed it open, a grating sound that he knew would carry. He heaved himself into the space above, the rain falling on his head as he registered the splintering of the wooden door behind him. He slid the metal cover back into place, dragging the corrugated sheets on top. He didn't have long and sprinted, the bag under his arm, towards the metal fence where, sliding the uprights aside, he slipped through and pushed them back into place.

He climbed the steep embankment to his camp above the tunnel and watched, the rain streaming down his face, the bag tucked between his legs.

9

Mary wasn't built for taking stairs two at a time and walked slowly behind, constructing her defence against Finistere who would automatically blame her for the loss of the bag. By the time she had arrived at the outside doors, the group had dispersed, Finistere was nowhere to be seen and the Frenchmen had disappeared to either side of the warehouse perimeter.

'You didn't tell me it was going to be like this,' Sophie said, drawing alongside Mary, the sound of the rain drumming on their umbrellas. 'But you did give me a very good impression of what he's like. He can't be easy to work with.'

The two women smiled at each other.

'No, he's not easy,' agreed Mary, nodding towards the bedraggled figure of her boss walking quickly towards them, his dark blue suit soaked and streaked with dirt. 'Stand by.'

'Secure my ass. Back of this place is like Selfridges on a Saturday. Anyone could get in and out. Where's Mollet? I want to give him a bollocking. Don't get wet,' he said to Sophie as he moved off to find the Frenchman.

'You changed your hair,' Sophie said to Mary. 'Overnight. I like it. Did he notice?' she asked, looking at the departing figure of Michael Finistere.

'Who knows,' Mary said. 'I don't really register on his radar, until he needs something that is.'

'Was the briefcase important?'

'I'm afraid so. It had most of the details of this deal,' she said, waving a hand towards the surrounding land.

'And he's going to blame you for losing it.'

'Of course, but he'll probably ask you to dinner first.'

The two women laughed, a strangely operatic chorus as the rain fell around them.

Finistere and the two Frenchmen appeared around the far corner of the warehouse and as they approached the two women were ushered back into the building where they all dripped on to the concrete floor.

'I've called the police,' said Mollet, now conducting all conversations in French.

'How could you have missed that way in to the building?' Finistere demanded although not in a way that expected an answer. And then he turned to Mary.

'What made you put the bag down? You knew what was in it.'

Mary thought that he had no right to admonish her publicly and refrained from saying that they had all been assured that the warehouse was safe and, anyway, the briefcase had been heavy.

'He was only a kid,' Claude Papon said. 'We'll find him.'

'Yes, and the details of this deal will be all over Paris by then.' Michael Finistere had his hands thrust deep into his pockets and the fine elegance of his suit was distorted. 'The Arabs will trade anything to anyone,' he said, while at the same time thinking that the events of the day were in line with his mood, one justifying the other.

'He just disappeared somewhere behind us,' Papon continued. 'The police will do a sweep of the land and the shacks over there.' In the distance they could already hear the wail of sirens and not long after a pair of police cars swung into the concrete car park.

The formalities were conducted in French and mediated through Sophie, the description of the briefcase and its contents, the means of entry and exit to the warehouse, the scant description of the thief and then, on the top floor, gathered around the model, a walkthrough of what had happened. Finistere wondered if he cared. There were duplicates of the documents and he doubted any of them would find their way into the wrong hands and even if they did, he couldn't imagine the facts could do him any harm. Already his mind had moved on and as the policemen were taking everyone's contact details, he beckoned Sophie to his side.

'I'm sorry about all this,' he said. 'I'm sure it's not what you were expecting. Perhaps I could take you to supper this evening. I have a table at the Grand Véfour.'

'*Le Grand Véfour*,' Sophie repeated, pronouncing the name of the restaurant correctly. 'This would be a business matter, yes?'

'Of course,' said Finistere, nodding his head slowly at her.

'I think it might be wise then if Mary came. Would that be a problem?' Her smile was as wide as her eyes.

'Naturally,' he said, walking away from her and then, over his shoulder, 'we'll meet there at eight.'

Youssef knew they wouldn't find him and he was certain that even if they discovered the way through the metal fence, they wouldn't venture into the camp. When the police did that they did so in numbers and from his perch under the protection of the overhanging buddleia, he could see only two police cars. He watched the loud one and the other two men run around the exterior of the warehouse in their smart suits and he enjoyed seeing them get wet. For the moment it was only the bag between his legs that concerned him for he would be vulnerable until he had hidden it and to do that he would need the torch, which he had left in the hut.

He put the bag under the low branches of the tree and scrambled back down the steep embankment. He didn't have long. Once the police reinforcements arrived he would be a prime target, for he was certain that at least one of the party had seen enough of him to give them a description.

He grabbed the torch from his hut and, sure enough, climbing back up to the camp, he heard them arrive, the threatening wail of a dozen sirens and the staccato slamming of doors. Even as he was sliding back down the embankment, he knew that later they would find the locker and that he would lose what tangible evidence he possessed of the life he had once lived.

Entering the gloom of the tunnel, he imagined them finding the photograph of his mother. The money didn't matter, but that precious memory of the past was irreplaceable. He pushed on into the gloom, edging past the wagons until he reached the platform. Down here it was still and dry, the air heavy with dust and he sat on the bench he had used before to gather his breath. If they followed, he would hear them long before they arrived.

He looked at the leather bag on his lap and wondered if taking it had been worth the loss of his mother's photograph. He undid the two buckles, holding the torch between his teeth, and slid out some of the documents, including a blue folder marked 'Les Merchandises'. Wiping his shirt over his wet hair so that no drops fell on to his lap, he began to read the various documents. Although they were in English, at first they made no sense and very soon the tables of figures danced before his eyes.

And then he stopped and the torch fell from his mouth. He'd made a mistake. He should have been alone in his hut when the police arrived, even if it resulted in a beating. He began to search for a place to hide the bag and as he did a plan began to form that would allow him to return to the camp with a plausible excuse for his absence. It would be too dangerous for him to retrace his steps to the mouth of the tunnel, so he had to find another way out.

He set off into the dark, remembering the caves he played in as a child, where he would go to escape the heat of the day. It was important that he didn't get lost and he decided to return to the railway line to see how much further it went into the hill. The torch was more effective here, picking out the walls on either side. The deeper he went, the more the air began to freshen, the smell he had sensed the first time he'd come to this underground depot. He reckoned he had walked about two hundred metres before the air began to change again and he didn't need the torch to see the shape of the tunnel walls.

Ahead of him he could make out the pale shape of another tunnel exit and he hesitated before going further, squatting down on one of the rails. He thought of what he had been through since he left home, or what had remained of it, two years ago and concluded that this was nothing, that he had already survived much worse. He brought forward the image of the woman on the train, the woman made real in the warehouse just minutes ago. Everything was possible. You just had to believe.

In the split second that Mary had looked up after Finistere had shouted out in the warehouse, she had seen the boy, only enough of him to register that he was young, but one detail she recalled exactly. He was wearing blue trainers marked by two zigzagged white lines that stood out in the gloom. It surprised her that she had kept this information to herself when being questioned by one of the policemen, but then it probably had something to do with the brusque way she was being treated by the officials, let alone by Michael Finistere. She knew she barely existed as a person to him, any more than she did to the police and in this she perceived that she was not much different from the boy, whoever he was. She saw the blur of his feet as he sped to the door, his escape with the bag and wondered if he did indeed live in one of the shacks as the police suspected. Michael Finistere had publicly berated her and then, immediately afterwards, asked Sophie out to dinner. Perhaps it was no surprise that she wanted to keep some information from him.

'I can't join you for supper,' she had protested to Sophie, detesting the idea of being a gooseberry.

'Oh, believe me, you wouldn't be,' Sophie had told her. 'If you said no, I wouldn't go.'

Mary had looked up the restaurant online and seen the gilded splendour of its dining room and, at one and the same time, congratulated herself for having the new haircut whilst imagining what the night would hold for the boy who had stolen the bag. Would he spend it in the misery of the camp, or thrown into a police cell? She couldn't imagine him being in a position to sell the contents of the briefcase, let alone understand them.

She was standing naked in front of bathroom mirror again, having peeled off her damp clothes down to the new underwear. Sophie was joining her in a bar around the corner so that they could fortify themselves with a drink before meeting Finistere at the restaurant. If she couldn't imagine what form the evening would take, Sophie had a fairly good idea.

'Cheers,' she said. 'I'm grateful for your support.'

Mary raised her glass in reply.

'Tell me a little of yourself,' Sophie continued.

'Irish girl, from Dublin. Went to university in London and never really left. And you?'

'Born in Paris, but my parents – my father is English, my mother Italian – are now divorced. My mother lives in Milan and I see quite a lot of her. My father is a different question.'

'You don't see him?'

'I might, if I knew where he was.'

'I always know where my father is,' Mary said. 'In the Harp, a bar on the corner of our street. It's where he's king of all he surveys. At home, my mother keeps him in on a short lead.'

'So, what are you doing working for Mr Finistere?'

'Now there's a good question. I did business administration at college and I thought it would further my so-called future career. And before you ask, yes and no. My boss is something of a maverick, prone to ignoring the rules, so some of the logic I was taught means nothing in reality. But I do get a close-up view of what goes on.'

'So…?'

'So I'm a glorified PA, well at least in his eyes. Have you always been a translator?'

'No, I'm a singer in fact, but needs must.'

Mary waited for her to continue.

'I was part of the chorus at La Scala in Milan, but I made the mistake of having an affair with the musical director, not a very clever idea, especially as he turned out to be something of a bastard. When I broke it off, he spread the word against me and work dried up. So now I translate to keep body and soul together. Drink up. We'll walk to the restaurant. I imagine the boss doesn't like to be kept waiting.'

IO

T he tunnel had disorientated him. He had emerged into the grey light to find a marshalling yard of half a dozen separate lines, each empty and ending in buffers. Youssef hadn't recognised the surrounding buildings, although they couldn't have been more than two kilometres from the camp, in the direction of the Gare du Nord. The protecting walls were all tagged with graffiti and the tracks were littered with rubbish flattened by the recent rain. He still had the bag with him and he had scanned the new territory in front of him for a place to hide it, for he certainly couldn't leave with the briefcase.

The problem in the end had been easily solved, for to his right had been a small concrete building and when he climbed the stairs to look inside he had found a series of levers that he assumed had once controlled points. A metal cupboard, similar to the one in the warehouse, stood against the far wall but he had dismissed it as too obvious. Having been caught once, he didn't want to risk it again, so he had pushed the case to the back of a dusty shelf above the door.

Now all he had to do was find a way out. The concrete building had given him a better view beyond the yard and he had been surprised to see, on top of the hill to his right, the white pinnacles of the church he knew to be called Sacré-Coeur. There had to be a simple way out of the yard but the double doors beyond the buffers appeared to be shut. He had been certain that retracing his steps and coming face to face with the police was not an option. And then, in a flash of memory so real it might have been about an event that had taken place yesterday, he had been reminded of his encounter with the bandits in the desert, shortly after he had fled home with his brother. He recalled the knife that had been brandished under his throat and the threats that had been made to his face, the sheer terror that had overwhelmed him. It was his desperate attempts not to wet himself that he recalled most, that and how calm Suliman had been. Standing now above the marshalling yard, he looked at his hand that had risen to protect his throat.

It was the wail of a siren passing close by that brought him back to his new reality.

From the end of the metal steps he had seen a road beyond the perimeter wall. He had lowered himself on to the wall and dropped to the pavement before setting off to walk to the market in rue de Bretagne, turning to mark the exact position of his exit in case he needed to go back in the same way.

Four hours later he was arriving back at the camp as dusk was darkening the underpass and it was from this gloom, as he approached his hut, that the two policemen emerged from the shadows. One of them hit him across the back, knocking him to the floor. It was no more than he expected.

'So where have you been you little fucker?'

From the floor, he remained still and the other policeman kicked him. He would have to be brave to survive this and he thought of what his brother would have done in the same situation. Very little.

'Get up,' the first policeman said to him, taking hold of his hair and pulling him to his feet. Maintaining his grip, he dragged Youssef through the camp and along the passageway that led to the road, where a police van was parked. He was thrown into the back, where he lay on the floor preparing for what was to come next. His head was burning and he could feel the shape of the baton across the top of his back. The journey was short and he was led to a room with a metal table and two chairs. Youssef was thrust at one of them and in front of him he could see the photograph of his mother and his possessions, pathetically few, spread on the tabletop.

This was a different policeman and he spoke in English. 'I don't suppose you have a name? No, I thought not. And I don't suppose you recognise your mother, do you?' he demanded, pushing the photograph in front of him. 'Let's try an easier question. Perhaps you can tell me where you were this morning?'

Youssef raised his head. 'At the market. I sometimes work at the market.'

'Where?'

'Rue de Bretagne.'

'And who will confirm that you were there this morning?'

'They all know me.'

'And their names?'

Youssef could only shrug. He didn't know their names.

'We'll check.'

Youssef knew that they would and it was the reason he'd been to the market after hiding the briefcase.

'And the bag, where did you put it?'

Youssef kept his head down.

'We know you took it, you little thief.'

The policeman hit him with his open palm and sent Youssef sprawling from the chair. 'Don't get clever with me kid. Where did you hide it?'

Youssef climbed back on to the chair and looked up at the policeman, his own face betraying nothing. He received a blow on the other side of his head and by the time he'd got back to his feet again, blood was flowing from his nose and on to his T-shirt. Wiping it away, Youssef watched the man pick up the picture of his mother, holding it between his hands in readiness to tear it in half. Youssef remained still, for he knew the policeman wanted him to react.

'So, Youssef Tigha, shall we send you home to your mother? Would you like that?'

Youssef had kept his papers in the metal locker in the warehouse, so he wasn't surprised to hear that they had found his name.

'If you'd like your possessions back, you can tell me about the bag. It's a fair swap. Once you've done that, you can go.'

He was lying, Youssef knew, and once again he chose to say nothing.

'Look at me, you little bastard, we could send you back for breaking and entering the warehouse.'

'I didn't break anything. It was open.'

'Don't get clever with me, you little shit,' he shouted, pulling the boy over the table towards him. 'We don't care for people like you. You stink.' And he threw him back into the chair, which tipped backwards so that Youssef lost balance and cracked his head against the wall. At once, everything became black.

When he woke it was still black and he had no idea where he was. Slowly his eyes got used to his surroundings and he could see that he was in a small room and that he had been lying on the bottom part of a bunk bed. His head hurt and there was dried blood in his hair. He sat up and the room began to move around him and he vomited water and bile on the floor in front of him. He lay back and groaned and shortly after blacked out again.

'Some more wine, Sophie?'

Finistere had already ordered champagne when they arrived in the mirrored restaurant and Mary saw him reflected several times before he appeared in person. She didn't really like champagne. He had arranged for Sophie to sit on the banquette next to him and she was allocated a chair on the other side of the table. How easy it would have been for him to put the two women next to each other on the velvet seat, but the truth was she would never have expected such a gesture. Finistere would have told them what to order if he could but first Sophie and then Mary voiced their different choices.

Mary took against the place immediately, the waiters patrolling their every move, the dishes overly elaborate and multiple reflections of themselves in every direction.

'So, Sophie, I'm sorry about this morning. It's not what you expected, I'm sure.' Finistere was gesturing at the waiter to pour more champagne. Mary covered her glass.

'Oh, I'm quite used to dramatic situations,' said Sophie. 'Have they caught the boy yet?'

In the walk from the Left Bank to the restaurant, crossing the Seine, they had discussed what had happened and Sophie too had seen that the thief had been a boy.

'I can't see what he would want with the briefcase,' Mary had said, looking down on a *bateau mouche*, lights gleaming in the dusk, slipping under the Pont Royal, the sound of music drifting up from its decks.

'Have you ever been to the Grand Véfour?' she had asked Sophie as they came off the bridge and entered the gardens.

'Once, when I was seeing the chap from La Scala. It's all very grand and very expensive. I wasn't paying, of course.'

'And you won't be paying tonight. It's just the sort of place Michael likes. He believes that his money deserves settings like that. He was at the Savoy Grill in London yesterday. It's as if the price of a place is a mark of its excellence.'

'Well, I suppose it usually is,' Sophie had said. 'But I know what you mean. It sounds like your Mr Finistere might not really be that comfortable in a place like the Véfour.' She had looked at Mary as she said this.

'Perhaps not. I don't get to go with him that often. The odd occasion that I have, he wants to take over. And he loves to have a waiter on his side by tipping him enormously as he arrives.'

'I know the sort,' Sophie had said.

Mary now looked at her in the restaurant. Sophie Arditti was in truth a quietly beautiful woman, tonight dressed in a black equivalent of what she had on during the day, only now her hair was pulled up from her face to reveal the shape of her neck. Mary was indeed going to be a gooseberry.

'I'm going to suggest the lobster and then the lamb fillet. Yes?' Finistere was already clicking his fingers at the waiter and Mary caught a glimpse of Sophie looking at her in the mirror.

'I think I'd prefer the terrine and then the plaice,' Sophie said.

'Yes,' said Mary. 'The same.'

'And a bottle of Chablis,' Finistere said, after he'd given his order.

'Which one, Monsieur?'

'The best,' said Finistere, not looking at the waiter but leaning forward to Sophie.

'So, translating must take you to some interesting places.'

Mary sat back.

'I've been on the inside of a few boardrooms, if that's what you mean. And I once had to translate for the minister of education in a discussion about curricula with his English equivalent. I'm sure Mary has a more interesting time with you. And, of course, her training is in business.'

Michael Finistere looked across to his assistant. If he was about to take this fact further he clearly thought better of it and instead turned back to Sophie. He was irritated that Round Mary was at the table tonight and made little attempt to hide it. There was something different about her that he couldn't quite put his finger on and he carried on as if she wasn't there.

'So, a boring job, then? Why do you do it?'

'There is a thing called money, Mr Finistere. I found I was in need of some and I happen to be a first-class translator in three languages, English, French and Italian.'

'I struggle with English,' he said. 'I read economics and you don't need much English for that.'

'And that's a shame, don't you think, Mary?'

Mary appreciated Sophie's attempts to include her in the conversation and she could see that Sophie was happy that she was there.

'I agree. I do think that the language of business is often couched in a way that is deliberately obscure. Which is probably why economists can never agree.' It was probably the most contentious thing Mary had said in front of her boss and she could swear that her Irish accent was more pronounced as she did so.

Finistere regarded her over his glass of white wine.

'I couldn't agree more,' said Sophie, raising her glass to Mary before turning to Finistere. 'What do you think your thief is making of the contents of your briefcase?'

'Don't remind me,' he said. 'I don't really want the whole of Paris knowing my business.'

'But he was only a youngster,' Sophie said. 'What good is that sort of thing to a boy like him?'

'An Arab would flog anything to anyone,' Finistere said, waving once again at the waiter and demanding more wine. Mary already knew what he'd ask for and sure enough a bottle of Vosne-Romanée arrived shortly afterwards and with it all the fuss of opening and decanting the expensive wine.

'I wonder if I might have a glass of Sancerre?' asked Sophie. 'It might go better with my fish.'

Michael Finistere caught the sommelier just as he finished his routines with the red wine and asked for a good Sancerre.

Mary watched her boss carefully for the rest of the evening, for her role, as she thought, and despite the best efforts of Sophie, was that of spectator. Michael Finistere was clearly quite struck with his translator, although Mary winced at his somewhat graceless attempts at courtship. She excused herself, diplomatically she thought, to go to the loo.

Finistere chose the moment to lean in further to Sophie. 'Listen,' he said, 'I find you quite fascinating. I'd like to see you again. Would that be possible?'

'Thank you, Mr Finistere. Shall we see how tomorrow goes? Mary tells me you have to be back in London for an important board meeting.'

Later, Sophie and Mary, in an unspoken pact, refused Finistere's offer of a lift back to their hotel declaring they would rather walk.

'He wants to see me again. Says he finds me "fascinating".'

'Well, there's a surprise. What did you say?'

'I said let's see how tomorrow goes.'

'Indeed,' said Mary.

Paris sparkled as the two women crossed the river, close to midnight.

11

Youssef had been dreaming of Suliman. In the hills near their home there had been a stream that on its downward journey sometimes formed the clearest and most perfect deep pool of water in a narrow crevice. They would regularly climb to find it, jumping off the rocks into the cold blue water and sinking almost to the bottom, before thrusting themselves upwards to the surface. It was an exhilarating gift and one they never took for granted. The brothers regarded it as their own and kept it secret.

Suliman, who was three years older, could be both protective and bullying, but back then Youssef understood that this is what brothers are like. Youssef saw himself climbing the outcrop before leaping off, tucking his legs into his chest to bomb the water, feeling the cold clean his body so that when he came to the surface he felt entirely new.

When he awoke from this dream, though, he was back in the reality of now and the pain in his head continued to weigh him down, forcing him to put his head between his legs while suppressing the urge to dry retch.

He opened his eyes to find daylight in the room, a brightness that merely increased the throbbing in his forehead. He stood unsteadily, reaching out to the upper bunk bed for support. He saw that his mother's photograph was still on the table and he snatched it up, holding it to his cheek before slipping it into his pocket. It was only then that he noticed the door to his cell was open. This is a trick, he thought, and sat down again to see what would happen next. He remembered dreaming about Suliman and, closing his eyes, tried to imagine where he was and what he was doing, bringing forward his face, usually defined by dark stubble on both his cheeks and his skull. He began to smile, although it hurt his head and his eyes screwed up in pain.

When he opened them, the door was still ajar. He walked towards it and tentatively pushed it further open. There was nothing, no human sound, only the distant whoosh of traffic. He turned in that direction and through another open door he could see the road. He was still proceeding cautiously, expecting a blow at any second, and he waited a few moments at this second door before drawing in his breath and stepping through.

There were no shouts, nor was there a blow from a truncheon. He knew then that it was a trick and that he was meant to escape, so he wasn't hurried as he made his way to the next junction in order to work out where he was.

A light rain was falling and for this Youssef was grateful. It wasn't as refreshing as the pool of his childhood, but it was something, a small gesture from above. He was aware that he was being followed, even though he couldn't prove it.

He worked his way back to the camp, his head becoming lighter as he went, only to find that his hut had been ransacked again and that his bedding was lying soaked in front of the open door. This was a small price to pay for freedom and he hung the damp blankets from the roof of the hut and hoped they might dry by the evening. Inside, he once again re-pinned the material to the wooden walls, devising yet a different pattern, hoping this new order would bring him more luck. As he did so, he thought about how he was going to retrieve the briefcase. When he'd finished, he stopped and propped himself in the doorway of the hut and casually looked around knowing that somewhere a pair of eyes was watching his every move.

Michael Finistere lay in his bed simultaneously cursing Round Mary while at the same time thinking about Sophie Arditti's neck, so beguiling that he marvelled he hadn't simply leaned forward and kissed its nakedness, almost more alluring than the sight of gap between her breasts just visible beneath her white shirt. He hadn't been so struck by a woman for, well, as long as he could remember. She had seemed particularly unimpressed by the restaurant and this made her all the more exciting. Just the thought of her had excited him and when he lay on the thickly carpeted floor to begin his exercises he was still partly aroused and his penis lay like a broken mast on his stomach.

He knew that his reaction to situations was often perverse. The more difficult they were the more engaged he became, so the resistance of Sophie

Arditti ran alongside yesterday's events in the warehouse. He wanted to get his own way with both.

He held his legs out in front of him for as long as he could, his feet just inches above the ground. There was sweat on his forehead and his penis has resumed its normal size by the time he had finished the exercise.

The board meeting in London was organised for later that afternoon and the helicopter was scheduled to leave Montparnasse at midday. As the cold water tumbled over his head in the shower he made the sort of decision that gave him enormous pleasure, one that would disrupt others as much as possible. Naked and dripping water on to the cream carpet, he called Mary.

'I hope you enjoyed the meal, Mary. It cost me enough.'

'It was a real treat, thank you.' Mary herself was standing in her new bra and panties, now clean and dry after yesterday.

'I want you to cancel this afternoon's meeting in London. Tell them that something important has cropped up but don't mention the bloody briefcase being nicked. And extend the booking of this place for another couple of days. Tell Mollet I want to see him at the warehouse later this afternoon, say four o'clock. Okay?' He rang off.

Mary Houlihan as messenger, the bringer of bad tidings, the one who would receive the wrath and indignation of the others. Not for one moment had Michael Finistere considered that she might have a problem rebooking her room. The phone rang again.

'And tell Sophie Arditti I want her there as well. And give me a contact number for her while you're about it.'

Naturally. Mary gave him Sophie's number and then began to fulfil her other instructions, but she started with herself, asking for another two nights at the hotel only to be told that she would need to change rooms. It could have been worse, she thought, as she extended the suite at the Lancaster for another two thousand euros a night. No need for Mr Finistere to change rooms. No, not at those prices.

She emailed the other board members, leaving the call to Sophie until last.

'Tell Sophie Arditti I want her at the warehouse at four,' she said, mimicking her boss as closely as she was able.

'I assume it wasn't a question about my availability,' Sophie said. 'You might tell him I have to go to Milan on Friday and that is fixed in stone. But I might be able to accommodate Mr Finistere today. For business, that is.'

Back in his suite Michael Finistere was still naked, although drier. He called Round Mary again. 'And get me duplicates of all the key stuff we had in the case.'

'I've already done that. If you open your computer, they're under the confidential file. I'll have hard copies available, should you need them.'

She had some uses, he supposed.

In her hotel room, Mary remembered that she had forgotten to call Mollet and she was about to do so when her mobile rang and she saw his name on the screen.

'Good morning, Mary. How are you?'

'Fine, thanks. I was just about to call you.'

'Perfect, then.'

'Mr Finistere wants another meeting. Four o'clock at the warehouse. Is that possible?'

'Ah, business. Of course. I expected it. Not an easy man your Mr Finistere. By the way, the police tell me that they're pretty sure who took the bag, but they haven't found it yet. They've released the suspect in the hope he'll lead them to where he has hidden it. I imagine, though, you have copies of what was inside?'

'Sure,' she said. 'We'll have copies with us later.'

'I was phoning, in fact, about something quite different.'

Erik Mollet paused, with a little cough, and Mary wondered what was coming next.

'What with the events of yesterday, I wasn't sure what your movements would be, but I suddenly have two tickets for a concert at Opéra Bastille tonight. I wondered if you were free to join me?'

Mary's reaction was strange, she later admitted to herself. At first she thought he had made a mistake and should have been speaking to Sophie. And then she wondered how he had 'suddenly' got two tickets for tonight and, anyway, wasn't he married and didn't he have friends he could take?

'Well, how wonderful, Erik. If you're sure?'

'Of course. Otherwise I wouldn't be phoning.'

She could hear him smiling.

'And you can make the meeting?'

'Both of them. Midday and tonight. Let's meet for a drink before. I'll let you know where.'

Mary was still in her underwear and she walked into the bathroom to look at herself in the long mirror. 'Thank you,' she said and returned to the bedroom. It was only then that a darker thought occurred, one that matched her own insecurity in these matters. Perhaps Mollet was taking her out as a means of getting closer to Finistere, a way to find out more about his so-called partner in the deal. It was with this thought she lay on the bed.

Every so often Youssef felt the bedding spread on his roof, willing it to dry. There had been a break in the cloud and the weakest of suns had appeared. He shifted some of the heavier blankets out into the feeble sunlight and hung them on the metal fence, glancing casually around him as he did. How was he going to find out what was in the briefcase when he was being watched? Although his head was still hurting, it was now merely a distant throb but the top of his back, where the baton has struck him, made it difficult for him to turn around.

He decided he would go to the market. If he was being followed, his destination would have been regarded as normal and perhaps, along the way, he'd be able to detect who was behind him. And while he was gone, the bedding might dry.

He left the way the police had taken him, through the narrow passage up towards Clignancourt, where he dropped southwards and then eastwards to his destination. He tried to clear his bruised and battered mind, not just of the events of the last twenty-four hours, but of the previous two years since he had left home. His life now was what he regarded as normal, his childhood a distant memory that would come back to him with utter clarity from time to time. He couldn't afford to try to recall it too often, for it would merely make him sad and halt him in his primary pursuit, that of staying alive.

He didn't see the crowds spilling out of the Gare du Nord and he was preoccupied as the road dropped down towards the river. He had walked through many kilometres of Europe like this, suspending his mind from the pain of his feet and the hunger that gripped his stomach every step of the way.

He was surprised when he reached the market and only then did he look behind to see if he could detect anyone who might have been following. It was later in the morning than he normally arrived and there was less work to do so he helped stacking the empty boxes and sweeping around the stalls. It didn't matter if he wasn't paid for his efforts. This was for show. He was given a glass of orange and he sat on an upturned box, thankful for the first refreshment in almost a day. He picked up an old carrot from the floor and ate it quickly and immediately felt restored. Yes, he sensed, he knew, that someone's eyes were on him but he didn't care. He'd got through another few hours and that in itself was an achievement. Sometimes five minutes could seem like a day, one day like a year and a week a lifetime.

12

ichael Finistere was still naked, sitting at the desk in his suite, Paris framed in the two large windows either side. Still in the perverse mood to challenge the orthodoxy of the events unfolding around him, he saw Sophie Arditti as a reason that it should go ahead. The logic was faulty, the reasoning absent but he had often used similar omens on which to rest his decisions, although never before on a woman. His fascination with her was sexual, of course, but he had detected, in the few hours they'd spent in the restaurant, the scent of mystery, that what he was seeing was just a fraction of the whole. This was a rare thought process for him. Usually the former, the sexual imperative, was enough and the ensuing relationship brief and quickly forgotten, by him at least. So it was with a degree of unexpected caution that he picked up his phone to call her. He hesitated, playing with a pencil on the desk top, drawing a series of overlapping circles on a sheet of hotel stationery and shading in darker circles at their centres.

'Sophie? It's me, Michael. I hope you enjoyed last night.'

'I was going to call to thank you, but Mary has just told me there is another meeting this afternoon, so I was going to do it in person. But now you're on the phone, let me say it was a beautiful meal and it was kind of you to take me.'

'It was my pleasure and I have to say you looked beautiful in that glorious room. It's a fabulous restaurant, don't you think?'

Sophie Arditti had a small apartment on the backside of Montmartre, walking distance, in fact, from Finistere's development. She had a living room, a tiny kitchen, one reasonable bedroom and another tiny room that doubled as a second bedroom, or study. From her windows it was possible to see and hear the rue Périphérique and, with such a view, Le Grand Véfour was too rich a contrast.

'You flatter me. I think you might say the restaurant belongs to the old school, now slowly disappearing.'

Not entirely sure what she meant, Finistere was for a brief second unsure how to continue, not a familiar predicament for him.

'Well,' he said eventually, 'the meeting's not until later this afternoon and I wondered if we might have coffee?'

He could hear her hesitate.

'So that I can tell you a little more about the project,' he said, filling in her pause, 'since a decision will have to be made one way or the other very soon.'

He knew the moment he spoke that it was a silly remark, but he couldn't withdraw it and had no time to castigate himself.

'You flatter me again, Mr Finistere. I would think that it was Mary who would be more use than me. A very bright woman, I think.'

Bloody Round Mary again. He'd never thought of Mary in this light, in fact he never thought much about her at all except as a reasonable organiser of his schedule.

'I'm sure she is,' he said, a concession he never thought he'd hear himself make. 'Nevertheless, I would appreciate another meeting with you.' He thought this response was vague enough, falling somewhere between business-like and personal, but even as he registered this compromise he was conscious of the unfamiliar tentativeness of his offer.

'I know a place that might amuse you,' he was relieved to hear her say. 'It's called the Louxor, a cinema just beyond the Gare du Nord. There's a coffee bar on top you might like. It's somewhat of an antidote to Le Grand Véfour, as you'll see. Shall we say eleven?'

Afterwards, sensing that he'd been somewhat out-manoeuvred, that he was being led instead of doing the leading, he Googled the cinema and wrote down the address for his driver. He had the feeling he was going into alien territory and for a moment didn't know what to wear. Fortunately, he had no option and he slipped on another suit, although as a gesture to the place he was going, he left off his tie, even if this did make him feel somehow incomplete.

It was approaching eleven when Youssef was asked to help unload a truck that was late arriving back from the wholesale market at Rungis. It meant that he had to trolley in loads of vegetables for the next hour or so, the perfect cover for him to scan rue de Bretagne each time he arrived at the truck. Whoever was watching him had to be in the sector to the right or left of the parked vehicle, which blocked the view straight ahead. Youssef made the journey more than ten times without observing anyone unusual and by the time the lorry was empty and he was sweeping the droppings into the gutter, he had come to the conclusion there was no one. After almost fifteen hundred miles of travel across the Middle East and Europe, suspicion was second nature to Youssef and with the beat of the brush against the pavement he calculated what he might be missing. By the time he turned back into the market to receive two five-euro coins from one of the stallholders, he had come to a sort of conclusion.

He retired to the loo with the wooden door at the back of the market and pulled off first his trousers, then his shirt and finally his trainers. It was there that he finally found what he had been looking for, cut into and hidden in the heel of the right shoe, a small, round metal transmitter. Youssef knew all about tracking and GPS. Without his mobile, and those of fellow refugees, he could never have found his way through the various countries of Europe. Now, in the palm of his hand, he understood why no one had been following, for he had been doing the job for them.

He put the tracker on one of the stalls, left the market and began to retrace his steps of the day before, the route he'd taken after he'd scrambled down the wall at the side of the marshalling yards. He felt lighter now, his head had cleared and his passage took him in a wide parabola south of the Gare du Nord, then towards Montmartre, up the long stairs to the church, whose pinnacles he'd been able to see from the yard, and finally down the other side. He didn't look back until he got to the wall, which he walked past once before turning to do so again. When he was sure, he shinned up and dropped quickly on to the metal stairway that took him along the inside of the wall towards the signal box. Once inside, he took the briefcase from the shelf above the door, sat on an old chair and tried to imagine the days when wagons would have been sorted into groups in front of him.

Youssef was delaying looking into the case and his hands lay possessively over the two buckles closing it. He recalled the last present his father had given him, a football he'd disguised in a square box, and how he had run his hands over it not wanting to puncture the excitement of expectation.

He slowly worked the buckles loose, sliding out the folder, the cover with its outline of the warehouses. He opened the document, smoothing the pages as he went, registering the plans for the area, made easier to understand now that he'd seen the model and watched snatches of the video. The mathematical figures were more difficult and at first they were just an indecipherable muddle, with headings and columns and numbers highlighted in red or emphasised in bold. He told himself that he had been one of the best in class when everything came to an end, the day the school had been bombed and many of his classmates killed. He stopped that memory from coming to the surface and concentrated on the numbers.

Eventually they defeated him and he ventured further on into the document. It was only at the end that he saw it was here he should have begun, under a section headed 'Summary and Conclusions'. What he needed was in front of him, clear, brief and in black and white. He took in the details and gradually felt the power the signalman would have had in this very box, controlling what was in front of him, directing what went where, switching the coupling of wagons, joining long with short until order had been achieved.

Another lesson learned on the trek across the thousand miles of Europe was memory. He couldn't, or didn't want to, write anything down, so it had to be stored and the information on the sheets in front of him was lodged firmly in his mind to go somewhere alongside the images of the woman on the train, and to serve the same purpose, to keep him going.

He put the document back, re-buckled the briefcase and once again put it above the door. He looked down at the tunnel, but decided he still couldn't go back that way, for it would have meant emerging just below the camp. He imagined by now the police would have deduced that he'd found the tracker, so he had to return via the wall.

Making his way along the metal staircase, he stopped, looking down at his feet but not registering the drop to the tracks beneath. His heart was thumping by the time he jumped down from the wall. This time he turned northwards, towards Clignancourt and when he arrived at the great intersection he registered the call box on the far side, beneath the graffitied flank of the old apartment block. He worked his way around to it and with the thrum of the car wheels on the cobbled junction, called 211.

'Police. Listen,' he said, slowly in English, holding his T-shirt to his mouth. 'Yesterday, an important bag was stolen near Port de la Chapelle. You will find it in the old signal box by the side of rue Poissoniers.'

Before there was any response, he replaced the phone, returned quickly to the passageway on the other side of the road and five minutes later was once again checking his bedding to see if it was dry. It wouldn't be long before they arrived.

In fact, it was an hour later when the policeman who had interviewed and then beaten him knocked heavily on the open door of his hut. Youssef was sitting on the bed.

'I suppose you know nothing about a certain phone call?'

Youssef cocked his head in puzzlement, which caused the policeman to bang the door again.

'And tell me this – and be careful how you answer – was there just one file in the case?'

This time Youssef didn't feign incomprehension but just kept perfectly still.

'I'll assume that is a yes,' said the policeman stepping into the door frame, darkening the small space and appearing as a giant silhouette to Youssef, who instinctively shrank back to the planked wall behind him.

'If I find this is not true, I promise you I shall kill you and no one will ever know you existed. I'll be back.' He pulled Youssef to his feet and his fist smashed into the boy's face.

Mary was tormented, unable to establish a state of mind for the rest of the morning. She needed her routines to keep her whole and so she organised the papers she would need for later and then, when midday came, filled the time transferring her possessions to the new room she had been allocated. It was two floors above and she took the narrow lift and rattled upwards to discover a much nicer room, with two dormer windows looking down on the leaded roofs between the hotel and the Seine.

She unpacked and then sat in a chair to enjoy the view but it was Erik Mollet that kept surfacing in her thoughts, a tantalising presence just out of vision. In the end, of course, he took over and she resumed her troubled reactions to his earlier call. She knew, though, that she wouldn't have an answer until she saw him, if not at the meeting in the warehouse, then certainly later. She believed, without conceit, that she was reasonably good at assessing people, a gift handed down to her by her mother, a canny woman not given to suffering fools.

Time couldn't go quickly enough, though, and it stretched ahead, an endless road to be walked towards infinity. Everything was up in the air and nothing was certain. With the view in front of her like the painted backdrop to an opera, it felt like she was approaching the end of act one, with the curtain about to fall on the stories that had been set in motion, their conclusions uncertain and just out of sight.

ACT TWO

13

Sophie Arditti was in that strange position of being at one and the same time part of Paris and separate from it. That tranche of her that was Italian, the bit that left Paris each weekend for Milan, more southern, more Latin, gave her a certain objectivity over the city where she lived and she saw that it was now at odds with itself, a little uncertain. The terrorist attacks had shaken it, leaving it both shocked and insecure. The true Parisian had a certain arrogance and swagger about their precious city and reacted with justifiable outrage and indignation and yet, this outsider could see, they were also guilty of a deliberate blindness to the shortcomings of their gilded capital. The mirrored splendours of the Le Grand Véfour didn't reflect anything of the very different reality that existed on its doorstep.

Sophie Arditti could see why she was entertaining these thoughts as she made her way up over the hill towards the Louxor and she knew with equal certainty that she regarded the upcoming meeting as more business than pleasure. She had intended to be early and was therefore surprised to see that he was ahead of her, perched uncomfortably on a bar stool that seemed too small to take his frame. He rose as she entered the café, the true English gentleman and she could see that he wasn't at ease.

They shook hands, an odd gesture, she thought, but one that she understood.

'We should go out here,' she said, directing him to the terrace and a table that gave them a view over the street and the railway.

'I love it up here,' she told him. 'Down there is the Métro in the open air and up there is the hill that rises to Montmartre.'

Finistere had twice walked by the cinema to be sure he had come to the right place. It was only when he stood on the other side of the road that he could see the café on the upper floor and he had to admit a certain discomfort as he entered in his suit, even without the tie. He looked out at the view she was describing and registered a visceral displeasure at the urban jumble spread in front of him.

'You don't like it, do you?' she said, assessing the look on his face. 'Perhaps a coffee would help? And perhaps a croissant?'

Finistere, who worked hard to keep his stomach flat, shook his head and he watched as she ordered their coffees with, he noted, a pain au chocolat for herself. How did she keep her figure, he wondered.

She saw him looking at her and laughed. 'I have a good metabolism, Mr Finistere. Lucky me.' She didn't add that the exercises she did for her diaphragm helped maintain her posture. 'Are you fond of this city of mine, Mr Finistere?'

'Call me Michael,' he said, which came out like an order. 'No, it's not my favourite. I've never had much luck here.'

'With work, or...?' Sophie could not keep the smile from her face.

'Both,' he said, returning the smile. 'I always feel hectic here.'

'Perhaps that has something to do with language, no?'

She was right, of course, for his preferred city was New York, a place for which the word hectic was invented.

Sophie could see that Michael Finistere was somewhat discomforted, and it was not entirely to do with the cacophony of sounds coming from down below. She had to admit that she found this quite endearing, somewhat different from the bombastic man she had encountered the night before and in the warehouse.

'But you like London?'

'My office is in London, but I live just outside, where the countryside begins. I have a villa in southern Spain that I disappear to when I can.'

'Do you have a family?'

Their coffees arrived, which gave him time to compose his answer. 'No, I've never been married. Close twice, but still single.' More or less the truth, he thought.

'And children?'

He couldn't tell her about Alan, so he shook his head.

'You don't seem sure,' she said.

'It must be frustrating,' he said, 'being a translator. You can't ask the questions you want, can you? Not your own, at least.'

She noted his evasion.

'So, here's a question of my own. Why do you want to build your development in Paris, then, if you don't like the place?'

'I was offered the opportunity to make some money. It's a business deal. Personal preferences don't come into it.'

'Really? It's just about money?'

'In a word, yes.'

'I thought you might have had some special affection for that part of Paris?'

'It's not the prettiest of places, let's face it.' Finistere was surprised at the combative nature of their exchanges, as much to do with him, he acknowledged, as her. 'Where do you live?'

'Just over the other side of the hill,' she said, pointing behind her, 'the north side of Montmartre. A small apartment.' She waited for him to ask her more, but he appeared to have run out of questions.

'Mary tells me you're very successful. From what I can see, you have a valuable assistant there.'

'So you keep telling me,' Finistere replied, irritated that Round Mary should be brought into the conversation. He looked at her directly and saw that her eyes were blue-grey, flecked like marble. Her dark hair was flatter this morning, not pushed back as it had been the night before. Her face appeared to pose a sort of challenge, her raised eyebrows almost mocking him. Or perhaps they were simply expecting him to say something else. A train rattled over the metal bridge just out of sight below them.

In the end it was Sophie who spoke. 'Was the stolen bag important?'

'Up to a point,' he said. 'In the wrong hands it would be, but I'm told it was a kid who stole it.' He shook his head, which she took to mean it didn't matter one way or the other.

'I have to make a decision about the development by the end of this week,' he said. 'I don't suppose you had the chance to form an opinion, did you?'

'I like those old parts of Paris,' she said. 'They remind me of what the place used to be like, the old warehouses, the canals, even the railway lines. There's something atmospheric about all that.'

'And completely useless, really,' he said. 'The new development will transform the district, super apartments, gardens, shops. It's not the smartest part of Paris, is it?'

'True,' she said, noting the steeliness of his response. Michael Finistere liked getting his way even in a gentle, unimportant conversation over coffee. 'Does Mary like it?'

'She's never commented on it.'

'The fountain is a good idea,' she said.

'Not you as well,' he said, looking at her again. 'I think it's going to cause problems.'

He saw her sit back and fold her arms, her breasts rising slightly above them. 'You seem uneasy about your project, if you don't mind me saying so,' she said. 'In the meeting yesterday, you were always looking for problems, as if you didn't trust your partners.'

'Perhaps that's why I'm successful,' he said, returning her comment back over the net.

'Of course. Perhaps your instincts tell you something is amiss, but you can't put your finger on what.'

It was a cross-court volley and it rather surprised him. In response, his return was rather lame.

'Something like that.' He laughed. 'And I've rather taken my eye off the ball.'

'Yes,' she said, aware that he was looking at her, 'it's not wise to get distracted.'

She was very beautiful, he thought, but difficult and not really what he was used to, more of a challenge than many of the women he had known who, he sort of conceded, he may have chosen for their very pliability.

'I do trust my instincts,' he said, continuing to look at her, 'and they seldom let me down, although some problems are more difficult than others.' It was an attempt at a drop volley but he expected her to get to it.

'Well, I imagine you'll find out more later, won't you?'

'I wonder if I will?' He leaned forward and picked up her left hand. 'No ring? I'm surprised.'

'It doesn't mean there hasn't been,' she said, withdrawing it slowly. 'I was married once but it didn't work out, or, to be more truthful, I made a mistake.'

'And now?'

'You mean, have I married again?' She laughed and clapped her hands. 'I think you say, once bitten twice shy.'

'And boyfriend?'

'How old fashioned you are. A few, yes.'

'I imagined so.'

'Why?'

'You're too beautiful to be alone.'

'Goodness, you make it sound like a penalty.'

As a passing shot it was perfect and although she was still smiling, she stood up ready to leave. 'I'll see you around four. Perhaps things will become clearer later. I think Mary will have told you I go to Milan on Friday. Thank you for coffee. I hope you get to like this place. Perhaps it will grow on you.'

He stood as she left and then, leaning over the terrace, waited for her to appear below, tracking her as she crossed the road. He felt somewhat a fool when she stopped and looked up, offering him a brief wave.

He sat back down, fingered his tieless collar and considered the meaning of the encounter or, more to the point, what it meant to him, for Sophie Arditti seemed blithely indifferent to him. Of course, this increased his interest but even that surprised him, for she was bright and combative and not his type. For a moment, he pushed her aside, leaving her to simmer on a back burner, and brought forward the problem of the development. He couldn't procrastinate for much longer but he had no clue to why he was hesitating. Not that this was necessarily a bad thing, for in many ways he welcomed the element of doubt in him, that feeling in his waters that his father told him he should never ignore.

He stood up to look at the view and imagined her climbing the hill ahead, the shape of her calves as she leant into the slope, going off into a life he didn't know.

Sophie knew that he would be watching her and in some small way it pleased her when she turned round to be proved right. What an odd man, she thought, aware of some of his emotions but a stranger to many others. Although he may have been interested in her, his approach was guileless, his overtures obvious and limited. She thought of him taking her hand and couldn't help but laugh. In some ways he was simple. Her mother would have found him most attractive and would most certainly have flirted with him. She could see that he wasn't at ease, that he was fighting conflicting instincts on what was perhaps new territory for him, and this she found interesting. In some ways she was looking forward to the afternoon and the strange drama that was to be played out in front of the model.

Her phone rang as she was putting the key into the door of her apartment.

'Hello?'

'It's me, Michael. I'm sorry, I don't think that went very well.'

'It was fine,' she said breezily. 'You had other things on your mind.'

'The thing is, I want to take you to dinner again. Alone? Would that be possible?'

She tossed her bag on to a chair and slumped on the small sofa and looked out over northern Paris. How was she to respond? She had been asked out by many men in whom she had no interest at all and a simple 'no I'm busy' was all it took. But she knew that Michael Finistere wouldn't accept this any more than he could sign the deal for the development of the site she could just about see from her window.

'What did you have in mind?'

'I got the impression that you might not have been overly impressed with the restaurant last night. I wondered if you might propose another.'

'To make it appear that I'm taking you out, you mean?'

'If you like.'

'When did you have in mind?'

'This evening. My hotel is booked for tonight and I go back tomorrow morning.'

She looked around her small flat, neatly ordered with her own possessions, uncluttered with the detritus of a partner. How simple it was to live like this.

'Okay, Mr Finistere, I invite you to the Café de L'Industrie, not far from the Bastille. It's a little different from Le Grand Véfour and your driver might have difficulty finding it. I'll book for eight, shall I?'

He had expected to be turned down so he was more than happy to comply.

'Perfect,' he said.

'But before that, I hope the meeting goes well this afternoon. I know what a big decision it is for you.'

Curiously, thought Michael Finistere as he ended the call, he had been more troubled about asking her out than finalising the details on *Les*

Merchandises. He mocked himself by thinking he was acting like a teenager, tentative, clumsy, unsure of himself. It was a new experience and he hadn't yet worked it out, which made two problems to tussle with as he climbed into his car to be chauffeured back to the hotel.

14

I t had begun over dinner three years earlier, when he had found himself sitting, not by accident, next to Erik Mollet. The meal had taken place in Chelsea, in the house owned by Stuart Phelps, the table laid in a large, wood-panelled room on the first floor with glorious views over the Thames.

Stuart had told Michael that Mollet had approached him recently with an interesting proposition in northern Paris. This is how these things begin, Finistere knew, tentative exchanges that slowly grow in complexity. He had been instinctively prejudiced against the plan, since it involved Paris, but Stuart had persuaded him saying that the prospect of a large profit should overcome his aversion to all things French.

He had been engaged by Mollet, the tales of his glory days as a French rugby international and the privileges it had brought him, financial and sexual. It was only after dinner, over a glass of cognac, that Mollet showed him one or two photographs of the site on his mobile. It was a low-key approach, the sort that Finistere liked, and a week later he found himself standing in front of the two large warehouses as Mollet gave him more details of what he had in mind. Later, the Frenchman brought rough plans to the Lancaster and over more cognac the business courtship became increasingly serious. It had developed without much trouble until now, when for some unknown reason Finistere had vague doubts that lurked in the back of his mind.

Today they were gathered around the model, on stage yet again, to play out what everyone hoped would be the final act in this extended drama. Mollet, in a *coup de théâtre* that surprised Finistere, arrived with the briefcase, holding it out in front of him like a trophy.

'*Voilà,*' he said with a flourish. 'And before you ask, no, I didn't look inside. It appears that the detective in charge was once a fan of mine and he delivered it to me about an hour ago.' He handed the bag to Mary with an elaborate bow. 'It was stolen by a kid, who didn't know what he'd got into.'

'I wonder who else read it, though,' said Finistere, somewhat ungraciously thought Mary, who found it hard to look Mollet in the eye.

'Mr Finistere,' Mollet said, suddenly formal, 'your instincts tell you that something is wrong. We have worked happily on this project for, shall we say, a reasonable length of time now and all has been well. I expect whatever there is in that bag outlines the cost, contingencies and likely profits for your group. Yes? I cannot add more than I already have. I hope that it is enough for you to finance all this.'

Mollet spoke in English and Sophie looked on, redundant. Finistere was watching her as Mollet made his declaration, more than ever taken in by the looks of the woman standing just a few feet to his right.

He clapped his hands and the sound rang around the empty space.

'You're right, Erik. What is it? What's holding me back? Something? But perhaps nothing?'

He walked around to the back of the model and picked up the orange figure, returning to the group, where he tossed it into the air and then kicked it into the gloom of the warehouse space. It clattered to the floor somewhere in the distance. 'There,' he said. 'As you might say, Erik, I've kicked it into touch. Let's go ahead.'

Sophie did translate this, but Erik had understood and was laughing his pleasure.

Was it Sophie who had made him do this, Michael thought, or his impatience with his own procrastination? He operated outside the tight straightjacket set for banks and the money he had accumulated was his own and although his company had a board, he could and usually did, act unilaterally. Cavalier, he had been described and he was happy to accept this misnomer, for he liked to give the impression that he moved more by instinct than reason. So what had the gesture with the figure been about? Was it the signal, as Mollet assumed, that he was putting his doubts behind him and the deal was sealed? Or was it a piece of schoolboy showing off in front of Sophie? He wasn't sure himself, but he walked over to Mollet and Papon and shook their hands.

Mary had known Michael Finistere long enough to be able to read his moods and despite the quixotic gesture she had just witnessed, she detected a look of discomfort in her boss, as though he, like her, thought his behaviour was not entirely in character. She risked a glance over to Erik Mollet, who was smiling but not looking in her direction and she momentarily entertained the thought that he might have engineered the stealing of the bag in the first place. She dismissed the suspicion, remembering his genuine shock when the bag had been stolen.

She looked down on the model. Who had put the figure there in the first place and why? Had this now been forgotten and swept under the carpet? What if the boy had stolen the bag deliberately, wanting to find out more about the development? She had yet to speak to Finistere about her walk through the underpass and even as she asked the question why, she knew the answer. He treated her as a glorified secretary and as she allowed this fact to settle on her yet again, she was aware of another change taking place. The concerns that Finistere had so theatrically booted to one side were in the process of being transferred to her and the chemistry of the group standing around her was in the process of undergoing fundamental change.

The men were still laughing and talking and Sophie walked over and stood by Mary. 'We're going out to dinner again tonight,' she said quietly. 'He's very persistent, isn't he?'

'You could say that, yes.'

'And I don't know really why he asked me here today.'

'Oh, I do Sophie. So he could show off in front of you. I've not seen him like that before. Shall we say, it was rather out of character for him.'

'I rather liked him for it,' she said.

'I think that's what he'd hoped for.'

Together they heard Finistere invite the Frenchmen back to the Lancaster for a glass of champagne before extending the gesture to the two women and coming over to sweep them up, his hand lightly touching Sophie's shoulder as he ushered them towards the door and down to his waiting car.

Mary, who knew as much about the project as anyone, had a strong feeling that nothing had really been solved, that Michael Finistere still had his doubts and that these had infected her and cast a strange shadow on her forthcoming evening with Mollet.

At the hotel, the deal was celebrated with the pop of champagne, although Mary barely touched hers as she watched Mollet clink his glass to Finistere's. Perhaps Mollet was conscious she was looking at him because he turned and, with a small gesture, raised his glass to her and she responded with a smile and a slow bow of her head. She didn't expect more of an acknowledgement from him, any more than she thought Finistere would make more obvious overtures to Sophie. This afternoon the two women were merely an audience for the men.

Youssef spat out the tooth and held it in his bloody palm. It had been loosened by the policeman but it had taken him a few hours to finally extract it. His eyes were blackened and there was a gash below the socket on the right that was in need of stitching. He would steal some plasters later and thought it was a small price to pay for the information in the bag and the retrieval of his mother's photograph.

He closed his hand on the tooth and surveyed the camp from his position above the tunnel, knowing now that it was all to be taken from him. He couldn't go back to the warehouse that, too, would soon be gone. His world continued to disappear before his eyes, his hopes dashed before they had time to form. He had very little more to lose and, opening his hand, he studied his tooth before throwing it down on to the tracks below.

To them, he was seen as an Arab, simply that, without further definition. It was a word that condemned him to a life that was continually being snatched from him. Arab, a general term that equalled thief, terrorist, dirt and poverty. He was an infection and existed to be exterminated. He knew the dangers. When you have nothing, you have nothing to lose and hatred takes over your life. Youssef didn't want this and resisted joining in with others in the camp whose anger had grown as they traipsed through Europe, rejected by one country after the next, heading for some distant land of hope that most of them were now beginning to perceive didn't exist. He thought about the man in the smart suit whose case he had stolen and tried to imagine his life, supported by more money than it was possible to spend, arrogant and noisy and used to getting his own way. Youssef was jealous too, he accepted, sitting in his camp listening to the raindrops pattering against the buddleia. His father had been wealthy, a lawyer and their home had a courtyard with a fountain that cooled the air at the height of summer. These details, let alone the name of his country, or the history of his family, one that ran back hundreds of years, could not define him in their eyes. He was an Arab, just that.

The rain was heavier and began to drip through the canopy of green on to his head. Youssef enjoyed the cool water running down his damaged face, through the red gash beneath his blackened eyes. Where are you Suliman? Can you take me from here? I know you're alive. Come and rescue me. It was a daily prayer and his faith that his brother was still alive never wavered.

He thought of the woman on the train, the very same woman made human in the warehouse. He would watch her on the train tomorrow, close his eyes and imagine her journey into her own fabulous world, far beyond the camp, a paradise that he could almost enter if he shut his eyes and forgot the pain of his face. Believe in fate, his father had told him and he saw her arrival in the warehouse as just that: fate, an omen. She had a purpose, whatever that might be and he was comforted by the thought.

Down below, the rain had doused the fire and the men who normally stood around it had sought the shelter of the bridge. A blue-and-grey train growled above them, another world slipping by oblivious of the one beneath it, heaven travelling over hell. He would not hate. He must not become like those who hated him. His childhood had been cut off, cauterised by trauma and overnight he had been forced into the shape and thinking of a man. He'd had to learn new rules in order to stay alive and he had done this, but there was a price, one that he couldn't yet see for it was too large to comprehend. He knew, though, that he carried it within him and that one day, in a future that was impossible to describe, he would be able to examine it, lay it out in front of him so that he could, rather like the figures he had read in the briefcase, work out the profit and loss in his life, what had been gained and what had been destroyed. Youssef believed this time would come, but it was hard to hold on to this hope, to summon the energy, mental and physical, to keep going, to drag himself from one day to the next, or, like now, simply into the next hour.

But he would.

15

They met in a bar just off Place Bastille, Mollet having given her one of his cards, with its address written on the back, as they had left the Hotel Lancaster. As romantic gestures went, it rated fairly low down on her scale of how these things should be conducted but, nevertheless, Mary understood the rules of the game, that business and pleasure should not overlap, and she was looking forward to the evening. She was glad that she hadn't drunk the champagne and back at her hotel she showered with a clear head and afterwards dressed slowly and deliberately. She was full of doubts, of course, but she broadly understood what they were and knew there was nothing she could do about them in advance. She couldn't imagine what Finistere would say if he found out that she was seeing Mollet, but was sure it would be dismissive and disbelieving. Well, too bad, Mr Finistere.

The bar was in a semi-basement and Mollet, she was glad to see, was already there. He rose and, without hesitation, kissed her on both cheeks, as he might have done his mother. He was only slightly taller than her and he too had about him a certain bulk, even if some of it had slipped southwards to his stomach. He was a swarthy man and even with the two chaste kisses she could feel the bristles and take in the pleasant aroma of his skin.

'You look wonderful,' he said and sounded as though he meant it. 'Now, clearly you don't like champagne. Yes, I watched you leave your glass earlier, so what would you like to drink?'

Mary was conscious of her beating heart somewhere in the blouse just beneath her chin. She ordered a gin and tonic.

'We are going to hear *Tosca*,' he said, as her drink arrived. They raised their glasses to one another. 'Do you know it?'

Mary, who had never been to an opera, thought she knew some of the arias and said as much.

'I must have heard at least half a dozen productions,' he said. 'It's an opera with one of the best-ever villains and one very spoilt and beautiful woman.'

'I don't normally associate opera with rugby,' she said.

'Yes, I know what you mean, but perhaps you'd be more surprised if a footballer said he liked opera, no? People make assumptions about sportsmen, that they can't be intelligent, or cultured. Stupid. But I sound too defensive,' he said, laughing.

Mary could see why she liked this man, although she still had to detect exactly what he saw in her. 'Why do you call Tosca spoilt?'

'Because she's aware of her own beauty and demands absolute devotion. If she doesn't get it, she becomes angry and jealous. You'll see.'

'I'm flattered you're sharing the evening with me when you barely know me.'

'Ah, you mean, don't I have a wife or girlfriend?'

'I suppose I did.'

'I have both, in fact. I'm divorced from one and, shall we say, estranged from the other. I don't think I am easy to live with. At least that's what they tell me.' He roared with laughter at this admission. 'Now, before we fall into the arms of Tosca, what about you?'

'I had a long-term boyfriend back in Ireland, but that ended when I left to work in London.'

'Do you miss him?'

'To tell you the truth, not at all. I think I escaped just in time.'

'You gave him Tosca's kiss.'

Mary frowned, not sure what he meant.

'When Scarpia, the police chief, tries to have his wicked way with Tosca, she stabs him and says this was her kiss, Tosca's kiss. Wonderful.'

'Perhaps not quite as dramatic as that. There was many a time, mind you, when I could gladly have stabbed him.'

'So, you'll find a companion in Tosca tonight. Come, I think we should go.'

As they left the bar, he offered her his arm and as they negotiated the busy roundabout to the new opera house opposite, she couldn't help but think what an easy man he was to be with.

*

Sophie Arditti seemed to be in the same combative mood she'd been in earlier.

'Not quite your cup of tea, is it?' She had watched him come into the large room, taking in the mismatched jumble of chairs and tables, the random collection of art on the walls and the motley group of diners, most casually dressed and what he might have called scruffy. At least he still wasn't wearing a tie and was carrying his jacket over his shoulder.

'Looks like some of these people have been in here all day,' he said, sitting opposite her, hanging his jacket on the back of the chair.

'Many of them have been. It's sort of their club and office combined. Not quite Le Grand Véfour, I do agree. Do you want the waitress to hang up your jacket?'

'No, it's fine.'

'Are you worried that somebody might go through your pockets?'

'Something like that.'

'How did you get here?'

'My driver brought me. Had a bit of a job finding it.'

'You must try walking sometime. You miss the best parts of Paris from the back of a car.'

His look at her was disbelieving. 'As you know, Paris and I sort of don't get on,' he said, the conversation already taking the tone of earlier. He certainly didn't feel at ease and this was not entirely to do with the surroundings.

'You're a man who likes to be in charge, Michael, and you can't be in a foreign language.'

'Is that what it is?'

'Well, tell me then, what is it you don't like about Paris? Or is it the French?'

'This is quite an interrogation so far. I thought I told you that I never have much luck here. Now, do I get a drink, or is that against the rules?'

Sophie was already drinking a kir and he ordered a scotch. She looked different this evening, but he wasn't sure why.

'Are we continuing the celebrations tonight? Today was important, no?'

He took a quick look at her across the ginger liquid and ice. The truth was, he couldn't tell whether she was teasing and before he could reply, there was another question.

'You don't seem that happy. Am I right?'

He hesitated, not quite sure of his response.

'Perhaps that answers my question. You aren't. So what made you change your mind so quickly this afternoon?'

He finished his glass and raised his arm for another.

'I thought you wanted more evidence of the "problems and pitfalls",' she continued, making speech marks in the air with her fingers.

He felt again like a schoolboy on a first date, hardly able to think straight let alone form a sentence. 'Do I get to answer?'

Above their table, directly in his eye-line, was a painting of a semi-naked woman fighting a snake and he wondered if she had chosen the table deliberately.

'Since I couldn't put any flesh on the doubts I had about the project, couldn't identify exactly what was troubling me, I decided enough was enough. The time for dithering, as my mother would have said, was over.'

'Was your mother a decisive sort of woman, then?'

'Not really, no. She just thought that was how men should be.'

'And you decided to stop dithering. In the meantime, what does Mary think?'

Mary again. 'Why do you ask?'

'I hardly know her, but I think she has good instincts. I watched her earlier and she could see that you were still not entirely certain.'

He frowned, taking in the information. 'I've got until tomorrow afternoon to change my mind.'

'And you would do that, after shaking hands with the Frenchmen?'

'That depends,' he said. 'Are you always like this?'

'Like what?'

'Exactly. Asking questions. Almost aggressive.'

'Do you like your women more compliant then?'

He sat back in his chair, clinked the ice in his glass and thought what answer would be correct. 'To be quite honest, that has been broadly my experience, yes.'

'Well, that's an admission.'

'And you, what sort of man are you used to?'

'Those with a good sense of humour. And who are interested in me.' Nothing like the musical director of La Scala, she thought, who really only ever existed for himself.

'That's not difficult, surely?'

'Oh, you'd be surprised.'

'I'd be surprised to find that a lot of men weren't interested in you.'

'Well, Michael, there's interested and *interested*, wouldn't you say?'

She looked at him coolly as she said this and Finistere, who knew exactly what she meant, couldn't meet her eyes.

'You say you trust your instincts,' she said, changing the subject, 'so why spend all this money in a place you don't like?'

'I expect doctors sometimes treat patients they don't like. It's simply what they do. And this is what I do. Use my money to finance projects like this one.'

'Yes, but you're not bound by an oath. You can pick and choose where to invest your money. And it's odd that you chose Paris. Maybe that's what's wrong with your deal.'

'Simple as that.'

'Why not?'

'Because it doesn't feel like that. I'm impressed with Mollet, even though I'm not keen on the city where he lives. I can put that to one side, though. I just have a hunch it might be something else, something I can't see.'

'Then why did you shake hands on the deal?'

'I told you,' he said somewhat curtly, aware that she'd observed him so well.

'Seems like I've touched a raw nerve. Shall we order?'

She told him what she had eaten on previous visits to the restaurant, running through the menu and making recommendations. The meal, when it came, was, she declared, just a delicious as the one they had eaten the night before.

'You're proving a point,' he said.

'I suppose I am,' she replied.

'To do with money.'

'Yes, and no. You give me the impression that money always gets you what you want.'

'And it doesn't?'

She shook her head slowly. 'You know it doesn't.'

He put his napkin on the table. 'It helps, though.'

'I don't think so. It can give the illusion that you're getting what you want. You're very rich and yet you give me the impression that you're not particularly content. No?'

'Dinner and therapy. Lucky me.' At that moment, Finistere thought of his father who in the last year of his life, having sold his business, bought a house on the south coast, which had always been his dream. He never got to live in it. Finistere believed his father had worked himself to death. 'Okay, I concede, you might be right and money doesn't always get you what you want.'

'Well, a concession. Bravo.'

Michael Finistere wasn't sure of how to respond, conscious of competing emotions but unable to describe them, give them shape or meaning.

'You've gone quiet.'

'Yes,' he said. 'It must be you.' And he meant it. The sensation of not being himself was powerful and new to Michael Finistere, whose evenings with women were normally orchestrated, loudly, by him.

'Tell me more,' she said.

'I'm not sure I can, any more than I'm able to work out what's worrying me about the project.'

'But did you enjoy the food?'

'I did. And this place is growing on me, as well.'

'Good, I'm delighted.'

'And, I have to admit, you're growing on me, too.' He leaned forward and put his hand on hers.

She looked at it for a second or two and then slid her hand from underneath.

'I think you'll have to work out why, Michael.'

'About you, or the job?'

'I think they're both about the same thing.'

'You're talking in riddles. Do you do this to all your men?'

'I don't have lots of men, as you put it.'

'I didn't mean it like that.'

'No?'

Afterwards, when he'd put her in a cab and was being driven home, he saw how the evening had petered out and, although he found it hard to take the blame, had to admit that it might have been his fault. He had been unable to dazzle this beautiful but difficult woman, to act with his normal swagger. The trouble was, he couldn't work out why.

'I have enjoyed working with you, Michael,' she had said, shaking his hand before getting in to the cab.

'I want to see you again,' he had said, lamely, as she had shut the door.

'There,' Erik Mollet said in her ear, 'Tosca's kiss.'

On stage, Scarpia lay dead and Tosca was in the process of placing candelabra on either side of his head. Mary turned to look at Erik and she saw that he had tears in his eyes. One rolled slowly down his face.

Afterwards, back in the same bar, she mentioned this and he laughed.

'I always cry in *Tosca*,' he said. 'And in quite a few other operas, as well. As I hope you'll find out.'

He leaned forward and kissed her gently on the lips and although it took her by surprise, it seemed entirely natural and appropriate.

'I'm frightened,' she said, adding immediately what was on her mind, 'that you want to see me to get, I don't know, closer to Michael.'

She couldn't prevent herself saying this and dreaded that it would spoil the evening.

'I can understand that. But I'm not. You'll have to believe me. Nor am I like Scarpia, forcing himself on Tosca.'

She looked at his face, still close. 'Thank you,' she said, although she registered that a tiny shadow of doubt still existed. 'Have there been many women in your life?' She knew, the answer, of course.

'Too many.'

He lowered his eyes as he spoke. Mary felt that it was an admission, rather than a boast. 'I'm bad at knowing what is good for me.'

Although she would have slept with him, Mary was glad that he had simply kissed her again. Later, alone and wide awake in bed, she thought about this and his declaration that they would meet again, and soon. But, as the small hours came and went, she still worried about why he had taken her out in the first place. She replayed his response over and over again until, just before dawn, sleep finally took her hand and dragged her under.

16

Mary Houlihan had been trained to tell the truth, a compulsion to honesty that had been handed down by her mother and refined by her church. That morning she knew, looking at her tired eyes in the sharp light of the bathroom mirror, that she would have to tell Finistere about her evening with Erik. It was just after seven and she was surprised he hadn't already telephoned for confirmation of the day's events. She didn't have to wait long, however. Her mobile buzzed angrily on the marble surface and she saw that it was her boss.

'So,' he said. 'Home today. What train are you getting?'

'I booked one for later this afternoon, in case there was anything we needed to tidy up before we left.'

'There is. I'm due to fly out from Montparnasse at midday, but I want to go to site again, first thing.'

'Okay,' she said. 'There's something I would like to talk to you about, anyway.'

'Can't you tell me over the phone?'

'I'd rather not.'

'Is it serious?'

'I'll leave that for you to decide.'

'Well, shall we say nine o'clock there.'

She put the phone back on the marble top and resumed looking at herself in the mirror glad, now that they were going back to the warehouses, that she'd decided to come clean about Erik. She attempted to wipe away some of the tiredness she felt.

Youssef stared at the ceiling and decided they were all different. He had lain under hundreds, sometimes the stars, often the canopy of trees or the stony mouth of a cave. When he couldn't sleep, those long nights when he was keeping the demons at bay, they were his theatre.

There was always a spill of light on the camp, an orange stain from the dual carriageway and he counted the planks in the roof, lined up the knots in the wood and tried to guess what shapes he could recognise in the grey fan-like stains. It was just before dawn, when the police normally raided, that Youssef decided that the man who had beaten him would return and, true to his threat, take his life. He would do it with impunity, without fear of recrimination, for Youssef Tigha was nothing in his world and his absence would not be missed, nor indeed celebrated. He collected some of his bedding and the few clothes that he owned, slipping out of his hut into the ambient hum of distant traffic where, any minute, he expected to hear sirens, followed by the tread of feet and the rhythmic beating of black batons.

The tunnel was less defined and more threatening at night, the black mouth larger, the darkness beyond more infinite. Youssef didn't dare switch on the small torch until he'd walked some distance into this unknown, using the feel of one of the rails under his feet for guidance. He knew he had to get beyond the two wagons, his destination the bench beyond the platform that, for tonight at least, would give him a bed and another ceiling to examine. The animals continued to scuttle around him and once or twice the torch picked out the white reflection of a pair of eyes. The deeper he went into the tunnel, the safer he felt and, squeezing by the wagons, Youssef congratulated himself for having earlier become familiar with this territory. By the time he reached the bench, he imagined that dawn would have broken outside and that his hut and the others in the camp, would once again become the clear focus of their hatred.

He was weary, his body still aching from the beatings, his tongue playing in the raw gap left by the missing tooth, and he laid the bedding on the dusty bench in the darkness and hoped that he might sleep, that he could keep the unknown day at bay for just a few hours.

Michael Finistere got to the site early, his impatience fuelled by recalling his exchanges with Sophie Arditti the night before. The rain had stopped but the heavy grey skies took the colour out of the scene, emphasising its rundown state by the railway tracks, bordered by the stained concrete supports for the bridge and dual carriageway that interlaced themselves to his right. Smoke from several fires rose straight into the air, undisturbed by any breeze.

Standing alone in the wide-open space of the large lorry park, he was motionless in his clean black leather shoes, white shirt and new suit, a fresh tie tucked into his buttoned jacket. He took in this alien, redundant landscape. In his mind he was listening to Sophie's words, weighing their meaning and registering the discord of the night before. He looked and felt out of place, disconnected from his surroundings, but Sophie's mocking observations of his motives for being here had merely brought him more resolve, a child's petulant desire, he could see, to prove her wrong.

He let himself into the warehouse and once again heard the scrunch of his feet on the broken glass, climbing the stairs to the top floor. Without the lights, the model appeared to be no more than detritus at the back of the open space. He walked to the row of tall windows that lined the wall to his left and stood looking at the view towards the embankment, the gantries of the railway just visible through the rising jumble of trees and shrubs. Rubbish had been discarded and spilled down the slope to despoil the land.

He heard the tread of feet on the stairs and moments later Round Mary appeared in the doorframe.

'Good morning,' he called, his greeting echoing in the great space.

'Shall I put the lights on?' she said, moving into the room, leaning down to a switch by the opposite windows. 'There, that's better. It looks human again.'

The model lay between them.

'I've brought a flask of coffee,' Mary said. 'I thought we might need it.' She produced two beakers from her bag, filled one and handed it to Finistere.

'Will I be needing this?' he said. 'You sounded rather ominous on the phone. Is there something I should know?'

It was typical of him to bulldoze straight in like this.

'I thought you should know that I saw Erik Mollet last night. He took me to the opera.' There, she'd said it and immediately felt better.

He saw the relief on her face and raised his eyebrows. 'Well, you do surprise me Mary. How long has this been going on?'

'It hasn't been going on, as you put it. He only asked me out yesterday, saying he had just been given tickets.' She waited, the confession delivered. 'It didn't seem right to keep this from you.'

'What's he like, off duty?'

'Charming, as ever.'

'I bet. He's a dark horse, isn't he?'

She thought for one moment that Finistere was going to voice her own fears, that Erik had only taken her out to get nearer to him, to discover more about the deal.

'And did he take you to dinner afterwards?'

'We had a snack in a bar near Bastille.' What Finistere really wanted to know, she thought, was had she slept with him.

It occurred to Finistere that he, too, had eaten in the same area and he flinched at the possibility that he might have run into them. Not that he was going to tell Mary about his evening with Sophie.

'And what was the opera?'

'*Tosca.*'

Finistere had little or no knowledge of opera. 'Not my cup of tea,' he said.

'Sophie is an opera singer, she tells me.'

That did get Finistere's attention and Mary could see that he was taken aback by the information, unable to fit this into his picture of the woman she knew he'd taken out the night before. Mary saw that he had decided to draw a line under the topic and he switched his attention to the model. Then he caught her unawares.

'What do you think of all this? You've seen the plans, you know the figures. What's your view?'

Up until this point, Mary had not intended to tell Finistere about her walk through the underpass, but he'd never asked directly for her opinion before and this seemed the right moment.

'I do have something else to tell you,' she said.

'Not another man?'

She laughed. Together, as they had been doing for the past few days, they moved round to the back of the model.

'Did you know about the tunnel?' she said. 'There's one just here.' She pointed to an area where several of the little figures were sitting on a grassy slope.

'There's one on the original plans, surely?'

She saw that she had his attention. She drew the duplicate information out of the bag and unfolded a scale map of the district, laying it gently on the model, adjusting it so that it matched, roughly, it's cardboard equivalent beneath.

'Sort of,' Mary said. 'You'll see here,' she said, her finger on the plan, 'that a railway line runs along this north side and the map indicates that it stops just here.' She moved her finger to indicate where. Then she shifted the map aside, to reveal the model. 'About there.'

Finistere peered down and saw that she was pointing to an embankment of toy trees, a neat slope painted green, with a boundary beyond. No road was marked, nor bridge shown. And there was no tunnel.

'How do you know this?' he asked, looking at her, back in the business mode with which she was familiar. His question was tinged with a curl of suspicion.

'This had nothing, I repeat nothing, to do with my evening with Erik. The other afternoon, I came here and walked along the underpass,' she said, pulling the plan that showed both the road and railway back towards her. 'The camp is here and, from what I could see, the tunnel runs along here.' Her finger described a loop back in the direction of the warehouses. Then she remembered she had taken the photograph and she fished in her bag for her mobile.

'Here. Look.'

Finistere stood looking at the photo of the camp and the tunnel.

'Surely we have reports of all this?' he said, but she could see that he wasn't sure. 'Let me have a look.'

He leafed through the documents, from time to time glancing down at the map and model. 'I don't get it,' he said.

'It's probably nothing,' she said. 'The tunnel might be filled in, who knows.'

By now, Finistere was moving back to the windows that gave him a tangential view towards the underpass.

'You went down there alone? Christ.'

He could only just make out the camp, lost in the giant supports of the bridge, but the smoke from the fires continued to mark its position.

This couldn't have been what had been worrying him, surely. How could he have been bothered by something he didn't know about? Then the image of Sophie came back to him, the conversations about Paris, her scorn that he should have chosen a place he didn't like simply to make money. It dawned on him, on this grey morning in Paris, that he was looking at this site for the first time. Before now, his dislike of Paris had meant he'd paid others a great deal of money to do this for him.

Mary watched the various stages of thought move across Michael Finistere's face, shades of anger, then disgust, both now converging into resolve.

Finistere had arrived at a conclusion. It was not often that he berated himself, but he now glimpsed that he might just have been at fault, that he'd not paid enough attention to his own instincts, the simple rule he brought to all his projects.

'Bugger,' he said.

Mary looked on and wondered what conclusion he had come to, aware that their exchanges up here on the warehouse floor were the closest they had come to a conversation of equals since they'd met, not perfect, far from it, but different at least.

'Do you fancy making that walk again?'

She looked down at his clothes. 'Do you think you're dressed for it? And what about the helicopter?'

'Delay it,' he said, reverting to form.

'I think you need a coat over that suit.'

He looked at her for a moment. 'Right.' He watched her turn off the lights, wondering why he hadn't known where the switch was when he arrived.

His car took them to a shop just below the Gare du Nord, where he bought a trenchcoat. She waited in the car and called the pilot. Ten minutes later, they were dropped back at the Porte de la Chapelle.

'Are you ready for this?'

She nodded. 'Are you?'

'Show me,' he said and they set off for the underpass.

'You'll see the camp appear on the left,' Mary said, 'but don't point and don't take pictures.'

Cars rushed by on their right. This was their territory, a hostile environment for humans.

It was only as they arrived at the slope leading under the bridge, that they saw the burning sofa smouldering across their path. Nevertheless, they walked on.

To his left, through the railings, Finistere could see the old railway tracks that soon became lost under the migrant huts. Mary nudged him when the tunnel came into view. They didn't want to stop, but he took in the graffiti that lined the walls either side of the tunnel's mouth, open to swallow the tracks that disappeared into its darkness. What happened beyond?

And then they entered the dark of the railway bridge and the smoke from the sofa was thick and chemical and their eyes began to water. Heads down, they began the long, slow climb up towards Clignancourt. Cars continued to rush by them. They were silent all the way to the top.

'And you did that alone,' he said finally. 'I don't know what to say.'

Clearly he didn't, she thought, and they sat at an outside table of the same café she had used only a few days earlier, to review what they'd just done.

'So what do you think?' he asked.

'Mollet did tell us about the track,' she said. 'Showed it to us on the video. It's just that the model really didn't account for it completely.' They sipped their coffees.

'Yes, and who put that orange figure on it? The warning?'

She shrugged. 'You weren't happy yesterday, when you agreed the deal, were you?'

'Sophie told me that you'd noticed,' Finistere said.

Mary waited to hear more.

'I saw her last night. She appears to have a high regard for you.'

'You sound surprised.'

'Well, I suppose, to be fair, I was. But after that...' he said, nodding in the direction of the underpass. 'What made you do it?'

'I didn't know enough. I wanted to see more.'

'I should have done the same thing.' He turned to look at her. 'When is a deal not a deal?'

'Well, you'll just have to find out more. Shall I cancel the helicopter?'

17

Sophie was packing her small bag for the weekend with her mother. She was humming a scene from *La Traviata*, occasionally breaking into song, folding and arranging as she went, a routine she repeated through each Friday. Paris was spread, nondescript and colourless, under her window. She berated her agent for not phoning to tell her that she'd been offered the part of Violetta. Or Norma, for that matter. Or Tosca. But, then, she had yet to be taken out of the chorus and given a lead and if she was truthful with herself, which she sometimes was, she could see that this was unlikely. Still, she could dream. And she could still sing.

Her phone rang and for the briefest of seconds she thought that her wish might have been answered.

'You never told me that you were an opera singer.'

Michael Finistere again, in typical style.

'You never asked.'

'I knew you weren't just a translator.'

'No, you didn't. You were too busy thinking about yourself and your *grand projet*.'

She could hear Michael Finistere absorb this response.

'Yes, you're right. Bloody thing.'

'I expect you'll want to blame Paris.'

'Sort of. But really it's all my fault.'

'My, this is a different Michael this morning. *Mea culpa*. Whatever next?'

Sophie stepped over to the window and wondered if he was phoning from the warehouse, somewhere in the distance down to her right. Whatever, she knew what was coming next.

'Listen, I've got to stay in Paris a little longer. And, yes, it's to do with my *grand projet*, as you say. So, can I attempt to give you a better evening than last night?'

It wouldn't be difficult, she thought. 'I'm afraid not, as I'm sure Mary will have told you.'

'Did she?'

'I go to Milan at the weekends. To see my mother.'

'Bugger. She did. Couldn't you change your plans?'

Sophie snorted. 'You might first have asked me more about my mother.'

'I don't understand.'

'It's polite and it helps oil the wheels of any relationship. Give and take, you know?'

'Okay, why are you going to see your mother?'

Sophie pondered whether she should tell him. 'She's not well.'

'Oh, I'm sorry. Is she very ill? What does she have?'

'It's not so much what she has, more what she hasn't.'

'I'm lost.'

'The French would say that my mother was a little *déprimé*, which is close enough to your word in English for you to guess.'

'Depressed?'

'Bravo, we'll make a French speaker of you yet, Mr Finistere.'

'What is she depressed about?'

'Men, in a word. She's going to be sixty soon, she's no longer with my father and she worries that it's all slipping away from her, if you know what I mean.'

Sophie could hear him take this in and for a while there was silence.

'What are you thinking?' she asked him.

'Well, to tell you the truth, I was thinking that a daughter as beautiful as you might not be the greatest help to a mother who regrets all that passing.'

Sophie registered that this observation was probably the most interesting thing Michael Finistere had said to her so far, and perhaps true.

'She's expecting me, however.'

'When do you return?'

'Late on Sunday evening.'

'Sunday evening, then? We'll go to your place, that café whatever it was called. Oh, I have to thank you for something else. You were right about Mary. She really surprised me today. I'll tell you all about it on Sunday. Shall we say eight thirty?'

Sophie hated getting back from these weekends, carrying with her, as she usually did, a potent mix of anger and guilt, so part of her welcomed the distraction of being taken to dinner that night.

'If you insist.'

'I do.'

He finished the call with a sense of triumph, an elation he hadn't felt since he'd been in Paris, indeed, for as long as he could remember. He had no idea if he would stay in Paris for the weekend, but he would be back on Sunday evening, that was for sure. Opera singer. Why hadn't Mary told him before?

He sat back in a comfortable chair, putting his feet on a matching stool, and closed his eyes. His problems were greater, but his head was clearer. Sophie Arditti rose in front of him, just out of reach, to take precedence over the other decisions he had to make. She had disturbed the controlled world in which he normally lived and each meeting with her was a skirmish, a battle that always left him wounded, but wanting more. He'd never felt like this before. Was she the first woman who had made him doubt himself? Or was she the first woman who had made him look at himself differently? Who knows, she'd certainly taken him over and, in the space of three days, arrived centre stage in his life, shouldering away his other routines and preoccupations. She'd made him see Mary differently, as well and it was she who he called first.

'What should I do about Mollet, do you think? You know him probably as well as I do.'

'Do I think he's hiding something? Is that what you're asking?'

'I think perhaps I am.'

'I don't know. My instincts tell me no, that both you and he need to know more about the tunnel and what's happening down there.'

'But...?'

'But, I can't imagine him having bought the land without knowing what he was getting himself into.'

'Unless...?'

'...unless he only found out afterwards, like we're doing.'

'And wanted to hide the problem?'

'Perhaps. There's only one way to find out.'

'Ask him. I will. But I'd like you there as well. We have some decisions to make this afternoon. Come over as soon as you can.'

*

Mary, in a café on rue Jacob, noticed that she'd used the plural when describing the problem of the tunnel to Finistere. She was talking about their problem and not simply Finistere's. Before she would have used the singular and she noted the step change. She considered phoning Mollet, but immediately reasoned that it would be disloyal to Finistere and if, indeed, the Frenchman was hiding something, he would have been similarly disloyal to her. She hoped he hadn't been and she crossed herself at the thought.

She was excited and as the taxi bounced across the river, felt for the first time she was not simply an occasionally useful object sometimes referred to as Round Mary.

When she got to his room at the Lancaster, the first thing she noticed were the trollies of food and a table laid for two. He couldn't be expecting Sophie, surely?

'I've ordered lunch,' he said. 'Sit down, sit down.' He tossed her a crisp white napkin. 'There's some cold salmon and beef. Shall we eat before we call, or after?'

'Definitely after,' she said, without hesitation.

'So, how should we approach it?'

The plural again.

Mary had thought about this. 'I'd tell him what happened this morning. That the other day I had noticed the tracks and the tunnel and I wanted to show you...' And here she stopped. 'No, that will sound just awful. Like I had been snooping.'

'I get it,' Finistere said. 'Why don't I just say that I wanted to take one last tour of the site and that I'd been curious about the camp, which he raised at the last meeting, and that you had come with me.'

It was true, up to a point, and she nodded. 'And along the way, we noticed the tunnel and wondered if he could tell us more.'

'Right. I'll put the call on speaker.'

He reached for the phone.

'Erik, good morning. It is morning, isn't it? Of course it is, we haven't had lunch yet.'

If Mary was watching Finistere, she was thinking of Erik's face, listening to his genial response and imagining the touch of his bristles against her lips. She was nervous and wanted the best to happen, but she couldn't think of a scenario where it might. She heard Finistere outline what they had discussed and she could hear Erik's breathing change.

'Yes,' he said, 'I know there is a tunnel but I think it ends pretty quickly and it poses us no problems. It's just a question of filling it in, as I said the other day.'

Finistere glanced over to her, raising his eyebrows.

'Do we know this for certain, Erik? The model rather gives the impression that all the problems at that end of the site can easily be smoothed over, beautiful green hills planted with pretty cotton wool trees.'

'Our engineers tell us that this is the case.'

'Do you mind if we have a look?' Finistere said, indicating to Mary with his fingers that he meant both of them.

'Of course, Michael. We have shaken on the deal, though, haven't we?'

'We have, Erik. This is just belt and braces.'

Mary could tell he hadn't quite understood and so had Finistere.

'I'll get Sophie to tell you about the expression. It means something like going over fine details.'

'It's going to be easier said than done.' Erik's voice had a degree of caution. 'Access is a little difficult, not least because of the camp.'

'Well, do what you can,' said Finistere, standing and walking over to the table to pour a couple of glasses of white wine. 'Call me back soon, one way or the other. I'm still here at the Lancaster. I'll wait to hear from you.'

He handed a glass of wine to Mary and raised his own in her direction.

'None the wiser, really,' he said.

Mary had willed the conversation to go well and the tension was still with her, her heart keeping time with her pulse, both of which she could feel against her skin.

'Let's eat. Cheers.'

Was it disloyal to Erik to be raising a glass with Finistere, who might at any minute pull out of the deal? Or was she being unfair to Finistere, who might be in the process of being deceived? She was grateful for the drink.

'In the end, it might not matter,' Finistere said, eating a piece of beef with his fingers. 'Perhaps we're both in the process of being surprised, in which case we either share the cost of putting it right, or don't.'

And if you don't, thought Mary, then Erik would be left with a plot of land whose value will have plummeted. This was business, she knew, the risking of large amounts of money.

'Nice food they do here, don't you think?' Finistere seemed entirely unconcerned, not a difficult position to take if you're protected by vast amounts of money, she thought. It was an easy decision and she wondered if she'd be the same. Perhaps Mollet was similarly wealthy?

'Have another drink.' He leaned over and filled her glass.

The phone rang and Mary froze in the process of raising it to her lips. 'What news, Erik?'

'We can go tomorrow, Saturday. The police will have some guys around the camp. There's access via the junction at Clignancourt. I'll meet you at the warehouse at ten tomorrow morning. I'll bring whatever's necessary.' His voice was tense and to the point.

During this brief exchange, Mary could feel the heat of panic rising in her and she slipped her hand into her pocket to turn off her phone. She couldn't cope with Erik calling her now.

'So, another night in Paris. Will we ever leave?'

Finistere was happy, even though nothing was clear with either the project or with Sophie. The feelings of doubt, however, were beginning to clear, even if he couldn't explain quite how to himself.

Mary looked at him. 'You'll need to have different clothes,' she said. 'You can't go into that camp, or the tunnel, wearing a posh suit.'

He looked down at himself. 'Right, Mary.' And raised his glass again.

Youssef retrieved his watch from behind the loose brick, polishing its face against his shirt before clipping it to his wrist and pulling down his shirt to cover it. He had returned to the camp in the early afternoon, going up to the den in the buddleia, commanding a view down on a scene he expected soon to disappear. The men came and went and the fires continued to burn. Change was about to happen.

He left via the gap in the metal fence, cautiously working his way around the warehouses, before setting off for the one fixed moment in his week. He had an even clearer picture of her in his mind and it led him down the canal towards Bastille. The rain had stopped, the sky had cleared and people sat along the edge of the water drinking coffee and wine. This was their life and Youssef threaded his way through it, ignored and, he saw from time to time, unwanted. This was not the place to check his watch, but he knew he had left plenty of time.

He arrived at the front of the Gare de Lyon about an hour before the train was due to leave, standing on the concourse to look up at the board announcing her scheduled departure. What would it be like to take the train, to disappear with her along those metal lines to the future?

He left and followed his familiar route on the roads that ran alongside the tracks until he came to the narrow bridge, the *passerelle*, that crossed the tracks. Half an hour to go. He slipped through the rusting gates, down the crumbling steps and sheltered under the bridge. Trains came and went until it was time to leave for the place he always waited, the graffiti-marked wall against which he could disappear.

And it began again. The anticipation. The distant thunder, first felt through the ground. And then the growing crescendo as the train came nearer. Finally, he stepped out from his hiding place just as the express came into view. Once again he counted the carriages, out loud, until fourteen.

And there she was, but now different. Not an imaginary spirit being carried away, but a real person, someone it was possible to stand against, to touch, to give shape to. She existed. She was flesh. And as quickly as she was in front of him, she was gone, the dust and rubbish flying in her wake, the hot air rushing by, the dream disappearing.

This time he knew it was different. Since she had been made real, she could also be taken from him. Like everything else.

18

Another storm moved in later that afternoon. Mary heard it beat against the windows of her top floor room, the thrum of the rain on the roof. She was sitting on the edge of her bed, her phone in her hand. She was looking at its face and its simple message, that she'd missed two calls, both from Mollet. She switched off silent mode and checked the times the messages had come through. The first, as she had guessed, was made shortly after he'd received Finistere's call and she blessed her foresight for having turned her phone to silent. The second call she'd missed only twenty minutes ago. She was composing herself before returning it.

A Friday in Paris. She couldn't expect him to be free, any more than she could guess his reaction when she called. She was between a rock and a hard place, damned whatever she thought.

The window frame rattled behind her.

She almost leaped in the air when the phone burst to life in her hands. She answered it automatically.

'At last.'

'Erik. It's you.'

'I tried before.'

'I know. My phone was on silent.'

'Where were you?'

It was the question she dreaded, for she knew she would have to tell the truth.

'With Finistere.'

'When he made the call to me.'

'Yes.'

'That must have been difficult for you.'

She was glad to hear him say this. 'Yes, yes, it was. And now it's difficult for you. For us both.'

'Does he know about us?'

She held her breath. 'Yes. I had to tell him.'

'I expect he thinks I want to see you to find out more about him?'

The wind rushed under the eaves and a squall threw rain at the window. She hardly dared speak.

'And do you think that?' he continued, his voice quiet.

'I wondered when you first asked me, but after the other night, no. Finistere is always suspicious.'

'And now?'

'He'll always be suspicious.'

'And you?'

She stood. The Seine was lost in the distance, obliterated by the storm.

'No,' he said, interrupting the silence. 'I'm being unfair. I'll just have to persuade you, won't I? I assume you're staying in Paris again tonight? And might I also assume that you are free?'

'You might,' Mary said, smiling.

'Perfect. I don't think the weather is quite right for a trip on the Seine, but a dinner somewhere nice, yes?'

'Yes.'

'Shall I pick you up at the hotel? Half past seven?'

'Yes.'

'Perfect.'

Mary kicked off her shoes and lay back on the bed. She was still smiling, although this disguised the two thoughts that competed for her attention and contradicted the look on her face. Mollet had not quite dispelled her caution about why he wanted to see her. And how on earth was she going to tell Finistere?

The phone rang again and she sat upright. With impeccable timing, it was Finistere.

'Do you fancy supper tonight? Since we've got to spend yet another day in this strange city.'

She couldn't help but give a small laugh at being asked out to dinner twice in a matter of seconds, not that she misunderstood Finistere's motives. 'Mollet's just asked me the same question.'

'The dirty bugger. Trojan horse, eh?'

Mary couldn't help notice the change in Finistere, not only towards her but in his reaction to things.

'He asked if I, and you, thought he had ulterior motives for wanting to see me.'

'What did you say?'

'Well, I said the thought had crossed my mind. And yours.'

'You're big enough to cope with it.'

Did he mean it like that, she thought, a put down to her size? Or was it a genuine compliment?

'You're a sort of double agent,' he went on, proving, she hoped, that he meant the latter. 'Well, should make tomorrow even more interesting. Have fun.'

Finistere put down the phone. It wasn't often that a night approached with nothing to do and the vacuum of the empty hours made him uneasy. The phone was still in his hand. He brought up her number.

'Hello?'

In the background, he could hear part of a message being given over a speaker. 'You're on your way to see your mother.'

'Yes, and I'd just dropped off to sleep.'

'I'm sorry. I just needed to hear your voice. As I thought, I've got to spend Friday night in Paris as well.'

'Poor you. Your idea of a nightmare. And no, I can't turn around and come back.'

'Tell me what a lone man should do in Paris on a Friday night, except hope that Sunday evening will come soon?'

'Well, I won't suggest Pigalle, assuming you know what I mean?'

'I suppose I could guess. Do you like going to your mother's?'

'Ah, a question about me. No, if you must know. But it's become a bit of a habit.'

'What a shame I couldn't change it. Is there lots to do in Milan at the weekend?'

'With my mother, you mean…?'

'Come to London to see me instead. It's an open offer.'

He could hear the train now and he imagined her alone in the carriage, her face reflected in the window.

'Can I assume that you like London, at least?' she asked.

'Up to a point. More than Paris, at least.'

'Doesn't sound like you'd be a good host, then.'

'You'll have to find out. I have an apartment in the middle of Mayfair.'

'I'm sure you have. Now, Mr Finistere, if you don't mind, I need a little rest before the rigours of my mother. To build up my strength.'

'I might need you to work on Monday, as well,' he said, not wanting to let her go.

'Work or *work*, Mr Finistere?'

'Both, if you like.'

'Good night. *Bon weekend.*'

Youssef was caught on the *passerelle* when the storm hit, blowing him against the side of the exposed bridge. By the time he had made it to the far side and stumbled under the awning of a small shop, he was soaking wet. The shopkeeper was watching from the window, so he hesitated before taking an apple and sprinting off into the downpour. He doubted that he would be followed in the deluge.

He gave up trying to stay dry. At least the rain would clean him, wash away the grime of the camp and the dust of the tunnel. He left a line of wet when he cut through first the Gare de l'Est and then the Gare du Nord but the last stretch, up rue Poissoniers, was open and bleak and he was thoroughly miserable when he reached the warehouses.

Worse was to come.

He worked his way up the steep slope, through the trees and shrubs, to the fence. As he moved the uprights aside, he heard the noises from down in the camp. He stopped, water from the trees running down his back. Several policemen were in the process of destroying some of the huts, including his own. Mallets were bashed into its sides and within moments it lay broken on the ground. Not all of the huts were smashed in this way. This was merely a warning of worse to come.

The police left but he waited for fear that there were more around he hadn't seen. Instead he watched some of the larger men from the camp pull the broken wood out of the rain before it became too sodden. On the tracks under the bridge they began another fire, although Youssef saw that his door and some of the uprights had been put to one side as the basis of a replacement hut. He doubted they would ever be used.

He saw the fire take, the smoke from the damp wood rising to the ceiling of the bridge to lick around the sides. Eventually the flames appeared and he went down to stand by their warmth. No one said anything about his hut. It happened all the time.

One of the Kurdish boys, a few years older but not much taller, came over to him and stood by his side.

'So what did you do? They were searching for you. You should be careful.'

Youssef looked at him. Was this a warning? However much the other refugees in the camp were faced with the same problems, Youssef was reluctant to say too much. He maintained the same silence he had with the police.

'You're a strange one.'

Youssef moved away. He needed to get up to his den in the buddleia and eventually to the tunnel but for the moment it was too dangerous. His world had shrunk again. Another home lay in ruins and the remaining hours of the day pressed against him with the promise of nothing. His damp clothes sucked themselves to his skin. He stood under the bridge and watched the drivers in their cars, secure and warm, looking ahead at their futures, near and distant. He slid the watch out of his pocket and looked at the second hand ticking forward into emptiness.

The boy who had spoken to him had left to join the Kurds at the other end of the camp, so Youssef returned to the fire, raking the embers with a broken stick to increase the warmth. Where would she be now? His journey could have taken him to Italy, but they had chosen to come through Greece and what he was told were the Balkans. What was Italy like? Was she going to Milan or Turin, the names on the train? How different from his mother, always at home, always at the centre of his life whilst the woman on the train travelled alone between countries. He looked over to the warehouse, almost lost in the rain. Other people's lives, filled with plans and journeys that led somewhere. Soon he would walk up to the camp and hide his watch and afterwards sneak into the tunnel and find his bed for the night. And that was it. There was no more.

Mary knew the outcome of her evening before it even began, but she couldn't think further into the next day, or the following week. She knew, though, that they beckoned her forward with promise. It wasn't that she conspired to make the events happen, well, not completely, but they followed the form she imagined, hoped, they would.

She felt his bristles against her face almost the moment they met in the small foyer of her hotel. This was not a kiss of politeness, a traditional peck on each cheek, but something much more, a coming together that had been predicted. The restaurant was near the new market off the boulevard St Germain, although it could have been anywhere. Not once did they discuss work, or Finistere, but instead began to fill the imaginary empty chequerboard in front of them with markers, each one an unknown fact, unloaded and swapped. It was a barter they entered into with equal enthusiasm, events big and small that had shaped their lives, presented and exchanged.

She watched Mollet eat with gusto, his napkin tucked into the neck of his shirt, his laughter infectious. The bistro had wooden alcoves and windows that, in summer, would open out on to the street. He was well known to the *patronne* and she second guessed most of the dishes he wanted and was polite enough not to mention the names of anyone else he might have dined with there before. He brought this up himself, another marker or two on the board. The drink came in *pichers*, with thick glass bottoms and there were several of them. By the time they had finished, the chequerboard was reasonably full, the childhoods in Gascony and Dublin, their Catholic schooldays, surprisingly similar, some of the stuff, thought Mary, that you need to get down before the next stage.

When they returned to the hotel there was no awkwardness about whether he should come up to her room and some things matched exactly the scenario she had created for herself that afternoon, the admiration of her legs and how beautiful she looked in the green underwear. There was no hesitation about the sex itself. For two big people, she thought they were admirably agile and the sound of the continuing rain and the wind in the eaves was broken only by their own sounds being exchanged for the very first time.

Laying down on the bench in the tunnel, there was a profound darkness above him, so Youssef could not tell whether his eyes were open or shut, or if a ceiling existed. The air was still and the space was almost without sound. It was the blackness of his life, no light at the end of the tunnel, nothing defined ahead of him. At home, when he slept outside in the relative cool of the night, the stars performed for him and however small he felt under them, they were a point of reference, something against which he could measure himself.

Now, down here in the darkness, all that was gone. He was in limbo.

19

ollet crept out of bed around five thirty, as he had told her he would. She watched him dress, careful and distracted. He leant down and kissed her, the bristles again and she wanted to pull him down but he was gone and the door clicked behind him. She piled the pillows behind her head. Sleep was impossible now. She got up to make herself tea and felt last night between her legs, a welcome dull pain. Just as she had predicted the events of the previous evening, so she expected the remorse of this early morning, the doubts that rose with the weak daylight. It was in her make-up to worry and what had seemed easy and natural the night before was now freighted with other meaning. He'd had many lovers, he had admitted, and was not successful at making relationships last. Was she simply another?

She wrapped herself in a hotel dressing gown and drank her tea, the dawn coming up on a cloudless day. In a few hours she would be seeing him again, but touching would be forbidden, intimacy out of the question. But that was all perfectly normal, she thought, and would give what happened last night an added piquancy even if, she had to admit to herself, it was never repeated. Having so recently experienced such extreme intimacy, though, its absence would be all the more marked, as it was now.

They hadn't discussed the project, or Finistere, and she added this to her list of worries, that perhaps it had been too deliberate, that he was being extra careful about revealing his hand. And then she posed the counter-argument: what secrets could he possibly learn from her?

She got up and paced the small room, her tea cooling in her hand, playing both defence and prosecution. If he really was the sort to use her in this way, he would have read the papers in the briefcase before handing it back. It contained all the details of the deal. Perhaps he had? It was typical, she thought, that she couldn't simply accept that he had been attracted to her and that this had nothing to do with her work.

She soaked in a bath, carefully washing herself and even as she did she felt aroused again, like she had with him, every part of her alive and electric. Wanton was a word her mother used from time to time to describe a certain sort of woman and if the word came to mind now, she thought it unfair and crude. She continued to touch herself and afterwards lay in the bath, her cheeks glowing.

She dressed slowly and despite a certain soreness, decided that she would once again make the walk to Finistere's hotel. The rain had cleared the air, the sun came up on a cloudless sky and even the Seine seemed blue. She had walked this way with Sophie and she stopped again on the same bridge. Somewhere, just a few kilometres to the north, beyond the beautiful stone facades of the glorious buildings of central Paris, was the migrant camp and on this clear, bright morning, the contrast could not have been greater. She headed up the Champs-Élysées and nothing could have been grander than the sweep of the road up to the Arc de Triomphe. What could be better? Striding towards a rendezvous with Erik Mollet on a crisp autumn morning with this view in front of her.

Finistere was waiting, sitting reading in the lush foyer.

'So, how was it?' He couldn't keep the smile from his face.

'We had a lovely evening, thank you.' Mary felt the blush cross her face.

'So I see. Did you talk business?'

'Not once.'

'Playing a waiting game, is he? Or does he simply enjoy your company?'

'You could ask him.'

'I might.'

'You've bought some new clothes.'

Finistere was wearing cream chinos, a pale blue checked shirt covered with a darker blue crew-necked sweater. On his feet he had rubber-soled brogues.

'You look almost French,' she told him.

'Dear God.'

Mollet arrived ten minutes later, also casually dressed and Finistere watched as he kissed Mary on both cheeks, before shaking his hand. Although the kisses were chaste, just the touch of his bristles on her face set Mary off again. Perhaps wanton was the right word after all.

Finistere wasn't going to miss the opportunity for a bit of mischief.

'Did you have fun last night, you two?'

Mollet was driving, with Finistere in the front and Mary in the back. She could see his eyes in the rear-view mirror and even without being able to see his face, knew he was smiling.

'We had a fine time, thank you Michael. A little restaurant just by the market in St Germain. I would recommend it. And you?'

'I had a roast beef sandwich in front of the telly and a good bottle of what you French do rather well, red wine. She didn't tell you any of our secrets, did she Erik?'

They were heading up towards the Gare de l'Est.

'Everything, Michael. As well as an industrial spy, she's also a beautiful woman.'

In the back, Mary blushed again.

'Could be she's working for me as well, Erik. My spy in your camp.'

'Who knows?' he said, turning quickly to look at her.

'I shall maintain a diplomatic silence,' Mary said.

Erik parked the car in a side street near Clignancourt. He handed each of them large torches. 'You'll need these.'

There were two policemen near the passage that led down towards the camp.

'Are you prepared for this?' he said, looking first at Mary and then Finistere. Mary was wearing a pair of trainers and under her coat, jeans and a sweater. They arrived at the rough ground, below which they could see the extent of the camp and the old railways lines.

'Jesus,' said Finistere, surveying the scene. 'How many are there?'

'It varies,' said Mollet. 'Between five hundred and a thousand, according to the police.'

Mary could see groups of policemen dotted around, standing clear of the migrants who acted as if the police weren't there. They scrambled down a steep path to the lines. Finistere looked at the graffitied walls, the rubbish strewn tracks and the fires burning nearby. Up ahead, he could make out the wooden huts standing unevenly against the concrete underpass and more thickly under the railway bridge. Why had he never seen all this before, he asked himself again? Looking the other way, he saw the tunnel, the lines entering the hill, the buddleia growing thickly above.

'Well, here we are.' Mollet nodded towards the mouth of the tunnel.

'So where are the warehouses? I've lost my bearings.'

Mollet pointed somewhere to the left of the tunnel entrance. 'One of the tracks continues over there, under the bridge, making the northern boundary of our development. This is a spur under the tunnel. Shall we go?'

'Have you done this before?' Mary asked.

'To tell you the truth, no.'

'But somebody did for you? A surveyor, yes?' Finistere said.

'Of course,' Mollet replied. 'Mary, you go in the middle, behind me.'

They walked into the darkness, the beams of their powerful torches bouncing off the sooty walls.

Finistere was almost reduced to silence, a relatively new experience. He was glad of the shoes and of Mary's instruction for him to buy different clothes. The tunnel curved around to the left and soon the light from the mouth of the tunnel was left behind. The air thickened around them, the tunnel blacker.

'Christ,' said Finistere, tripping on a rail. 'This wasn't on the fucking model.'

They stopped as a carriage loomed ahead and their powerful torches played over its bulk. Mollet stepped to one side. 'There are two of them, I think. We can squeeze by.'

Finistere found it claustrophobic to have the great weight of the wagons on one side and the tunnel wall on the other. After another hundred metres or so their torches picked out the low platform and they climbed up to it, Mollet helping Mary. She tried to see his eyes, but it was too dark. She thought of their touches in the dark of the night before.

'Must be a sort of depot,' Mollet said, his torch locating the door in the wall. Tentatively, they made their way towards it and pushed it open.

Youssef heard them only at the last minute. The darkness had tricked him into believing it was still night. He heard someone speak and then saw the cracks in the door outlined by torchlight. He had no time to gather his bedding or put on his trainers but he snatched up his torch and moved carefully into the heart of the great space, heading towards the far corner, where he sat on the floor. It would take a very powerful light to pick him out there.

He heard the door push open and saw the beams of light cut into the darkness. He sank lower into the corner and hoped.

*

'Jesus,' Finistere said again. 'What is this place? It feels enormous.'

'It is a depot,' Mollet replied, also repeating himself. 'An underground warehouse.'

The two men were ahead of her when Mary's torch picked out the dirty white trainers. The moment she saw them, she moved the beam elsewhere. She had recognised the distinct logo. The others had moved further into the room, so she walked towards the shoes and as she did she saw the bedding laid out on the bench. Someone had slept here. Could it be the boy who had stolen the briefcase? She slid the beam along the wall either side of the bench, expecting to glimpse a figure. She could see the searchlights of the other two, now some distance away. Mary began to walk along the wall, to find its limit. Once she had, she turned left, keeping the wall on her right, her torch lighting her way along the perimeter. She estimated that it was over fifty metres before she picked out the wall ahead of her and she was beginning to turn and follow it, to join the others, who she could see further along, when the beam panned over an unexplained shape. Uncertain, she redirected the torch. Then she stepped back. In the corner was a figure hiding his face, who now stood and began to race back across the floor.

'What's that?' she heard Finistere shout, his torch and then Mollet's, following the direction of the noise.

'There's someone in here,' Finistere said, following the light of his torch.

Mary still had the brief image of the boy's face, frightened and filthy, burned into her mind. She began to walk across towards the other two, the boy's face still with her, but turned more to her left, heading for the spot where she had seen the boy's possessions. Eventually, she located the bench, but the shoes and the bedding were gone. Finistere and Mollet joined her moments later, Eric taking her hand in the darkness.

'Did you see who it was?' Finistere asked her.

'Not really, no.' But she'd recognise him again, she thought.

'Must be living down here,' Mollet said.

'I must say, I've seen better hotel rooms,' Finistere added. 'What a place.' He pointed his torch at Mollet, lighting up his face. 'And where exactly on that model of yours, is all this, Erik? It's a hell of a big hole to fill in, wouldn't you say?'

Mary stretched out her hand and touched Finistere's arm, pushing it down so the blinding light left Mollet's face.

'I agree, Michael. But all this is new to me, too.'

'How much more of it do you think there is?' Finistere asked, directing his torch back to the door. 'And where does our land begin and end?'

They left through the door, Mollet leading them further on along the tunnel. 'We'd better find out.'

Mary was now at the rear and wondered where the boy was and, more to the point, who he was. Did he live in the camp?

And his face remained with her, the image of his eyes, wide and frightened as her torch found him crouched and alone.

20

They emerged into sunlight. After the blackness of the tunnel, they had to shade their eyes.

'I see,' said Mollet.

'Well, I'm glad somebody does.' Finistere surveyed the marshalling yard with his hands on his hips.

'That's rue Poissoniers over there, beyond the old signal box. This is nothing to do with us.'

'And the rest of it, Erik?'

It was like a discarded toy, a companion to the model in the warehouse, thought Mary. A giant hand might appear at any minute and place a train and wagons on the track.

'I'm afraid we're going to have to go back through the tunnel.'

'I want to take a photograph,' Mary said, holding up her mobile. 'Hold on.'

She walked along to the metal steps that led up to the signal box. As she rose, she first saw the old levers and then a broken-down metal chair. Finally the boy, crouched under a counter. She hesitated on the last step and the boy, wide-eyed, stared back at her. He raised a finger to his lips. She moved forwards, looking back on the splay of empty lines, towards Erik and Finistere, their faces tilted in her direction. She took several photos and returned to the steps, going down backwards, with the view of the boy slowly disappearing.

The last thing she saw were his distinctive trainers.

Moving back through the tunnel, Mary thought of the boy and her decision not to reveal him. Mollet slowed ahead and in the darkness she bumped into him. She felt his hand on her legs and for a moment the boy was forgotten. They resumed their passage, Finistere's torch lighting the way ahead. Would she tell Erik, she thought? Or would it remain her secret? There was something in the boy's pleading eyes and desperate request for silence that made her an instant conspirator and for now, until she had made more sense of him, she decided she should keep her counsel.

Up ahead, Finistere was thinking about Sophie and his need to call her again. He had this ability, he knew, to compartmentalise his mind, sealing off the problem of the underground depot so that it didn't contaminate any other thought or activity. Yes, he needed to pursue Sophie Arditti. Perhaps the courtship of the two following behind – he'd heard Mollet slow down and imagined what might have been going on – had produced an element of envy.

'C'mon you two. What are you up to back there?'

They passed the depot platform and then the two carriages, the tunnel curving round towards the light. They gathered in the mouth and from the camp they were being watched by several groups of men, who in turn were being monitored by the police, hands on the batons tucked into their belts.

'What do they think we're up to, Erik? Do they know?'

'I would imagine so, Michael. The police have started knocking down some of the huts already. They know they haven't got long.'

The faces of the men, and they were all men, were blank, thought Mary, empty of emotion. She felt uncomfortable, not through fear but as an intruder might in someone else's territory, a trespasser. She caught Erik looking at her and wondered if he felt the same.

Finistere held out his hands, streaked with soot and grime. 'We need to talk, Erik. And us too, Mary. But first I need a bath.'

Youssef stayed in the signal box until they were gone. The big woman had not betrayed him and he didn't know why. There was goodness in her eyes, though, a softness in her face and it was this that had stopped him running. He had gestured for her to remain silent and perhaps he wasn't surprised when she agreed. She was the opposite of the policeman, who would have killed him.

He got to his feet, leaving his bedding in the shelf above the door, where before he had hidden the briefcase. A half plan was forming in his mind, a comfort for at least it gave him direction for the next minutes, an immediate structure to his day.

He left the yard along the metal walkway, dropping down on to rue Poissoniers before making his way up to Clignancourt. He was sure that eventually they would leave this way, taking the passage that ran alongside the café. There was a bench on the other side of the road and he sat there in the warm sun and waited. It was hard for him to know how long he had been in Paris. His days compressed into one, his weeks passed unnoticed. Time, like the days of the week, had no meaning, for there was nothing to look forward to, or plan for. Perhaps he'd been here for three months, perhaps more, certainly one summer. The people who walked by him did so with purpose, enclosed in days where the hours were all allotted tasks and pleasures, meetings and appointments. He was in freefall, untethered from the framework of time.

Youssef was so distracted that he almost missed them leaving. At first, he thought they were going to cross the road towards him, but they turned and he followed at a distance. They left the main boulevard for a side street and Youssef waited, now more exposed. He saw them stop by a grey Mercedes and climb in, the car reversing in the road before heading back in his direction. The big woman was in the back and as the car reached the intersection with the main road, she looked in his direction. For a second their eyes met and he knew that she had recognised him.

There he is, she almost said but stopped herself just in time. She held the boy's eyes as the car turned into the boulevard and he was left behind. She understood in that moment that this was the boy who had put the figure on the model, who had quite literally flagged their attention. The orange worker carrying his red flag was protecting the smaller figures of a couple with a child. Quite simply, it was a call for help. The boy, with his own way of entering the warehouse, had discovered the model and perhaps even watched the presentations given by Erik. He saw what was going to happen to the land that contained the camp, understood that it was all going to be destroyed.

She let this information sink in and align itself with the other events of this notable few days in Paris. For now, the boy fought for attention with her more basic instincts, as Mary hoped that Erik would drop Finistere at his hotel, before taking her on to the rue du Bac.

And so it turned out.

'I'll see you here later, say three,' Finistere told them both as they left him at the hotel.

They had three hours, which turned out to be both more languorous and more erotic than the night before, slower and more deliberated and yet more deliberately physical. They barely spoke and the boy with the pleading eyes and the great cavern under the ground were both replaced by more immediate concerns, more urgent needs. The distant Seine was also forgotten, place lost its meaning and time was suspended as she abandoned normal boundaries, all points of reference swept aside. If the previous night was enjoyable, it was also a surprise and it liberated this Saturday lunchtime, gave it more freedom. It was both conscious and understood and Mary knew, even before they had finished, exhausted, that remorse would not follow, that she could relax into herself and enjoy the sheer physicality of what had taken place.

Their legs were intertwined, his hand resting lightly on her pubic hair. 'I suppose we have to go to a meeting,' he said, patting her down below.

'How will I keep a straight face?'

'Finistere knows, Mary. You can see it.'

'Who cares?'

'Who cares, indeed.'

'I saw the boy who took the bag,' she said, not knowing in advance that this was what she was going to say. 'He was the one in the depot. I recognised the trainers.'

Mollet had propped himself on his elbow.

'And then he was in the signal box. He asked me not to give him away.'

'And you didn't.'

She shook her head. 'I didn't have the heart to. He looked so lost.'

He took her hand and kissed it.

'I think he put the figure on the model in the first place. He was trying to tell us something, wanting us to stop, perhaps.'

Mollet's eyes were on her, following what she was saying, listening.

'We'll destroy the camp, won't we? And where will they go, the people there? They have nothing and then they'll have less than nothing.'

'You have a good heart, Mary Houlihan. When we bought the land, the camp didn't exist.'

'And what do you think of them, the migrants, the refugees?'

'Most of them are Arabs, from North Africa. A fact of life, I'm afraid,' he said, rubbing his hand on her rough hairs.

She moved her body under his hand.

'Do we have time?'

'Of course.'

He had begun calling Sophie even before he arrived in his room. He stood by the window, hoping the distant tone would be answered, but it clicked to voicemail.

'Bugger.'

He dropped the phone on to a chair, but then immediately picked it up.

'Stu, it's me. Still in Paris, as you know. Could you tell the others there's still a bit of problem. We may have hit a snag. I don't know whether to come back, or stay.'

'A snag?'

'I'll call you later and explain. I've got a meeting at three. Now I need a bath. I've been underground for the last two hours. And, yes, I'll explain that as well. Just tell the others.'

He tossed the phone on the chair again and stripped off his clothes. He lay in the bath before submerging himself, rising like a whale and blowing air from his nose and mouth.

'Bugger,' he shouted at the mirror. He was imagining Sophie in Italy and he saw her in the black linen suit, the thin material barely disguising her shape. What was she doing now? Shopping? Lunching, probably, trying to reassure her mother. Why wasn't she here with him?

'Bugger.' He submerged himself again.

Moments later, he was pacing the floor of his suite, water dripping on to the pale carpet, drying his hair, looking at his watch on the table and seeing that he had half an hour before they arrived.

He threw the towel away, sat down and picked up a pencil. On hotel stationery he made a list, a rough agenda. He then tried Sophie again and was frustrated once more. He put on the same chinos but this time with a pink shirt that he'd also bought. He brushed his hair in the mirror, sat and waited. He could imagine what Round Mary had been doing with Mollet, the old goat. The thought made him cross at his own failure with Sophie.

'Bugger.'

The look on their faces when they arrived told him all he needed to know. He felt like a stern father ushering in his daughter and her inappropriate boyfriend.

Noticing the wet towel on the floor, he picked it up and threw it into the bathroom and shut the door.

They sat at the table in the window, the blue sky beyond.

'So, Erik, cards on the table time. You had no idea before this morning that the tunnel and all that space existed?'

'I knew about the tunnel, sure, but not about the rest. I thought the tunnel would be easily filled.'

'What about this surveyor of yours?'

'He didn't indicate anything more.'

'Why the fuck not?'

'Your guess is as good as mine. Maybe he simply didn't know.'

'Simply didn't do his job, you mean.'

Mary watched this exchange, not quite the partisan supporter she might have been a few weeks earlier.

'What I don't get,' Finistere said, rising from the table, 'is exactly where all that is, the depot and so on, in relation to the warehouses. Do you, Eric?'

'A little, yes.' From his back pocket, he produced a piece of paper, unfolded it and got up to spread it in the middle of the table. It was a rough plan of the development. 'Here are the warehouses, the railway running along the north side, the spur going into the tunnel and these dotted lines are my guess as to where we walked earlier.'

Finistere leaned forward for a better look.

'It's rough, of course, and something of a guess, but I reckon the underground depot is here.' His finger traced the dotted line.

Finistere looked up at him. 'To one side of the warehouses, you think? Fuck, what does that mean? That's a hell of a lot to fill in.'

Mollet shrugged.

'Who owns it then?' It was Mary who spoke, not really looking Erik in the face but wanting to. She hoped that her own face didn't show signs of his rough stubble on her skin.

'That's a good question, Mary. I will need to look into it,' Mollet replied.

'You need to look into sacking your surveyor while you're about it. How much time do you need?'

Another shrug. 'I think my lawyer will tell me. End of the week, perhaps.'

'Can't I ever get away from Paris? Christ.'

Mary was thrilled, but kept a straight face with, once again, her eyes firmly averted from Erik's.

'I'll need to talk to Mary, Erik. I'll call you later.'

Mollet left and there was nothing Mary could do to say goodbye, no gesture that was adequate after what had so recently taken place.

'Well?' he said.

It was the sort of question, she thought, that a headmaster might have asked a pupil who'd been caught flouting school rules.

'I think we need to know more.' An idea was forming in her mind the moment she spoke. She didn't have to announce it.

'You should stay here. It's probably what you want anyway. I'm not asking you to spy on him but we can't go ahead with a fucking great cavity under the plot.'

What a strange turn of events. A week in Paris with a lover now loomed ahead and with it a proper role, far beyond that of being a mere dogsbody to Michael Finistere.

She went to cross herself, but stopped.

21

Mary remembered the morning of her eighth birthday, the blissful comfort of knowing what awaited her downstairs. The day before, she had seen the wheel of a brand-new bicycle poking out from the tarpaulin that was failing to cover it in the garage. So, dashing out of bed the next day, she had the certainty that all was well with the world, that her prayers had been answered.

Finistere had decided to fly back to London and she had just finished fixing the helicopter and a car to meet him when he landed at the office. For a moment, she was back in her old role, but she didn't mind, for she was going to be alone in Paris and it was the pleasure of this that reminded Mary of her eight-year-old self.

She called Sophie's number and heard it click to voicemail.

'Sophie, it's me, Mary. I'll need your help on Monday. Michael has had to go back to London and he's asked me to stay in Paris and do some research for him. Give me a call and I'll tell you more.'

She would ask Erik to help as well, but she would need Sophie's support with some of the calls and meetings she expected to have in the coming days. There was also, she acknowledged, a certain conflict of interest working for Finistere whilst asking Erik for help, even if Mollet and Finistere both needed the same answers. She imagined that Finistere had done this deliberately, knowing that she had become close to Erik and was therefore at the heart of the enemy camp, as he might have put it. As soon as she had made the call to Sophie she felt better, knowing that employing her would help formalise things. It would, as her mother might have said, 'keep everything above board'.

She called Erik and told him the news. He laughed.

'He wants you to keep an eye on me.'

'And I'm happy to comply, *Monsieur* Mollet.'

'We'll be able to have Sunday lunch together, my favourite meal of the week.'

'And tonight?'

'Alas, no. I have a family dinner to attend.'

A small cloud passed in front of Mary's perfect sun. 'Can't you take me?'

'One step at a time, Mary. I don't think you'd like to be interrogated by my mother, let alone my aged grandmother. These are formidable women. Are you going to be staying on at the hotel?'

'Unless you ask me to your apartment?'

'I'll need to get the cleaner in first, then. Let's discuss it tomorrow. Shall I pick you up at midday?'

Afterwards, Mary knew she had no right to be disappointed. She had wanted to be with him again immediately and she thought once more of her younger self and the stubbornness she displayed when she didn't get her own way. She told herself she wasn't being fair, but she couldn't dissipate the feeling. Her phone rang and she saw that it was Sophie.

'You got my message then,' Mary said.

'Yes, and about half a dozen from Michael. Persistent as ever. Does he always get his own way?'

'I'm afraid he quite often does.' Mary laughed, thinking of her earlier reaction to Erik.

'He wants me to go to London and see his apartment in Mayfair.'

'Well, there's a surprise, Sophie.'

They arranged to meet at the hotel on Monday morning at ten and as soon as she had said goodbye, Mary saw the hours ahead of her looming until tomorrow at midday. She looked at her bedroom, which bore all the evidence of their recent activity and his absence was palpable. Her suitcase lay propped open against the wall, her one set of clean clothes reminding her how little she had to get her through the next few days.

To fill the void, she would go shopping.

Youssef looked for the Kurdish boy, whose name he learned was Baha.

He walked through the camp, the others regarding him coolly, knowing that his hut had been destroyed and the policeman had beaten him up. He was tainted, bad luck and their eyes showed it.

Youssef and Baha were recent arrivals, but most of the others, Arabs from North Africa, lived here. This was their permanent home and Youssef understood that his presence threatened their security, however precarious. They spoke in Arabic.

'I have some important information about the camp,' he told Baha, who he'd seen with two men Youssef thought looked important. 'Who should I talk to?'

Baha, perhaps taken by the seriousness of the look on Youssef's face and his calm approach, nodded towards a larger hut in front of which a make-shift porch had been added. Underneath it was an old armchair in which a man sat, one leg draped over an arm. Youssef walked over. The man was handsome, with short curly hair and intense eyes. His look alone, thought Youssef, marked him out as a leader.

'My name is Youssef. I'm a refugee.'

'I know who you are. The policeman beat you up. Why?'

'I stole a bag.'

'Was that foolish?'

Youssef shook his head.

'*Salaam.* I am Hakim.'

Youssef wiped his mouth. He had kept himself to himself since arriving at the camp, a wariness gained by bitter experience during his long journey from the south. He was about to share a piece of information and like feeding an unknown dog, he didn't know if his hand would be bitten.

'The camp is going to be knocked down.'

'That is always a possibility,' Hakim replied, but his face told Youssef that he wanted to know more.

'There are some men who are going to destroy the two warehouses over there and make a new development. All this will go.' Youssef spread his arms behind him.

'And was this information in the briefcase?'

'Yes. And there is a model. I've seen it.'

'A model?'

'It shows what it will look like when it's finished. It's in the bigger of the two warehouses, on the top floor.'

Hakim leaned forward, taking his leg off the arm of the chair.

'And did you learn anything else?'

A slow nod from Youssef.

'Are you going to tell me?'

'I need to find out if my brother is alive and where he is. Can you help me?'

Hakim stared hard at him but Youssef held his ground.

'A barter?' He stood up and walked towards Youssef, a tall man, well built, imposing. 'Show me.'

'I need to write,' Youssef said.

Not taking his eyes off the boy, Hakim produced a biro from his pocket and handed it to Youssef. He turned and went into this hut, returning with a piece of paper.

'There,' he said, pointing to a small, stained wooden table. 'Write.'

Youssef, the figures he'd read in the document clear in his mind, wrote them down, the costs of the development, the number of apartments and shops, the estimated profit, the ground rents and finally the proposed start and finish dates. Below, he wrote that the land was owned by Erik Mollet, with the finance for the development from Michael Finistere.

He pushed the piece of paper away from him and it was picked up by Hakim.

'How do I know this is true?'

'It would be hard to make up,' Youssef said, his head turned away.

Hakim looked down on the figures. 'That much profit and we are bull-dozed out of the way for nothing.' He carefully folded the paper and put it in the pocket of his shirt.

'Can you get into the building, Youssef, to show me the model?'

'It is difficult now. They found out how I was getting in and they've blocked it up.'

'Can you get from one warehouse to the next?'

Youssef shrugged.

'What is your brother's name?'

'Suliman. Suliman Tigha.'

'And where do you think he is?'

'We were split up when our boat capsized. We were going to Calais.'

'Might he be dead?'

'No.' The reply was so quick and loud that Hakim flinched.

'But you don't know?'

'I know he is alive.'

Hakim took the paper out of his shirt pocket. 'Write your name and your brother's. And where you come from.'

Youssef did what he was told.

'Where are you sleeping now?'

'Over there.' He didn't want to say more.

'Yes, I've seen you, Youssef Tigha.'

With a gesture of his head, Hakim dismissed him and as Youssef walked away he wasn't sure whether he felt better or worse. What could he have done with the information, anyway? He stopped and turned round. He saw that Hakim, the paper in his hand, had gathered three other men around him and from time to time they all looked in the direction of the warehouses.

Everything was taken from him in the end, Youssef thought, heading into the darkness of the tunnel.

Finistere arranged to meet Stu Phelps that evening in his club in Mayfair. He had phoned from the car on the way to Montparnasse. He then tried Sophie, expecting the same anonymous voice to tell him to leave a message. He was surprised when she answered.

'I thought you'd disappeared,' he said, more gruffly than he'd meant.

'I did. I went for a drive with my mother. When I'm with her, I'm not allowed to have an outside life.'

'I've got to go back to London. Do you fancy coming over for lunch at the Savoy?'

'I'm seeing you tomorrow, don't forget.'

'So, Saturday as well as Sunday.'

'I think not, Mr Finistere.'

'What does it depend on?'

'It's a long list.'

'So I gather. Well, the offer is there. And I'll see you on Sunday night.'

In Milan, Sophie Arditti raised her eyes, wondering if Michael Finistere might want to know what was on the list, but he was just as incurious about that as he was about where she had driven with her mother, or where they were going to eat that night. His world began and ended with himself. But, as he said, one way or the other they would meet again soon and she wasn't entirely displeased at the thought. To be sought after was a virtue. Well, up to a point.

'And what will you do tonight, Michael, while I take my mother for pasta in her favourite little restaurant?'

'I'm seeing my partner, my business partner,' he quickly added, 'to discuss Paris. There have been a few problems.'

'What, more *pièges*?'

Finistere thought she used the word almost mockingly.

'You have your mother and I have Paris.'

'Ah, *touché*. A *piège* apiece.'

The sound of her laughter played down the phone.

He wished he could see her face and it was not beyond him, he knew, to change the helicopter's destination to Milan. Once again, he thought back to the courtship of the important women in his life. There hadn't been many and they had all followed a similar pattern, brief, intense and, except for Alan, without consequence. He'd met Marilyn, a banker, at some conference and the conquest had been quick, the result permanent. He loved his son, at least that's what he told himself, although he rarely saw him and Alan had been brought up by Marilyn who, he thought, had got what she wanted out of the bargain.

'Are you still there?'

'Sorry, Sophie, I was thinking of something else.'

'Well, I'll let you go then.'

'I'll see you on Sunday.'

'Indeed.'

He could see the Montparnasse tower up ahead, a ghastly landmark the city deserved, he decided. He felt disappointed.

'Bugger,' he said out loud. Why was it so difficult with Sophie Arditti and since it was, why did he persist? He didn't need this aggravation and there were other women, more biddable, that he could call. But he couldn't, could he? She had stepped into the forefront of his thoughts and refused to move off stage. Why, though? He fancied her, yes, but there was more than simply her looks, though he didn't know quite what he found so alluring.

The lights of Paris were just coming on as the helicopter rose from the tower, making the city seem softer. They banked and headed northwards and through the grey dusk and in the distance, coming closer, he could see the two stations, the Gare de l'Est and the Gare du Nord, and the rails running into them.

Somewhere, nearby, his development lay in the half light, neither clear nor completely lost.

22

'There's a fucking great big hole underneath.'

The walls of the Mayfair club were painted midnight blue and Finistere was sitting in his favourite corner, with Stuart Phelps opposite, both dressed in business suits. It was not really acceptable to wear anything else, even though it was Saturday night.

'I don't get it,' said Phelps. 'Surely this would have shown up on the plans.'

'That's what I said. Fucking French surveyors.'

'Do you think Mollet knew?'

'That's the sixty-four-thousand-dollar question. Did he? I could go either way, but my instincts tell me yes, he did.'

'Your instincts being your natural prejudice against the French?'

'If you like.'

Finistere had more wine brought over.

'Whatever,' he continued, 'it's too big a hole to simply fill in. And we're not sure who owns it.'

'After all this time.'

'Indeed.'

'I've asked Mary to find out more. She's having a fling with Mollet, so she'll be quite close to the action.'

'Mary?' Stuart Phelps, smart, young, naturally good looking, blond hair flopping on his brow, couldn't keep the mocking surprise out of his reply.

'Are you shocked that she's having an affair?'

'That and the fact you've given her such an important task.'

'Yes, well she's clearly got talents we hadn't seen.'

'Evidently.'

The two men looked at each other.

'It should be simple enough to find the original plans to fix exactly what's underneath the properties,' Stuart volunteered.

'Sure, but you know what French bureaucracy is like.'

'But Erik's got a name. He's a French hero. He might be able to cut through the crap.'

'Or maybe he wants to keep it deliberately confused.'

'Not really in his interest is it?'

Finistere was thinking he just had to get through tonight before he could see Sophie again tomorrow evening. Behind him other men in suits leant towards each other across tables in the discreetly lit dining room. For the first time, Michael Finistere wondered if life was passing them by, that whatever deals and difficulties they were discussing were merely a way of filling in time, of playing at what was important.

'I seem to have lost you.'

'Sorry Stu, I was suddenly thinking of something else.'

'We need to sort this, one way or the other.'

Finistere looked at his colleague.

'We do, indeed.'

He was thinking of Sophie.

'I'm going back to Paris late tomorrow afternoon.'

Stuart frowned. 'But I thought you were leaving Mary by herself to find out more?'

'Yes, I am. This is something else.'

'Oh, yes. Tell me more.'

Michael Finistere didn't really feel like telling his partner about Sophie. Normally he might have bragged about a woman he was seeing, especially one as beautiful as Sophie, but now he felt that anything he said would not have been appropriate. Exactly why, he couldn't be certain.

'It has to be a woman. C'mon, what's she like?'

Finistere shook his head.

'It's not like you to keep it to yourself,' Stuart persisted. 'And flying back to see her. She must have made quite an impact.'

This was not something Michael Finistere wanted to admit to, although it was true.

Stuart Phelps sensed he shouldn't continue. 'So when will you be back?'

Finistere checked that there wasn't a smirk on Stu's face.

'I don't know. I don't want to get in Mary's way. She's better off alone with Mollet.'

'And you don't know how things are going with this mysterious woman, is that it?'

Finistere supposed there was a part of him that wanted to tell Stuart about Sophie, to describe her looks and the power she seemed to hold over him, but the words he had used in the past about women seemed crude and inappropriate and he didn't have any new language to call on.

'Whatever, I'll let you know. We should know this week about whether Mollet is being straight with us. And once we've established the scale of the new problems, we can decide what to do.'

'So you might come back and you might not?' Stuart Phelps was smiling now.

'You could say that.'

Saturday evening was difficult for Mary Houlihan. It had been easy during the afternoon to distract herself with shopping and she had walked around the narrow streets off rue du Cherche Midi, looking at the shops. She was both focused and vague, if such a combination was possible. In the beautifully dressed windows the clothes were seen in relation to Mollet, how he might approve or not. In between shops, her mind wandered in step with her body. She found a beautiful pair of linen trousers in pale stone, comfortable on her hips and tapering free form to her ankles, and a sleeveless T-shirt in dark grey. She now wanted a shirt or cardigan to complete the look. And a pair of flat shoes.

She wove in and out of the narrow streets around Place St-Sulpice, where she stopped for a cup of tea. The weather was kind and late autumn in Paris was blessed with warmth.

At first she didn't see the family on the pavement ahead of her for she was looking at the towers of the church of St-Sulpice, dramatically lined up to the east. They were sitting, resting against bundles of clothes and bedding, a mother, father and children. There was an ordered calm about them, a lack of fuss. They didn't want to be observed and by resting still and being expressionless became merely part of the background, as indeed they had been when Mary sat down. The woman's face was delineated in red, the sort of look, Mary thought, that you get after being buffeted by a strong wind day after day. Her dark hair was held in place by a blue spotted head scarf that came down across her cheeks and was tied under her chin. She sat on the pavement with her legs clasped in her arms. Opposite, her husband sat in a mirror image, his jacket buttoned to his throat, his trousers old and baggy, revealing trainers that were battered but clean. He had a son by his side, the mother a daughter, statues in the square, motionless.

Mary looked at the bags on her own lap, the clothes she had just bought. She scanned the square and with her eyes now readjusted, saw several other figures, equally still and unobtrusive, that she could only assume were migrants. They weren't begging, but waiting. For what, Mary thought? If her instinct was to stand and offer them food, she checked it for fear of giving offence, for there was about them a quiet dignity.

She paid and walked past the family but they didn't look up. Although later Mary bought a pair of shoes and found a pretty burnt orange cardigan, she did so with different eyes and she saw, on her way up the slope to the Luxembourg Gardens, other men and women carrying their possessions in bundles on their backs and she imagined them sleeping at night under the trees and by the great clipped hedges in the gardens, until she saw the gendarmes patrolling the paths, their machine guns pointing to the floor, their fingers on the triggers.

She sat on a bench in the sun and watched the different figures come and go and for a moment Erik Mollet and Michael Finistere were forgotten.

Did her mother resent her looks, Sophie thought, watching her spoon up her pasta before carefully wiping around her mouth so as not to disturb her lipstick? She was surprised that the question had been prompted by Michael Finistere, for it was a rare remark for him to have made. Nevertheless, she thought it contained more than an element of truth and she looked at her mother slightly differently, seeing a woman who was, perhaps, taking advantage of her, having her cake and eating it, so to speak.

'You're not hungry?' her mother now asked.

'No, not really. I'm tired I think.' Not really true, thought Sophie, although she carried a certain mental weariness from going through these same hoops with her mother. What did these weekends achieve? Perhaps the opposite of their given purpose, neither helping a lonely older woman, nor assuaging the guilt of a dutiful daughter. Perhaps the visits were damaging them both.

'I was wondering if I might stop these weekends with you,' Sophie ventured.

Her mother didn't pause in her eating. 'But I thought you liked coming?'

'But I wouldn't mind a weekend to myself now and again. Don't you feel the same?'

'No, not really. I like your company.'

Sophie then thought, perhaps unkindly, that her mother was using her as bait, someone to attract men to their table. It had happened several times.

'I have been invited to London,' she said, not entirely true but good enough to be going on with.

'A man?'

'Yes. He's a financier working in Paris. I'm not sure if I really like him.'

'It's nice to be able to pick and choose. Chance would be a fine thing.'

'Perhaps I'm getting in the way? Had you considered that?'

'Of course not.'

But you might entertain the idea for a moment, thought Sophie, turning over her uneaten pasta with a fork.

'Let's not spoil the evening,' her mother said. 'At least he doesn't work at La Scala.'

The dials of his watch shone on his wrist.

Youssef was sitting against one of the stone columns holding up the entrance to the church. He was in the shadow, his back to the square and he was listening to the music coming from inside the great building. He'd heard it first by accident, not long after arriving in Paris, and he occasionally came back to feel the music, just like the noise of an approaching train from the Gare de Lyon, seemingly transferred through the stone into his body.

His watch ticked silently on.

Youssef recognised one or two of the faces in the square, people who roamed the centre of Paris, filling in time each day, hunting for scraps of food, until they could find a safe place to bed down for the night. Today he'd come from the Place de la République, now claimed by the demonstrators protesting against the terrorist attacks in Paris and thus making it unsafe as a place to stay overnight. He walked over the Île St Louis, up the Boulevard St Germain and he would spend the evening here watching the shadows grow longer until they disappeared.

The dials were clearer now and although he activated the second hand sweep, the red-tipped arrow speeding on his wrist, time stood still for him as the music swelled inside the church behind.

Youssef knew he couldn't spend much longer in the darkness of the tunnel, that the camp would soon be destroyed and the warehouses bulldozed.

The sun had disappeared from the far side of the square and he set off for his journey northwards, deciding that this would be his last night underground. Walking was as automatic as the mechanisms on his wrist, actions that took place whilst he was thinking of other things. He crossed the river on the little Pont St Louis, having walked by the buttresses of Notre Dame without giving the great church a glance. Up through the Marais he trudged and although he had no pack to carry, it might have appeared to others that he was supporting a great weight. On up the canal to the railway stations, a journey that he could do in his sleep, that he now felt he was doing in his sleep, until finally, as night closed in and his watch shone clearly on his wrist, he arrived back in front of the warehouses.

He stopped and looked at them, outlined by the glow of the Paris nighttime. White letters had been painted across the brickwork, three metres tall. He moved closer to read them.

SOS. PEOPLE BEFORE PROFIT. The words were in English, running the length of the warehouses.

It must be the work of Hakim, he thought, and when he moved onwards to what remained of the camp, he saw that other words had been painted on the concrete of the underpass that framed the remaining huts. And in the half light he could just about make them out and saw that they were repeated on the lip of the bridge, under which drivers sped towards their various rendezvous.

ET NOUS ALORS?

The French that he'd accumulated told him this meant:

AND WHAT ABOUT US?

Youssef felt the emptiness in him dissipate. For the first time in as long as he could remember, he didn't feel alone.

He looked at his watch again and closed his hand over its face. No one could see the tears in his eyes.

23

The sun came up on Paris and Mary watched the view from her window grow clearer by the moment. She thought the weather matched her changing moods. The room faced north, she decided, and the scene was brushed with grey, including the brief glimpses of the Seine in the distance.

Her anticipation of the day ahead was shadowed by her speculation of what Erik might have been doing the night before. She cursed her suspicion, the insidious doubts based as much on her own insecurities, she thought, as on fact. Her mother would have had nothing of this: he's too flighty by half, she could hear her say.

The clothes she had bought yesterday were arranged on a hanger attached to the wardrobe door and, as the light rose, their colours became clearer. Mary couldn't help but feel that they mocked the day ahead, daring her to try them on, to prepare herself for seeing Mollet again.

This is ridiculous, Mary thought, getting out of bed and flicking the sheets back in place. As she was showering, she thought she heard her phone buzz in the bedroom and in her mind she listed the messages she hoped it conveyed. With a large towel wrapped over her breasts and another encasing her hair, she picked up the phone to find that it was, indeed, from Erik. The message it contained, though, was not one that she had considered in the shower.

She sat on the edge of the bed and looked at the photograph she had been sent, the two familiar buildings and across their fronts, the message daubed in white. And then a second picture of the different message in French: ET NOUS ALORS?

'This was sent to me this morning,' said Mollet's message. 'The photos are all over social media. Would you mind if we went there before lunch? I'll pick you up at 11. x E.'

She looked again at the images. What did she think? Her reactions came in a series of waves, one after the other, eventually merging in turbulent waters, jumbled together. Her first thought, the one she would cling to afterwards, the one she regarded as honourable, was in line with her feelings about the boy, heightened by the migrant family in the square the day before. She had sensed, from the moment she saw the orange figure on the model, and then later when the boy stole the bag and, finally, in the signal box, that something larger was at stake than merely a building development in northern Paris. The writings on the walls were her doubts given shape.

Her second reaction was one of pure selfishness, frustration at the thought that her day was in the process of being spoiled, that the anticipation of lunch with her lover was now rudely interrupted by the imperative of work. In this she saw her eight-year-old self stomping her feet to get what she wanted.

Finally, though, out of the colliding waters of the two waves washed up a conjunction of both feelings, a justification. She was now going to see Erik earlier, to be with him longer and that, anyway, work was why she was here in Paris in the first place.

She texted Erik to say she would be waiting for him and began the slow process of preparation, finishing with the deliberate assembly of the new clothes and the tentative appraisal of herself in the long mirror on the bathroom door. Did she see herself, or did she imagine Erik looking at the image in front of her? What would he think? She put her hands on her hips and then struck a pose. You get what you see.

Mollet was early, but then so was Mary, waiting in the small foyer of the hotel. They kissed and he barely registered what she was wearing. It was Sunday and the roads were emptier than normal.

'It was the briefcase,' he said, almost his opening words. 'Someone knows about our plans.'

The car crossed the Seine on which the sun had now risen.

'It was bound to happen, sooner or later,' Mary said.

'Yes, but it should have been in our control.'

Mary, disappointed at the coldness of their meeting, wondered how much the contents of the briefcase really mattered. Assuming the slogans had been written by someone from the camp, what power did they have against the combined strengths of Erik and Michael Finistere, let alone the French police?

Erik glanced across at her, aware of her silence.

'You look very nice, by the way. I should have said.' And he laughed.

'I thought Sunday was a day of rest.'

'It will be, Mary, I promise.'

Mary could just see the entrance to the Gare du Nord and the spill of people in front of its grand facade. Tomorrow it would be a week since she had walked across the same forecourt unaware of what was ahead of her, no possible way of looking down the road and seeing a passing car carrying her future self, driven by a handsome Frenchman who was her lover.

They had dressed for Sunday lunch, not to clamber over the derelict remains of industrial buildings. Mary assumed that Erik wanted to confirm that the statements on the warehouse were real and not cleverly doctored photographs. They stood together in the car park to read the first statement, moving to one side to observe the second slogan on the bridge above the camp.

'C'mon,' he said and they made for the entrance.

Mary wondered if the door might have been forced but the lock seemed intact and once again they climbed the stairs to the top floor. The broken orange figure lay on the floor where Finistere had kicked it and the model, once Mary had turned on the lights, appeared untouched. Erik moved across to the window that Finistere had looked through on their last visit and peered down on the camp to his right. He turned and leaned against the window, so that Mary saw a black outline of him.

'Come here,' he said and she walked over to stand in front of him. He put his hands on her hips and pulled her towards him until their faces almost touched.

'I'm sorry I wasn't such good company earlier,' he said, leaning in and kissing her. She felt him grow beneath her. He now put his arms around her waist, slipping his hands down the back of her new linen trousers. He wheeled her round, still kissing her, so that her back was against the wall and window. His hands explored further.

'No, Erik.'

He stopped and looked at her.

'Not here. I don't know why, but not here.'

Mary thought she did know why, but didn't want to say.

Erik removed his hands and placed them on her shoulders.

'I'm sorry,' he said.

'Oh don't be. I don't know, it just didn't feel right.'

He held her then, her chin on his shoulder and she looked outwards into the great space.

Youssef had seen them arrive in the lorry park and by the time he had got to the warehouses, they were already inside.

Earlier he had sought out Hakim, sitting in his usual position outside his hut.

'What do you think?' Hakim had said, not waiting for Youssef to speak.

'Thank you.'

'No. Thank you,' Hakim had told him. 'What we need in this world, Youssef Tigha, is facts. And you brought them. We cannot win, but we can be difficult. Do you want to be difficult as well?'

Youssef had nodded, although he didn't fully understand what Hakim was saying.

'I believe you,' Hakim had said, standing. 'I believe your figures.' He held the paper in front of him. 'As you said, you couldn't make these up.'

Youssef had waited, conscious that he was being included in something larger and that, for the first time here in Paris, his life wasn't singular, alone.

'You'll see.'

And with this statement, Hakim had held up his mobile phone. 'This comes without colour or class.'

Climbing the stairs, Youssef thought that he understood. He had lost his mobile, or it had been stolen, somewhere near the border into France. Until then, he had used it to tell him where he was, not just geographically, but with his fellow travellers and what friends he had left behind. It also guided him towards food and shelter and warned him of dangers ahead. He could see how Hakim might use the information he had given him online.

He arrived at the fifth floor and peered around to see the Frenchman by the window and the big woman walking towards him. He was surprised to see them kiss and he watched as he turned her around and pushed her against the wall. He could see the man's hands inside her trousers and he didn't know if he should continue watching but he couldn't stop himself. Was he glad that she pushed him away? She spoke to him but softly and he couldn't hear. The man removed his hands and hugged her instead, the woman's head appearing over his shoulder.

He stood, watching, and he followed her eyes as they looked into the space of the warehouse, moving around until they came to the place where he was standing. He didn't move. Even from a distance, he could see the moment she saw him, the second her face changed. She remained still, though, looking over the man's shoulder and her gentle eyes fixed on his own.

And he waited and saw that she stepped back from the man and kissed him on the forehead. Perhaps she spoke some words, he couldn't see. He thought he knew what she was going to do next and he stepped back into the protection of the doorway, his eyes still following her. He saw her move away from the man and walk slowly towards him. For some reason, Youssef didn't want to run, but waited behind the partition. He heard her feet coming closer until she came through the doorway, where she headed towards the stairs but instead of leaving, turned to him and looked into his eyes. For a moment, which seemed like a long time, they looked at each other and he saw her raise a finger to her lips, just as he had to her, and gesture for him to follow.

Together they went silently downstairs to the next floor, where she stopped and held her mobile phone to him. It showed the photographs of the slogans outside.

He studied them and nodded.

She leaned towards him. 'My name is Mary,' she whispered.

'Youssef,' he heard himself say.

'Are you still living underneath?' she said, pointing downwards with her finger.

He nodded again, even though he had decided not to spend another night there. He trusted this woman. It was something about the look of her face.

He watched her take a pen from her bag and write on a piece of paper, which she then gave him. It had her name and the number of her telephone.

'I will see you tomorrow, Youssef. Now I must go.'

She turned to leave and he saw her pause and take something else from her bag. She gave him a fifty euro note.

'If not for you, then the others.'

She climbed the stairs and he watched her disappear.

*

'Where did you go?' Mollet called across to her as she reappeared in the doorway.

'Call of nature,' she answered, but she saw that he hadn't understood.

'I had to have a pee,' she explained and she was reassured to hear him laugh. 'And where's this fabulous Sunday lunch you promised?'

She held out a crooked arm to him and he came towards her and took it, kissing her on the cheek as he did. What a strange morning, she thought, the look of the boy's face still with her, the large dark eyes, the vivid red scar under one of them, the black unruly hair but, above all, the set of his jaw that seemed to say that he was prepared for the worst, for this was no more than he expected.

The restaurant was full and noisy but their table was by the window with a view on to one of the bridges leading to the islands. She couldn't see the river, but every now and again a mast or a funnel floated by.

'I'm sorry,' he said, for the second time that morning. 'I shouldn't have mixed work with pleasure in the warehouse.'

'It wasn't that,' she said, happy though to hear his apology. 'I think it was the thought of Michael Finistere standing there and watching. Believe me, I wanted to make love to you.'

'What a thought,' laughed Mollet. 'Not the idea of making love with you, you understand, but with Finistere looking on. I think we need a drink.'

If she had wanted to ask him about the night before, the moment, like the boats, drifted by and the occasion took over, the dishes arriving and disappearing, the drink being poured and the noise in the restaurant steadily increasing.

Perhaps it was the drink that made her ask, 'Did you know about what was beneath the buildings?'

He shook his head. 'As I said yesterday, Mary, I knew about the tunnel, but I thought it ended fairly soon.'

'But you didn't feel the need to explore more?'

He shrugged, which might have meant he was admitting his shortcoming, or that it didn't really matter.

'It could be a problem for you. And for us,' she added.

'I know, I know.'

'Will you come with me tomorrow, to the planning offices, wherever they are? I'll ask Sophie to come as well. There must be maps of the original layout.'

'Of course,' he said, taking her hand and looking into her eyes. 'Although I have other things on my mind right now.'

She smiled back at him and felt herself become aroused.

They returned to the hotel and it never really crossed her mind that he was driving after what they had both drunk. It was even easier this third time, the pleasure increased with the beginnings of familiarity and as he lay there on top of her, she looked upwards to the ceiling and saw a pattern of narrow creases and cracks. Then she felt him in her again and what was in front of her disappeared. She once again entered a zone where time had no function and her surroundings receded and evaporated.

Afterwards, lying in her arms, she wondered what the boy, Youssef, had been doing this Sunday afternoon. What was the order of his day? Where had he come from? And why was he haunting this project, his big eyes seemingly always on them?

The conflict of waves, or perhaps currents, was beginning again, the power of the immediate, the passion of what had just taken place and the calmer, but insistent, weight of what was taking place elsewhere, the messages that were coming from the warehouses, that seemed to speak to her in a way she couldn't ignore.

And in front of it all, the boy.

24

The emptiness of Sunday morning yawned around him. He watched from his bedroom window as Mayfair went about its business, detached from the rest of the world as only Mayfair could be.

Michael Finistere had done his exercises and read his emails. He considered giving his son a call but a sort of listlessness seemed to overtake him. He recalled seeing himself reflected in the mirrored lift in Paris and the sensation the multiple images, none of them real, all of them beyond touch, created, that if he stretched out a hand he would touch nothing. He hated these interregnums between activity and tried always to fill his time so that he wasn't left in the loneliness of the present. The helicopter was booked for the early afternoon and he contemplated bringing it forward, but that would merely shuffle the vacuum to late afternoon Paris and he'd rather endure it here.

He'd done some work on Sophie Arditti and he sat at his desk, his computer already open. He clicked on an image of her and brought up the control bar. He'd played the piece the night before, when he returned from the club and now he heard it start again. The music had been new to him, *Cosi fan Tutte*, and she was performing in a small-scale production with only four other performers and just a handful of musicians. He would never normally listen to such music, although he admitted to be taken by some of it, especially when she was singing. The opera was silly, not that he really knew what was going on, but, as far as he knew, she was good and her face and voice conveyed the sort of confidence he'd already encountered over two suppers. The morning had drifted into afternoon by the time the piece came to an end.

Within a stone's throw of the flat, Michael Finistere had a car, wrapped in a plastic bubble, in an air-conditioned garage whose annual rent would be a substantial deposit on a modern semi in an outer London suburb. A classic car of some beauty and great cost, he had driven it only twice and it remained a hidden trophy, a securely banked asset. As he peered down on to the junction of the street where it lay underground, he knew that it would not impress Sophie Arditti, that if he arrived in it outside her apartment in Paris, it would make no impression. The fact was, he didn't know how to impress this woman.

'Bugger,' he said, kicking the skirting board beneath him.

One thing he would get right for this evening was his clothes. He would not arrive at the restaurant in a suit, to stand out like a sore thumb and once again be the butt of her humour. Although there were still three hours before the arranged departure time from Farringdon, he felt better as he began to dress and prepare for the journey. He checked his watch and then made what was, for him, a strange decision. He called his driver and arranged for him to take his bag to the office. He had decided to walk, a distance of no more than two miles, but a journey he had never made on foot. Could he put this down to Miss Sophie Arditti as well?

He was crossing Piccadilly Circus when Stu Phelps called.

'Well, what are your thoughts this morning?'

'About what?'

'The project. Unless you want to talk about the other thing?'

'I haven't given it a thought.' This was true, Finistere realised, as he negotiated his way through the crowds towards Leicester Square.

'Don't you think you should?'

'Yes, yes, don't hector me, Stu. We're still short of facts.'

'But what about your celebrated instincts?'

'Gone to pot,' he said, but then he was referring to Sophie Arditti.

'Well, keep me posted.'

It was true, Finistere thought, entering Covent Garden, that Les Merchandises had not crossed his mind that morning. He checked his mobile for directions to the office in Farringdon Road. He couldn't remember the last time he'd been on a bus and the Tube journey he'd had to take a few days earlier was a rare and not to be repeated experience. He was chauffeured everywhere in silent comfort, the air constantly refreshed, the seats smelling of leather, the outside world kept at bay.

He was directed up St Martin's Lane, where tourists wandered in groups not entirely sure where they were.

His instincts about Les Merchandises? He thought he knew, that if left to him he would walk away now but – and he was surprised to engage this thought – he wanted to maintain this link to Paris. He kicked an empty cigarette packet into the gutter with an elaborate swing of his leg. Out here in the streets, dressed casually, he was just like everyone else. He might even have been a tourist and, he thought, to some extent, he was, a stranger to these streets along which he'd travelled so often. It was like being introduced to *Cosi fan Tutte* for the first time, a new experience. He tried to hum one of the pieces he'd heard earlier that Sophie and two others had performed, a melody that, to his surprise, had stayed with him and took him across the junction by Holborn Tube station. By Gray's Inn he thought he'd almost mastered it, and not long after he arrived at the Farringdon Road, turning down it towards his office, a journey sponsored by Sophie Arditti. He quickened his pace for the final few hundred metres.

Finistere had made flights like the one ahead of him before, trips beyond the imagination of most people, certainly unimaginable to his mother or father. A helicopter from the centre of London to Paris in order to have dinner with a woman. He didn't have to think about the thousands of pounds it cost, nor of the lives of the people who made it possible. When once again he clattered over the Thames, he felt a simple pleasure, that the purpose of the day had been restored, the vagueness of the morning forgotten.

Somewhere over mid-Channel, he began to compose a series of questions for the evening ahead, so that he could be better equipped to scale the formidable walls of Sophie Arditti. He knew, for example, where she'd trained, what she'd graduated in and some of her major productions. He was approaching seeing her in the same way he would a business meeting, carefully checking the facts in advance, being clear about his aims.

In a morning of firsts, this was another, for he'd never before approached a woman in this way.

She watched him come into the restaurant, casually dressed but still not at ease in a territory that wasn't his own. He leant down to kiss her on one cheek, although when she automatically offered the other, he'd already sat down.

'So how was your mother?' he opened, an improvement from their previous encounters, she thought.

'So so. She assumes that I enjoy the weekends with her.'

'Did you tell her you didn't?'

'No, not in so many words. I said I wouldn't mind the odd weekend to myself, however.'

'It's a start.'

She watched him raise his arms towards a waitress, a proprietorial gesture with a cupped hand that assumed she would immediately be at his beck and call.

'What would you like?' he asked, as she came over.

'A gin and tonic,' she said to the girl in French, smiling at her. She watched as he ordered a whisky, immediately turning away from the waitress once the command was delivered.

'So you might be free next weekend?'

'Next weekend is a long way away, Mr Finistere.'

'It is indeed, Ms Arditti.'

'You know I'm working with Mary tomorrow?' She knew this would surprise him, as indeed it did.

He shook his head.

'She didn't tell you?'

Here we go again, Finistere thought, combat already.

'She didn't have to. As long as she finds out what we want, she can hire whoever she needs.'

'So you've taken my advice about Mary.'

He looked into her eyes, wonderfully grey-flecked and he thought that this was the way she was, abrupt and direct.

'I did indeed. She's having a fling with Mollet, which I assume you know.'

It was her turn to nod.

'So she'll be near the heart of things,' he said.

'Perhaps that is a good choice of words, Michael.'

'Oh, I'm glad it's Michael, at last.'

'You should try the crayfish,' she said, ignoring the remark. 'Chef tells me they are delicious.'

A boyfriend, he wanted to ask, and it was as if she had heard.

'Her name is Miriam. You'll meet her afterwards.'

Over the crayfish he told her he had listened to her singing. Sophie had to admit she was surprised, if not a little sceptical.

'What, exactly?'

'*Cosi fan Tutte.*'

'And what did you think?'

For the first time, Michael thought, she seemed engaged with him and he congratulated himself on his homework.

'It's a silly opera, but I liked some of the music.'

'Such as?'

He had anticipated this would be her response.

'Where the three of you sing together, the slow bit. I was very impressed.'

And so, she had to admit, was Sophie. '*Soave il vento,*' she said.

'Is that it? I was humming it to myself when I walked across London this morning.'

'You walked? My goodness. Opera and now walking. Whatever next?'

He pressed on and wondered, perhaps, if this automatic spikiness was how she was with most men.

'You have a very strong face on stage. I believed your singing, even if I didn't know what you were singing about.'

It was a compliment and probably the second most interesting thing he'd said since they'd first met.

'I'm not sure what good it's done me, though. I did that with a small group I was with for a year or so. I hardly earned a thing.'

'Well, I saw it. So it did do some good.'

'I'll take your word for it.'

He ate steak, which she had expected him to order, and she had the three different cuts of lamb. For a while they didn't speak.

'Are you going to return to London?' she asked, eventually.

'I haven't decided. I don't want to get in Mary's way. I think she'd be better off without me.'

She was conscious he was looking at her. He was different this evening, less bombastic and he'd made some attempt to accommodate her. She knew, though, that whether he stayed in Paris or went back to London might be dependent on her.

'I thought about what you said about my mother resenting my looks.'

'You didn't tell her, I hope.'

'I almost did. But then I took your thought a little further. I wondered if she was using me as, well, bait, for her own ends.'

'I'm sure you're right. I would have come to your table.'

He poured her some wine. 'A weekend in London would do you good.'

'Oh yes?'

'Think about it.'

He tried to sound off-hand, take it or leave it, but the truth was that Michael Finistere felt as though he was treading on eggshells and that one false word from him would have him back at square one.

Sophie noticed that he'd left most of his steak and he was in the process of shovelling his food to the side of his plate, like a schoolchild might to try and hide the amount he was leaving.

'What time are you seeing Mary?' he asked.

'We're meeting at ten, although I'm not sure where we're going after that.' She noticed that he'd made no attempt to hold her hand, as he had the time before, nor pressed his claims on her. She saw him slightly differently tonight, somewhat muted, his foot deliberately on the soft pedal. And so it was at the end of the evening, when they kissed on both cheeks and he told her, almost off-hand, that he would let her know if he was going to stay on in Paris.

Michael Finistere had begun the day cursing himself and this was how he finished it, critical that he hadn't been himself, that he'd been reading someone else's script and that he'd not said what he'd wanted.

'Bugger,' he said, before finding a taxi to take him to the Hotel Lancaster.

They came at midnight and obliterated the camp.

The bulldozer drove through the fencing alongside the car park and then, like some terrible beast, followed the railway line, collecting the huts as it went, the simple wooden structures snapping and splintering in its path. On the slopes the police herded the men who hadn't already fled and drove them up the passageway towards Clignancourt.

Youssef watched on from within the buddleia, unsurprised. The slogans had made the inevitable arrive even sooner. The bulldozer roared up the steep slope to reach the final huts under the bridge and they tumbled, broken, on to the tracks. Finally, when the wood had been pushed together, the huge machine ground it down even further, so that nothing could be reused.

The detritus of what had once been a community was then swept towards the broken fencing, where several lorries waited to take it away, out of sight somewhere, just like the men who were now being dispersed into Paris, to haunt the doorways and shadows, to struggle once again in the art of staying alive.

25

Mollet was driving. Mary sat in the front, with Sophie in the back. Mary wanted to ask him about the dinner with his mother and grandmother, about which he'd said not a word yesterday, but hesitated to do so in front of Sophie. They were driving to the office of Mollet's surveyor, somewhere out in west Paris where, Mollet had told her, Renault cars had once been built. Her father had once driven an ancient Renault 16 and she wondered if it had been built there.

Mary had expected old industrial buildings, but these had been swept away and replaced by silver-sided new office blocks interspersed with smart, trimmed, gardens.

Everything was waiting for them, laid out on a large glass table in a bright meeting room, the sort you might find anywhere in the world, Mary thought. The surveyor was small, dark and efficient to the point of brusqueness.

There were a series of unfolded sheets and as the surveyor spoke, his delivery abrupt, Sophie translated quietly in her ear.

'Here we have the several stages of the development that concerns us.' He moved to point at the first plan. 'From the eighteen-eighties, when the industrial complex was first laid out, through the various additions and subtractions that took place over the next hundred years, before the site became, shall we say, redundant.'

Like the Renault works, thought Mary, craning forward to look at the relevant parts of the map.

As if anticipating her, the surveyor moved one of the plans closer to him. 'These tracks were added at the turn of the last century, when the site was just entering its busiest years, years that were to last until the late fifties when the slow, some would say inevitable, decline began.'

Mary edged closer and, once she had oriented herself to the map, could see the sweep of the track along the northern boundary of the site. To help her, the surveyor placed his finger at the appropriate point.

'You will see,' he said, 'that although the line does indeed go into the hillside at this point, it stops about a hundred metres into the tunnel. I presume it was a place to store wagons before use, who knows.'

'But no underground depot?' Mary asked, the question translated by Sophie.

'Indeed, no. Not even on these later plans,' he said, gesturing to the others in a line along the table. 'So let me anticipate your next question. Why not? This plan was made in nineteen thirty-five and shows nothing and neither does this one, the last one made.'

If he was enjoying his audience, he didn't show it.

'We can only assume,' he said, 'that the development was secret, that it took place during the last war, by the Nazis, for their own purposes.'

Mary frowned. 'But surely, in the seventy-odd years since the war some evidence of its existence must have come to light?'

Sophie's manner conveyed the same surprise in French.

The surveyor shrugged. 'Many such things lie hidden underground, *madame*.'

'And these are all the maps?' Mary persisted.

'Facsimilies of the originals, yes.'

'You see,' Mollet added, 'this is what we based our development on. The tunnel, as shown here, would be easy to fill and pose few problems.'

Mary looked at him but he was peering down at the plan.

'I will leave you to study them further. I shall be outside in the office,' the surveyor announced, his work done, his case for the defence complete. Mary sat in the high-backed chair at the head of the table.

'So,' she said, 'is it as simple as that Erik? You didn't know because no one knew?'

'*C'est ça*. That's about it. When we bought the site, this is what we knew.'

'And now?'

Mary was going to ask where the originals were kept, but then she thought, did it really matter? The problem existed; it was real.

'We need a new plan,' she said instead. 'We need to know the scale of what is underneath Les Merchandises.'

Mollet nodded and left the room. Mary looked at the plans spread before her. Finistere would walk away from it all, she knew, his instincts proved right in the end.

Mollet returned. 'He'll do it. He can give us a rough plan by the day after tomorrow, one that will at least show the extent of what is underground and where ownership begins and ends.'

Mary noted that he said this in French, which Sophie now translated. There was a strange atmosphere in the room and Sophie's presence prevented Mary from further investigation. Something wasn't right and she couldn't put her finger on quite what but her doubt had transferred itself to her stomach, a physical manifestation of her unease.

Mollet drove them back to the centre and along the way Mary said that she had further work to do for Finistere. Mollet dropped them at Mary's hotel with a casual 'see you later'.

'What's the matter?' Sophie asked Mary as they stood on the pavement.

'I don't feel so good,' Mary said. 'I'm sorry. Do you mind it we call it a day? I'll call you.'

They parted but instead of going in to her hotel, Mary walked to her café in rue du Bac. She sat, glad to be alone. What she'd felt in the surveyor's room was still with her, but had now shifted from her stomach, moved from being a doubt into fact. Erik was lying. The consequences of this she was still exploring, from the moment she first caught the scent of it standing above the plans, to now, with the taste of it in her mouth, she had been waiting for the full impact to strike home. She looked down at the new clothes she had bought and immediately wanted to take them off. She was keeping her anger at bay, but she sensed it inside her. Had she been taken for a fool from the start? No, she decided quickly, she had doubted his motives at the outset, but to be proved right after what they'd done made her clench her fists and grimace.

Mollet and the surveyor had rehearsed this morning's charade like a play, with Mollet the innocent bystander as the plans were quickly presented and the underground depot dealt with as simply the legacy of the occupying Nazis. Did Mollet take her for an idiot? Yes, she suspected he did and had from the start. He had got what he wanted, and her body in the bargain. She had become both a smokescreen and a messenger, a manipulated go-between.

She had no proof but she didn't need it, for every fibre in her body told her she was right.

Her coffee was cold in front of her, the croissant untouched.

And then, just as every door appeared to be slamming in her face, another popped open and through it she saw a glimpse of clear blue skies. At the same time, her phone rang and she saw that it was Mollet. She ignored it.

As much as she now saw that he'd known about the depot from the start, she was also pretty sure there had been no dinner with a mother or grandmother, that his apartment was out of bounds for it would have revealed a life that he didn't want her to see.

She maintained her composure, refused to give in to the feelings that were pushing upwards inside her, holding them at bay so that she could think more clearly, moving steadily towards the open door.

Damn him to hell.

Youssef looked at the phone in his hand, running his fingers over its smoothness, hardly believing it was his. He had spent the night in the tunnel, unable to sleep properly in case the police had mounted a search.

That morning he'd left via the marshalling yard and he'd found Hakim sitting on a bench at Clignancourt, not far from the one where he himself had sat a few days earlier. He had got the phone from Hakim, after showing him the fifty euro note. The older man had not asked him where the money had come from and Youssef responded in kind when, an hour or so later, Hakim had presented him with the mobile and twenty euros change.

Now, on another bench in a different square, protected by the shadow of a large plane tree that was in the process of shedding its leaves in brown heaps around him, Youssef was deciding whether he should phone the woman he now knew as Mary. To do so would mean his number would be public and that he would be traceable and that knowledge unnerved him, his immediate instinct to protect his previous anonymity. His phone was empty, the SIM new and unused, its potential untested. Like his watch, it had to remain hidden, unflaunted. If a policeman saw him with it, he would become an automatic target, the assumption of theft made instantly. The watch was worse, which is why he hardly wore it.

The small square was off rue Mouffetard, in an area of Paris where he felt less conspicuous. He took out the piece of paper she had given him and tapped in her number.

*

When her phone rang, she assumed it was Mollet again. When she saw that it was an unknown number, she was still inclined to ignore it, but then she remembered giving her number to the boy. She picked up the mobile.

'Hello,' she heard him say, cautiously. 'It's me, Youssef.'

'Hello, Youssef. How nice to hear your voice. Can I help?'

She wondered where he was calling from and for some reason looked around to see if he was nearby.

'They destroyed the camp last night. They came at midnight with a bulldozer and now it's all gone.'

'How awful,' she said, trying hard to fully comprehend the boy's feelings and not sound too trite. 'Did you spend the night in the tunnel?'

'Yes, but they will find me soon. They always find me.'

'Will you take me down there again, Youssef?'

She could hear the atmosphere on the line.

'Or is that too difficult?'

'It is difficult, yes. But it can be done.'

'Tomorrow? Midday?'

'Yes. Outside the old buildings, where you go in,' he said.

'Will you be alright?'

'I have to be,' he said and she could see again his mouth set against the inevitable. 'See you tomorrow.'

The decision enabled her to draw a veil over the events of the morning, a deliberate refusal to engage. She had a lot to do before tomorrow's meeting and she set about it with practised efficiency. It was more than simply a displacement activity.

'I'm sorry about earlier,' she told Sophie afterwards. 'I wasn't myself.' She was grateful that Sophie didn't question her further. 'Could you be free this afternoon? I have some things I need to buy and my French simply isn't good enough.'

And so it was, early that evening, with a glass of wine each, Mary surveyed the results of their afternoon's work, laid out on the bed in front of them. She deliberately refused to think about what had happened in this bed only twenty-four hours earlier, banishing it to exist with her reactions to the morning's events in a dark place to be explored later.

On the bed were two rectangular torches, bigger than the ones that Mollet had brought before, several lamps with candles and two electronic devices for measuring distances.

Mary was conscious of Sophie watching her over the rim of her glass and was prepared for the questions that would surely follow for so far Sophie had not inquired why all this was necessary.

'So,' she said, 'you're going underground again?'

'Yes,' Mary said. 'Tomorrow.'

'After this morning?'

'Yes,' said Mary.

'I thought you didn't look very happy.'

Mary carried on looking at her, but didn't say anything.

'So you're doing some surveying yourself?'

'Yes.'

'Call me if you need me again.'

'Thank you, Sophie. What's happening with Finistere?'

'I saw him last night and I have to say he was somewhat different.'

'Go on.'

'He'd watched some of my music, one of the operas, *Cosi fan Tutte.*'

'Goodness gracious.'

'That was my reaction. I thought he'd be in touch with me today, but so far, nothing.'

'Is that a relief?'

'I'm not really sure. He said he might fly back to London today. I know he didn't want to get in your way, but I've no idea if he's left.'

'Good,' said Mary. 'He would be. But if he's listening to opera now, I can't imagine it will be long before he contacts you again.'

'He's probably doing more homework,' Sophie said.

When she'd gone, Mary moved her purchases from the bed and lay on top. It was impossible not to think of the night before.

Later she fell asleep, surrounded by her own sadness.

26

Monday had been a lost day and early that Tuesday morning Michael Finistere surveyed its ruins and asked himself what was going on, why was it that twenty-four hours came and went with no purpose? And in this process of self-examination he thought yet again of the multiple images of himself in the lift, both there and not there, real but untouchable, and, lying in bed with his hands folded behind his head, wondered if he'd known then that something strange was taking place just beyond his comprehension.

He had brooded all day on his meal with Sophie, diverted himself by calling several of his chums and refused to phone the office or even think of Les Merchandises. He was in a self-imposed free fall and he refused to allow Tuesday to follow the same downward spiral.

He was in a smaller room at the Lancaster, for no amount of money would have made the suite available, he'd been told by the manager in a voice no louder than a whisper, since it was currently booked by a Saudi prince. As rooms went, though, it wasn't bad but as Finistere was a creature of habit and used to getting his own way, he wasn't entirely pleased with the compromise.

There was only one thing on his mind this Tuesday morning. He wanted to call Sophie immediately but he feared she would be with Mary again and he didn't like the idea of her hovering in the background while he spoke. He didn't want a repeat of Sunday and Monday, days that brought back memories from his childhood of rainy school holidays, looking out of his bedroom window with nothing to do, the raindrops running down the glass in front of him, the endless empty day stretching ahead.

Of course, he had stayed on in Paris, even if he'd led Sophie to believe he might go back to London. This was where he needed to be even if, right now, he didn't know what to do. Sophie was up there ahead of him, out of reach and he debated what he had to do to make her turn around, to register him.

He was here in Paris without his normal driver, with no itinerary to take him through the day, without a dinner booked in the evening. He was annoyed at his own feebleness, an inertia that was new to him.

In the end, it was sheer frustration that forced him out of the hotel into Tuesday morning in Paris. He had picked up a map from reception and he decided to study it over a coffee, if he could find a café that took his fancy. So much of this detail was usually taken care of by Mary and the cohort of lesser women at the office who filled his diary and structured his days.

He wandered down the Champs-Élysées, in the direction of the Grand Palais, passing various cafés and deciding which to choose but not really taken by any of them. He admired the Grand Palais in a detached sort of way and saw that there was an exhibition of Mexican art, which he thought might be a contradiction in terms. He came to the river shortly after, crossing it on what he thought was the ludicrously decorated Pont Alexandre, the Eiffel Tower poking up to his right. With another woman he might have taken a boat trip there and then the lift to the top, before supper in an expensive restaurant nearby. He couldn't imagine doing the same with Sophie.

He found a café on the other side of the river and as he waited for his coffee to arrive, mused on what advice Mary might give him in this situation. She appeared to have had no difficulty having a fling with Mollet, so why couldn't he follow suit with Sophie?

When he brought out his phone, he saw that he had a missed call from Phelps, chose to ignore it and at the same time remembered that he couldn't call Mary, so he drank his coffee and peered at Les Invalides, which is rather how he felt. He shoved the mobile back into his pocket but even as he did an idea came to him sponsored, he realised, by Round Mary herself. The opera. Could he not do the same with Sophie? It was a risk on several levels. He hated the idea of following in Mary's footsteps, had no idea what opera she and Mollet had seen, or indeed what operas Sophie liked. But, for now, it was all he could think of.

He Googled Paris Opera and quickly found Opera Paris at Bastille. They had a production of *Tosca*, a name that sort of rang a bell. He tapped his way through the information and saw there was a performance that night, but tickets were limited, a few rear stalls and one box. He knew, even as he confirmed the box, that Sophie would have expected him, in typical fashion, to go for the most expensive seats, but he wasn't going to sit behind a pillar a hundred metres from the stage to listen to something he was fairly sure he wasn't going to like. This assumed, of course, that Sophie was free and wanted to come. The mechanics of transactions like this were normally done by Mary and as he clicked through the final details of his credit card, he felt a sense of minor achievement.

He finished his coffee and looked at his watch. It was just coming up to midday. He composed a quick text to Sophie.

Two seats booked for Tosca tonight. I hope you can join me? 7pm in the foyer? x Michael.

He thought about the kiss and decided to keep it in.

Mary glanced anxiously at her watch. It was midday and she was standing outside the warehouses, rucksack on her back, feeling conspicuous. Ahead of her, the two messages had now been eradicated from the walls and, as she could just about see to her right, the camp had been similarly removed, only the rough scars on the concrete lorry park to show where the bulldozer had turned, its job complete.

At first, she didn't hear the whistle and even when she did she failed to relate the sound to herself. Then her vision focused and she could see Youssef partly hidden by some bushes to the side of the right-hand warehouse. She walked across to him and ducked into the undergrowth, seeing his figure ahead of her indicating that she should follow. The rucksack made it awkward and she climbed after him, finding it hard to bend under the branches of the sharp trees, which she assumed must be hawthorn. The slope got steeper until she saw that Youssef had stopped by a metal fence. As she approached, she wondered how they were going to go any further.

She arrived, panting, by his side. He gestured to her to keep quiet. Down below, the bare earth showed where the camp had been but there was little to tell that hundreds of people had once lived here.

Youssef slid aside the two metal uprights and squeezed through, indicating that she should stay. She saw him slither down the other side until he was out of sight. She imagined him doing this on the day that he'd taken the briefcase, escaping on this private route that he'd created, to disappear below. She slipped the bag from her back and waited, concerned with tackling the steep slope and waiting for his signal. A few moments later, she heard the whistle, pushed the bag through and followed. The rucksack acted as a break behind her as she slid downwards.

He was waiting at the bottom, signalling that she should hurry so, as quickly as she was able, she ran to the mouth of the tunnel. Once inside, gathering her breath in great gulps, she felt safer. The anger she felt about Mollet, that she knew was still contained within her, drove her on and she walked a little further into the tunnel before unpacking the two lamps and handing one to Youssef. Mary turned hers on and immediately the bend in the tunnel ahead was revealed, the shadow of the boy projected on to the wall. What truths might the sooty brickwork tell about this subterranean passage?

Youssef was moving confidently ahead, his lamp lighting the way, so Mary switched hers off to save the batteries for later. She remembered her fears the first time she had ventured along the tunnel in what seemed a lifetime ago, but it was less threatening now with the broad beam of light ahead.

She slid by the wagons and soon after climbed on to the platform before finally pushing open the doors to the depot.

'Youssef,' she said, whispering at first but then more loudly, her voice disappearing into the great space.

'Youssef. Good morning. How are you?'

His face, upwardly lit by the torch, looked back at her.

'Youssef, I need to measure all this,' she said, raising her arms.

He moved his head in understanding.

She pulled the electronic device from her bag and held it up to him to see.

'Shine your torch over there,' she told him, pointing into the distance. The beam was just about strong enough to make out the far wall, but it was good enough. She set off for the wall nearest to her and held the device against it, pointing it in the direction of Youssef's beam before turning it on. She registered the reading and turned her torch to her bag from which she took a pen and notebook and recorded the measurement. Redirecting her own light, she then made her way to the wall on the right, telling Youssef to point his torch the other way. She stood with her back to the wall and repeated what she had done before, noting the distance on the pad. She drew a rectangle, roughly to scale, adding the two figures.

'I need to go to each corner,' she told the boy, heading towards the nearest. Here she stood and from her bag brought out the GPS tracker, activated it and noted her position. Together, they worked their way to each of the four corners of the rectangle. Once complete, she aimed her lamp at the space above her, just making out a series of brick arches that made up the roof.

To make this exercise work, she knew she'd have to replicate the depot's footprint above, or at least take readings from the extremities of the proposed development, to see where one fitted against the other.

Youssef came over, directing his torch at the floor so that he wouldn't blind her. Standing in front of her, he pointed to her face, rubbing his own with his other hand to indicate that she had a smudge of dirt across her cheek. She brought out a handkerchief, spat on it before wiping her face. She looked at the boy for confirmation that she had been successful. He nodded and she put her hand on his head in thanks.

She shone the torch towards the bench where he must have slept the night before. They sat down together and she showed him her rough drawing with the added dimensions. She leaned towards him.

'I need to find out where this is,' she said, pointing at the outline on the paper, 'in relation to the buildings above,' her eyes turning upwards.

She could see that he had understood.

'We have to be careful,' he warned. 'The police come often. They don't want the camp rebuilt.' He picked up the GPS tracker and held it in his hands.

'You know how it works?' she asked, but she could see that he probably knew better than her.

'I will do it,' he said. 'I can hide better than you.'

Mary smiled in the gloom.

'Where do you want me to take the measurements?'

She looked at the boy, his serious face and the dark, dark eyes.

'You must go to the four corners of what will be the development. You remember the model upstairs? The edges of the car park on both sides and then behind, the corners of the fences along the roadside and the one along the railway embankment.'

On another piece of paper, she drew the outline, placing the two warehouses in the middle, putting in the perimeter and marking with crosses the four points she meant.

The boy stood. 'Wait here,' he said and set off towards the doors that led to the tunnel.

Mary, who trusted Youssef, took the two lanterns from the rucksack, put the candles inside each and lit them. She placed them either side of the bench on which he slept, turning off her torch. She had bought them for him, imagining him down here in the darkness.

She lay down and waited and in her mind replayed the charade that she'd been through in the surveyor's office, convinced the dark and abrupt man, whose name she didn't know, would never come here to confirm the measurements, for he already knew them, the dimensions marked on a plan he hadn't shown. How she knew this for certain, she couldn't be sure.

And Erik, where was he now? How would he be with her when they next spoke? More to the point, how would she react? Down here, in the soft light of the candles, she felt that she would strike him across his face.

It was almost an hour before the boy returned and she had begun to worry that he'd been stopped by the police. She held her breath as the light appeared on the other side of the doors and breathed a sigh of relief when he appeared.

'There,' he said.

She looked at the references, smiled at him and touched his cheek. 'I've got some candles for you. And some food.' From the sack she removed two bundles wrapped in foil. She handed them to him.

Those eyes again, regarding her, still perhaps expecting a trick, not quite accepting that this was an honourable exchange, one that didn't demand anything from him in return.

She put her hands against his cheeks. 'I will speak to you later, Youssef. I promise. And I will see you again soon, somewhere different.'

'You cannot leave that way,' Youssef said, pointing behind him. 'You must go the other way. Follow me.'

So Mary returned to the marshalling yard, up beyond the signal box and along the metal staircase to the wall. Youssef lowered himself over the rim and dropped to the ground. She wondered if she was able to follow. She tossed the bag over first and then moved herself into position, gripping the top of the wall before letting go, landing and half falling on to the pavement. She was looking up to the sky when his face slid into view.

He was smiling.

27

S ophie Arditti looked upwards to the ceiling and contemplated the two problems she had been posed.

As an outside observer, she had watched the scene in the surveyor's office with a degree of detachment, able to stand back from events. She had seen Mary's face change, move from genuine curiosity to barely concealed hostility. She had been able to record the surveyor running through his allotted task with perfunctory efficiency while Erik Mollet remained to one side, distanced from what was taking place. The atmosphere in the room was, she thought, charmless and without warmth, like the building in which the meeting was taking place.

Something had changed, but Mary had refused to discuss exactly what and when they parted she was unusually remote. It was just after midday and Sophie had expected a call by now.

Instead she had received the text from Michael, which she now examined, holding the phone above her. *Tosca.* The word released several distinct emotions in her, the primary of these being disappointment. The name brought back, as it always did, the moment she had been told that she was being considered for the lead at La Scala. She could picture this clearly, the musical director in bed with her, his voice soft in her ear, but this was always followed by the memory of the crushing blow a few weeks later when she heard, almost by accident, the role was going to someone else, that she had been discarded. By then the relationship was over and her hopes had been dashed and pushed aside.

Her arm fell to the bed. She had not been able to watch the opera since, nor even hear it on the radio and now Michael Finistere wanted to take her to a performance, to relive those terrible days that she had done her best to block out.

Some small part of her, which she wasn't entirely happy to see or admit to, saw that she was becoming bitter, that a vain, selfish man had wilfully damaged her for not playing second fiddle to him and she was full of resentment. It didn't take a career in opera to remind her that art imitates life.

Michael Finistere, in all his innocence, was now asking her to confront some of those demons and her decision was loaded with a significance beyond whether she should simply accept a date with a man.

When she stood looking out over Paris she was unwittingly humming the music that accompanies Mario to his execution at the end of the opera. As soon as she registered the fact, she stopped. The end was tragic, no good came of it, Mario was shot and Tosca threw herself to her death.

No, she wouldn't be a victim as well.

She texted back.

What a lovely thought to cheer up Tuesday. I will see you there at 7. Looking forward to it. S

She knew that he would note there was no kiss in response to his own. He would have to work harder for that.

Mary's bedroom, up under the eaves of the hotel, had lost its charm, so full of the memories of what had taken place there so recently that she thought she could still smell his aftershave. She slammed the door and set off for the café in rue du Bac. Erik had called several times but she hadn't been sure enough of her emotions to speak to him. In her pocket she carried a large-scale map with grid references of the area around Porte de la Chapelle, along with her notebook. Her excitement about the task in hand pushed her anger to one side.

The day was dull but calm and she was able to open the map on the small round table, find what she was looking for and then refold it to a more manageable size. It took her some time to correlate the readings from her notebook to the squares in front of her, but gradually they began to make sense. After two coffees she had a fairly accurate picture to confirm what she had already concluded. The footprint of the underground depot lay directly beneath the two warehouses, tilted at a different angle but contained within its boundaries.

Mary sat back. She felt a sense of achievement but accepted that this was just the beginning, that she had simply arrived back at square one. She turned the page of her notebook and on a blank sheet began to make some notes. Taking the copy of the dossier that Youssef had stolen, she turned to the plan of the development and with several pens, began to rule a series of lines and shapes that she then blocked with colour. An hour slipped by before she was happy and she carefully cleared the table, refolding the map, clipping her notes and drawings together and putting them in her bag.

'So there you are.'

Erik Mollet stood above her. She looked up but was unable to respond. Mollet was smiling.

'May I join you?'

Mary moved her chair to one side and he pulled over another.

'How are you? You haven't returned my calls.'

Mary had no idea how she was going to speak, or indeed of what she was going to say. Cat got your tongue, her mother might have said, waiting for a response to accusations of some misdemeanour.

'Are you okay, Mary? Is it something I've done?' Erik leaned towards her.

'I've been busy,' was all she could say, but what words might follow she had no idea.

He put his hand on hers and she felt its warmth.

'I'm sorry,' she said, and she was.

'Is Finistere with you?'

She shook her head.

'Only, the surveyor will have the details you need this afternoon. That's why I was contacting you.'

She lowered her head to indicate she had heard. Could she go to the surveyor's office with him again?

'What is he going to say?' she said, in a small voice.

'We'll find out.'

'But he must have told you already?'

'No, I thought we'd find out later.'

She didn't believe him, but along with all her other doubts, she had no evidence and this was merely a gut response. This wasn't enough, not so much for Mollet, but certainly for Finistere.

His hand still covered hers.

'I'll meet you there. I have some things I need to do,' she said to the table.

He was looking at her and she shrank back into herself, not so much in expectation of a blow but because she didn't know how she would react to whatever he said next.

'Whatever it is, Mary, I'm sorry. We're due there at three. You know the address. See you later.'

She felt his shadow leave the table.

Would she go to the surveyor's office? Did she need to? Did she not have all she needed to know in the bag by her side? Instinctively, she confirmed that it was still below the table by her feet. She could hardly breathe and her body was still, like that of a frightened cat. Although he'd been reasonable, she didn't believe him any more. All her trust had seeped away, the trust that had made her offer him her body and the very thought of that made her go cold.

She laid her mobile on the table. There was a text from Mollet.

See you later xx

She deleted it. In some ways, she thought, she should speak to Finistere, wherever he was, but she had no desire to, sensing that she first had to justify her reaction to Mollet with hard facts. She could hear Finistere mocking it all as a lover's tiff. It was now shortly after one. She would skip lunch. She wasn't hungry and she set off for the Métro, but then paused, turned back to the hotel and photocopied the papers.

The touch of Mary's hands on his face had loosened something in him, shaken some far corner of his soul. He had fallen asleep in the gentle light of the candles. But the softness was deceptive and it had seduced him into believing his demons would be held at bay. Instead, they returned with more force and with a frightening clarity, with details he had never seen before, or chosen to pretend he hadn't. Now, in the pictures that came to him, there were other images before his mother floated towards him, a scene in the classroom of children shouting and screaming. The wall where the teacher sat was missing and so was she. In his mind he saw the bodies, the limbs and the heads, the building still falling around him, although he could hear nothing. And then he was running along the corridor towards the door and even in his dream he could feel his fear rising. He pulled the door open and there, in the air, his mother was coming towards him, her eyes wide open but now, behind, he could see the bright orange of an intense flame made even more vivid by the black cloud that darkened the sky.

He woke up, his hands in front of his face, waiting for a blow that never came. His face was covered in sweat and at first he thought the yellow of the candles was part of the dream, that he was in the ruins of his school. He gripped the sides of the bench, expecting to see the broken remains of his classmates, smashed and bloody at his feet. But the candles burned on and gradually Youssef came to see where he was, in the depot underground in the heart of Paris. Placing his hands together, he silently thanked Mary for the lights, for he knew that if he'd woken to pitch blackness his fear would have been profound and might well have broken him.

He never saw what had happened to his mother, nor did he ever see her again. Now that his memory had been nudged to life, he recalled waking up in hospital with Suliman sitting by his side, holding his hand. It was the look on his face that told him their mother was dead, that a line had been ruled under their lives that divided past from present. That past had now become a fading picture, occasionally punctuated by images of quite brilliant clarity, almost too clear to be real: the blue of the mountain pool where they had played, the brown hills at sunset and now, in this great underground cave, the smell of coriander so fragrant that he had to look round for its source. And there, by his side, the sandwiches that Mary had made.

But his hunger had disappeared.

Mary stood outside the silver building and squared her shoulders. This was not the woman, she thought, who had watched Michael Finistere's helicopter rise from the roof of the office in the Farringdon Road for the journey to Paris just the week before. Round Mary had been left behind and she wanted to keep it that way, to maintain her new identity.

Mollet and the surveyor stood together as she was shown into the same long room. They sat on one side of the table, Mary on the other, and she was glad of the division.

'So,' she said, her voice returning, even if her script was out of sight. 'What have we?'

The surveyor, with the same air of disinterested purpose, brought forward the same sort of large-scale map that Mary had in her bag. Then, like a conjurer he produced two sheets of tracing paper, placing one over the map and the other to one side.

'So,' he said, echoing Mary, 'this is what we have. The development, *Les Merchandises*, fits here. *Voilà.*'

She stood and registered the clear outline of the plot in black ink.

The surveyor, waiting for Mary to absorb the information, then moved the next sheet of tracing paper into place. Mary registered the red lines as the surveyor slid the grid squares until they matched.

No one spoke. Mary leaned further forward, certain what she would see, but needing further confirmation. The thick black lines were clearly visible on the lower sheet. The lighter red markings on the top sheet showed that the underground depot was to one side, partly under the railway embankment, touching the footprint of the development only in one corner.

Mary absorbed the details.

'Might I take a photo?'

'Of course,' said Mollet.

Mary carefully moved the plans towards her, bowed forward over the table and took several pictures.

'That seems conclusive,' she said to them both. 'Thank you.'

As she was leaving, Erik appeared at her side.

'And later?' he asked. 'Are you free? For supper, I mean?'

For the first time that day, she looked him in the face.

'I'm afraid not. Something has cropped up with Finistere. I'll speak to you later.'

He made to kiss her on the cheek but Mary had stepped away and begun walking quickly towards the Métro. She lifted her bag and tucked it firmly under her arm.

28

The weather was changing again, autumn and winter fighting for supremacy. A sharp wind had begun to whip the remaining leaves from the trees and they swirled in the air before settling in drifts in doorways and gutters. Finistere was glad to be back in a suit, not simply as protection from the newly arrived cold, but because it was the uniform that made him feel at one with himself. He had been out and bought a white silk scarf, one of several activities he'd invented to while away the afternoon, and placed it around his neck, his preparations for the evening complete. He had read up on *Tosca*, learned about Puccini, played parts of a recording and intended to get to the opera house early so that he could read the programme. Round Mary, let alone the millions of pounds waiting to complete the deal on Les Merchandises, had been temporarily forgotten.

He took a taxi through streets over which dusk had already fallen, intimation that winter wasn't far behind. Two days had been wasted for the encounter ahead of him and bouncing along the right bank of the Seine he tried not to think about those empty hours and the anxieties they had produced. He raised his hand to touch the knot of his tie, perhaps to confirm that he was real and not one of the reflections in the lift. He smiled at his ridiculous gesture but he knew it was a temporary reprieve and he pushed aside thoughts of the strange emptiness he'd felt during those lost hours.

He was unable to read the programme notes, not simply because they were in French, but because he was too distracted, his eyes on the main doors in expectation of her arrival. As it was, he failed to see her entry and he was startled to hear her voice from the stool next to him at the bar.

'Mr Finistere, I presume?'

She sparkled. This was his first thought and afterwards he imagined that the bright shiny flecks were dotted on her face and in her hair and not only on the sequined waistcoat she wore over a dark silk shirt.

'I'm sorry,' he said, tipping forward from his stool and dropping his programme. 'I was trying to read about *Tosca* in French. You look stunning, if I'm allowed to say so.'

'You are, Mr Finistere. And what would you like to know about *Tosca*?'

'It's my first opera.'

'A good choice, then.'

'What would you like to drink?'

They carried their flutes of champagne to seats overlooking Place Bastille and Finistere felt that he was an actor in a play he'd under-rehearsed desperately trying to remember his lines.

'How was Mary?'

'She's not spoken to you?'

Finistere shook his head, surprised that he'd asked the question in the first place, for he hadn't given her a thought all day.

'She wasn't herself, I thought,' Sophie said, hoping that she wasn't betraying a confidence.

'Do you know why?'

'I thought you might. Yesterday we were in Mollet's surveyor's office. I think something might have happened, but I'm not sure what.'

He was watching her mouth move as she said the words and wanted to lower his head and kiss her.

'Did you hear my question?' she said, eyebrows raised.

'No, I don't think I did.'

'Well, never mind. I think you and Tosca might have got on rather well.'

'And why's that?'

'You both like getting your own way. Some might say Tosca was wilful, although, as a member of her sex, I like to think of her as strong.'

'Headstrong, perhaps.'

'You've been doing your homework again, Michael.'

'Did you ever play Tosca?'

He saw her face become more serious and he wondered if he'd blundered in some way.

'I have sung the part, yes,' she said. 'For that small company that did *Cosi*.'

'Do you like it?'

Again, a brief hesitation.

'Oh, yes. You have to be very hard-hearted not to like Tosca, both as an opera and as a woman. You'll have to let me know what you think afterwards.'

'We're in a box,' he said. Her response was as he'd predicted.

'I wouldn't have expected anything less.'

He thought it wise not to tell her he had ordered smoked salmon and champagne for the interval.

At first, the box felt exposing, poised above the main auditorium, the stage spread below. When he saw her face, he thought Sophie might be feeling the same. She looked distant, concerned, an expression that Finistere had not seen before.

'Are you okay?' he asked, his hand on her forearm.

She studied him before replying.

'I am. Thank you for asking.'

The rumble of noise from the audience grew and rose around them, a mix of excitement and expectation, similar to what he was experiencing. He saw how beautiful she looked and he imagined many men glancing upwards in her direction. For the first time since he'd arrived, he was glad he'd booked the box, for it suited her.

The audience clapped the conductor and the opera began.

He had expected to be bored. He'd read the story in advance, which he thought might help, and the opening scene confirmed his expectations. It was only when Tosca appeared that the mood changed and this was transmitted in the most vivid way through Sophie's face. She was mouthing the words that were being sung, at times closing her eyes. Later on, during the love scenes, he sensed that she wasn't by his side, but down on the stage.

When the interval came, she was still elsewhere and she appeared not to notice the champagne and food as it arrived and was laid on the table behind them. He poured her a glass and handed it to her, watching her face but seeing only the distant look. Gone was the jousting, mocking woman he had encountered over their previous encounters. They didn't speak much in the interval, or if they did it was minor talk of no significance. He was glad of this since he was trying to work out her mood and for the time being had nothing to offer.

There was a moment in Act Two where he ceased to exist altogether, when she might just as well have been alone in the box. Scarpia, the chief of police, was forcing himself on Tosca and both were singing against each other, Tosca's voice rising higher and higher. Finistere was watching Sophie's face, completely caught up in the drama, her mouth forming the words, her fists clenched on her lap. Her forehead was creased and a line of perspiration glistened on her upper lip. When Tosca kills Scarpia, her head dropped, as if she'd held the knife herself. Finistere was transfixed not only by what was on the stage, but what was taking place by his side. He put his hand on her shoulder but the gesture went unnoticed.

He knew there was no happy ending, but the operatic intensity of the final scene took him by surprise, Tosca's scream as she threw herself to her death reverberating around the theatre. As the audience erupted, so he watched Sophie's head drop once again, her shoulders shaking as she wept. He was at a loss, caught between offering comfort and standing to join the applause. He chose the latter and after a while she was standing by his side as the curtain calls came and went.

Afterwards, he poured the remains of the champagne and they clinked glasses.

'Thank you,' she said.

He knew she wasn't thanking him for the box, or the drink in her hand, but he wasn't sure to what she was referring.

'I was surprised,' he offered. 'I didn't think I'd enjoy it so much.'

'And nor did I,' Sophie said, again mysteriously.

The audience was thinning away, shuffling through the doors and leaving them alone in their nest above the stage. She was looking down, more towards the stage than the departing crowds. He would have liked to escort her to the car he had in the garage near his office. It was a Jaguar saloon from the early sixties, beautifully restored, with pale leather upholstery, chrome spoked wheels, a wood-rimmed steering wheel and dark green bodywork that seemed to emphasise its graceful lines. It was one of a number of classic cars he owned but rarely drove, possessions, trophies that he accumulated, comfort blankets. He liked them well enough, but they were also assets and their value had quadrupled in the last year or so. With the Jaguar, though, he could now see its value in different terms, as an accompaniment to great beauty, one setting off the other.

'I owe you an apology,' she was saying, her voice surprisingly loud in the empty auditorium. She took a sip of champagne. 'Once upon a time I was offered the chance to play Tosca in a performance at La Scala, Milan.

At least, I thought I was. It was later withdrawn, to my huge disappointment. This was two years ago and, until tonight, I was unable to listen to this wonderful music.' Another sip of champagne. 'But, thanks to you, that spell has been broken. *Tosca* has been restored to me.'

She leaned forward and kissed him on the cheek. 'Thank you,' she said. 'I could not have done it alone.'

The first kiss arrives by accident, when you're least expecting it, thought Michael, wanting more than ever to whisk her away in the car. He knew, though, that he was expected to say something more, that what she had just told him begged further questions.

'Do you know,' she said instead, 'I feel exhausted. A combination of *Tosca* and champagne. Would you mind if I went home?'

'Of course not,' he said, in truth rather glad that he had not been called on to question her further. 'I'll get us a cab.'

Outside, the wind had become even colder and the leaves swirled over the new concourse.

'I'll take the cab on to my hotel after I've dropped you,' he told her. There was no suggestion that anything further was going to happen tonight and they were silent as the cab took them around Place de la République. From the window he could see the slogans hung on the statues and monuments of the square proclaiming the solidarity of the French in the face of terrorism. How little all this impinged on him, he thought, caught up as he was in the drama of this woman.

He had anticipated what she was going to say as the cab drew up in front of her apartment block.

'I won't invite you up,' she said.

'I know,' he said, taking her hand and kissing it. 'I know.'

He watched her go, the elegant sway of her body, her slight stoop and the sadness she seemed to carry with her tonight.

Back at his hotel, he ordered a fillet steak and a bottle of claret and settled himself in front of the window. He couldn't get her face out of his mind, the tortured look with the tears on her cheeks, and he understood then, looking out on the trees waving madly in front of the street lights, that he knew nothing of this woman, that tonight she had afforded him the merest hint of her world, one he would have to work a great deal harder to enter.

*

Below ground, Youssef lay awake, protected from the cold wind that had sprung from nowhere that afternoon. The candles in the lanterns barely flickered by his side and the sandwiches had been eaten. It was guilt that Youssef now experienced, imagining the men from the camp seeking shelter in Paris, tucked into doorways, huddled down in the Métro or, if lucky, shacked up in one of the cheap hostels where they would sleep four to a room. Tomorrow he would find Hakim and bring him down here, show him the space that others could share. They would have to enter by the other route and Youssef decided to suggest a ladder to help negotiate the wall, one way and the other. He was using these thoughts to keep him from sleep, not wishing to be revisited by the horrors of the night before. It was thoughts of Suliman that eventually claimed him, the picture of his face staring at him in the hospital, willing his recovery, his eyes imploring him to get better. He had to find him again for without Suliman Youssef saw no relief from this endless struggle for survival.

The candles continued to burn and he felt comforted that they would see him through the night.

She wept again and from the belly of Paris beyond her windows came the faint sounds of *Tosca* and the distant cries of a tortured lover, overlaid with the ever-present backdrop of sirens. Slipping into sleep, she thought the boil had been lanced, the poison released and although her body was still accommodating this change, her mind had become easier, the endless repetition of the same events broken, their menace scattered.

Midnight came and went unseen, the new day arriving unheralded.

29

ary knew she should talk to Finistere. It was the logical time to deliver the results of the task he had set her. And yet.

It was too cold to sit outside, so she had taken a table inside, now covered with her notes and the remains of a baguette. The night before she had prepared a paper with her conclusions and spent some hours copying the documents along with the map of the development, adding in red the footprint of the depot below. She held it up in front of her and if she declared herself moderately pleased with the results, it failed to make any indentation into her primary feelings.

After several texts and two unanswered phone calls, Mollet had given up trying. It was Mary's turn now, for she had concluded that she needed to add a body of hard facts to her instinctive reaction to Erik. Only this would allow her to be coldly rational with Finistere, who would simply mock her if she became emotional.

She picked up the mobile and returned Mollet's last call.

'Mary, good morning. I was giving up hope.'

'I need to see you. Are you free this morning?'

'Of course, of course. Where?'

Mary had thought about this and she was torn between wanting to see where he lived, to take in what clues it might offer about the man with whom she'd made love, and a reluctance to discover what such a visit might also confirm.

'What about your place?'

She could hear him hesitate, weighing up the pros and cons just as she had done. She could imagine what one of the pros might be and, sure enough, it won the day. Men, her mother would have said, are all the same.

'Okay,' he said and he gave her the address. Just beyond Bercy Village, he said and she imagined old houses and a village green, but he went on to describe a flat in a modern block with the railway on one side and the Seine on the other. Mary allowed him two hours to get organised and for her to prepare the armour of defence she would need for the encounter. Just three days ago, she would have longed for this rendezvous, for the symbolic role it would have played in their burgeoning relationship. How quickly her motives had changed, how abruptly hope had been extinguished. She gathered up her papers and brushed the crumbs from her clothes.

He had directed her to take the Métro to Liberté and then, in a series of instructions she had been forced to write down, to cross what he called the *Passerelle de Valmy*, the footbridge across the tracks to Bercy and his new apartment block. Or you can take a taxi, he had added, but she thought she'd see more of Paris this way and would also have longer to prepare herself for what was to follow.

When she stood at the end of the footbridge she saw it stretch out ahead of her, ruler straight, for about, it seemed, three kilometres. It led over a mass of railway lines, twenty or more, she counted, as she walked slowly above the trains coming and going below. Half way across, she stopped to watch, the wind blowing over the open space so that she had to pull her coat up to her throat. An old signal box stood forlornly between the spaghetti of lines and she could see how a disused and rusting gate to her side would have once provided access. It was a forlorn place.

She shivered and imagined what it might have been like to cross the bridge at night.

The footbridge took her towards what clearly had once been an industrial area but was now in the process of change, for beyond it rose the shiny new blocks that spoke of an expanding, modern Paris. She came off the bridge and the wind dropped. An old bar, with a peeling, cracked exterior, stood to one side but her directions led the other way and she set off, the sound of the trains on one side and the drone of a motorway a block away to her left. She found Mollet's road, located his block, steel and glass, and stood before the array of buzzers that would give her access to, what?

Mollet's distorted voice told her which floor and she was buzzed through. She took a lift to the top and as the door slid open, Erik was standing there. He came forward to kiss her and she offered him her cheek, feeling the familiar bristles but experiencing none of the emotions that had so recently accompanied such a touch.

He took her into an apartment that was all light, a big window framing the Seine below which lines of traffic sped, silently, along the motorway that followed the embankment.

'Please, sit down,' he said, pointing at a modern leather sofa supported on impossibly thin steel legs. 'Coffee?'

The kitchen made up the opposite side of the big room and along its length ran a glass-topped table, at the centre of which a large bunch of flowers burst from the top of a beautiful red lacquered vase. Another small posy of flowers, violets, graced the coffee table in front of her. There were magazines and books and the total effect was a one of comfort and, Mary concluded, the work of a woman.

He carried over a tray with a *cafetière* of coffee, a jug of milk, some biscuits and napkins. This was a domesticity she would never have expected from the man she'd known for no more than a week.

He sat in a beautiful grey chair opposite, again supported on two arches of shining steel.

'What's wrong?'

She had to suppress her anger at his hurt innocence.

'You don't know?'

'You think we knew about the space beneath the development but didn't tell you?'

She waited.

Mollet spread his hands in front of him, hands that had sought out the most private corners of her body. 'I've told you, but you won't believe me.'

'And what about the surveyor?'

'What about him?'

She looked hard at his face and thought of the combat and dirty tactics he might have used and encountered in top-class rugby, ideal preparation for this challenge.

'I don't believe details of the depot don't exist,' she said finally. 'I think you knew about them from the start.'

He shook his head. 'It's not true. I had no idea. I've told you once and I'll tell you again.'

She let this go.

'Then he is lying. Or you both are.'

'What do you mean?'

Again, the hurt innocence of his response, the look of bewilderment.

'How well do you know your surveyor?'

'He's helped on several jobs. I don't know him personally, but why do I need to? I work with lots of people I don't know well.'

'He's lying.'

His face was perfectly still and she scanned it for any trace that he was complicit in the deception.

'How would you possibly know?' Mollet said, shaking his head.

Mary wasn't going to declare her hand and the papers in her bag would remain by her side.

'I know, Erik. Believe me, I know.'

He leaned forward to pour more coffee.

'You surprise me, Mary. Perhaps you embarked on our relationship in order to spy for Finistere.'

'Let's stay with the surveyor, shall we? This is a plot of land owned by you. I cannot believe that the presence of such a space underground was not known to him and therefore to you.'

'Well, you'll just have to,' he said with anger, rising to his feet and turning towards the big window. 'Does Finistere know?' He still had his back to her and she thought for a second before she replied.

'No.'

'Is he here in Paris?'

'I'm not sure.'

'Perhaps you'd better talk it through with him.'

His reply was offhand, the casual dismissal of the messenger. How had she been so deluded, so taken in by this man, so open to his charms? She was glad he was facing away, for if he'd turned, he would have seen her flush of anger.

She rose and walked to the door. She turned, but he was still looking out of the window. She let herself out.

On the footbridge, the wind was behind her and she felt it pushing her coat against the back of her legs, speeding her along, away from Erik Mollet. Her heart was dead, but in its stead was a steely resolve that grew with the roar of a large express on the tracks underneath, beginning to speed away from the capital. By the end of the narrow path, she had begun to cry, the tears finally released following the original meeting in the surveyor's office. Mollet couldn't quite carry it off. In the end, the pained innocence was transformed into a withering dismissal issued by a man who assumed his natural superiority.

If she had lost Eric Mollet then she had gained something else, as he would surely find out.

By midday, they had begun to arrive, scaling the wall in rue Poissoniers, entering the other end of the tunnel, led by one of the two scouts Youssef had instructed first thing that morning. Hakim had told him that it was too dangerous to use social media, but word of the underground depot had spread quickly among the dispersed former inhabitants of the camp and they began to arrive in ones and twos, carrying their possessions strapped to their backs. The weather, colder even than the day before, added a new urgency to their journeys. By early afternoon, a ladder had been added to speed up access over the wall. Hakim had organised further lanterns and a runway had been marked out along the centre of the space in which the new arrivals were directed to place their bedding. It was a precarious new home, but it was warm, dry and protected from the elements. And there was nowhere else.

Hakim called him over. 'You've done good work, Youssef. Sit.'

They were on the same bench at Clignancourt, only now their collars were tucked up against the wind. In just twenty-four hours, Paris had become a crueller place.

'I have put out word about your brother,' Hakim told him. 'If he's...'

Youssef was certain he was going to say 'alive'.

'...around, then we will, *inshallah*, find him for you. Be brave.' On his phone, he showed the message and then he forwarded it to Youssef, whose phone pinged shortly afterwards.

After Hakim left, Youssef sat alone and thought of warmer days in a different country and a brother whose importance grew by the day.

Did Michael Finistere sense in some small way he was beginning to learn the rudiments of how to react to Sophie Arditti? He knew without question, for example, that he shouldn't phone her that morning, that she needed some time alone after the emotion of the night before. In the background, *Tosca* was playing again and it was growing on him, like ivy works its way up a wall. His friends might laugh at this sudden conversion to opera and they might assume, correctly, that it had been brought about by a woman.

It was Wednesday midday, time he phoned Mary but, he noted again, he had very little impetus to do so and he slipped the phone back into the pocket of his dressing gown. Afternoon had begun and he still hadn't got up. He slipped off the dressing gown and lay naked on the floor to begin the exercises he had neglected for the past few days. He thought of Sophie, tears slipping down her cheeks to her lips, as she silently mouthed Tosca's words, to drip finally on her top of tiny sequins. It was, he thought, an image without sexual connotations, one that matched the intensity of the music, the tears the distillation of the emotions contained in the story, on the one hand ridiculous and on the other so perfectly exact.

He showered in cold water, dressed and declared himself ready for the day now already half finished.

30

Hurrying towards the end of the footbridge, Mary looked at her watch and saw that it was after midday. Her indignation was driving her forward, the thought that she might once again find herself back as Round Mary, leading a singular life in London, nothing more than a glorified PA to Michael Finistere. Cutting through a small square on her way to the Métro, her head was down with the determination that her life would not slip back, that she would cling to her new-found status no matter what.

The blow when it came was so unexpected that she had no time to prepare her defences, the grass of the park coming towards her with alarming speed and spinning away from her even as she crashed to the ground.

And then the strange collection of sounds, hushed voices, a siren that failed to come and go, the bleep of machinery and a voice speaking in French. She closed her eyes, to be woken immediately by a face looming down at her.

'N'allez pas dormir, madame.'

Another voice.

'Elle est Anglaise.'

'No sleep, please, madam. You must be awake.'

Mary knew then that she was looking at the ceiling of an ambulance and the voices belonged to paramedics, and with the realisation came the nausea and she began to retch. A paper bowl was placed under her chin, her head supported and held forward. The moment passed and she lay back, trying to piece together what had happened and why she was in an ambulance. Had she been hit by a car? Mary began to panic when she found it hard to recall the last thing she remembered, her past obliterated. She tried to sit up.

'It's okay, madam. Calmez vous.'

More lights above her, coming and going and then a different voice, speaking English.

'My name is Selena, I'm a doctor. You've hit your head, but you'll be okay. We need to do some routine checks.'

And she was being wheeled under the lights again, still struggling to make sense of the void that was now her memory. The roar of a machine blocked out all thought and then once again she was on the trolley and under the lights, to be slipped, finally, into a bed where she closed her eyes and gave herself up to blackness.

When she woke, she was frightened. Where was she? In her head she heard the noise of trains and saw the blurred image of grass. She could smell it now. And then another face looking at her.

'Miss Houlihan, I am a policeman. Are you able to talk?'

Mary wasn't sure.

'I think so.' She was surprised the words had emerged and felt better that they had.

'You were found unconscious in a park near the Métro station, Liberté. Can you remember what happened?'

She went to shake her head but the pain stopped her. But her mind was working and she remembered the Métro station and the instructions that were written on the paper in her bag.

'My bag,' she said, attempting to rise on her elbows.

'We have it,' the policeman said.

'Let me see.'

She knew, even before that bag was handed to her, that the papers would be missing, for her mind had been piecing together the splintered fragments of memory, each one sponsoring another. Her purse was there, but the money was missing and, zipped in a side pocket, her passport remained. There was the blue handkerchief her mother had given her and the scrunched-up piece of paper with the direction to Mollet's apartment. It all came back in a rush and, apart from the final moments, she assembled the events of the morning.

'What day is this?'

'Wednesday, *madame*. Wednesday afternoon. Can you tell us what you were doing?'

'I had a meeting on the other side of the railway and I was coming back from that. Did I fall?'

'No *madame*, you were attacked. Is there anything missing from your bag?'

'Money,' she said.

It wasn't a lie, nor was it the complete truth. Why was her instinct not to tell the police about the papers? Was it simpler to leave them out, or was she somehow protecting Mollet?

'And nothing else?'

'No.'

'It appears that you were mugged. I think this is your word.'

The doctor who had seen her earlier appeared at his side.

'The scan showed no damage, *madame,* so after you have rested, you are free to go.'

'Thank you for looking after me,' Mary said, her mind now fully engaged with the confusing events of the past few hours. The policeman said that he had taken her details and explained that they would be in touch, but in such a way that made her certain that to them this was simply another mugging, one to add to a long list.

The hospital was in the twelfth arrondissement, she was told, and when Mary explained where her hotel was they gave her directions on how to get there. She left the hospital feeling somewhat vacant, wanting only to lie on her own hotel bed and sleep. Which is what she did forty-five minutes later, falling into a strange sleep in which images came and went but none made any sense and somewhere, in the distance, a phone was ringing.

Sophie had expected Finistere to call and was somewhat relieved, not to say surprised, that he hadn't, for she was still licking her wounds from the night before and hadn't the energy to cope with his demands. Sophie wanted to thank him for taking her to the opera and contemplated texting, but this seemed somehow inadequate. In the old days, she could have written a letter that would have been delivered by the afternoon. It was difficult to be electronic and personal.

Should she phone? What message would she be giving? She thought about their night together and how she had shown so much emotion in front of him. At first, she found it strange that she'd done this, revealed herself in this way. He had chosen to take her to the opera, for this is what he assumed she'd like. That it was *Tosca* was, indeed, chance and he could not have predicted the impact it would have had on her, nor the reasons why. She, too, was taken aback by the emotions that had flooded to the surface. He had behaved impeccably and although she was aware he might have been at a loss to probe further why she had felt so vulnerable, she was nevertheless glad that he had remained quietly supportive. Strange, she had to acknowledge.

It was the thought of the approaching weekend that made her decision. The anticipation of having to shoehorn her life to accommodate her mother yet again was already beginning to sap her energy.

'Michael. It's Sophie. I wanted to thank you for last night.'

Finistere, who was walking along the street when he took the call, found a seat in the café he was passing.

'It was a great pleasure, Sophie. I've been playing the music all morning.'

'Well, a convert.'

'Perhaps. Who would have thought it? I'm not sure I dare tell my friends. They'd never believe it.'

Was he going to refer to her tears, she wondered, or would this be venturing into territory where he felt uncertain?

'You were clearly upset,' he said, answering her unspoken question, confounding her expectation.

'Yes. I told you a little of the story, but it's all quite complicated.'

'Reason for another meal, then?'

She laughed. Michael Finistere true to form, but she was, she had to admit, slightly pleased at his obvious good spirits. She guessed what might follow and this time she wasn't wrong.

'And what about standing up your mother in favour of me this weekend?'

'Let me think about it, Michael.'

His response anticipated her thoughts.

'I have two bedrooms at the apartment in London, by the way.'

'And what about Paris, Michael? What's going on with the development? How is Mary getting along? I haven't heard from her for over a day.'

'I'm ashamed to say,' she heard him say, following it up with a laugh, 'I have no idea. I've been neglecting my duties. How has that happened, do you think?'

'Is it a good idea to become so distracted with so much money at stake?'

'Very unprofessional, you're right. I'll call her immediately.'

She could hear he wasn't being serious.

'But what about later?' he continued. 'Shall we meet? Nothing grand. Take me to one of your places, you know, where ties are banned and the waiters look like diners.'

It was her turn to laugh. 'If you insist. I'm not sure you'll like it.'

'I'm sure I won't,' he said.

'It's noisy, cramped and full of French.'

'Sounds just right.'

She gave him directions to the restaurant in rue de Bretagne and they fixed on eight o'clock. When she put down the phone, she was pleased.

Finistere let out a whoop of delight, so that the waiter heading in his direction stopped in his tracks.

'I'll have a glass of champagne, please.'

The waiter turned on his heels.

While he waited, Finistere took out his phone to call Mary. He heard it ring, the smile still on his face.

The phone rang and vibrated on the bedside table, although it was some time before Mary registered it was her own. She picked it up and saw that it was Finistere and that she had another missed call from Sophie.

'Well, Mary, what have you been up to?'

The ebullience of his tone, in sharp contrast to the way she was feeling, told her that all was going well.

'Quite a lot,' she said. 'I was going to call.'

'Such as?'

She didn't want to tell him on the phone. In her mind it was all planned. The meeting would be hers and she would take Michael Finistere through the conclusions of the previous three days.

'I need to show you,' she said, mustering as much strength as she could.

'Give me a clue.'

He really did sound very chirpy and she didn't have to think hard to find the reason.

'He's lying.'

'The little bugger. How do you know?'

'I'll show you.' She wasn't going to reveal how bad she felt, or what had taken place earlier. She knew she wouldn't receive much sympathy.

'When?'

Mary held the phone from her ear.

'This evening?'

'Can't. I'm busy. What are you doing in an hour, say three o'clock?'

Mary needed longer.

'Could you make it four? There's some stuff I still have to do.'

'Four it is. We'll have tea at the Lancaster.'

The bump on her head was still tender but the skin had not been broken, even if the bruise was so big that it felt like a horn. In the bathroom she examined her face and the stare it returned showed a pale woman with flattened hair and wild eyes. She stripped off and showered, turning up the power and alternating between hot and cold. She needed to be at her best for the meeting as Finistere did not countenance weakness of any sort.

She dressed as formally as she could, in the dark skirt and jacket she had originally travelled to Paris wearing. Her hair still retained the new cut and her face now showed signs of colour. She rehearsed her pitch out loud, speaking to her reflection in the mirror in what she hoped was the same voice she'd use later.

She gathered the papers, the copies she'd made at least and smiled as she did so. She had learned a lesson when the briefcase had been stolen in the warehouse.

She declared herself happy and was about to leave when she remembered the missed call from Sophie. Feeling somewhat guilty at her silence, she called back.

'Sophie, it's me. I'm sorry I haven't been in touch.'

'Are you alright?'

'Yes and no. I've got to dash now, can I explain tomorrow?'

'Sure. Finistere is taking me out again tonight.'

'Yes, I rather guessed that. He was on such good form when he called just now I knew it had to be because of you. But I must dash. Have fun.'

Mary felt the weight of disappointment as she took the narrow lift down to reception, exactly what she didn't want to feel. She had no right to be jealous of Finistere and Sophie but she couldn't help but feel angry at what had been taken from her, and why.

She stepped out into the cold air and decided, however, that revenge was in her hands.

3 1

F inistere's euphoria was clear to see and if Mary knew the reason why had nothing to do with her, she still marvelled that he was able to remain untouched by the problems of Les Merchandises and the tens of millions of pounds that remained on the brink of being spent. It would have worried her sick and it was her mother who once again came to mind. He's got more money than sense, she might have said.

Tea was laid out on a low table covered in a white tablecloth, cakes and sandwiches on pretty plates, a silver tea pot and matching strainer and napkin rings.

'Perfect timing,' he announced as she walked in. 'You look a bit pale. Cake might help, don't you think?'

She thought it might. He was already pouring her tea. This is my meeting, she reminded herself, but with Finistere in such form she saw that it might be hard to take the floor.

'So,' he said, pushing the layered cake stand towards her. 'Tell me all.'

She unclipped her bag and removed the plan and laid it, along with her other notes, on her knee.

'Talk me through it.'

She sipped her tea.

'On Monday Mollet took me to his surveyor's office and I was shown a collection of maps that covered the time from the construction of the warehouses, back in the eighteen-eighties, through until today. None showed the underground depot.'

'So,' he said, 'how could they have known it was there?'

'Because one of the plans was missing.'

'How do you know?'

Mary ignored the question.

'The surveyor said that it must have been built by the Nazis in the last war, a secret underground store for which there was no record.'

'Perfectly reasonable, no?'

Mary knew Finistere was playing devil's advocate, but she would present her case calmly and in the order she wanted. She had rehearsed it this way in the bathroom mirror.

'I knew they were lying.' Mary held up her hand to stop him asking why. 'And so I asked if the surveyor could prepare a plan of the depot showing its layout in relation to the warehouses above.'

'So?'

'And that's what he did.'

She handed Finistere a print of the photograph she had taken of the surveyor's results.

Finistere looked at it.

'But it shows that the depot's not part of the development, doesn't it? Isn't that what we wanted to know?'

'They were lying.'

Mary was in her stride now and she knew she had Finistere's attention.

'You'll find the truth here.'

Finistere took the document from her, holding Mary's eyes before looking down at the plan she had drawn. He was quiet for a moment and Mary felt that she had wrested control of the meeting from him. She watched as he held both documents up in front of himself for comparison.

'But this one is completely different,' he said, tapping Mary's version.

'Completely.'

'Where did you get this one?'

'I made it.'

Finistere moved aside the various plates and the cake stand to put the papers side by side on the table.

'You?'

'I took measurements and GPS readings.'

'How?'

Mary brought out the GPS tracker and electronic ruler and presented them to him, one in each hand.

'As simple as that?'

'Sort of. I needed help.'

'Couldn't have been Mollet, could it?'

She shook her head. 'I'll introduce you some time.'

Finistere turned back to Mary's plan.

'It's directly under the warehouses.'

'It is.'

'What does this mean?'

She had turned Michael Finistere and the floor now belonged to her.

'It could mean lots of things. That the foundations of the new development might need to be looked at again. And we don't know what was kept in the depot. It might have been contaminated. There's lots we need to know.'

'And Mollet was lying.'

'He was. He might not have found out about the depot until after he'd bought the land, I accept, but he tried to keep it from us and then had the surveyor draw up a false plan.'

'The bugger.'

The cakes lay untouched in front of them.

'We'll just walk away. I had my doubts from the start. How did you find out? When did you know?'

You know when a lover is lying, she wanted to say, and it was perhaps what Finistere wanted to hear.

'It was all too pat,' she said instead. 'The first presentation they gave me, on Monday morning, felt rehearsed. They thought they could pull the wool over my eyes.'

'So you went and bought all that stuff,' he said, nodding down at the electronic devices on the table. 'Would you believe it? I'm going to phone Mollet now and give him a piece of my mind.'

'Don't you think we should know more, first?'

'What do you mean?'

Mary judged that she had Finistere's full attention, that the meeting was being mediated by her.

'Foundations can be strengthened and contaminated land cleaned up.'

'But why would I let those bastards have my money?'

'Because you could make a lot more from them.'

Finistere took a bite from a chocolate gateau.

'Go on.'

'Look again at the map I drew. It's roughly to scale.'

Finistere picked it up off the table.

'See the black gates indicated on either side of what is now the lorry park. I've added the dotted lines leading from them. Imagine one is an entry and the other an exit.'

Mary waited, watching his face and she saw the moment the penny dropped.

'A car park. An underground car park. Fucking brilliant.'

He took another bite of the cake and wiped his mouth with a napkin.

'Do you reckon Mollet's thought of this?'

Mary shook her head. 'If he had, he would have upped the price. He was too busy keeping its existence from you. He's worried about losing the money he's already invested.'

'And you know this, do you?'

She could see through what Finistere was saying, the question he wasn't asking. Did she discover all this because she had been Mollet's lover?

'I do,' was all she was prepared to say.

'So, next moves?'

She wondered if he would thank her, but even as she had the thought she was aware he didn't operate like that. She could see that he was in his element, that an opportunity to make more money had presented itself and one which would allow him to pull off a business coup.

'It's almost five o'clock,' he said. 'Time for a glass of champagne, I think. Don't you?'

Mary supposed it was close enough to a thank you.

'White wine, if you wouldn't mind.'

He went off to find a waiter and she ran her hand gingerly over her bruised head. Why had she not told him about the assault? She knew the answer, of course. He would assume that it could only have happened to a woman, the weaker sex. To mention it would serve no purpose and so, for the time being, she kept it to herself, tucked away alongside her disappointment and anger with Mollet. It remained unfinished business.

They raised their drinks to one another, the clink of the glasses signalling the official change in their relationship, she thought. Mary's presentation had increased Finistere's good humour.

'I can't believe it, Mary,' he told her, with a shake of his head. 'You caught Mollet with his pants down, so to speak.'

He laughed at his own joke, one she could imagine him making with his business chums.

'And how's that going?'

She knew that he would ask the question in the end.

'It's gone,' she said.

'Just a fling.'

'Yes, just a fling, the sort of thing that happens in Paris. You know what I mean?'

At least he laughed at her response.

'Indeed. I'm seeing Sophie tonight. She keeps taking me to these out-of-the-way places.' He brought out a piece of paper from his pocket. 'Here it is, in the rue de Bretagne. Small and full of French, she told me.'

'Sounds perfect,' said Mary and for her it would have been. The feelings of envy began to surface again and she fought to quell them along with her desire to eat the rest of the chocolate gateaux.

'I want to go again,' Finistere said. 'To the warehouse and depot. Can you fix it?'

'Without Mollet and his mob, you mean?'

'Of course.'

'I want you to tell me exactly what you had in mind.'

Finistere was smiling at her, but she doubted if he knew exactly what she was thinking.

Youssef couldn't believe it. He estimated that almost two hundred people had spent the night with him underground and more were arriving. A generator had been conjured from somewhere and the great space was now lit. Work was under way to provide water, although it was necessary to leave the site to go to the lavatory. It had been the same problem in the camp. Some cafés nearby, run by Arabs, accepted them using their facilities, but Youssef saw that this many people coming in and out of the depot would attract attention and that once again their time here was limited. At any moment he was prepared to hear the police drumming their batons against their shields and he lived in fear, the mark of a baton still livid on his back.

He had kept his bed on the bench, but for how long? He thought about Mary and her hands on his head, the touch of kindness, the sort that had disappeared from his life. He had helped her measure this place and he thought of the model above them, of the bright new buildings that would sweep all this, and them, away. He wanted the doors behind him to open and his brother to arrive, to take him away to a life that had some purpose, a life that had a future. He had been told that there were many more people just like him travelling across Europe, needing shelter, wanting food, clinging to survival. He had seen the little children in Paris, unnaturally quiet, remaining by their parents' side, too uncertain, or unable, to act like young children should at their age, with noise and freedom. They had absorbed their parents' anxieties, had become the manifestation of their bewilderment. Youssef understood it, for this was what was happening to him. Each day he was bent further out of shape, distorted from the boy he once was, who had played with his brother and been noisy in the streets. Now he moved furtively, secretly, not wishing to draw attention to himself. The people in front of him now made it more difficult. The more there were, the harder it was to hide. Out of the goodness of his heart, what remained of it, he had told Hakim about the space, but he feared that he would have to make another decision soon, for he was now too vulnerable.

Down here it was neither day nor night and he was not part of the world. Would he cry out at night when he saw his mother once again floating towards him above the broken bodies of his friends? He didn't want to share this horror with others, and didn't want to be questioned about it. He wanted it locked away. He had almost stopped thinking of home, the smells of the kitchen and those from the hills had almost vanished, along with his hopes of ever being there again.

His exile was permanent.

32

Finistere's feeling of bonhomie was still with him when the taxi dropped him off in rue de Bretagne. He had no idea where he was and had he been forced to walk home he would not have known which direction to take.

The Charlot was a strange name for what Finistere thought was neither a bar, nor a restaurant, a smallish place crammed with tables where the noise almost repelled him at the door.

He saw Sophie on the far side, tucked into a corner one table in from the window. He could see that she had been watching his arrival.

'You look very happy,' she said as he squeezed into the chair opposite. 'I don't believe it's all to do with seeing me.'

'And why shouldn't it be?' he said, although he was surprised that she had detected his extra delight at the news Mary had given him earlier. Just above her head were a series of dials indicating either water pressure, or electricity output. He wasn't sure whether they were for real or merely decoration.

'I bought you a kir,' she said, pushing a glass towards him. 'What do you think of the place?'

'Busy,' he said. 'Do you live near here?'

She laughed. 'No, but I used to. It's just north of the Marais, if that helps.'

It didn't. He supposed this was the sort of place that set designers came up with when they wanted to show an authentic Paris restaurant and he had to admit that it had a certain charm, although he preferred the Grand Véfour, a different sort of reality.

'When you had a place around here, were you living alone?'

'That's a very personal question, Mr Finistere. Some of the time, is my answer.'

Finistere imagined a series of different lovers coming and going, some staying longer than others, a complicated life that lay somewhere out of vision.

'Quite often, by myself. My partner was in Milan most of the time and my work also kept me there. I hung on to my apartment and we would come here occasionally.'

'Has this anything to do with being let down for the part as Tosca?'

'My, my, Mr Finistere, you have been listening. Yes, as a matter of fact.'

'And is that why we're here tonight?'

Sophie thought about this and wondered if, subconsciously, it was. She and Claudio had come here certainly and she had not been back since.

'I think you might be right, Michael. Although, to be truthful, I hadn't really thought about it. You'll have to believe me.'

Finistere, who had about as much interest in psychology as French irregular verbs, didn't fully believe her and Sophie could see that he was sceptical.

'Okay,' she said, leaning across the table towards him, 'perhaps something happened last night that allowed me to resume a life I'd put on hold since the events that took place with *Tosca*. Going with you to see it again helped me confront that terrible time and tonight is one of the results.'

'Well, I'm glad I've been of some help,' he said, not entirely following her logic but glad, at least, that she'd leaned towards him. He did the same in return. 'And food, can we eat here?'

'On the board just over there,' she said, looking at him properly for what she thought was the first time. He wasn't good looking in the traditional sense, but then those men had barely interested her. His hair was traditionally cut and neatly parted and his face, which she could see would quickly lose its shape if he didn't keep fit, was nicely toned. His eyes were restless and properly summed him up, she thought, always alert and never entirely relaxed.

'What should I eat?' he asked, his face still with the smile he'd had when she watched him get out of the taxi.

'Fish or meat?' she asked, but continued before he could answer. 'We'll go for both. Grilled oysters followed by veal. *D'accord?*' She didn't tell him exactly what part of the veal she was suggesting.

'Fine by me,' he said, not knowing whether his good mood had made the evening easier, or whether she was different towards him, warmer and less combative.

'Your good humour when you arrived, Michael, was not all to do with seeing me, I think?'

'You're right. All the result of Round Mary.'

The nickname was out before he could stop himself.

'Round Mary? Is that what you call her?'

'Sure,' he said, deciding to brazen it out. 'Well, it's what I used to call her. She's been different in Paris.'

'In what way, Michael?'

He couldn't say thinner, but that's what he meant, at least he thought he did, so he embarked on giving Sophie an account of their meeting earlier and hoped she would draw the right conclusions.

'She has done a remarkable job and has opened up new possibilities with Les Merchandises, ones that I had never considered before. To tell you the truth, I never thought she had it in her.'

'Or you never gave her the chance, Michael.'

'That's true, I suppose. She was always so efficient, though.'

'So you kept her on as a PA, when she was able to do so much more. Perhaps you see all women in this way?'

Here we go again, he thought, back to pistols at dawn, although he had to admit there was considerable truth in Sophie's conclusions, at least as far as Mary was concerned.

'Do you think so?' he conceded.

'I went to the surveyor's office with her on Monday. Mary's a formidable opponent, easily the measure of Mollet and the surveyor. What more did she find out?'

Finistere turned over a napkin and drew a rough approximation of the warehouses and, using dotted lines, the depot beneath.

'Mary has discovered that the space below the development, here in dotted lines, lies exactly below where we propose to build and she's made a brilliant suggestion.'

He looked at Sophie, the grey marble flecked eyes.

'But this needs to remain confidential.' He enjoyed the notion of sharing a secret with her. 'She thinks we could make it an underground car park, solving a problem that we'd had about the site from the start. It means we can charge more for the apartments and yet pay the same for the land.'

They were interrupted by the arrival of the oysters.

'With champagne and shallots,' Sophie told him, 'and then briefly grilled. They're delicious.'

Finistere, who liked oysters, had never had them prepared in this way and he wasn't sure he liked the idea of a heated oyster. Nevertheless, he had to agree they were delicious and he could well have eaten the same again.

'I gather you enjoyed them? So what's your next step?'

Well, I wouldn't mind kissing you, he thought, but judging the right moment was going to tax him, for an ill-judged advance might destroy the progress he appeared to be making.

'I think we should conclude the deal before they realise what an asset they're sitting on.'

'Good old Mary. I hope you've told her?'

'Not in so many words, no.'

'You should. It makes a difference, you know?'

It was true he'd taken Mary's results without showing proper appreciation, but he reasoned that this was the result of being so flabbergasted at the new talents she was showing. He said this to Sophie.

'Perhaps Michael, but I think you have a tendency to take women for granted, if you don't mind me saying.'

Sophie thought Claudio had been the same, so wrapped up in himself that he assumed all others were there simply to serve him. Her voice, for example, which she knew to be good, he had taken for granted and had used it merely as a vehicle to enhance his own career. When she'd finally objected, his indignation that anyone should challenge the way he did things was complete. From then on she saw him differently and before long the separation became permanent and her career was correspondingly shunted into a siding, where it had been for too long.

'I'll make amends to her tomorrow. We're going to the site again. Do you want to come along?'

'No, Michael. I wouldn't want to get in the way of Mary. I think it's going to be her day.'

The veal was placed in front of them, although it wasn't any part of a young cow he recognised. He peered at the stew-like mound and smelled the slightly astringent aroma it was giving off.

'I'm not familiar with this,' he said. 'What exactly is it?'

'Try it first,' she said, taking a mouthful. 'And then I'll tell you. It's delicious.'

He did as he was told and the red wine sauce, slightly vinegary, was as she described, both smooth and slightly sharp. He took another mouthful and was further convinced.

'It's veal brain,' she said.

Finistere stopped and looked at his fork and then at Sophie's face, which was smiling, before completing his movement.

'You're right. Delicious,' he declared, smiling back at her, feeling the comfort of the evening beginning to take him over, the woman opposite a strange mixture, both combative and warm and still, for now, beyond his grasp.

They were offered cognac on the house and he couldn't help but think this is what used to happen before, with the other man. He held her hand as they left and she didn't appear to object. They took a cab to her apartment in Montmartre although he couldn't have said what would happen once they arrived and made no plans in his mind.

Sophie invited him in for a further night cap and he walked up the long stairway behind her, again uncertain what to expect. The flat was as he imagined it might be, a reflection of her, neither too neat nor too tidy, perfectly judged. She opened the window to show him the view down on to the northern slopes of Montmartre, pointing behind her to indicate the location of the vineyard. Finistere had no idea that wines were grown in Paris, let alone here. She directed him to look at the line of lights moving across the middle of the view and told him this was the road that ran alongside the far boundary of Les Merchandises. When he turned, she was sitting down and two brandy glasses were on the table between the seats.

'This is nice,' he said.

'You're the first man I've invited here since you-know-what,' she told him.

'I'm honoured.'

'In a way, you should be and in another, you shouldn't.'

'Explain.'

'You're here because you helped break a cycle of events for me, made me conscious that I'd become somewhat sorry for myself, not to say bitter. Going to the opera, to *Tosca*, was the start and you did that.'

Finistere was waiting for the 'but'.

'And why shouldn't I feel honoured?'

'Because it happened by accident, so you're here because I've invited you, rather than to say thank you.'

'I think I get it,' he said.

'I'm going to kiss you Michael, but that's all I'm going to do.'

He watched her stand up, stooping to put down her glass. He did the same and she took a step towards him, coming very close to his face. He didn't move and slowly she put her lips against his, opening her mouth slightly. He responded, not wanting, perhaps not daring, to do more. And then it was over and she turned to pick up her glass, which she raised to him. Once again, he followed her cue.

'When you leave,' she said, 'turn left and go to the end of the road and then left again. It will take you to some stairs that lead up to the Sacré-Coeur. Climb them and you will come to a view of Paris that perhaps you have never seen before, that is spread before you like no other view. Sit for a while and take it in, the Eiffel Tower to your right, the west, and the ugly tower of Montparnasse to the east. Contemplate for a while, take Paris in, let it overwhelm you.'

They parted formally, with him kissing her hand and then he did as he was told and the night, cold but clear, did just what she'd predicted, made him see Paris differently. But, he thought to himself sitting on a bench with Paris below him, she'd begun to do this about many things. He accepted she was leading and that he was happy to follow.

After half an hour, he used his phone to work out how to walk to his hotel and descended the south slope of the hill of Sacré-Coeur with the smell of Sophie Arditti still vaguely on his lips.

33

Mary stood alone in the centre of the forlorn lorry park, the cold wind making no concessions as it whipped from the north, over the dual carriageway, disturbing the shallow puddles of water around her, blowing her hair forward over her hidden face, on its wild passage across the city. Mary's heart was as cold as the leading edge of the wind, in union with its bleakness. She was early for her rendezvous with Finistere and, hunched and alone on the acre of bleak concrete, she brooded on the night before, the demons that had assailed her, just as the wind was doing now. Envy and anger are natural bedfellows, she thought, feeding off one another, and they conspired with her jealousy, powerful allies. The trapped fury of her feelings about Mollet intensified when she thought of Finistere and Sophie together. She was warmly dressed in protective clothing, but the coldness was coming from within and invaded every corner of her body.

She heard a car draw up behind and turned to see Finistere walking towards her, his face and step still carrying the warmth of the night before, a smile on his face despite the best efforts of the wind.

'You look cold, Mary. Let's find a bit of shelter.'

He took her by the point of her elbow and they retreated to the far side of the warehouse, out of the wind. Even in that short distance, Mary decided that work should now supersede the powerful alloy of her other feelings and, resting her back against the brick wall, she already had the plan in her hand. Towards the early hours of the morning, she had abandoned sleep to think about this meeting and from her coat pocket she produced one of two spray cans in dayglow green and red.

'I'll show you,' she said. 'Stay there.'

In her other hand she held the GPS tracker and she walked a few metres back across the car park before she stopped and marked the spot with a squirt of green. As she returned to him, she indicated that Finistere should follow and made off to the back side of the block, through the tangled buddleia, to the left of the metal cover that Youssef had used to enter the building. She made another mark, this time in bright red, on the dirty earth. She called Finistere to her side.

'Look along this line,' she said. 'This is the southern limit of the depot.'

They moved across the back of the warehouses, Mary leading, their heads down against the north wind blowing directly into their faces, until she'd located the north-westerly extent of the underground space, which she marked, again in red. Finally, they crossed beneath the northern wall of the second warehouse, to make the last mark on the concrete of the car park. From this point they could make out three of the extremities of the irregular rectangle that made up the void underneath.

'And I've been thinking,' she shouted, the wind attempting to steal her words and toss them in the air, 'that, once upon a time, there must have been access between down there and up here, probably somewhere under the floor of one or both warehouses. It makes sense, doesn't it?'

This time Finistere put one arm around her shoulder as he guided her, the wind blowing behind them, towards the door into the warehouse, before unlocking it and climbing to the fifth floor and its relative warmth.

Finistere turned on the lights and they both stood in front of the model, where it was easier to see what they had just done in relation to the development as a whole.

'We'd be mad to wait any longer, wouldn't we?' he said. 'You've done great work here and it's changed my view of the whole place.'

She nodded, speculating whether Sophie had told him to be more grateful for her efforts, for his praise was anything but natural. Finistere took out his phone and she watched on, a spectator, and her stomach turned when she heard his first word.

'Mollet. It's me, Michael. How are you on this cold French morning?'

Finistere rolled his eyes at her as he listened to Erik's response.

'Let me cut to the chase, Erik. I've been back in London and my board have signed off on the purchase. Good news, eh? Congratulations. I'm sorry for the delays. I'll have the first tranche of money in your account by late this afternoon. What changed my mind? Something you French will understand only too well. I've fallen in love and I've thrown caution to the wind.'

How very clever, Mary thought, to mask a hard financial decision behind the smokescreen of emotion, thus diminishing any suspicion Mollet might have had over his sudden change of heart.

'I've brought the documents with me and we'll sign today. Shall we say the Lancaster at five? Fine. I'll book one of the downstairs meeting rooms.'

He snapped shut his phone, the smile still on his face.

'So, Mary Houlihan, you are now responsible for spending fifty million pounds of my money this morning. How does it feel?'

'I'm glad,' she said, knowing that Mollet was ultimately the loser in this deal, one in which she saw herself as collateral damage, a victim of friendly fire.

'Come with me for the final signing,' he said, stooping to switch off the lights.

'No,' she said, with more force than she intended, her words echoing in the room. 'No,' she repeated, more quietly, 'this is your deal.'

'But this is your success, Mary,' Finistere said before he remembered, for the first time that morning, that Mary and Mollet were an item and, as he did, recalled it was over and that this no doubt explained a certain remoteness in her behaviour.

'Fine. As you will. I'll catch up with you afterwards when everything's been signed. You and I will have lots to do, but we'll be able to celebrate. I wonder if Sophie will be free?'

'I think we should go downstairs to the depot now,' Mary said, looking him in the face. 'One last time. Belt and braces you might say. I've brought the torches.'

'Is there something you're not telling me, Mary?'

A few things, Mary thought.

'I want you to meet someone.'

He saw Finistere frown and a few seconds passed. 'You continue to surprise me, Mary.'

They filed down the stairs, out into the cold wind and around to the back of the warehouses, Mary leading the way to the fence that Youssef had shown her, where she moved aside the metal spears.

'How do you know all this?' he asked, squeezing through behind her.

'You'll see. Mind the drop here, it's quite tricky.'

They slithered their way down to the railway track and the emptiness of what had been the camp. She hurried across to the protection of the tunnel and he followed. They switched on the torches and the wind dropped as they moved inside and along the now familiar curve towards the abandoned wagons.

It was only as they shuffled by the massive vehicles that they heard the babble of voices somewhere in the darkness ahead. There was more light, too, and for a moment they both paused, before Mary encouraged him forward. The noise grew louder and the shape of the doors that led into the depot were clearly outlined by a light beyond.

Suddenly two figures emerged from the darkness of two alcoves set into the brick walls of the tunnel.

'*Oui?*'

They were tall, well-built and carried what might have been baseball bats. Mary felt Finistere stiffen at her side and she placed a hand against his chest.

'*Bonjour*. We are here to see Youssef. Youssef is a friend of mine. Tell him it's Mary.'

The two men spoke to each other and one peeled off, through the doors into the depot, a shaft of bright light falling across the tracks on which they stood. Not long after, he returned and beckoned them to follow. When they stepped through the double doors they were met by a sight that Mary could only think of as biblical and behind him she heard Finistere mutter, 'fuck me.'

They sat in long groups, each with their own tiny space on which were laid bedding and possessions. Finistere thought there might have been two hundred and fifty people, but in that space they appeared more numerous and the browns and greys of their clothing, lit by the yellow lamps, transformed the scene into a giant medieval painting.

'Christ,' Finistere said. 'How did this happen?'

Mary knew the answer.

Youssef was sitting on his bench, watching them approach, the two lanterns that Mary had given him burning by his side.

'Youssef, this is my friend, Michael.'

Youssef's big eyes regarded the man he called the Loud One.

'Michael, this is Youssef.'

'Are you the one that stole the briefcase?'

The boy's eyes remained on him.

'He is, Michael. But you need to hear his story.'

'You know him?'

'I do. He lived in the camp until it was destroyed, before he moved in here.'

'He was the one we saw that day? Bugger me. And everyone else followed, by the look of it.'

'Did you tell them about it, Youssef?'

Almost imperceptibly, the boy nodded.

'That was kind of you.'

Mary felt Finistere turn to look at her and sensed his rising anger.

'Is there anything you need?' Mary asked, a ridiculous question, she knew, but the boy would understand.

'Lavatories and water.'

Mary looked across at Finistere, feeling that he needed more of an explanation, only too aware that his elation upstairs was now in the process of being confounded. She, herself, had been astounded to see the number of people here underground, but she understood immediately how it had come about.

'I have known Youssef for a few days. It was he who showed me the route through the railings that we have just taken. And, more important, it was Youssef who helped me measure out the depot. I couldn't have done it without him.'

Finistere regarded the boy again and the look they gave each other, Mary thought, was similar, defiant and unshifting. They might be cut from the same cloth and in different circumstances she would have laughed. On one level, they deserved each other and at this she did allow herself a smile, one that Finistere picked up.

'You find it funny?'

'I was thinking how similar you two are,' she said.

'Similar? Jesus.'

He looked again at the boy. It was the sort of remark that Sophie might have made, Finistere thought, and for that reason he viewed the boy differently, his dark, inscrutable eyes and wild hair. Because he had detected the strange impact Sophie was having on him and bearing in mind the work Mary had done to bring him here today, Finistere offered the boy his hand.

Youssef was not expecting this and at first he didn't know how to respond, looking across to Mary for guidance. He saw her smile and so he offered his hand and felt the Loud One's close over his. Too late he realised he was wearing the watch and with his other hand he quickly pulled down his sleeve.

At first, Finistere couldn't believe his eyes. Perhaps it was his imagination, but he thought he'd just caught a glimpse of a most unusual wrist watch. The boy, he noticed, had now put his arm behind him and the big black eyes looked hard at him, challenging him to do more. Finistere turned to Mary.

'Would you ask Youssef to show me his watch?'

'What?'

'Would you tell Youssef that I know about watches and I think he has a most beautiful possession. Tell him not to worry, I'm not about to take it.'

As bizarre exchanges go, thought Mary, this was verging on the surreal, a multi-millionaire asking a migrant boy if he could see his watch in a camp beneath Paris.

'Youssef, Michael says you have a most beautiful watch. He is interested in such things and he does not want to take it from you. Would you show it to him, please?'

Youssef, who had only retrieved the watch from the buddleia camp that morning for fear the colder, wetter weather might harm it, hesitated. It was one of the last of his possessions and behind his back he closed his hand over its face. He could trust Mary, but the other one, the man she called Michael, was different and it was with reluctance that he produced his arm and pulled back his sleeve to reveal it.

'It is,' he said. 'Fuck me.' He knelt down and when he went to hold the boy's arm, Youssef withdrew it sharply.

'I'm sorry, I'm sorry,' Finistere said, 'I only want to look.'

Youssef again offered his arm and he watched the man examine his wrist.

'Extraordinary,' he said, looking up at Mary. 'I've been after one of these for ages. It's a Bremont Spitfire. Costs a fucking fortune. Where on earth did he get it?'

Youssef took back his arm.

'He thinks you're accusing him, Michael. I don't think you should.'

'Okay, okay,' he said and changed tack. 'It's a beautiful watch, Youssef. And very rare. Thank you for letting me see it. What now, Mary?'

'We might be able to help you, Youssef. But aren't you worried the police will come again?'

Youssef nodded.

She went into her purse and brought out all the notes she had, around eighty euros. She rolled them up and gave them to him.

'I know this is not much, Youssef, and you need a great deal more, but it might help. You have my number, so please call when you need me. I wanted you to meet Michael for reasons that I think you already know.'

Finistere watched this exchange with growing astonishment, finding himself, as he often did with Sophie, catching up with events after they'd happened. Mary placed her hand on the boy's head and so he offered his hand. At first Youssef was hesitant to take it, for it would show his watch again, but eventually he responded and his palm was covered.

Walking back along the tunnel, Finistere couldn't contain himself.

'Where the fuck did he get a watch like that? It's worth about twenty grand. Nicked it, I don't suppose.'

Finistere's accusation ricocheted along the tunnel.

Why don't you buy it from him? she nearly said, thinking that such a large amount of money would transform his life.

'He's not got much else, has he?'

It was as if Finistere hadn't heard.

'How the fuck are we going to get rid of them? Do you think Mollet knew about this?'

Mary allowed him to rant on, back on familiar form, at the same time remembering they should have left the other way, via the marshalling yard. Once outside, it was too difficult to climb up the embankment to the railings, so they headed towards the passageway that would lead to Clignancourt. Half way along it she stopped and turned to Finistere.

'Whatever happens, you must go through with the deal. What you have just seen, the migrants, is nothing, nothing at all. We can deal with it.'

Finistere regarded her carefully. 'You're not in bed with Mollet about this, are you?'

'Oh, for God's sake,' she yelled at him. 'Don't you understand anything?'

She hurried on without him.

34

Finistere watched Mary's ample figure disappear along the passage and followed slowly after, weighing up the words that had produced this sudden outburst. She'd been having a fling with Mollet and for a moment earlier he'd had the chilling thought that, as he'd put it, they might still be in bed together, so to speak, in partnership against him. On reflection, he thought this unlikely and he could see why she might have been angry. He knew he ought to apologise, but when he reached the road she was nowhere to be seen, so he called her, with no luck. He had four hours before the final meeting with Mollet and he wanted to see her before then.

He saw a sign that told him that the Sacré-Coeur was only a couple of kilometres away to his left, so he began to walk up a street that became steeper as it went. It was a decision that was, at one and the same time, both irrational and perfectly logical, out of character, certainly, but he was overcome with an urge to speak to Sophie, to hear what she might have to say about the events that had just taken place with Mary.

It was towards the top of the street that he recognised the stairs up ahead and he looked to his left to find what he was fairly certain was Sophie's road. He couldn't remember her number, nor even what her building looked like, so he called her.

'Sophie, it's me. Where are you?'

'At home.'

'Oh good, because I'm outside. At least, I think I am.'

He could imagine her walking to the window and sure enough, a few metres further along the road, her face appeared through an open window scanning the road below. He waved and walked along to hear the buzz of the door being released. He let himself in and climbed the stairs to be met by her at the door.

'Well, hello, what brings you here unannounced?'

'I'll tell you.'

He didn't greet her with a kiss, but walked past her into the room.

'It's like this,' he said, sitting on the arm of a small sofa. 'I've just pissed off Mary and I wanted to discuss it with you. Would you mind?'

Sophie, who had been told on more than one occasion by Mary that Finistere pissed her off, was interested to hear Michael acknowledge the fact.

'She's done amazing work on the development, as you know. We went there this morning and she made it all quite clear, so much so that I've confirmed the deal with Mollet.'

He stood up and she could see he was agitated.

'The trouble is, she then took me down to the underground depot and it was full of people. Crammed full. All migrants. And she knew about it, or at least knew some kid that had made it possible, she told me. And so, as we left, I had this peculiar feeling that she might be in cahoots with Mollet and that I was being taken for a patsy.'

'And you told her?'

'Sort of.'

'Oh Michael, what a fool you can be. Mary would never betray you. It's not in her, how do you put it, it's not in her DNA.'

'I know, I know, for heaven's sake, but it just slipped out.'

'Have you apologised to her?'

'Her phone must be off.'

'Well, for goodness sake, try again.'

He did and he shook his head, slumping down into the sofa. 'Still off. And it was all going so well.'

'It *is* going so well, Michael. I told you, she's a super bright woman that you've been taking for granted and once again this morning you misjudged her. You have to put it right. What did she say to you?'

Finistere looked towards her. 'She said, "don't you understand anything?"'

Sophie laughed, not a single outburst, but a series of laughs that made her shoulders shake.

'She's right,' she said eventually. 'Sometimes you don't.'

He stood and faced her. 'As bad as that?'

She came forward and kissed him, not sexually, although to him any touch from her was charged.

'Well, at least you knew that you'd insulted her.'

'Will you come with me later, five o'clock at the Lancaster? We'll be signing the documents. The first of the money will be in his account by close of play.'

'Of course,' she said and he took her hands.

'Thank you.'

'Will Mary be there?'

He shook his head. 'She said it was my deal and that she didn't want to be there.'

'You really have pissed her off, as you put it. Get her to change her mind. From what I can see, this is as much her deal as yours. Now go. You have work to do.'

For the first time since arriving at the apartment, he looked at her and felt moved to say something more, but it seemed to be locked in his chest, so he simply kissed her on the cheek and left.

On emerging from the Métro, Mary saw that she had two missed calls from Finistere and her guilt at her outburst fought with her anger at his words. There is nothing wrong with anger, Mary's mother had taught her, except when it becomes trapped and then you never know when it's going to appear and what damage it might do. Better let it out than keep it in, she cautioned.

Her mother's words came to Mary as she walked towards her hotel, all the euphoria she had experienced earlier that morning draining out of her. Finistere's reactions had been inappropriate, but he hadn't deserved her angry dismissal. However, the idea that she might have had to explain what had happened between her and Mollet had her quickening her pace. He would have to wait.

She took the tiny lift up to the top floor, her mind and body sad, as much with disappointment with herself as the events with Mollet. The lift door closed behind her and she slid the key into her door, heard it click and pushed it open. She screamed with shock as she felt the body behind her shove her into the room and turned in fear, her hands coming up to protect her face.

Then she saw it was Mollet.

'I'm sorry, but I need to see you and this was the only way.'

She was breathing heavily. 'What do you want? You frightened the life out of me.'

'You know why I'm here, Mary. Why does Finistere suddenly want to do the deal?'

Mary was frightened. There was a look to Mollet that she hadn't seen before, a turn of the mouth, a narrowness of his eyes, that spoke of cruelty.

'Why don't you ask him? You're partners in this, aren't you? You want the deal, he wants the deal, so what's wrong?'

'You tell me, Mary, you tell me.'

He came closer to her and his menace was palpable. He put his hands on her shoulders and she could see his face soften. 'Remember what we did here, Mary. It was good, wasn't it? You wanted it, didn't you? Didn't you?' he repeated the words, tightening his hands on her body.

'I misjudged you. You were lying and I didn't see it. You used me and I was blind.' Her anger lay just beneath the surface, but she was frightened of showing it.

He squeezed her shoulders more and she thought she would faint, her legs weakening. He brought his face even closer and through her pain she thought this was the very opposite of intimacy.

'What did you discover, Mary? Tell me. What made our Mr Finistere change his mind?'

'He told you,' she shouted.

Mollet hit her with the side of his hand and she fell against the bed, her ears ringing. He knelt down so that his face was once again in front of hers and for the first time Mary thought that she was in real danger, that behind this face there lay real evil and no remorse.

'I persuaded him to take the risk because I thought I was in love with you.' It was a lie but one she thought he might like, that would at least give him pause for thought. 'I told him that the space below was no problem and that you were keeping it from us because it might have been contaminated, something we'd be able to sort out later and that we may need to strengthen the new foundations. And Michael was happy. He'd met a woman himself and he was predisposed to do the deal.'

Mollet looked at her and she could see him take in the information. She knew that he had seen her plans, that he'd had someone mug her and she plucked up the courage to go one stage further. She deliberately pushed him away.

'Since he made the phone call to you, we found out something else.' Her face was now close to his and she hoped he could see her dislike of him. 'We went underground, through the tunnel. It's full of migrants, hundreds of them. They're living there. Do you want them to be your problem as well? Finistere has committed himself, but he's worried. It won't take much for him to pull out.'

He smacked her again, across the other cheek and she fell against a small table and crashed to the floor.

'Bloody whore,' he said, taking hold of her hair and shaking her head before thrusting it against the wall.

She could barely see him now, her eyes filled with tears, her vision blurred. His bulk towered above her and she braced herself for another blow. He kicked the side of her leg and the pain was so immediate, so total that she blacked out.

The table was the first thing she saw, her forehead creased against it, the pains in her body not allowing her to move. There was too much for her to cope with so she shut her eyes again, but she was conscious now and she could sense the room swaying around her. She needed to get up and she attempted to roll on to her back but the side of the bed prevented her from moving. She pushed the table away with one hand and forced herself along the floor with the other until she was able to prise herself into a sitting position. She ran her hands slowly over her face, looked at them for signs of blood and then turned to a kneeling position before finally, using the bed, half stood before sitting on it, her head throbbing. She looked at her watch and saw that it was four o'clock. When she located her phone, she saw further calls from Finistere and one from Sophie. The thought of calling her made her tearful.

Sophie answered almost immediately.

'It's Mary.'

'What's wrong? You sound terrible.'

Mary broke down, as she knew she would.

'Mary, what's happened? Where are you? Let me help.'

'Can you get a message to Michael for me?'

'Why? What's going on, Mary? You're in trouble.'

'Listen, tell him Mollet is suspicious about his change of mind. I've told Mollet about the migrants. Get Finistere to sound doubtful about going ahead with the deal. Please do this.'

'I don't fully understand, Mary. What's going on?'

'Michael will understand, Sophie. Get him to call me if he doesn't. Thank you.'

She fell back on the bed, exhausted, her head banging, the pain in her leg preventing her moving any further.

She knew why she didn't phone Finistere herself. She didn't want to be emotional with him, for he wouldn't have offered sympathy, merely a series of questions that she didn't have the strength to answer, the most important of these being to do with Mollet. She was ashamed of her affair and wanted to hide her head about it, not explain it. She had been taken in and she felt a fool. She wanted the deal to go through, for Mollet to be caught by his own duplicity. For her, it was a small revenge and would only go part of the way to compensating for what had taken place in this room, the two extremes of physicality. For the moment she was beaten, in body and in soul, and she would curl up and lick her wounds, waiting for her strength to be restored. She closed her eyes, but as she did she saw his face, close to hers and the eyes that had no warmth, that carried in them the cold of deep winter.

35

Youssef Tigha looked at his watch, unclipped it and put it in his pocket. He knew he shouldn't have worn it and had told himself so when he took it from behind the brick in the buddleia camp early that morning. The Loud One, who Mary called Michael, wanted to take it from him, a man who clearly had all that he needed, who would destroy this camp to build something new that would make him the enormous sum of money he had seen and remembered. Despite all this, he wanted to take his watch.

After they had left, Youssef had decided that he must get to Calais. He had been here too long and if he'd learned one thing in these many months fleeing through Europe, it was how to smell danger. Right now, underground, it was the smell of hundreds of others that was driving him out, back into the cold autumn air. He would leave in the morning and the decision, once taken, gave him a different purpose, allowed him to think into the future and however thin his hope might be, it was there and he would hang on to it, for without it he was lost.

Mary had taken a shower and she examined herself in the mirror. The bruising around her eyes was just beginning, a smudged darkening that would soon deepen. Her leg, which still hurt, was marked by a blue-black explosion beneath her skin. The damage to her mind was the most painful, but that was hidden.

It was four-thirty. In the shower, she'd heard her phone ring and she saw that Finistere had tried again. She sat on the edge of bed, the phone in her hand, her body rebelling beneath her and she pictured Mollet, all charm and smiles, his doubts and motives hidden, with Claude Papon at his side, in the hushed splendour of the hotel. On the table in the private room, the papers would be laid out, the cold facts that made both parties very rich, more money to add to their coffers. She closed her eyes and saw the scene like she might an opera, the players going about their parts, with the audience only too aware that this was a tragedy, this scene merely a prelude to what was to follow. Order was about to be destroyed, the smiles torn away and in her mind she could hear the music begin to suggest this, a darker theme signalled by a series of base notes like she'd heard at the end of *Tosca*.

Mary dressed painfully, but her resolve was fixed and not open to negotiation. She took one final look at her face and it was unknown to her.

bass

Finistere received Sophie's call as he was preparing the papers in the meeting room at the Lancaster. It would have been easier with Mary to help and once again he cursed what had taken place that morning and his ill-judged words.

'Bugger,' he said, kicking the leg of the table.

He answered the phone without looking to see who it was and at the sound of Sophie's voice, he sat down on the nearest chair.

'Am I glad to hear from you,' he said.

'Listen, Michael, I'm worried. I've just had a call from Mary and something's happened to her. I don't know what, but she's not right.'

'What do you mean?'

'I don't really know, but she wasn't herself. Listen. She asked me to give you a message and I'm not sure I fully understood. I think she'd just seen Mollet.'

'What?'

Finistere got up from the chair and, despite himself, his first thought was that Mary could indeed be conspiring against him.

'Michael, are you listening? She told me to tell you that Mollet is suspicious, couldn't work out why you'd suddenly changed your mind and now wanted to go ahead with the deal. But, and this was the important bit, she said that you'd subsequently seen the migrants in the depot and were now having second thoughts. It was important that you conveyed this to Mollet. She said you'd understand, but I'm lost. She sounded bad, Michael.'

Finistere was pacing around the board-room table, trying to make sense of what he'd heard.

'Why couldn't she call me herself?'

'I think she was too upset. She cried on the phone with me.'

'What the fuck is going on?'

He glanced at his watch. They'd be here in twenty minutes. He tried to put together the pieces of information Sophie had just given him and see them in relation to the events of the morning. Mary had been triumphant in the delivery of her information about the warehouses and her plan for the car parking. She'd wanted the deal to go ahead, even if she'd refused to come along to the meeting that was about to happen. Why would she want him to once again express doubts about going through with the deal?

'Michael, have you tried calling her again?'

'Several times. Nothing. When are you getting here?'

'I'm about ten minutes away.'

'Hurry.'

He tried Mary's phone again, but again it remained unanswered. Something had happened, Sophie had said. But what? He replayed the events of this morning again and recalled it was Mary who had insisted on going down into the depot. She'd known what to expect. And it was Mary who had taken obvious pleasure at the idea of pulling the wool over Mollet's eyes and getting the land on the cheap. Perhaps she was worried that the deal wouldn't go through, that Mollet had smelled a rat. Yes, this was it. She was asking him not to be too keen, to use the migrants lodged in the depot, which he'd only just discovered, as yet another reason not to sign. Yes, that must be it.

He banged his fist on the shiny tabletop.

Minutes later he was looking at himself in mirror of the bathroom attached to the meeting room. He was in the process of deconstructing his face from that of a man delighted to be completing a deal, to one who was now assailed by doubt. The look he gave himself was now flat, concerned, with a touch of suspicion.

Sophie arrived in the black linen suit he'd so admired at the Grand Véfour.

'Have you heard from her?' she called across the room.

He watched her come towards him and the purpose of the meeting, the reason the papers lay in neat piles on the table, even the concerns about Mary, receded at the sight of her face.

'I'm glad you're here,' he said, taking both her hands.

'She's not been in touch?'

He shook his head.

'I think she's in trouble, Michael. Something bad's happened to her, I'm sure of it.'

There was a knock on the half-open door and Mollet walked in, closely followed by Papon.

'Sorry, I didn't mean to interrupt anything,' Mollet said, with a smile. 'Is Mary joining us?'

Finistere had released Sophie's hand as soon as he'd heard the knock, but Mollet had seen, he was sure.

'Come in, gentlemen. No, Mary is involved somewhere else this evening, but I was with her earlier. You know Sophie, of course. I'll call for the coffee,' he said, matter of fact, picking up the phone on the table to speak to reception.

'Sit down, sit down.'

He could see Mollet watching him, carefully assessing his demeanour for signs that might tell him which way the wind was blowing.

A large tray of coffee with a range of patisserie was brought in and placed on the table and the door closed.

'I wanted this to be merely a formality. As I told you, my board in London has sanctioned the deal and the money is waiting to be transferred electronically.'

Finistere picked up several papers and shuffled them to neatness against the table. Mollet was waiting, his eyes on his every move.

'Mary and I visited the site this morning, as I said, for a final viewing and at the end we went underground to the depot.'

Finistere paused, looking across at Mollet, meeting his eyes.

'Have you been down there recently?'

Mollet's face didn't move.

'I would say there were about three hundred migrants living there now. At least three hundred. Surprise you?'

Again, no response from Mollet.

'No, perhaps not. As you know, there have been several problems that have delayed the signing of these papers. And this is perhaps another.'

Mollet remained very still and Finistere imagined him like this just before a rugby international, focusing his mind on what was directly ahead of him, allowing no distraction to break his concentration.

'When you called me this morning,' Mollet said finally, 'before you went to the site, you sounded so sure. What had changed your mind?' He spoke the sentence slowly and with icy precision but Finistere had been prepared for it, had, in fact, wanted it to be delivered.

'Partly this woman,' he said, gesturing to Sophie. 'She's made quite an impact and has made me see things differently.'

Sophie looked at him, her face quite still.

'And, to be honest, boredom. The whole thing has been going on too long. But then I saw the migrants this morning.'

'The migrants. But they're no problem, as you well know. The police will have them out of there as soon as we say so.' He paused. 'So,' he said, placing his hands on the table as a pianist might, 'why are you now so keen?'

'Put like that Erik, I'm not. I've always had doubts about this and as you know, I can take or leave Paris. If you want to pull out and not sign, so be it.'

Mollet continued to look at him and Finistere saw a coldness that he'd not observed before and imagined what he might have done in the darkness of a scrum, out of sight of the referee. Mollet stood, glancing across to Sophie as he did.

'If you'll excuse me, Michael. I need to talk with Claude.'

The two men rose and left the room.

'Try Mary again,' Sophie said, even before the door had closed.

Mary was just leaving the sports shop with a package under her arm when she heard the phone. She knew who it would be and ignored it. The meeting would be underway and she hoped that Sophie had conveyed her confused message to Finistere and that he had deciphered it correctly. She was glad not to be there, for it would have been impossible to conceal her emotions, let alone the marks on her face.

Walking was difficult, but the more she did, the easier it became and she slid that long package into the rucksack on her back. She had cleared her mind of everything else and crossing Place Bastille she refused to look at the opera house. Just beyond, she climbed the stairs to the raised garden indicated on her map, planted on the top of railway arches that ran for a kilometre or two. She walked between trees and benches and looked down into the rooms of apartments close by. So many lives, each with their own dramas in the process of clouding existence.

Her leg was easing up, but one or two people coming the other way gave her second glances as they passed. Somewhere off to her right, she could hear the railway in the distance. She was in another world and her bruised body made her aware of its extremities and how it contained her, remote and removed from everyone else.

She continued on her way into the autumn afternoon.

It was thirty minutes before Mollet and Papon reappeared to resume their positions at the table.

'I'll come straight to the point,' Mollet said. 'It is our belief that we are underselling the plot and we'd like you to make a counter offer.'

Finistere waited for less than a second before standing, bringing the papers towards him and storing his pen in his pocket.

'No, gentlemen. You're welcome to your plot and the migrants underneath. It's a good deal and you know it. I have reached the limit of my patience and it's a case of take it or leave it.'

He placed his case on the table and began to put the papers carefully inside. He'd done this a few times before in similar situations and he felt certain it would work. Anyway, for him, it was a win-win situation. The loss of Les Merchandises wasn't the end of the world for it came laden with problems, not least the migrants and it meant he could put Paris behind him. He smiled at Sophie as he fastened the case.

'Gentlemen, I bid you good day and thanks.'

He had reached the door before Mollet spoke.

'Wait,' he said. 'Sit down.'

Finistere paused and then did as he was told.

'Get the papers out again.'

Again, Finistere responded, knowing that he'd won the game of bluff.

Mollet produced his own pen to sign the various documents. As important occasions went, it lacked any sense of importance and the final signatures were placed in silence.

'There,' Mollet said in conclusion. He stood and offered Finistere his hand. The two men shook but neither was smiling.

36

Sophie was looking across to Finistere.

'Did you mean it? What you said about me? Or was it just a device to use against a business rival?'

'Of course I did.' He was repacking his bag.

'I wish you hadn't.'

Finistere stopped what he was doing.

'But I meant it. You have made an enormous impact on me.'

He stood and walked towards her, pulling out the nearest chair. He was about to speak when she held up a hand.

'Don't Michael. It wasn't right. You failed to respect my privacy, my feelings, like you did with Mary. You used me to get your own way. If you were going to do that, you should have asked me first.'

Finistere was confounded. What had come naturally to him, he thought, was now being rejected. He dropped his head. To lose Mary in the morning was one thing, but to find the same thing happening with Sophie, spoke of his clumsiness.

'I'm sorry,' he said. 'But I meant it. You seemed to have invaded every corner of my life. I think I'm in love with you.'

These were words he hadn't planned to say and he was taken aback.

'Well, you have a funny way of showing things, Michael. You should not conduct your love affairs over the boardroom table. It's a blurring of what is public and what is private. It looks like you got your way today by using me as a pawn.'

She got up and he stood in unison. She walked past him and left the room.

He sat again and looked straight ahead. The signing of the deal meant nothing and he cursed the signed papers in his bag for his victory was pyrrhic. He kicked the table leg again.

'Bugger.'

*

Mary reached the Gare de Lyon and she walked in front of its grandeur without giving it a second glance. She was looking for rue du Charolais, which she knew would bleed into rue Coriolis, her phone once again ringing in her bag to remind her of the world she'd turned her back on. The tracks were beyond the buildings to her right and every so often she saw through the gaps between them to the bridges and gantries beyond. Eventually, the road ran alongside the embankment and the trains on the nearest track seemed almost to brush the apartment blocks. Another one was approaching and she stopped to watch it pass, the great weight of the train transferred through the earth so that she felt its power in her legs. She estimated she must have walked two or three miles and there was still a way to go.

Rue Coriolis took a dogleg to the left and she came up to the main road and the green of the Bois de Vincennes on the other side. The scale of the railway was now clear to be seen, the splay of lines and the long sheds where, she guessed, the trains were stored and repaired. She was not far away from her destination and if she had forgotten the pain in her leg, her mind wasn't so easily overcome. She'd deliberately sought Mollet's face as it stared at her in the bedroom, the eyes transformed and without emotion, the mouth that she had once kissed narrowed and ugly. The image propelled her forward.

She turned off the main road. It was around here that she had been mugged, but she crossed the same grassy square without any qualms. This time, no one knew she was coming and she stood at the end of the footbridge looking along its length. She imagined the meeting would be finished by now and she was sure that one of the calls that she refused to take would have confirmed this. She wrapped a scarf around her face and set off over the tracks, darkness already closing in on her route. A brightly coloured commuter train scuttled by beneath, in front of the ruined signal box.

Mary's plan was only half formed, but she was carried forward by her anger and her resolve would make it happen. She came down the stairs, the windows of the old bar like eyes watching her and when she saw the apartment block, she paused in a doorway. There would be CCTV here, although she couldn't see any cameras. A calmness came down on her as the purpose of her mission was so close.

She watched his door and waited, blocking out her mother's voice demanding what are you doing girl? She was no child anymore.

She saw a young couple approach the entrance and she moved towards them as they pressed the code to open the door. She arrived as they went so it was perfectly normal for them to hold the door to allow her in. She nodded her thanks, the scarf still around her mouth. She didn't want to get in the lift with them, so she took the stairs to the next floor, where she waited before calling it again and taking it to the top floor. She estimated that Mollet, if he was coming back to the flat immediately, wouldn't get here yet. She would wait by the door that led to the stairs. She might be here for hours and from her rucksack she slid out what she had bought in the sports shop along with a bottle of water and a banana. She had all the time in the world.

Mary wouldn't answer her phone and he was uncertain whether to try Sophie. He called Stuart Phelps instead.

'Yeah, it's me. I've done the deal.'

He heard the whoop of delight and wished he could share some of the joy.

'Well done, Michael. You must be so pleased. When are you coming home to celebrate?'

'I'm not sure, Stu. I've one or two things to tie up here. Could you make sure the first tranche of money is released before close of business tonight.'

'Are you okay, Michael? You don't sound yourself.'

'It's been a long day already and I think this whole business has rather taken it out of me.'

'That's not like you. Ah, is it anything to do with that mystery woman you won't tell me about?'

'I'll fill you in on my movements later, Stu,' he said, irritated. 'Spread the word, would you? Cheers.'

He, Michael Finistere, was now an owner of part of Paris, one that would soon be transformed, but he remained untouched by this fact. In some part of his memory, he recalled a history master telling the class about one of Napoleon's great victories, he couldn't remember which one, that he couldn't take any pleasure from because when he rode back to his campaign tent there was no letter waiting for him from Josephine. He knew how he felt.

Night had fallen when she saw the yellow lift button glow. She began to prepare herself. If it was Mollet, she hoped he wouldn't look in her direction but do exactly what she'd imagined and move automatically to the door to his apartment. The hum of the lift came closer and in unison she felt the tension rise inside her. She pressed herself against the wall and her breathing became shallow. These were the last seconds of the life she used to know, she thought, watching the lift door slide open.

Mollet stepped out, searching in his pockets for his key. He walked towards his door unaware that Mary was approaching him from behind. She heard the key engage and she saw him drop the handle.

'Erik.'

He span round at the mention of his name and she saw the bewildered look on his face.

'I thought you might like to apologise to me. In person.'

She saw him smile.

The scarf was still around her mouth but she knew he could see her blackened eyes.

'Aren't you ashamed of what you did? How could you make love to me and then beat me up? What sort of man are you?'

'And you, Mary? What game were you playing? Getting close to me to soften me up for Finistere. Bitch.'

He spat the word at her and she took a step back.

'No, I did it because I found you attractive. I was wrong. I was deluded. You're a monster.'

He made a move towards her, faster than she expected, but she still had time to take the baseball bat from behind her back and swing at his head. She heard it strike home, a strangely hollow sound accompanied by a metallic ping. He crashed to the ground and lay still.

'That's Tosca's kiss for you, Erik Mollet.' And she kicked his leg, some-where to the side of the thigh at the same spot he had kicked her. She heard him grunt.

All her fury had gone into those blows, the pent up anger that had begun to accumulate in the surveyor's office and had grown ever since. She stared at the body, her energy ebbing away to be followed, she was appalled to register, by remorse. She could suddenly see what she had done and dropped the bat, her hands coming to cover her already hidden mouth.

'Oh, dear Lord, make him not be dead.'

She knelt down at his side and could see that he was still breathing.

'Thank you, thank you.'

She sat by his side, tears forming in her wounded eyes.

His feet were half inside the open apartment door and eventually she got up and propped open the door before holding his feet and attempting to drag him inside. He was surprisingly heavy and an irrational thought entered her mind, that this was the man who had lain on top of her, a weight that she had welcomed. The rugs on the wooden floors helped her slide him unceremoniously into the room, where she put him into the recovery position. She was about to leave when she saw the candlestick on the glass table. She picked it up and placed it by the side of his head.

'Whatever, Erik, God bless you.'

And she shut the door, before picking up the bat, putting it back into the rucksack and making for the stairs. The scarf was firmly in place as she clicked open the downstairs door and went out into the street where the last of the day was completely extinguished and night had taken over. She didn't want to take the footbridge back to the Métro, but instead turned right and headed for the Gare de Lyon from the river side of the tracks. She was strangely calm now, all the tension having left her chest. What she had done was entirely out of character, she thought, but then absolutely appropriate. It was a gesture that you saw in opera, that she had seen in an opera only last week.

When she got to the station, she sat on a bench under the great roof and took out her phone. Four missed calls from Finistere, two from Sophie and once again she tried her first.

'Where have you been?' were Sophie's first words, even before Mary had announced herself.

'I went to see Erik,' she said, in a small voice that reflected the exhaustion she was feeling.

'And?'

'I had one or two things so settle,' she said.

'I don't understand, Mary. Anyway, the deal has been signed. Erik did it this afternoon.'

'Good,' said Mary, although she experienced no sense of achievement. She might just as well have been told that it was going to rain in the morning.

'Where are you, for heaven's sake?'

'The Gare de Lyon.'

'Why? When can I see you? Have you contacted Michael yet? He knows he shouldn't have said what he did this morning. He's been trying to get you to say he's sorry.'

'I know. I just didn't feel strong enough to face him.'

'Why, Mary? What's happened?'

'I'm not really sure, Sophie. For the past few days I've been living someone else's life, not my own.'

'Speak to me. Tell me about it.'

'I can't for the moment, Sophie. I will, but not now.'

'Do you want me to phone Michael?'

'Would you? I'd appreciate that. I feel terribly tired.'

'Let me see you tomorrow morning.'

'Okay, that would be nice.' Mary could feel her voice fading away. 'Thank you Sophie.'

Mary took a cab back to the hotel and was asleep within seconds of collapsing on to her bed, fully clothed.

'Michael, it's me. Listen. I've just spoken to Mary and she's not herself. She went to see Erik this evening. I don't know what took place, but her voice was strange. I'm worried.'

'I'll go and see her immediately.'

'No, don't. She won't want that. I've arranged to see her in the morning at the hotel. I'll call you after that.'

'I'm sorry about earlier, Sophie. I thought I was doing the right thing.'

'It seems, Michael Finistere, that you simply don't understand how women work.'

37

The decision had been made for her, Sophie reflected, while straightening the cushions on her small sofa, beginning the routines she normally did before leaving to see her mother in Milan. Friday had arrived again, but this time it was different. She called her mother and told her that a friend needed her help and she would be unable to come. Although her mother remained silent, Sophie could feel her disappointment transmitted across eight hundred kilometres.

She had reclaimed her weekend, Saturday and Sunday belonged to her, although she found it hard to exult in the freedom it promised.

She texted Mary to warn her that she was on her way, deciding that she would leave talking to Michael until later.

The weather remained cold but the sky was a uniform blue and Paris continued its capricious ways with resident and visitor alike. For Sophie, walking down the hill towards the river, it ill-prepared her for what she saw when Mary opened her bedroom door.

'Oh Mary,' she said, shocked. 'You poor thing.'

Mary's bloodshot eyes stared out from her blackened face, both cheeks marbled with a red-blue crazy paving, her upper lip bruised and swollen and distorted. Sophie took her in her arms and she could feel Mary begin to weep. She guided her back into the room and sat her on the bed, pulling up a chair to sit opposite, taking her hands as the woman in front of her sobbed.

'Take your time, Mary. And then tell me who did this to you.'

Mary wiped her painful eyes and drew a deep breath.

'Mollet. It was Mollet. Here, in this room. He was waiting in the hall when I got back. He thought I had been spying on him.' She broke down, weeping and then, between sobs, struggled on. 'Except it was the other way around. He had used me. Oh, Sophie, I have been so stupid. I was taken in. I believed him, but it was a lie. And he beat me up, hit my face and then kicked my leg, up here,' she said, pointing to her upper thigh, 'and it was so painful I must have fainted.'

Sophie tightened the grip on her hands, knowing there was more to come. 'And I became someone else, someone I didn't recognise. Honestly. I was so full of hate, Sophie, taken over with it. I bought that.' She nodded her head to the corner of the room where the metal baseball bat was propped against the wall.

Sophie looked at her, half knowing what was coming next and already shaking her head in disbelief.

'I went to his flat and did to him what he'd done to me. I hid in his lobby, on the top floor, and waited until he was opening his door. And then I hit him as hard as I could and after he'd fallen I kicked him on the leg, exactly where he'd kicked me.' She dropped her head. 'I was glad, so glad and then, almost immediately, full of sadness. Do you understand?'

Mary's panda eyes were full of tears and Sophie could see that she was both appalled and frightened at what she had done and needed support. She smiled, which broke into a small single laugh.

'An eye for an eye. You were brave, Mary Houlihan. You beat him twice, once around the head and then again in business. Michael finished off the job, doing just as you said he should. Had this just happened, when you spoke to me?'

'Yes, he'd just left. I had to get to Finistere before the meeting, but I couldn't face speaking to him.'

'I knew something pretty bad must have taken place. I'm only glad Michael understood the message, because I didn't.'

'It's the sort of intrigue he likes,' she said and her broken lips formed a small, joyless smile.

Sophie pushed her chair further forward to examine Mary's face more carefully. 'I'll get some stuff from the chemist that will help. Lie down here and I'll be back.'

Mary did as she was told and found herself looking at the ceiling before the memory of the two Eriks in this room, the good and the bad, made her close her eyes, the pain unspecified but somewhere deep inside.

When she returned, Sophie carefully applied arnica cream to the bruised face of her new friend, smoothing it carefully with the tips of her fingers.

At first it simply deepened the bruising, but in time it would sooth and soften the damage.

'What will happen?' Mary asked the ceiling.

Sophie thought about the answer, her fingers continuing to work on the bruising.

'I assume he wasn't dead,' she said quietly.

'He was breathing when I left. Oh my God, I hope he woke up.'

'I imagine he had a pretty hard head, given what he was used to in the past. And, do you know, I don't think there's anything he can do.'

Sophie stood up and reached into her bag for her phone, before leaning over Mary to take a photo.

'There,' she said, 'evidence for the prosecution. Or defence.'

'Thank you, dear Sophie. And what of you and Michael?'

'He can be something of an oaf, can't he? I wonder if he's ever had to think about anyone else other than Mr Finistere?'

Mary had tilted her head and was watching Sophie from the bed.

'He wants me to go to London with him this weekend.'

'It might be a better bet than another trip to your mother.'

Sophie glanced across to her.

'I think you might be feeling a little stronger. I used you as an excuse this morning, when I told my mother I wouldn't be coming. I said a friend needed my help.'

'She did. I don't want to see Michael just yet. I don't feel strong enough. Will you tell him about Mollet, please?'

'Of course, Mary.'

'Do you want to go to London with him? You've changed him, Sophie, perhaps not enough yet, but he's different.'

Sophie patted her hand. 'I've brought you a few things for lunch. I'll call later and tell you what's going on. Be brave. And lock this door.'

Michael Finistere was not given to brooding. Introspection he regarded as an indulgence, but on this bright Friday morning in Paris his thoughts were racing through what had taken place the day before, events that seemed to run away with him and culminated in his purchase of the land. Along the way he appeared to have lost the assistant who had made the deal possible and the woman to whom he'd declared he was in love. How was this possible?

The perfect blue sky mocked him.

The bluster that would once have had him phoning Sophie had deserted him. He had to admit that he was a little afraid of her acerbic put-downs and knew that he was clinging to the relationship by his fingertips. Against his instincts, he decided discretion was the better part of valour. As to Mary, he had wounded her to the point of exasperation and, unable to speak to either woman, he blocked them out and busied himself with the details of work, answering emails, making sure the documents from yesterday's signing were copied and filed. The odds on Sophie coming with him to London were so small as to be negligible and rather than spend another weekend in Paris without her, he contemplated arranging the helicopter to take him to London. He was on the verge of calling Stu and asking to meet him at the club later.

When his phone began to ring and he saw that it was Sophie, he was stopped in his tracks. It was with a very tentative voice that he wished her good morning.

'A good morning for us, perhaps, but not for Mary. I'm at the Louxor, the place we went. Can you meet me here?'

He told her he'd be there as quickly as possible. It was more than he could have hoped for. He called reception for a taxi and ran to the bathroom for a rapid survey of how he looked, before dashing downstairs.

In the cab he thought about Sophie's words and wondered what had happened to Mary. His impatience almost overflowed as they ploughed slowly through the heavy traffic and he had reached no conclusion by the time they pulled up outside the old cinema. He was frustrated and apprehensive as he reached the top floor café, where the sun was just warm enough to allow her to sit on the terrace.

'I'm sorry,' he said, sitting by her side, opening lines that were now becoming all too familiar.

'I suppose I should have been flattered,' she said, rather surprising him. 'It's only I wasn't expecting such a declaration in those circumstances. Don't take it too badly.' She patted the top of his hand. 'Now, even more important, Mary. Mollet beat her up.'

She watched Michael stare back in astonishment.

'Christ. When?'

'Sometime yesterday, not long before the meeting.'

'The bastard. And then he sat with us, cool as that.'

'She was badly beaten. Her face is black and blue.'

'I'll kill the bastard.'

'Mary's already tried that.'

'What?'

'She hit him with a baseball bat?'

Michael half rose from his seat and then slumped back.

'She did what? Mary?'

'She knocked him unconscious and then she told me she kicked him hard, just as he had kicked her.'

Finistere was having trouble taking it all in and she watched him shake his head.

'Mary. I can't believe it.'

'No, she's surprised you again, hasn't she? You underestimate that girl at your peril, as I keep saying.'

'Is he okay? Not that I really care.'

'She thinks so, yes.'

'Does she want me to see her?'

'No, Michael. She thinks you wouldn't fully understand.'

'She's right.'

'Exactly. Mollet was on to you, couldn't quite work out why you'd changed your mind and wanted to complete the deal all of a sudden. In the end, it was Mary who made it possible, but only just and at considerable personal cost. She told him that you were probably in love with me and that I had, shall we say, softened you.'

She looked at Michael and she could see that once again he wasn't sure how to respond, that he was frightened of making another false move.

'And then she had the masterstroke, although I didn't understand it at the time, of telling Mollet you were having cold feet again, because of the depot and the migrants. It tipped the balance, but only just.'

This time, Finistere did get up and walk to the edge of the terrace to look down on the Métro tracks and the busy street. He had been in Paris for approaching two weeks and it was hard to piece together the process of events that had led to this moment. They appeared as chaotic as the people crisscrossing the pavements below and the two trains passing on the great metal bridge.

He returned to the table.

'Where is she?'

'At her hotel.'

'Is she safe?'

Sophie looked hard at him before answering.

'I think so. I told her to bolt the door from the inside. I said I'd be in touch after I had spoken to you.'

He thought of the helicopter and the flight back to London.

'I can't leave her.'

'We can't leave her, Michael.'

Now it was his turn to look more carefully at her.

'You're not going to your mother's?'

'No.'

'So we'll both be here in Paris?'

She watched him consider what this might mean and for the first time that morning, she saw him smile, a smile that touched every corner of his face.

'I don't know what to say.'

'Well', she said, 'that's a start, given what happened yesterday.'

Mary lay on the bed, her face calmer with the arnica and her mind more relieved now that she had spoken to Sophie. An eye for an eye, she had said, but was it? She knew she was more damaged, that the exchange wasn't equal. Mollet was untouched, the sex between them for him merely a means to an end. For her it had been so much more, the natural consequence of the comfort and trust she felt with this man. She was deceived and badly wounded, not just in body but in mind and she hoped the damage was not permanent, that it wouldn't colour all her future relationships.

Right now, alone in the room with the ceiling above her, she feared that it might and that the shadow of these days in Paris would haunt her forever.

38

There was an order to the camp, an unexpected neatness. It defied the numbers that now congregated below ground and Youssef saw that the floor space had been carefully apportioned, marked out with coloured rugs and patterned sheets, giving it a certain dignity. In just a few days, this had become a home.

Youssef's watch told him it was Friday and he knew that he would have to see her one more time before he left Paris, to reassure himself that the route to the future still existed, even if it meant spending another night down here, below ground. He resigned himself to fate, of which she was an integral part.

Walking the familiar route across Paris, he thought about the significant role she held in his life, a magical figure who represented the possibility of change, of freedom and of the world beyond. In the warehouse she had been given a name, Sophie, but this was too specific and he held firm to her larger significance, the spirit of a different life where, somehow, she was leading him. He had to see her today, to salute her one final time.

Did anyone notice his familiar route along the canal, across Place Bastille, in front of the Gare de Lyon? He had been taking this journey each Friday for several months, a pilgrimage of his own making, part of the faith he maintained in his own future. It was a ritual he couldn't desert, for it would mean abandoning hope, giving up, and without it, without this fixed point in his life, he would become untethered and even more at the mercy of uncertainty.

Through the narrow corridor of rue Coriolis, where he could almost reach out and touch the trains, onwards, wrapped in himself, alone in the strange city that had become home, but where he was not loved. The *passerelle* over the tracks focused the passage to his goal and he hardly saw the man walking towards him holding a bloody handkerchief to his forehead.

It was best not to meet the eyes of such strangers. On, through the old gate and down the concrete steps to the tracks, to pause as he always did under the footbridge. Here, his territory, beyond the city, with its own smells and secrets. The blue sky was brushed with grey as the late autumn dusk arrived and he followed the passage over the tracks, between the ever-present trains ready to swat him aside.

The graffiti was waiting to welcome him and he rested against the multi-coloured background that granted him immediate anonymity. He closed his eyes and let the moment take him, his body becoming lighter, his weariness and despair banished for these precious seconds. He remained still until he felt the first tremors, the future approaching, heavy with purpose, the ground shivering in anticipation. This was the only point in the week when time mattered and his watch, just beginning to glow, confirmed exactly where he stood in the world.

Louder now and, just as he always did, the exact steps of the ceremony observed, he moved away from the wall and stood in preparation. The train loomed on him, pulling its way forwards, taking with it those who were gifted with this essential journey to another world. And he waited, as he always waited, full of expectation, counting the carriages, part of the litany he knew by heart.

Twelve, thirteen and now, at last, fourteen. The windows, flashing the final seconds, came and went.

And then there was nothing, only a golden rectangle where she should have been and his eyes followed its emptiness. His arm rose in protest, a tiny gesture that meant nothing against the giant hulk of the train. She was not there and in that instant everything was gone, the rush of air whipping his clothing, his arm slowly falling to his side, his hopes crushed.

Youssef stood there as the night prepared to claim him, just as his future disappeared along the curve of the track.

Mary looked at her watch. Just after six. She had been asleep for several hours and she approached the bathroom mirror tentatively, keeping her eyes lowered until the last minute. The bruising had receded, although she still looked what her mother might have called a fright. Despite the hollowness inside, she had gathered just enough strength to observe her predicament and decide that she had to move forward, or risk falling apart. She stripped off her clothes, rubbed the blue patch at the top of her thigh in the hope that she might erase the ugly colour and stepped under the water. It was a beginning, the first stage of recovery, a small gesture but one that enabled her to dress and at least entertain the idea of what she should do next. The void of the weekend appeared before her, a black hole into which she was frightened to fall. She would have to phone Finistere and the thought made her sit, naked, on the bed. It was almost two weeks since she'd taken the Eurostar to follow Finistere's helicopter and she considered how much of that woman, Round Mary, still existed. She had been eviscerated and the remains of what she had been lay scattered in pieces around her.

You can't sit there moping, she had been told by her mother and some part of her felt the same as the teenager being admonished all those years ago.

It was inevitable that she called Finistere. She had the distance of the phone, at least, and if she cried she could always end the call. But she didn't and her head became surprisingly clear the moment he spoke.

'You've been in the wars,' he said and she thought there was concern in his voice.

'Yes, it was unpleasant and something of a shock. I hadn't thought that Mollet could do that.'

'Do you want me to call the police?'

'No.' Her answer was lightening quick.

'So, what next? What would you like to do?'

'You signed the deal.'

'I did. Thanks to you. Your idea was perfect. I called his bluff by saying he could keep the depot with all the migrants. Thank goodness you spoke to Sophie.'

Mary could feel her brain begin to stir, a bear moving after a long winter's hibernation, slow and clumsy at first.

'I don't suppose you feel like celebrating your success?' he said.

She thought about this statement and what it represented. Did he really see the purchase of Les Merchandises as her achievement, or was it said to make her feel better? Soft soap. Her mother again.

'I could take you to the Plaza Athénée. Michelin stars, just right.'

She thought of her wounded face and imagined how she would stand out in grand surroundings, fussed over by waiters at her side and with nowhere to hide.

'Somewhere quieter, perhaps. And darker.'

'Leave it to me,' he said and she knew he would phone Sophie. Could she cope with sitting with them as a couple, her on the outside looking in?

'And perhaps not tonight. I think it's too soon. Tomorrow. And we need to talk first.'

'Whenever you're ready, Mary.'

'Are you free tomorrow morning?'

'Of course. Ten o'clock at Les Merchandises? Are you sure?'

'I'm sure, Michael. Thank you. I'll see you in the morning.'

She was getting cold and so she dressed, avoiding any clothing with connotations to Mollet. She was beginning to take charge and bit by bit her old self was creeping back, limping and licking its wounds.

Youssef was sitting under the footbridge when his phone rang and he saw it was Mary. He waited for a train to rattle by outside before responding.

'Yes,' he said quietly, hoping the light from the phone didn't show, curling his body to block it off.

'Will you be at the depot tomorrow morning?'

'Depot?'

'The camp, underground.'

Youssef thought about this, for it had been his intention to leave early and begin the journey to Calais. He had only a rough idea of how this was possible, but he had travelled across Europe this way and the journey held few fears.

'Why?'

'I am bringing Michael and Sophie with me to talk to you.'

Sophie. Is this the reason she wasn't on the train? He was going to meet her? It was meant. The emptiness he experienced when he saw the blank window of coach fourteen was suddenly banished, miraculously justified. Fate had taken his hand and was showing him the way.

'Yes,' he said, more firmly. 'Yes, I will be there.'

'Will you tell your guards to expect us, about ten o'clock? Thank you, Youssef.'

He stood and looked towards the horizon, where a halo of light formed a dome over Paris, a glow he imagined emanating from Sophie, a single figure somewhere in the heart of the city.

In the darkness it was dangerous on the tracks and it was easy to trip and fall. A train approaching on the next track hooting a warning, although Youssef doubted that he could be seen. What folly it would be if he was knocked down and killed, finished in this no man's land he called his own. He climbed the old staircase with some relief and sat on the top step.

Sophie was ironing, a repetitive task that enabled her to think of other things. The window was open behind her and although the night was cool, she enjoyed the freshness that entered the room to finally clear out the stuffiness of summer.

She had just finished talking to Michael, who had told her about Mary and the proposed celebration the following night.

'Do you think it's a good idea that I'm there?' she had asked.

'Why not?'

His response had irritated her.

'Well, think about it Michael. Mary has just been beaten up by the man she'd just begun a relationship with. She doesn't want us holding hands in front of her, don't you see?' She had thought he didn't. 'If she wants me there, she'll let me know.'

'Well, Mary wants to go somewhere not too grand and not too bright,' he said, clearly put out.

'I'll come up with somewhere,' she had said, and that had been that.

She ironed a crease in the sleeves of her favourite black linen jacket and slipped it on a hanger just as her phone rang again. She thought it might have been Michael again, but Mary's name showed.

'How are you feeling?'

'Somewhat restored,' Mary said. 'Thanks to you. I still look ghastly but not quite the monster I was earlier.'

'Michael phoned. Said that you were going to celebrate tomorrow night.'

'He suggested the Plaza Athénée. I've just looked it up. Me, in there, looking like this. I asked for somewhere darker and more casual.'

'Yes, that's what he's just told me. He doesn't understand sometimes, does he? He wants me to choose somewhere for you.'

'I thought he might. Will you come, please?'

'You don't want me there, surely?'

'I think I do. And, one more thing. Can you meet us at Les Merchandises at ten tomorrow?'

'But of course, Mary. This is your success.'

'It doesn't quite feel like that, Sophie, and I have to admit that it's strange to think that the land now belongs to Michael.'

'Yes, he owns part of a city he hates.'

'I think he looks at it slightly more kindly knowing that you're part of it.'

Yes, Sophie thought, I believe he does.

'*À demain*, Mary.'

Sophie stood at the open window, holding herself in her arms and thought about what Mary had just said, the lights on the Périphérique continuing on their relentless way in the distance.

39

Michael Finistere left a trail in the first frost of winter, faint footprints on the concrete car park, the marks of ownership. It was early and the sun had yet to show on the horizon. Sleep had eluded him and it was a relief to leave the hotel and take a taxi to the site, the new outpost of his empire.

It was even colder in the warehouse and he walked around each of the floors, his every breath revealed in the air as he paced out his territory. On the fifth floor, he turned on the lights and warmed himself under the faint heat they emitted, remembering the time they had gathered around the model and he had met Sophie Arditti for the first time. Just twelve days divided the man who was disinclined to buy the land in the city he disliked and had no intention of falling in love from the one who stood here now, hands shoved deep into his chino pockets, a grey scarf wound around his neck. He would see them arrive from up here and it would allow him further time to prepare himself to greet the two women to whom he'd been blind that Monday morning.

In two years or so he would sell the completed development and, based on the figures that Stuart had emailed him late the night before, the profits would make the initial investment in the land, on which he now stood, appear ridiculously small, all made possible by the instincts of Mary Houlihan. He walked slowly across the floor and through the far window he saw the blue-and-yellow livery of a Eurostar train slide towards the Gare du Nord. She might once again bring hot coffee in a flask, but the woman who would hand it to him would be different. Just how different he could not see until some time later when, even from the height of the top floor, he observed her damaged face and the way she carried her leg.

He came down the stairs to meet them in the car park and in the cold light of the morning that face was almost unrecognisable. The relationship he had with Mary was formal to the point of severe, but this morning in Paris he took her in his arms. He felt uneasy doing so, but it was the only gesture that matched the damage she had suffered on his behalf.

'I'm so sorry, Mary. I had no idea.'

'It was worse yesterday,' Mary said, pulling away, 'and soon you won't know it ever happened.'

Sophie stood to one side and watched this curious exchange, the artificial embrace and Michael's awkwardness. He was having to change his approach to the woman who worked for him, a new entity, and he was still learning. He was equally unsure when he turned towards her, but Mary intervened to help the moment.

'We should go down. They'll be waiting for us.'

If Finistere wondered exactly who she meant by they, he kept it to himself.

As they set off towards the back of the warehouses it dawned on Mary that this means of entry, Youssef's route, was now redundant, but having come this far there was no point in turning back.

'We should have entered at Clignancourt,' she said over her shoulder by way of apology, as they slipped through the railings, 'but too late.'

All this was new to Sophie and she slithered down the embankment even further amazed by Mary, a feeling that increased tenfold in the tunnel when the two dark figures stepped out of the shadows and escorted them along to the doors and the depot.

The great space was now full, the access lines neatly dividing the floor, stamping it in just two short days as a refugee camp. Sophie was astonished at the number of people spread before her, an underground panorama that was almost beyond her imagination. She paused to take in the quiet and ordered humanity that had reduced Finistere to silence. Mary was already ahead of them and they hurried to catch up.

Youssef saw them arrive, his eyes fixed on Sophie, hardly believing that she was real. It was magic that had transported her from the train to be here, now, by his side and he whispered a quiet *inshallah*. Then he saw Mary's blackened face and knew at once she had been beaten, for his own face had looked like this on more than one occasion.

'Sophie, this is Youssef, my friend,' Mary said.

Youssef saw that she held out her hand and he wondered if he dare touch it for fear of discovering it wasn't there, that what he was seeing was just part of a dream that didn't really exist.

'Hello, Youssef.'

She was smiling and her hand was in front of him. He reached and touched it, its warmth and softness sending a slow charge of energy through him, bleeding through his arm to his body,

'You weren't on the train,' he said, almost to himself, his wide, dark eyes seeking an explanation. 'Every week I have watched you leave.'

If Sophie wondered how this was possible, her face didn't show it and she kept her surprise to herself.

'No, not this week. This week I knew that I would be meeting you.'

She watched Youssef nod, as if this was the explanation he'd been expecting. He was still holding her hand and she leaned forward to take the other, his big eyes still watching her. She couldn't think how he'd seen her on the train, but it somehow didn't matter, just another part of the extraordinary morning that was unfurling before her.

Finistere, who had been shocked into silence by the sight of the migrants in their orderly lines, even more than had been there the day before, watched the strange play between the boy and Sophie. Youssef's look was caught between reverence and disbelief and it appeared to Finistere that he held her hands for fear she might disappear, for proof she existed. Perhaps he was drawing something from her, that her touch was vital and in this he felt sympathy.

'What do you think of them all, Michael, the people down here?'

Even through her bruising, Finistere could see Mary's eyes, the look of determination with which he was becoming familiar.

'They're extraordinary, don't you agree? Youssef helped this happen, as you know. I have a question for you Michael. Will you let them stay?'

Finistere, who had turned to look at the hundreds of figures laid out before him, was thinking of the artist Lowry and his stick figures milling around a Northern street scene. He shook his head, unable to respond.

'Winter is coming and they have nowhere else to go. They need help. They need you.'

'How long have you been thinking this?' he asked, still not prepared to answer to her questions.

'Probably since I made the walk alone through the underpass, not long after we got here. Certainly since I met Youssef.'

Sophie looked on at a drama in which she was, once again, only a bit player, waiting for Michael to answer, and what he said was suddenly very important to her.

'I'll have to give it some thought,' she heard him say and, for her, it was the wrong answer.

Finistere could see the steeliness in Mary and he thought he saw something of himself there. His life had been lived beyond the troubles of these migrants, in a world where they barely touched his consciousness. He had never given them a second thought and, if he was truthful, when he'd seen the camp originally, he'd seen them merely as a nuisance, one that the French police could deal with easily, as Mollet had explained.

'You own this land,' Mary said, almost as though she'd heard his thoughts, 'and you can decide whether they stay or go, whether this young boy, Youssef, has a place for the night, or not.'

Finistere wanted to say that the migrants had nothing to do with him, that his decisions were pragmatic and economic and shorn of emotional demands. He knew it was not what Mary wanted to hear and, given the way Sophie was regarding him, it wouldn't go down too well with her either. He said nothing and tucked his chin into his scarf.

Youssef still had hold of one of Sophie's hands and from time to time he looked up at her face. He believed that fate, in the form of Sophie, had literally taken him by the hand, that to fight it was impossible and that what was happening was inevitable. If kindness was an almost forgotten experience for him, this was beyond even that and belonged not to the world of the here and now, but to somewhere much higher. His walk to Calais broke to pieces in his mind, pushed aside by the woman who held his hand, a hand he feared to release. Perhaps it was she who would lead him to Suliman.

'Tell me, Youssef, do you have any family?' he heard Mary ask and in that instant his mother was flying, open-armed towards him once more, so quickly that he ducked, the image so real. It lasted no more than a second, a flash frame and it was gone.

'Are you okay, Youssef? I'm sorry, perhaps I should not have asked.'

The flashback had been prompted by her question and Youssef thought

that in that brief, vivid second, his brother must have been standing somewhere as well, waiting for him to leave the smashed school.

In the end, he spoke. 'I have a brother, Suliman. I think he is in Calais.
I was going to leave today to find him, but you came instead.'

'Perhaps we can help you find him?' Mary said.

Finistere watched with a detached fascination at what was taking place,
so far removed from his day-to-day experience, far distant from the agenda
he had set out with barely a fortnight earlier. Sophie appeared to have overwhelmed the boy and Mary was talking as if he, Michael Finistere, didn't
exist. The look of concern on Sophie's face made her twice as beautiful, the
only reason, he thought, that he remained part of all this.

'Michael,' Mary said, cutting across his thoughts, 'you need to speak to
the police. Tell them that this land is now yours. That you're aware that the
refugees are down here and they have your permission.'

Mary had never spoken to Finistere in this way, but her statements were
out before she had time to think for their logic, she thought, was beyond
question.

Finistere heard her with a certain coolness, his attention shifting from
her to the mass of humanity enclosed by the depot and the low murmur
of conversation that rose into the great space. He wanted no part of them
and what they represented. He could afford not to. He turned back and
saw that the boy was still holding Sophie's hand. The shape of the watch
showed just below the jagged ends of his pullover and despite the innocent
look on his face, Finistere still believed it had been stolen. When he looked
at the boy's face, he saw that his eyes were on him and Finistere turned to
Mary, who was watching and still waiting for an answer.

'You don't know the first thing about the boy,' he said.

'I know that he needs help.'

Finistere shrugged and at that very moment entertained the smallest
doubt about the deal he'd just completed. Sophie was also studying him,
also waiting for an answer, he thought. He felt trapped between the women
and the mass of humanity behind him.

'I need to give this some thought,' he said, registering the look that
flashed between the two women. Bugger them, he thought.

Mary could see the set of Finistere's shoulders, a bullish resistance, and
it signalled that her hopes for the morning, that his shock and resulting

sympathy from her appearance would somehow soften him, had failed. She supposed that later Sophie, if she felt so inclined, might persuade him, but for now the purpose of their time in Paris appeared to have come to an end.

'I will see you later,' she said to Youssef, who slowly released Sophie's hand.

He watched them leave and an awful sense of finality came over him for he knew that he would not see her again. Sophie turned by the doors and saw his face, all hope beginning to drain away. She decided she would walk back to her flat alone.

Finistere was quiet in the taxi as it dropped down the hill towards the Lancaster and Mary knew that her suggestion about the people in the depot had fallen on stony ground. At the same time though, as far as Sophie was concerned, it had left him in a quandary.

She was glad that he hadn't asked more about Mollet, for her emotions were still raw as the taxi bumped over the cobbles at Place de la Concorde and crossed the Seine on to the other bank. She was disappointed that Finistere, who stood to make even more money from the project than he'd planned, could not entertain the idea of spending even a little of it on the refugees. She thought his attitude singularly ungenerous. And she had a fairly good idea what Sophie would make of it, too. As for Youssef, just as they left the depot, departing through the double doors, she had turned to see him watching their leaving, his face that of an abandoned child alone in a window.

40

Youssef watched until they disappeared and a coldness ran through his body. His hand, which had been warmed by Sophie's, was now icy and he was gripped by an ominous feeling that even his disorganised and fractured world would never be the same again. He was being left behind and the trust that he'd felt for the few moments he had been with the two women had now evaporated leaving him, even amongst these hundreds of people, entirely alone.

It was no surprise to him when later in the morning Hakim sought him out.

'You've heard?'

Youssef knew that it would be bad news even before he spoke and inside he prayed that it had nothing to do with Suliman. His prayer was only partially answered.

'It's Calais. The camp has now been completely destroyed. The French have moved everyone out, taken them to places all over France. Hopefully your brother is one of the lucky ones.'

Youssef knew he should receive this as a reassurance, but he could take no comfort from his words. He was predisposed to believe that nothing good could happen now. He returned to his bench and lay on his bedding.

Mary and Finistere barely spoke in the taxi which, having dropped him at the Lancaster, took her along to her own hotel.

Back in his suite, Finistere picked up one of the delicate silk cushions from the nearest chair and flung it across the room, knocking over a vase that bounced harmlessly on the thick carpet. He knew what he felt, but he wanted someone to tell him he was right. He called Stuart Phelps.

'The place is full of migrants,' he said without preamble. 'The depot, underground, full of the buggers. And I'm supposed to do something about it.'

Phelps, who was used to disentangling these typical outbursts, calmly asked for a little more detail.

'They knocked down the migrant camp just outside the development, then the buggers all came inside. And now Mary wants it to be my, our, responsibility. I ask you.'

'What a bore,' Phelps said in sympathy. 'But if I know the French police, they'll move them on pretty soon. If you wanted, you could give them a call.'

Finistere, now walking up and down the room, thought this wasn't a bad idea. No one needed to know and it would solve the problem without getting his hands dirty.

'It's a thought.'

'But...?'

'Mary couldn't find out?'

'Why would she? It's not her decision, surely?'

'No.'

'You don't sound certain.' *(should it be Phelps ??)*

And then Finistere heard the penny drop.

'It's that other woman, isn't it?'

Finistere took a few more paces before answering.

'Could be.'

'And she wouldn't like you to call the police either. Well, you could always just wait and I'm sure it would happen anyway. One way or the other. Whoever this woman is, she's obviously really got to you.'

'But we don't want them, do we? The migrants I mean. They're not our responsibility.'

'Heavens, no. Pain in the ass.'

It was what Finistere wanted to hear. 'Thanks, Stu. Despite all this, we've got a bargain. I'll call you later. I may even fly back.'

It was only as he said this that he remembered he was having supper with Mary and Sophie the following day. Did he think it would happen? The phone was still in his hand but something inside told him he couldn't phone Sophie. But what? Could it be because he didn't want to, or was it that he knew he would receive a fairly frosty response? Or perhaps the former was the result of the latter. If things had been different, if Youssef and his mob had not materialised on his doorstep, he might have been in London with her now and the very thought of this made him pick up the cushion from the floor and fling it back to the sofa.

The walk had been good for Sophie. Her progress up the steep slope to her road was slow and deliberate, in line with her thoughts. The boy's eyes were still on her and the coldness of his hand remained on her palm. Her breath smoked the air and Paris was unnaturally still. She was weighing in her mind the fine margin between right and wrong, how people are defined by their reactions and decisions. But for the boy and his fellow migrants, she might now be in Mayfair, a world a million miles removed, and she would not have witnessed Michael's behaviour underground.

She let herself into her building, up the worn wooden stairs to her flat that this late morning seemed more like a sanctuary than ever. Still preoccupied by her thoughts, she made coffee, brought a tray over to the table by the window and sat looking over the slopes she had just climbed. She imagined that from here she might later be able to see the construction work on the site, the building of the two blocks to replace the warehouses and the landscaping of the development. It wouldn't be long before memories of what that corner of Paris once looked like had been forgotten. And somewhere in London Michael Finistere, who would probably dislike the replacement as much as the original, would be richer than ever.

Sophie refilled her cup, the sharp aroma of the dark coffee mixing with the softer smells of the flat. She supposed she had known in the meeting with Mollet in the hotel, although it wasn't simply his inappropriate declaration of love. His reaction to the boy was strangely cold and, as far as she could see, he viewed the refugees as a mild irritant that could and should be brushed away. Michael Finistere was relentless in the pursuit of what he wanted and she, Sophie Arditti, was simply another goal for him. Looking at it now, sitting here above Paris, she couldn't even feel flattered. For her, he had been a means to an end, however unwitting for both of them. He had helped her break the repeated cycle of regret she had been trapped in since the breakup of her affair and the resulting loss of her role as Tosca.

Somehow it felt like an end and she couldn't imagine the dinner tomorrow night could ever take place.

*

Mary's dissatisfaction was profound. The colours in her face appeared to have darkened in sympathy with her thoughts, the edges of her blackened eyes turning a sulphurous yellow. The futile exchanges in the depot with Finistere had exhausted her, his lack of sympathy a shock. He gave the impression that he didn't care for the humans gathering for shelter under the property he now owned. A small gesture, however temporary, would have been a concession but as far as she could see, he remained unmoved by their plight.

She didn't have the energy to confront him again now and slumped on the bed, her eyes closing on her wounded face.

Something told Youssef that this might be his last Saturday in Paris and he had climbed once again to the buddleia camp above the tunnel. He was reversing what he had done earlier, unclipping his watch to replace it behind the loose brick to join his other possessions. He pushed it back into place, wiping away with his sleeve any mark that might give the hiding place away. The day was still and cold and he felt that a heavy hand was pressing down on Paris. He returned underground and lay on his bedding on the bench, the ceiling far above him, and waited for what he regarded as inevitable.

ACT THREE

42

The police came from two directions, but silently this time, surprising and then disarming the men posted as guards at either end of the tunnel. There was no banging of baton against shield, no deliberate attempt to induce fear and chaos and this approach was altogether more sinister.

Youssef, lying on his bedding that late Saturday afternoon had already imagined it, given himself up to whatever fate had in store for him next. Even when the lines of police burst through the double doors, three abreast to spread out in line right, left and centre, he didn't move from his bench but turned his head to watch the dark blue figures filter menacingly into the great space. It was only when the first object was hurled at them, followed by the raising of sticks and other improvised weapons, that the mood changed and the police came together in two giant sweeps and, standing side by side, began to corral the migrants at either end of the depot.

Youssef watched the men and boys react like trapped animals, screaming and joining forces to push against the black lines of police, who had now raised their batons and were beating back the figures that confronted them, the roars of pain and anger echoing and magnified in the enclosed underground space.

Youssef, on the bench against the wall, was partly hidden under his bedding and he now pulled this further up so most of his face was hidden. Fighting had broken out, with tightly grouped teams of quick-moving police allowed through their own cordons to pinpoint and subdue key individuals, which they did with practised brutality. Heads were beaten and Youssef watched as men fell unconscious to the floor. There were fewer police than migrants, but they were armed and organised and showed no restraint in their suppression. He saw the policeman closest to him, a big man, his face hidden behind a tight balaclava, knock two refugees to the ground and set about them with his boot and baton repeatedly hitting the men's heads until they lay still. This was a secret arena, hidden underground, free from the gaze of others and the violence of the police was uncontrolled and abandoned.

Youssef was waiting for the big policeman to turn in his direction and had given himself up to the inevitability that this would happen. He was irrationally glad that he'd had the foresight to hide his watch.

The police, drilled and working as two units, began to encircle the migrants at opposite ends of the depot and would soon begin to push them towards the doors and drive them into the tunnels. When the smoke began to billow in the farthest corner, Youssef's first instinct was that it had been deliberately started by the refugees as a way of confusing the police. However, when he saw the police begin to slip on breathing apparatus he changed his mind.

It was now that fear overtook Youssef's resignation. The smoke was billowing from both ends of the depot and against the far wall, beyond the fighting, he saw the first flames lick into life and he quickly dampened one of his blankets with water from a bottle under the bench. There was panic and a wildness took over, migrants desperate and fighting their way towards the doors, seemingly oblivious of the repeated blows they received, bodies falling unconscious to the floor, tripping others as they lay.

The smoke had thickened and Youssef, his blanket over his head and lower part of his face, worked his way along the nearest wall towards the doors. As the smoke belched and drifted, he could see the broken bodies lying on the ground, the blood gathering around their heads. It was impossible to get near the door and people ahead of him were being crushed in their desperation to leave. Youssef slumped to the ground, his back against the wall and pulled the blanket around his head. He waited and what happened next was played out as a series of terrible sounds that he could only think came from the gateway to hell.

Youssef, curled up in himself, thought he could survive the smoke, but if the flames took hold there would be no hope. He could hear the muffled roars of the police behind their masks, shouting insults, the sort that he'd heard many times before and he wondered, as he always did, at their unrestrained hate. He assumed it must be from their own fear and dislike of anyone different, who didn't conform to their way of life. Perhaps he could entertain these rational thoughts because some part of him had given up the will to live, the limbo of his existence and his exhaustion from his endless journey combining to finally defeat him.

When his mother appeared again it was different. He saw it not through shock and surprise but with a mind that had finally made sense of this moment. He had accepted the truth, allowed it into his consciousness to take its correct proportion, however terrible, in his memory. He knew now that the second bomb had landed outside the school, where she had been standing, in the seconds before he and his other classmates, who had survived the first, were running towards the school exit. As he pushed open the door, the blast had lifted his mother off her feet and flung her towards her son. For the space of perhaps less than a second he saw her, or perhaps more truthfully he had subliminally registered one frame of the image of her in flight before the blast had knocked him unconscious. That terrible instant, which had been with him ever since, one tiny moment that had taken over his life, he could make sense of for the first time. It had taken one horror to release another.

It was the sound of the fire coming closer that brought him quickly to his feet. The bodies were piled around the exit and there were a few people still left standing around him, lost and bewildered. Piles of bedding were on fire and Youssef peered through the smoke at the figures laying sprawled around him, human beings who had so carefully and neatly organised themselves over the past two days, only now to be smashed into chaos. Although he held the damp wool against his face, the smoke was making him cough, burning his chest, and he began to crawl over his fallen comrades to the tunnel. The draft was sucking the smoke towards the marshalling yard and he stumbled off in that direction. And then he stopped and turned. An orange glow of flame lit up the doorway and he was caught, his instinct to flee checked by the thought of all the bodies still trapped underground. He let out a yell, a roar that filled the tunnel and rebounded along its length.

When he reached the tunnel entrance he fell gasping to the floor, sucking in the clean air, his chest at first unable to give him much, before coughing doubled him up. He lay there, on the dirty sleepers, too exhausted to move.

He slept, or blacked-out, he wasn't sure but a buzzing in his chest woke him and he moved his hand towards the noise, thinking it might be something physical in his body, an organ giving out. When he discovered his phone, he wanted to stop the noise for it would only attract attention. He pulled it out and answered it as quickly as his aching body allowed.

'Hello, hello? Is that Youssef? Youssef, speak to me. Are you alright?'

After what he had just been through it seemed impossible that he would ever hear Mary's voice again.

'Yes, it's me. Youssef.'

His words were thick and almost inaudible.

'What's the matter, Youssef. Has something happened to you?'

'It's the end. It's finished.'

'What? What are you saying, Youssef?'

'They have come for us.'

Even as he said this he heard the sound of approaching feet and he looked up to see the figure of a big policeman looming towards him, beating his baton into his palm, his silhouette blue-black and featureless in the dusk.

'Youssef, are you there?'

The man stood above him and then sank to his haunches and Youssef saw that it was the policeman who had beaten him up and threatened to tear his mother's photograph. As he stood, he ripped the blanket from Youssef's face.

'In the bushes above the tunnel,' Youssef said into the phone seconds before the boot smashed it out of his hands.

'It's you again. Fucking Arab.'

He yanked the boy to his feet. 'I told you what I would do, didn't I, you little fuck? Didn't you believe me?' Picking the boy up so his feet didn't touch the ground, he took him into the mouth of the tunnel and thrust him hard against the dirty wall.

'Now you have a phone. Stole that as well did you? We don't want your sort here. Understand? Don't. Want. You. At all.'

Youssef looked at the man, encased in the dark uniform padded with armour, the helmet on his head and the coldness in his eyes. He was pulled yet further into the tunnel but continued to look the man in the face, knowing what was to follow but unafraid, giving himself up to destiny as he was swallowed into the darkness.

'Youssef. Youssef,' she continued to yell at the phone until she saw that the connection had been broken. 'Oh Youssef.'

For Mary, Sunday evening had approached as a threat, reminding her of the same day a week ago, a time that belonged to another world. The memory mocked her, the thought of what they had done in this room that day. She was feeling sorry for herself and it wasn't until she tried to imagine how Youssef might be spending his evening that she had begun to pull herself together. Mollet had received her response and if parity would never be fully restored, Mary had acquitted herself reasonably well. But the boy's life remained unchanged, all his days the same, no difference between weekend and weekday, nothing to look forward to and plan for. It was this thought that made her phone him and the resulting, staccato exchanges continued to play in her head.

What was happening and what could she do? And what did he mean by 'in the bushes above the tunnel'? Hadn't Youssef said that 'they had come for him'? It was dark outside and dusk was beginning to close on the Paris weekend. The camp would soon be in darkness, but what was happening underground? Mary wrapped herself in warm clothes, found the torch, anxiety growing in her all the time. She took a taxi to rue Poissoniers, intending to be dropped off at Clignancourt but the road was cordoned off with tape.

She paid the taxi and stood in horror. Blue lights flashed everywhere and the sirens from arriving and departing ambulances shrieked in her ear. Beyond the wall surrounding the marshalling yard, she could see billowing smoke lit by powerful lamps. A door into the wall was open and paramedics, their faces hidden by breathing equipment, were entering with stretchers. Mary's hand was covering her mouth, not as a defence against the smoke but as an involuntary action of despair. As much as she was held in place by what was happening in front of her, she knew she had to get to the warehouses on the other side of the yard and she forced herself away. She began to run, not really sure where she was going but guided by further lights and sirens. When she arrived at the lorry park, she saw several fire engines in the process of spraying great columns of water over the brick warehouses, lines of hoses feeding through the doors into the buildings. The cordon was only rudimentary here and not patrolled so she worked her way forward. It was only as she arrived close to the buildings that she understood that they weren't on fire and in that awful moment knew that the flames had to be underground. She steadied herself against the body of a fire engine and thought she might faint. Pushing herself away, she began to run towards the side of the second warehouse but stopped at the sudden darkness she encountered the moment she turned the corner. She waited for her eyes to adjust before feeling her way forwards towards the shrubs and as she did she could see the metal fence above her, powerfully lit from behind. She worked her way forwards over the damp ground until she reached the top where she stopped, hardly able to believe the scene below. Smoke belched from the mouth of the tunnel from which relays of stretcher bearers crossed each other, some leaving carrying bodies, others running into the smoke carrying their stretchers upright. In the distance she could see the casualties being ferried like a line of ants up towards the passage that led to Clignancourt.

Mary moved the two uprights aside and slid through. She sat and watched between her fingers, her sobbing unheard, the white light from the emergency lamps taking the colour from her face and highlighting the tears that ran uncontrolled from her blackened eyes down her face. Never in her life had she felt so helpless, so small and so lost.

She had to get down there, but she began to take the slope too quickly and rolled forward, her hands desperately trying to get a grip on the wet grass, tumbling and skidding before crashing to the level of the tracks. Two men were shouting at her in French and they helped her to her feet. She was winded and between breaths, pointing at the tunnel entrance, she tried to tell them about Youssef. The policemen called over a colleague.

'You cannot be here, *madame*. This land is private and there has been an accident. You must leave.'

'But I know someone in the tunnel.'

'How is that possible, *madame*? They are all migrants. You must go home. Take her,' he said and the first two policemen took her arms and guided her to the path up to Clignancourt.

'You don't understand,' Mary said, but it was to herself. 'He's just a boy.' She screamed out Youssef's name but her voice was lost in the commotion.

They led her up the path that narrowed before emerging at the road, where two ambulances flashed their angry lights.

'*Allez*,' they said, gesturing for her to walk away. She sat on a bench and when it became too cold she took a taxi to the hotel, her body, like her mind, numb, empty and finished.

*

It was around eleven that Finistere called Stu from the Lancaster. In his hand he had a large glass of cognac.

'Cheers,' he said, banging the glass against the phone. He knew that Stu would be at the club and he heard a reciprocal echo.

'Her name is Sophie, Stu. And before you ask, there's not much to tell.'

Phelps waited for him to continue.

'I met her a couple of weeks ago and before you ask again, nothing has happened. She's the translator we've been using.'

'Sounds like quite a lot has happened, if you don't mind me saying. I've not heard you like this before.'

'Well that's as maybe. Trouble is, she thinks the same as Mary.'

'About the migrants?'

'About a lot of things.'

'I don't get it,' Phelps said. 'When have you ever listened to Mary, or anyone else for that matter? It must be this Sophie woman.'

'She's an opera singer.'

'Good lord. Not your usually territory then.'

'I thought she might be coming here with me to London this weekend. I don't get it.'

'I think I'm the one who should be saying that. It's not like you, this hesitation.'

'That's why I'm here in this bloody hotel in the middle of Paris. By myself. Couldn't stand it any longer. The whole thing's been difficult.'

'Still, we've done the deal.'

Michael Finistere had to admit that he felt little joy in the celebration, but, as he usually did, he pushed his mood to one side.

'Bloody women.'

'Did you make the call, by the way?'

There was a short pause.

'That would be telling, Stu.'

'Bloody women,' he agreed.

42

Mary woke fully clothed and slumped in a chair in front of the television in her hotel bedroom. On the screen, a woman in white, in an all-white room, was advertising tampons. It took a few seconds before the memory of the night before flooded over her and despite the ache in her body, she stood, compelled to take action but uncertain what to do. The sight of the stretchers streaming out the tunnel remained with her, played on a never-ending loop. Once back at the hotel, the news channel had told her what had happened, a tragic fire that had trapped the migrants underground. At some stage she must have fallen asleep and she sought to remember the facts that had been relayed to her just a few hours earlier. As they came tumbling back, she woke and wept again.

At first she didn't hear her phone ringing as it was muffled in her coat pocket. She retrieved it and saw that it was Sophie.

'Are you okay?' were her first words.

'Not really, no,' Mary said, wiping the tears from her eyes.

'It's terrible news. What happened, do you know?'

'They say a fire began underground. Poor Youssef.' Mary knew that over a hundred bodies had been recovered and that the same number had been taken to hospital.

'I don't know what to do, Sophie.'

'I'll come over. Stay there.'

Later they sat and watched the continuous news relay and Sophie translated the parts that she knew Mary wouldn't understand.

'They're saying that the *pompiers*, the fire brigade, received an emergency call around eight o'clock and together with the police they attempted to evacuate the space. They say it was hell down there, with almost five hundred migrants. They say the fire must have been started by them.'

She didn't have to add that the number of casualties had now risen to one hundred and twenty-six, for this was displayed on a strap at the bottom of the screen.

'What can we do?' Mary said quietly, looking down at her hands.

'Does Michael know?'

Mary shook her head. 'I haven't told him. Perhaps he's seen the news.' The truth was, she didn't care and at that moment she thought that she'd never again come to Paris.

The two women sat together and for a moment said nothing. Even when Mary's phone started ringing, they appeared frozen in position. Mary picked it up and only when the voice spoke did she recognise Finistere.

'What the fuck has happened?' he said.

Mary looked across to Sophie, who was frowning and looking at her. She flicked the phone to loudspeaker.

'There was a fire underground.'

'How, for Christ's sake? What's the damage?'

Again the two women looked at each other.

'Over a hundred and twenty dead,' Mary said.

'What a bloody mess,' said Finistere, still shouting at the phone. 'I knew they shouldn't be there. We should have got rid of them.'

'Well, now someone has, Michael. Someone has. They're no trouble anymore. You have what you want.'

It wasn't Mary who spoke, but Sophie, unable to believe Finistere's response to the situation.

'Well, it wasn't my fault they were down there.'

Sophie stood up and yelled across to the phone. 'What's the matter with you? People have been killed. Perhaps Youssef. Do you have no feelings for them?'

Mary switched off the phone.

'We have to find out,' she said. 'Will you help me, please Sophie? I spoke to Youssef last night, just before all this. It was as if he knew what was going to happen. The last words he said to me on the phone were "in the bushes above the tunnel". I think he's put something there. But we have to find him first.'

What followed next, Mary would think in years to come, was beyond understanding. It didn't accord with anything she had been taught to expect and she had no means of accommodating the experience, no yardstick with which to measure it and give it proper proportion.

The bodies had been taken to a temporary morgue, a series of hastily erected army tents on land which was part of the big hospital next to the Gare du Nord. The French police were cautious, preparing for a backlash from the city's considerable Muslim population, so it took some time for Sophie to explain why they wanted to confirm if one of the dead was Youssef Tigha, a friend.

'We have very few of their names,' they were told. 'To be sure, you will have to see the bodies of all the deceased. Are you ready to do this?'

Both Mary and Sophie nodded, holding hands as they walked under the canopy of the first dark green tent to be met by a sight that neither would forget. A white-coated nurse led them along the lines. Some bodies were badly burned and an awful smell forced its way through the antiseptic spray that had been used to keep it at bay. Here they were, the men and boys who just twenty-four hours earlier had lived in peaceful harmony on the depot floor.

They moved on to the second tent and it was in the middle of the last row that they found Youssef, his face perfectly still and more at rest than Mary had ever seen him before. He was unmarked, but there was no chance that he would wake and stand. He was empty and entirely still. Mary began to weep, quietly, and when she touched the boy's hand it was ice cold.

Mary nodded at the nurse. Before they left, Mary turned and, leaning down, kissed the boy's forehead. It was like marble.

'His name is Youssef Tigha. I have no idea where he came from, but he wanted to find his brother, Suliman. And now he is dead. His journey is over.'

The sweet air outside the tent was overwhelming and Mary and Sophie held each other, glad of the warmth their bodies gave. They said nothing on the short walk back to Sophie's flat.

'Do you believe,' Sophie said as they reached the long stairs that led up to the Sacré-Coeur, 'that Youssef, God bless him, used to come each Friday and watch me as I left for Milan on the train? I imagine he used to stand by the tracks and watch for my carriage. He attached to me some special importance, as you saw.'

'You were his escape,' Mary said. 'You were doing what he wanted to do. Get away to some magical place that wasn't his own life. Perhaps he's there now.'

Upwards they climbed until the white spires of the church came into view. They were breathing heavily at the top and they sat on a bench and looked over Paris.

'It's not what is seems, is it Sophie?'

'Not always, no.'

'I feel so sad. Everything has been taken away.'

'I know.'

The two women hugged and they didn't feel the sharp wind that blew up the slope and caused the pedestrians behind them to lower their heads.

The following morning the papers told Michael that it was a tragic accident. Stuart had flown over to be with him for support and to assess the damage to the site. He had been trying to call Sophie and Mary again, but without success. He felt nothing but irritation and he knew this would be his last visit to Paris for some time. The development could take place without him. He never liked the city in the first place and if he had the chance again, he would have walked away from the deal.

At the Lancaster, he finally got through to Mary.

'I'm at the hotel.'

'He's dead.'

'Who?'

'Youssef, the boy. Died underground. Sophie and I went to identify him.'

'I'm sorry.'

'Are you? You didn't want him, them, anyway.'

Finistere adjusted his position by the window and wondered how best to respond. Mary was right, of course, and the truth was that he felt little sympathy for what had taken place.

'Life must go on though,' he said, 'and we'll have to go to the site again. Can you meet me there later. As owners, we've got permission to be on-site. See you there midday. Bring Sophie.'

He was glad to shut down the phone.

Mary called Sophie.

'I need you with me today, Sophie. I feel rather alone. Finistere's here and he wants to meet at the site. He told me to bring you. Come for me, would you?'

'Of course, Mary.'

'He wants to meet at midday, but could we get there at eleven? I want to try and find what Youssef told me about, in the undergrowth above the tunnel. Will you help? I don't think I could do it by myself.'

'I'll be with you Mary, don't worry.'

'By the warehouses.'

The smell of smoke remained, although to Mary's eyes everything had changed. She could not look upon this scene in the same way anymore. Whatever joy or purpose it once held had been removed, torn away. The day was suitably grey and she waited for Sophie, dreading moving further into the site.

She heard her name called and Sophie approached with her arms wide and for a moment they held each other.

'C'mon,' Mary said and they set off to climb the slope behind the second warehouse before slipping through the railings. This time Mary was more careful climbing down although they held hands on the descent. When they stood on the track, not far from the tunnel mouth, the smell of smoke was stronger and for a moment they stood still and stared.

'I've never noticed the buddleia before,' she said finally, nodding above the tunnel. 'I think that's where Youssef meant. We'll have to get to it by climbing the slope over there.'

It wasn't easy and Mary could see why the boy had chosen this place to hide, even more so when they pushed through the thick shrub to find the near perfect camp, enclosed but with views all around. They found the loose brick without difficulty and it was only as she slid it out that Mary hesitated.

'I'm frightened,' she said.

Sophie put her hand on her friend's shoulder.

Mary felt inside and pulled out a cardboard box, only slightly smaller than the brick. She looked at Sophie for support. Mary took off the lid and the two women looked down on all that remained of the life of Youssef Tigha.

Mary picked up the watch and saw that it was still working, a fact that brought tears to her eyes. She wept even more openly when she held the picture of the woman she assumed must have been Youssef's mother. They were both crying now, the power of this strange ceremony above the railway tracks taking hold. There were some coins and finally a folded piece of paper, which Mary carefully opened.

If you are reading this, I am dead. I have known it would happen soon. My life is impossible and I cannot go on. Mary, I want you to give the watch to the person who I call the Loud One. It was found on a train when I was helping the cleaners. Sophie, you will have my most important possession, the photograph of my mother. She was always a constant in my life until she was killed. I think you helped me understand how she died. For a while you were a dream to me, someone beyond this world. When I watched you from the railway, you were my vision of hope. It was difficult to meet you. When you were real, I knew you could be taken away, like everything else. To you and Mary, I thank you for showing me kindness, a quality I had forgotten existed. May you continue to have good lives.

Inshallah.

Youssef

43

They could see that Finistere was impatient, looking around him, his face a scowl, Stuart Phelps standing just behind. The letter had rendered them motionless and they had sat under the buddleia unable to speak. By the time they had retraced their steps it was gone midday.

'What have you been doing?' barked Finistere, looking at his watch. 'Sophie, this is Stuart Phelps, who works with me.'

The two shook hands. Sophie's face was half-covered by a scarf and she didn't meet his eyes.

'Where were you?' Finistere persisted.

They were standing in the middle of the forlorn lorry park, the cold wind blowing their coats and hair. Impatient for an answer, Finistere began to move towards the warehouse door.

'Wait.' It wasn't a request, but an order and Mary's word had an edge that Finistere had not heard before.

'This is for you,' she said. She held out the watch in the palm of her hand, like she might give a biscuit to a dog.

Finistere, caught by her tone of voice, stopped and looked around. He was still impatient and irritated and at first he didn't focus on what Mary was holding out to him. When he did, he stepped forward and hesitated before picking up the watch and putting it into his own palm.

'How did you get this?'

'I don't think that's really the question, Michael. You know that Youssef is dead. You might show some sympathy, no? We have seen his dead body and those of many others who perished down there.' Her eyes looked towards the warehouses. She took a pace towards him. 'The boy left the watch for you. This is his will.'

She offered Finistere the sheet of paper and watched him read it.

'You will note that he didn't steal it, as you accused him. When he died he had nothing left but that watch, a photograph of his mother and a few coins. You might have helped him, and the others, Michael, but you chose not to, to retreat to wherever you go instead. And now he's gone. He doesn't exist. But, then, he never really existed for you anyway, did he?'

Finistere looked at her and wondered how he had got involved in this mess in the first place. He should have obeyed his instincts and refused to take part in anything that included Paris. Now he was being accused by one of his own staff of killing a migrant kid. He smoothed the face of the watch against his overcoat. Of course the boy stole it.

'Shall we get out of the cold?' he said, moving off towards the warehouse.

'No, Michael.' It was Sophie. 'Don't you have anything to say? The boy you met just twenty-four hours ago is dead. Does that not mean anything to you? No, it doesn't. It just gets in the way of what you want, doesn't it?'

Finistere was stopped in his tracks again. Sophie's grey-flecked eyes regarded him above the line of her scarf. Is this something else I should have avoided, he asked himself, part of the Paris package he let himself into?

'It's sad, yes, but it's not my responsibility to rehouse hundreds of bloody migrants.'

'Why not, Michael?' said Mary. 'What are your millions for? You can't spend them all, can you? A few nights underground here, out of the cold, wouldn't have cost you anything. But you couldn't even do that, could you?'

'I don't need this, Mary.' Finistere was only just controlling his anger. 'We need to talk, but not now.'

'Wait.' It was Sophie again. 'You can't talk to Mary like that. She's right. Do you know that? I was deceived, Michael. I thought there was part of you that might have been open to change. But I'm afraid not. I was wrong. But I know you won't care, will you? Because you can't own me, you'll just move on.'

Finistere saw the two women standing together, linking arms. Would he miss Sophie, he thought? Well, there was nothing to miss was there? Nothing had happened. She was an unfulfilled promise, simply that. He would walk away from all this as soon as he could.

A thin rain began to slant across the open space, but they stood there, mannequins, the two women watching Finistere, he in turn looking back at them, the figure of Stuart Phelps a spectator. From a distance, they might have been a group of modern statues, or figures from the model that stood in darkness on top of the warehouse that would soon become Les

Merchandises, or perhaps, singers frozen in the final act of a tragic opera as the lights went down.

Then the group broke up, the women, still arm in arm, moving towards the road, the two men, watching at first before turning to the warehouse, the taller of the two strapping a watch to his wrist as the wind pushed the rain into their faces.

Four months later, Mary and Sophie, both wearing black, met for the memorial service to the dead migrants and watched as the pomp and splendour of France was deployed and lined up for those who had died. In those eight weeks, Mary had accepted a job as a coordinator for UNHCR, the refugee relief agency, spending much of her time abroad. Sophie was about to appear in a production of *Norma*, as Adalgesa, who forms a bond of friendship with Norma despite the fact they both love the same man. Both Mary and Sophie found this somehow appropriate and saw Michael Finistere as the catalyst.

Some months later, Mary managed to track down Suliman, who had been dispersed to a refugee camp on the outskirts of Lyon. She told him of his brother's final days, of his stoicism and bravery and it was only as she described her final moments with his body and how she had kissed Youssef's head, that Suliman broke down and wept.

Work had begun on Les Merchandises, but Finistere had seen another opportunity in Leeds, which he regarded as safer ground. He intended to sell the Paris development as soon as it was finished. He wore Youssef's watch, but although the story that Michael Finistere told of how he came to own it was very different from the truth, it always made people laugh.

Thanks

This book had a long journey, which began in a hairdresser's chair some three years ago. I was in the hands of Sabrina Lefebvre, who was telling me that she had just returned from the Jungle in Calais where, as a volunteer, she helped cut the hair of migrants. The next time she went, I accompanied her. I had wanted to write about extremes of wealth and poverty and on that freezing day in late January, nowhere could have been poorer, more forlorn or inhospitable than the camp. People had walked across Europe to be there, cold, wet and uncomfortable. Nevertheless, they were full of good manners, offering me sweet tea wherever I went. The visit was the start of what would become this book and I am indebted to Sabrina for helping launch it.

Throughout its writing, I was encouraged by Rita Dallas and Chiara Messineo, as always valuable touchstones, as are Tim Hailstone and Jon Henderson. It was Jon, not only a stickler for all things grammatical but also a font of useful information, who first told me about the tunnels under Lord's cricket ground in London, which would lead me to transpose them to another city. Richard Barber again deployed his forensic skills on the manuscript, as did Peter Jacobs of Quartet and Peter Denton. Above them all stands my wife Sally, whose eye and judgement are as sharp as the winds that blew across the Jungle that day in Calais.

Paris is at the heart of this book, a city of contradictions. Our eyes are drawn to its golden centre but barely a short walk away is a very different city. One cannot be viewed without the other and I acknowledge the part that the lesser-known Paris has played in this book.